KW-223-765

ACKNOWLEDGEMENTS

So many people have been involved in my writing of this novel, and I thank you all.

Sister Geraldine Costello for her invaluable knowledge of Ireland in the 1950's/'60's which provided the information I needed to get started. I am grateful to Gerry and Susan Walsh and Kitty O'Malley-Harlow for help with the Irish.

Fellow writers, Gwen Chessell and Carol Norris, who read the first draft.

In Australia, Noela Mattiazzi and my cousin, Marie Livingstone who also took the time to read and encourage me.

For the map and illustrations, thank you to my friend of many years, Barbara Walsh whose empathy with the subject of the book was exceptional. And to Kit Foster for the work done on the cover.

I would like to mention my appreciation to Anitra Mehl and the Balzer family for agreeing to use their mother's painting for a cover image. Jean-Caroline was a very special friend to me and deeply missed.

I would also like to thank David Jones who proof read the novel first and the editorial work done by Mauve Publishing.

A very special thank you to Oliver Eade, fellow writer and friend, whose support and encouragement has been with me from the beginning.

And finally to my family, my husband, Iain and my daughter, Isla. Thank you for always being there for me throughout.

BALLYBEG

PART ONE

CHAPTER ONE

When Bernard Kelly brought Annie Smith home to the West of Ireland there was much speculation followed by a good deal of discussion in the small community of Ballybeg in which he lived. For it seemed to all that Bernard, aged thirty-two was set for a life of bachelorhood, destined to live out his days with his elder brother, Mick.

It had been decided between them after the death of their father that the two men would share the work and the profits, meagre as they were and that the division of labour thus agreed, would be in many ways a binding contract, verbal though, not tied to any legalities. Mick, being the eldest by four years, would have the final say in any dispute arising in the day to day running of the farm.This worked well enough and would have remained so had not a series of events caused Bernard to make choices. It was these choices that changed his life. He rarely made decisions. Decision-making was left to Mick. It was easier that way.

"See what Mick has to say," he would murmur, for the two brothers had their roles carved out, so the good people of Ballybeg said, as unmoveable it seemed as the stones that lay heaped all around them on the barren soil.

"What do ye make of this, Mick?" Bernard asked cautiously as he handed his brother a page of neat handwriting from his cousin Sinéad in London. Sinéad had left the West twenty years before with her husband, Pete and never returned. She wrote regularly to the brothers for she had a woman's sympathy for the unbending routine of their bachelor lives and had thought often of Bernard, alone with Mick. Her husband worked on the building site and there was work to do. It was 1949. London was rebuilding after the war and a strong young Irishman could do the work. So she wrote to offer Bernard board and lodgings for two months at the end of the year.

As Bernard studied his brother and awaited his decision, he felt that wonderful sense of timing some people call coincidence and others, perhaps more enlightened, live their lives by and are not in the least surprised when events fit perfectly into place. The offer of work in this case could not have been better. Bernard was off to Scotland in September to dig up potatoes as his brother and father and grandfather had done before him. Tattie-hoking, they called it, and it was hard work but an adventure. When he was younger, he would go with a squad of young folk but this time he was travelling most of the time on his own, for the Kellys were hard workers and welcomed on many of the farms. Their work always ended in East Berwickshire. Grandfather Kelly started the trend. His individuality set the Kellys apart from their companions but it had never bothered him and it didn't bother Mick or Bernard either. If Mick agreed to Sinéad's proposition, Bernard could catch the train to London from Berwick-upon-Tweed and return to Ballybeg from London just before Christmas. It seemed to be an ideal proposition.

Bernard bit the nail on the index finger of his right hand. He always did this when he was nervous. If anyone had ever loved Bernard enough to notice, they would have known the sign. But no one ever had and Bernard nibbled away, waiting to hear what Mick would say. Mick read the words, letter by letter, studying each word while Bernard's heart beat faster and his nail got shorter. Finally, Mick handed the letter back to his brother and rolled himself a cigarette.

"Maybe ye should go."

At this, Bernard's heart seemed to leap into his throat. It would be hard physical work both in Scotland and in London but London was an unknown. Somehow, life in the city would break the monotony of farm life and give him a chance to stay with Sinéad and Pete. He liked Pete, although he hadn't seen him or Sinéad for many years. He could remember all of them leaving, twenty years it was

3

now, and Sinéad crying like a baby as the train took her, Pete and their children away.

"Should I write to her and say I'll go then?" He needed reassurance. He wanted Mick to totally agree to his going. He would not go without it.

"Don't see why not", was Mick's reply.

It was decided. Bernard set about the task of writing to his cousin. He wrote carefully in almost joined-up writing, spacing each word and dotting the "i's" and crossing the "t's" the way Sister Bosco had taught him. This is what he wrote:

> *An Teach Ban*
> *Ballybeg*
> *Ireland*
>
> *15th May 1949*

Dear Sinéad

Thank you for your letter. Tell Pete I would like a job. I am coming with the squad from Ballybeg to Scotland in September to do some tattie-hoking.

We start in Ayrshire and I finish up myself at the McNultys farm in Berwickshire. You might remember Father talking about them. I would catch the train from Berwick upon-Tweed at the end of October.

May Our Lady watch over you and Pete and the children.

Your loving cousin
Bernard

PS Mick says he can manage fine without me. We got a good price for eight of our pigs the other day.

He smiled as he sealed the envelope. Had he known the transformation in his life that would occur through writing this one letter, he would have accepted the proposal without asking for approval, decided at once and he would have written, "Yes, yes, yes" and played all the joyous songs on his fiddle to celebrate. But at the time, Bernard just thought Sinéad's letter was a delightful coincidence and nothing more.

Bernard worked hard in Scotland and the days flew by. True to his word to Sinéad, his last farm was in Eastern Berwickshire with the McNultys. Mick had worked there a year before. He helped Farmer McNulty tidy up. Mrs McNulty took quite a liking to him and Bernard had his meals with the family.

"E's a braw laddie," she said to her husband. "A wirry aboot im gaun doon yonder."

She was preparing a mountain of sandwiches for Bernard's train trip to London.

"Yer ower saft, wumman," teased her husband. "The Irish aye lan on thar feet gin thay stey richt lang eneuch, thit is," and he chuckled at his own wit.

"Bernard's nae a drunkart," protested his wife.

"Yer richt eneuch thare. Ay. E's a guid laddie. Wush thare wur mair lik im..."

They insisted on taking Bernard to the Berwick Railway Station. He piled into the farmer's old pick-up truck, squashed awkwardly between the two of them with sandwiches, flask and tatties for Sinéad balanced on his knees.

At the station platform Mrs McNulty, short and rounded, stood on tip toe to give Bernard a kiss on both of his cheeks and a hug.

"Noo, ye bi carefae doon yonder," she said, wiping a tear from her eye. "Pit yer siller in yer buits."

"Ay, shae's richt," added the farmer. "Thaim toon fowks ir a different cleck, laddie. Thare's a wheen o bad yins doon yonder."

He held out his hand to Bernard. His hand was rough and calloused like Bernard's.

"Hez kizzen wull jyne im it King's Cross," Mrs McNulty fussed. "Bi carefae, laddie," she added. "Thaim toon fowk isnae lik uz." And she hugged him again as the train drew into the station.

Bernard coloured to his hair roots and looked at his boots. Then he was climbing onto the train with sandwiches and tatties and his old black bag. Bernard never forgot the kindness of the family. To the end of his days, he would defend the Scottish people.

"They're good people," he would say. "Hardworkin'. Just like us."

In London, Bernard fitted neatly into the lives of Sinéad and Pete. He worked hard beside Pete and enjoyed the camaraderie of his fellow workers.

"You're all right, 'Paddy'," they would say and teased him, getting him to fetch and carry for them, sometimes on futile missions which caused much joviality. They sensed Bernard's naivety but admired his stamina and willingness to work.

"Why do you want to go back to dig up potatoes?" they said to him, "You could stay... there's a lot of 'Micks' here now... look how we've tamed this one!" And they laughed at Pete as he sat with them, contented, eating his sandwiches.

"I've a farm back home and a brother there too. No, I have to go back," Bernard replied, though in his heart he wished he could stay. London was grim but here was excitement too and he wondered what it had been like when the bombs came down. There was so much work to be done if only he could stay, Bernard thought to himself as he loaded bricks for Pete and whistled an old Irish song as he did. It seemed no time at all and he had already been in London three weeks.

A few days later, Pete and Bernard were making their way home from their day of toil, talking to each other in the friendly way that two men who like each other have. They were busy discussing the day's work and the progress they were making when Bernard noticed a girl in front of them. She was in her twenties, he thought, and beautiful.

"Hello, Annie," said Pete as the two men passed her by.

She smiled, recognised Pete and smiled a lovely smile... a smile that completely transformed her face, making her seem even more beautiful to Bernard.

"Why, hello, Pete", she replied, looking all the time at Bernard.

As she gazed at him, he could feel himself growing redder and, in his nervousness, he stared at his boots but all the time he was aware of the girl and wanted to speak to her. He was dumb. He had been chatting so easily to Pete a few minutes before. It seemed impossible for him to believe that he was now unable to utter a sound.

The two men kept on walking, silently now. They were close to Pete's home and the warmth of the fire. Sinéad would have a meal ready for them. Bernard basked in the joy of a woman's care. Sinéad spoiled him, fussed over him, knowing a little of the situation back home with Mick. He dared not speak to Pete of the girl. His heart beat in his chest when he thought of her. Annie. Pete must know her, he thought. She was so beautiful, he kept thinking of her and was distracted all evening until he took his courage in hand and spoke as casually as he could, but his face coloured as he did so and he thought his cousin would notice his embarrassment, but he had to know. He had to know.

"Sinéad," he stumbled over her name, paused, formulating the question in his head, "Sinéad..."

"Why, what is it, Bernard?" She looked up, puzzled.

"Sinéad... Pete and me, well, Pete seemed to know this girl. I think he called her Annie... well, she seemed to know him too?"

Sinéad laughed, sensing Bernard's unease, amused but interested.

"Annie?" She looked at Pete who was busy cleaning his boots.

"Oh, that's Annie Smith," said Pete, with no interest in the conversation whatsoever.

"Annie Smith. She's a nice girl, Bernard. Been through a lot but we all have, haven't we, Pete? Why, after the war we thought of coming back to Ireland, didn't we, Pete? But I said, this is our home now and we have friends and there's more work here than back home, so we stayed, didn't we, Pete?"

Pete nodded. He always nodded when his wife spoke – it was easier that way.

Bernard wanted the conversation to get back to Annie, now that he had started, but Sinéad rambled on about the war and the bombs and the rationing until she suddenly remembered Bernard's questions:

"Oh, you'd like Annie, Bernard. Her mother, she's a lovely woman, isn't she, Pete? Has the butcher's shop in the High Street, ye know. They have a butcher working for them these days and a messenger boy, well, they had to, ye know. Her father was killed at the beginning of the war. She only had one brother and he ended up dead in Italy. Poor Annie... and poor Mrs Smith. But she's lovely, Bernard, and would make a lovely wife. And you'd like Mrs Smith too... if ye could get a word in edgeways. Talk? Oh, that woman can talk! But they're good people, Bernard. They're Catholics, too!"

At all this, Bernard's face grew redder and redder but excitement entered him as well and at that moment, he made up his mind that he must somehow speak to Annie. The thought of Annie burrowed into his brain and affected his concentration. He had six weeks left on the building site. Then he would have to go back to Ireland. There was no way out. Mick would need him. The money would help them both, improve the farm a bit, but Mick would need Bernard over the winter. Bernard had made enough money this year, and with a bit of luck he mightn't have to go to Scotland the next. Work was drying up there, anyway, and their farm might begin to make a decent living for them both. Annie, too. The thought of bringing Annie back to Ballybeg as his wife, made Bernard's heart beat faster. He now knew where she worked and where she lived... in the flat above the butcher's shop. Bernard had just six weeks and a fear rose up within him. If he didn't act soon he would lose Annie and he would never know the joy of her. His life with Mick would remain unchanged and he would just grow older. He wished he had been able to bring his fiddle with him. The fiddle for Bernard was an extension of himself. Without it, he felt a part of him was missing. Playing the fiddle gave him confidence and he hid behind his playing, insulated. In truth, he missed his fiddle more than Mick. But that didn't solve the problem of Annie.

He was caught between a desire and a dream and he wasn't sure if he had the courage enough to bring his dream into reality. However, life being such that once a plan had been hatched in Bernard's mind it only took a series of events to bring it about. And so it was with Annie.

Bernard's mind, dwelling constantly on Annie, brought into manifestation the object of his desire and in practically the same place and time as the day before. Pete noticed her first. He nudged Bernard and mumbled,

"Go for it, man," and walked away. He had been instructed by Sinéad.

Bernard stood, noticed the rounded comfortable shape of Annie and determination overcame his shyness. He resolved to speak to her. He had to or he would blame himself forever for his missed opportunity. He swept his old tweed cap from his head and approached the object of his desire. He planned to introduce himself as politely as he could. He was awkward and shy around girls. But Annie saw him coming towards her, this tall Irishman and in the instant moment of attraction between the sexes noticed everything about him – his black curly hair and blue eyes, the tweed coat with the hole at the elbow and the brown trousers and boots with their repaired laces. She spoke before Bernard had a chance to utter the words he had carefully formulated a few moments before.

"I know you," she said. "You were with Pete Nolan yesterday," and she smiled the smile that so disarmed him.

The ice was broken in that instant. The next moment for Bernard was ease itself. He grinned from ear to ear – he had a cheeky grin when he wanted to.

"Pete's married my cousin, Sinéad. I'm down here for two months on the building site... then back to Ireland."

His gentle Irish accent fell softly onto Annie's ears. She felt she had known him for ages. It was a magic moment between two young people who, in their different ways, had suffered so much. She liked him and her eyes told him so.

Bernard's heart hammered in his chest. He was suddenly aware of his hands. They were so clumsy, he thought and he was conscious of the dirt under his fingernails. But elation rose within him and he heard himself speaking with a certain amount of urgency because time was passing and he knew he must not, could not, let this girl go.

"Perhaps ye would do me the honour of coming out with me?"

Formal, but he loved her so much. He didn't want to seem too forward in case she rejected him. But he needn't have bothered because Annie smiled and said, "Yes, that would be nice." And Bernard felt his world change and happiness exploded within him. He thrust his hand onto hers and began to shake that small hand with great vigour and excitement until she had to get him to release his hand and, laughingly now, told him her name and where she lived. Arrangements were made for an outing and Bernard walked, or rather ran, to Sinéad's place, so great was his pride in what he had done.

All things that happen in life are relative and for Bernard this was his defining moment. The thrill he felt at that moment would remain with him for the rest of his life. When future circumstances sometimes brought pain to his life, he would look back at the precious moment that Annie spoke to him for the very first time and it would ease the pain. Such is the power of love.

As if by magic, the lives of Bernard and Annie changed and their happiness brought happiness to those around them. The garrulous Mrs Smith took one look at Bernard... and knew. It was impossible for her not to like the quiet Irishman. He grew more confident and his gentle banter made her laugh. A few short weeks after they had first met, Bernard proposed marriage to Annie on one of their walks by the river. He had rehearsed the words a hundred times but to his absolute amazement when she said "yes" and slipped her hand into his, he could hardly believe it and, whooping with delight, took her in his strong arms and swung her round his body. His joy was profound and clasping this gentle woman in his arms, he vowed he would remain true to her forever.

Annie was kind but within her was a resilience toughened by circumstances beyond her control. She was just sixteen years of age when Hitler unleashed his insanity onto Europe and the twin pain of losing both father and brother to the madness that is war, gave her courage in adversity. This was the sort of woman that life had taught Annie Smith to become. This courage in one so young would be surely tested as the years went by but for now there was just the moment of finding love.

Whether it was apprehension about taking Annie back to meet his brother, Mick, or just a desire to make their love legal, Bernard insisted on being married before his return to Ireland. Although surprised by the urgency of the proposed wedding, Annie had no doubts about the outcome and acquiesced. Arrangements were made, the banns were read and Father John at St Mary's was asked to perform the ceremony.

Bernard was in a daze. His every waking moment seemed to be spent thinking of Annie. Never before had he experienced the joy of having someone to focus on to the exclusion of others. The only thought that cast a shadow was Mick. He would try unsuccessfully to suppress the thought but it kept coming into his head. He was nervous to the point of anxiety when thinking of Annie and Mick. He feared his brother's reaction but he feared even more that somehow Mick would spoil his happiness, that somehow he would come between himself and Annie and what he was experiencing now was too good... too good to last. He was unable to talk about Mick to Annie. He dared not.

It was as if Sinéad read his thoughts because one evening, quite unexpectedly, she remarked:

"Are ye goin' to tell Mick yer gettin' wed, Bernard?"

Bernard looked uneasy. He wasn't prepared for the question.

"There's no point," he replied, wriggling slightly in his chair and avoiding Sinead's eyes. "He couldn't come. Not able to leave the farm."

Sinéad was puzzled but she suspected a lot. She had known both brothers all her life and was aware of the tension between them. Why, her own sister Doreen had written ages ago that she had been over to the farm and disturbed Mick and Bernard having an almighty row! She didn't stay around to find out what it was about but it was serious enough for her to write to Sinéad about it. Sinéad guessed things had probably got worse between the two of them, especially since their father had died. She looked at Bernard and decided not to pursue the subject. The look on his face warned her.

"At least I tried," she said to Pete when she told him the story.

"Aye that ye did," replied Pete. "That ye did."

Sinéad decided that Bernard should have a new suit for his wedding and that it should be a wedding gift from her and Pete. Bernard started to protest but Sinéad was adamant. Pete agreed with his wife. As far as money was concerned, Pete had a wonderful attitude. The man earned it and the woman spent it! He was happy to hand over his pay cheque to Sinéad and he was in awe of her ability to make a small amount go a long way. She had successfully fed and clothed their five children, owed no one anything. Now, with just the two of them, she had a little left over.

"Why, we're millionaires now, there's just Pete and me," she joked to Bernard.

So Bernard was duly taken to a tailor friend of theirs and fitted out with a 'nearly new' brown pin-striped suit, double breasted. His thin frame meant that the jacket appeared a little big for him, especially across the shoulders, but apart from that small matter, he looked quite handsome. Sinéad was proud of her young cousin of whom she had become very fond.

"I couldn't have ye gettin' married in yer old suit," she said to Bernard when she saw him in the new one. "We mustn't let the family down, ye know," because although Sinéad and Pete had been in England twenty years, they still considered themselves Ballybeg folk and she was keen to make an impression on those back home. *The Ballybeg News* was delivered weekly to their door and both she and Pete read it from cover to cover. She would have loved to have a mention of Bernard's wedding in the paper, but she dared not.

But Bernard was just happy to go along with his cousin. If it meant that Annie thought him handsome, he would have agreed to anything. He bought himself a new pair of brown shoes, a white shirt and a navy blue tie and, on his wedding day, Sinéad made sure he had a white chrysanthemum in his lapel. Bernard Kelly was getting married!

Annie and Mrs Smith were so liked in Camden it was natural that on Annie's wedding day a small group of onlookers, mostly women and children, gathered outside St Mary's to see the bride and groom. It was one of those cold December days when a thin sun tried unsuccessfully to emerge from between grey black clouds and brought some

13

light but no warmth. So everyone huddled together and talked about Annie and Mrs Smith. Annie, dressed in white and with a bunch of white and yellow chrysanthemums for her bouquet, walked down the aisle, nervous but excited. She held onto her Uncle George's arm and he reassured her as he always had. Dear Uncle George, her mother's widowed brother. She would miss him. But she had eyes only for Bernard and when Father John pronounced them "man and wife", she felt a wonderful, wonderful surge of happiness as they kissed at the altar in front of a small number of guests.

It is sometimes the most unexpected surprise that brings the most pleasure. Uncle George knew a couple in Brighton who ran a small bed and breakfast in the town. Unknown to everyone, he had contacted them and they had agreed, even though they were officially closed for the season, to open for two days for Annie and Bernard. Uncle George paid the bill. Bernard wasn't used to generosity, he being the recipient of such, so he was on the point of arguing when Annie frowned and, taking her Uncle's hand, she said to him in the sweetest voice imaginable:

"That's very kind of you, Uncle George. I'd love to show Bernard around Brighton."

Uncle George's round face beamed with delight.

"Well, it seems a shame that you two lovebirds can't have a bit of a honeymoon. It's been tough for all of us these last few years. Go ahead and enjoy yourselves."

Annie and Bernard did just that. Brighton was cold and wet and the wind was relentless. They had to cling to each other as they struggled along the Promenade. The grey waves tumbled in, scattering more pebbles onto the shingle beach and the wind stung their faces, blowing a thin spray over them, freezing cold, and they giggled uncontrollably. It was magic to eat fish and chips out of newspaper, to huddle together, to laugh and love.

As he watched the waves Bernard became quite philosophical and remarked how that small bit of water had kept the Germans away. And he told Annie how unaffected Ballybeg had been by the war. It was as if what happened in Europe was happening on another planet. A lot of Ballybeg folk had friends and relatives living in Scotland and England who had joined up so people were aware. Nothing happened in Ballybeg. In fact the closest thing that had happened, and Bernard chuckled as he recalled the story, was the sighting of what they thought was a German U-boat. No one was sure. Then all of a sudden everyone became an 'expert' and for weeks after heated discussions took place in Murphy's Bar as to whether it was indeed the enemy or some other vessel. He was away in his thoughts, remembering, and Annie was remembering, too. She thought how that little bit of water was still big enough to keep her father from getting back to England. She felt a lump in her throat and tears behind her eyes but she didn't want to cry in front of Bernard and spoil their happiness because if she started to tell him about her father she would think of her brother, William and then she would cry. She would tell Bernard but not today. Not yet. Perhaps... never.

"Let's not talk about the war, Bernard," she said, slipping her hand into his, "It's all over now, thank God."

And Bernard squeezed her hand ever so gently, as if he did, perhaps understand a little.

*****

The night before Annie left for Ireland she had a vivid dream. She dreamt that she was rowing a small boat but she was unable to move the boat along in the water because of the waves that kept crashing into it. Everything was black and dark. Bernard was there but not there as is the nature of dreams. She cried out, "Help me!" and then another man appeared in the boat but, instead of helping her, he started to fill a bucket with water from the sea and kept pouring this into the boat. Annie felt the boat disappearing beneath the waves and she feared she was going to drown in the dark sea. She cried out and woke with sweat on her brow. Woke and knew it was just a dream because Bernard was snoring gently beside her and she was in the flat above the butcher's shop and safe. The dream kept coming into her mind all day, disturbing her thoughts and it was a dream that would come again and again into her conscious moments as the years went by.

There was just Uncle George and Mrs Smith, Sinéad and Pete to say goodbye to Bernard and Annie as they waited on the platform for the boat train that would take them to Holyhead and Ireland. When the time came to say goodbye they clambered aboard with their cases and coats and eyes full of tears because partings are sometimes like a little death and this was one of those times.

*****

The Owenbeg River divides the town of Ballybeg neatly into two parts with one side filled with a line of houses and the other more devoted to shops and hotels. It's a picturesque place with the sea not far from the centre of the town and Slieve Geal, that bright mountain, overlooking the back of the town, so that Ballybeg is effectively hemmed in between mountain and sea. A sense of resignation prevailed. Here was the end of the line with the wild Atlantic throwing its might onto the shore and the next stop, America. This geographical isolation of Ballybeg somehow insulated its people from the rest of the world. A sleepy haze hung over the town especially in the dark days of winter when its inhabitants slept happily on till the late morning and the shopkeepers refused to open their doors until well past half past nine.

The town had been quite prosperous before the Great Famine and its busy port had employed hundreds. This prosperity spilled over to the layout of the town and there were many grand buildings along the Owenbeg. The north side of the river was by far the most salubrious and the grandest building of all was the church of St Peter and St Paul. A wit once remarked that the misdemeanours of the Ballybeg folk were such that it needed two saints to mediate on their behalf to the Almighty. The church was certainly an imposing building, grey brick with a dozen steps leading up to a beautifully carved solid oak door. The design was classic Gothic and the spire could be seen for miles. The church of St Peter and St Paul faced the Protestant church of St Michael uneasily across the Owenbeg and while the former was filled to overflowing on Sundays with people sometimes spilling out onto the steps, the latter could barely summon twenty loyal parishioners and was forever in danger of closure. The other fine building on the north side of the river was the four storey Ballybeg Hotel with its beautifully executed Georgian windows, also grey brick but with an imposing entrance where an ornate chandelier in the foyer impressed visitors and locals alike. The view from the attic windows was splendid, with sea, river, mountain and town providing a much described view. In Victorian times Ballybeg was considered as desirable a location for the English upper classes as Zermatt or the Scottish Highlands and the coming of the railway brought a considerable number of prosperous visitors to the town. Walking tours were fashionable and the more intrepid would climb Slieve Geal and enthuse about the panoramic view far below them. From its peak, it was possible to see across to the upper reaches of the Owenbeg. There a fine salmon run attracted hosts of eager fishermen and women. Many a fine specimen was pulled from the Owenbeg.

Four bridges crossed the Owenbeg. The river meandered in a giant semi-circle so it had been necessary to connect both parts of the town. The grandest bridge of them all was the North Bridge while the second and less imposing road bridge was named the South Bridge. The naming of the bridges had been the subject of bitter argument as various people wanted the two bridges immortalised with names of famous Ballybeg folk. Ballybeg's most illustrious son became a Congressman in the American House of Representatives and his descendants were determined to give his name to one of the bridges – North Bridge being the preferred choice with its ornate stone carvings at either end. But finally, to settle the disagreement the two bridges were named for their geographical position alone. Such was the acrimony of the dispute that the Congressman's family and subsequent generations vowed never to walk upon North Bridge and, as far as anyone ever knew, not one of them ever had. They took the long route round and crossed over the South Bridge instead. With the coming of the railway two other bridges were built to cross the Owenbeg. Again, imagination seemed to have little part in the naming of them and the road bridge became the Railway Bridge. Alas, the rail bridge, unnamed, was always referred to as "the other bridge".

In 1950 Ballybeg was a faded glory of its former self and despite its superb views, the population had dwindled to a mere six hundred from about fifteen hundred in better times. Life was cyclical and the seasons and the church dictated that resignation and acceptance of their fate to the population so that people like the Kellys, who had lived in Ballybeg for generations and had survived famine, emigration, English landlords and, as many personal difficulties as any other family anywhere, were a catalyst for the wider community.

Mick and Bernard Kelly, bachelor brothers, who were held to the soil by the seasons, the weather and the economic necessities of making a living, found relief in two different pursuits. Routine controlled the lives of the two brothers but half a mile out of Ballybeg and situated conveniently on the Galway Road was Murphy's Bar, a place frequented by both Mick and Bernard. Every Saturday night, Bernard would play his fiddle and drink pints of dark, smooth Guinness. Sometimes Mick came with him, sometimes not. Bernard loved his fiddle and in another life he could have made a living playing it, but he was content just to sit on a stool and let the rhythm flow. Mick, for his part, spent his free time reading and went

18

once a week to the small lending library situated next to the Post Office on the north side of the Owenbeg. These two different activities provided the only break in the otherwise relentless routine that the brothers experienced and neither could imagine any change in their circumstances.

Now there was just Mick and Bernard, two brothers bound to the farm after all those generations, and only a few scattered cousins around the place... relatives, but of no consequence to the brothers. The four years between them gave Mick the advantage of being the first born and also gave to him a certain degree, in his eyes, of superiority as far as his younger brother was concerned. "Ye do it this way", was Mick's favourite expression and he used it frequently so that Bernard, with his quieter nature, would acquiesce. Sometimes though, in a fit of pique, Bernard would object, silently. But Mick had the infuriating habit of always being right so that after a while, and no one quite knew when it happened, Bernard just gave up arguing with his elder brother and would simply shrug his shoulders, set his mouth a little tighter and go about his business.

The Kellys touch the sky! Bean poles... and Mick was Jack, climbing to the top for wasn't Mick a strange one, even at school, and stranger still as he grew older? No one knew what he was thinking and that caused a certain amount of uneasiness amongst the men and women who lived in Ballybeg. Not quite right, that's Mick Kelly they said, and gossiped about his life with Bernard, the two of them together on the farm... and wondered. But the Kelly family loyalty kept whatever secrets there were and Bernard never spoke against his brother. Ever. Not even Father O'Malley knew the secrets. Father O'Malley, Parish Priest, ruled Ballybeg but even he knew nothing. Father O'Malley, staunch upholder of the letter of the law as far as the church was concerned, was not quite trusted by the Kelly family. He might have a direct link to God but that link could be broken, the Kellys thought, especially after their priest had had too many pints!

19

It was the agreed opinion in Ballybeg that Mick dominated Bernard. Everyone in the town knew that Mick, too, took a drink and often a drink too many. Why, once Mick had been found dead drunk and lying in the middle of the road by Doctor Ryan returning about two o'clock in the morning from one of his night calls. Doctor Ryan, who as far as the people of Ballybeg were concerned, was only a little lower than the Angels, had come across the supine figure, thought for a moment that here was death but, looking closer, saw that it was Mick Kelly and he was out cold from the effects of the alcohol consumed no doubt at Murphy's Bar. Doctor Ryan, that good doctor, had lifted and dragged the unfortunate Mick into his car and taken him back to his own home much to the consternation of his wife who did not share her husband's altruism and spent all the next day muttering about "the curse of the drink". But Doctor Ryan couldn't bear to think of Mick out in the cold as the winter was coming in and Mick was known to all.

When Mick awoke the next morning, instead of being thankful to the good doctor who had possibly saved his life, became quite belligerent when he discovered where he was and accused the Ryans of abducting him for the purposes of medical research. Aghast at this tirade of unjustifiable accusations and also feeling a little unsure of their not-so-welcome guest, Doctor Ryan, firmly but politely asked Mick to leave. This story would have remained with Doctor Ryan but for his wife. She was prone to feeling important in the community and took great pleasure in telling and retelling the story. And with every telling, Mick became more outrageous and even more violent so in the end, if there ever was an end to it, the doctor represented all that was good and Mick all that was evil. So for a long time after, Mick was ignored by the community and Mick, in his turn, would not speak to Doctor or Mrs Ryan, refusing to have anything to do with either of them.

What Doctor Ryan had observed about Mick on the morning in question was an aspect of Mick that he kept to himself. He glimpsed a certain irrationality which he noted could be a mental problem and should be looked at more closely. But how, with limited knowledge and no cooperation from Mick, could that problem be solved? Doctor Ryan took the path of least involvement and hoped that things might resolve themselves if Mick could just control his drinking bouts.

Mick could be quite pleasant. He would go for months before another drinking session manifested itself. Bernard never knew what triggered the mood swings and the sudden irrational behaviour. Mick would usually go out drinking after days of querulous behaviour. Laconic, he would sit huddled in his chair refusing to work so that Bernard was left to run the farm. This silent fury could last for up to a week and then Mick would disappear to Murphy's pub, sometimes returning in a belligerent state; other times, similar to the incident when Doctor Ryan found him, collapsed somewhere behind a wall or on a park bench. Then, more often than not, Garda O'Sullivan would find him and take him, sometimes protesting, back to the Gardai house to sleep it off. In the morning he would be none the worst for it except his eyes would reveal the haunting inside. And those about him would wonder.

*****

What tangled webs are relationships, and when decisions are made how life-changing those choices become. The decision to go to London at the time he did and the moment he agreed to go, was for Bernard Kelly a choice that would change his life forever and would so alter his brother Mick's life in the process. Into this strange and isolated world, so far from the London she knew, Bernard brought his new wife, Annie.

CHAPTER TWO

The journey from London to Dublin for Annie and Bernard was not an easy one. Delays for some inexplicable reason boarding the ferry at Holyhead were further combined with a wild winter storm that hit them half way across the Irish Sea. The vessel ploughed through the waves, up and down, up and down, lurching sideways as the force of the sea crashed onto the bow. Annie, in particular, found the crossing very difficult. She clung to Bernard's arm as the black skies outside and the rain, in unabated fury, lashed the windows. She decided she wasn't much of a sailor and was glad of Bernard's support. For his part, he was happy to reassure his new wife that all would be well when the ferry finally got to its destination.

Even getting into the harbour at Dun Laoghaire proved difficult but at last, thankfully, the spires and the houses on the harbour front came into view and the lights along the promenade shone through the dark night signalling a welcome to Ireland. The ferry, safe from the storm, was tied securely and the passengers disembarked with mutterings of: "What a wild night," and "They'll be lucky to get another crossing if this keeps up..." from the relieved souls.

Two streets away from the seafront at Dun Laoghaire, stood a neat row of houses with a small pocket handkerchief garden in front. This was Mrs Slattery's Private Hotel. Mrs Slattery, in her fifties, a widow and childless, was a neat cheerful little woman whose hotel had become known to the people of Ballybeg as a place for a good night's rest and a full Irish breakfast either before boarding the ferry to England or returning home. She welcomed the two travellers warmly. With a wisdom gained from years of studying her guests, she guessed they were newlyweds and gathered them into her hotel with all the concern of a mother hen with chicks.

"Oh 'tis a wild night to be sure," she said as she bustled around, making them a welcome cup of tea. "But isn't it grand, the two of ye," and she took Annie by the arm and led her into the front parlour of floral chintz and neat settee, with its curtains drawn.

"Now, ye two just sit here and get warm and we'll have ye ready for a good night's sleep." And Mrs Slattery winked, giving them a mischievous grin as if to say, I know it all!

"It's so nice to be on dry land again," Annie replied politely as she was wondering whether she would ever want to go on water again.

Mrs Slattery smiled at Annie and the two women knew that they had found a friend in each other, a friendship that would last. Annie felt happy in this cheery little hotel which was more like a home and she said as much.

Mrs Slattery positively beamed; her brown eyes twinkled more than ever.

"Now, yer to feel at home, dear and when ye get tired of the West," as Bernard had already told her they were Ballybeg people, "or," she added, with what was to be a prophetic statement, "when ye need to cross over to England, this is the place to come. Ye'll always be welcome here, the both of ye."

"Why, I've never even been to Ballybeg", she laughed now, "and I don't know how Ballybeg people got to know of me, but they always come – and one day, well, I'll just come and visit ye all!"

"And you'll be very welcome, Mrs Slattery," replied Annie, issuing an invitation to her hostess even though she, too, had never been to Ballybeg either.

The irony of this wasn't wasted on Bernard who added, in his quiet way, "Mrs Slattery, the whole of Ballybeg will come out to greet ye, to be sure."

The three of them smiled in a conspiracy of togetherness and the evening passed as pleasantly as it had begun.

The next morning the adventure of crossing Ireland by train began after farewells to Mrs Slattery who insisted on packing sandwiches and cake for their journey. Her kindness was appreciated by Annie who had learnt the lesson of gratitude during the difficult years of the war. She had also learned the lesson of the transience of human life and was very glad to have met this cheerful little woman even for such a short time. Annie felt sure she would meet Mrs Slattery again. Her first introduction to Ireland was a happy one.

Annie was glad too of Bernard. This quiet Irishman had swept her off her feet, so to speak, but she felt in her heart that he was the man for her even though she was a little nervous of what was before her. She was mystified by Bernard's refusal to talk about his brother, Mick. Loving her own brother as she had and still feeling the pain of losing him so cruelly a few days before the end of the war, Annie could only wonder at the relationship between her husband and his brother. Bernard refused to be drawn about Mick and would quickly change the subject whenever Annie questioned him. She didn't like to pry into her husband's world at this stage and was just happy to be loved by him, this quiet, tall Irishman with the cheery smile. It was his smile that had first attracted him to her along with his soft gentle accent. Accepting his proposal so soon after they had met hadn't seemed at all hasty in her eyes. In fact, it was all part of a great adventure, even though the ferry crossing had been frightening, it was all behind her now, and she was glad to be away from London with all the bombed out buildings and memories. So she accepted Bernard's reticence about his brother with memory of her mother's words, "Best left alone", her mother had said and Annie could only agree. She loved Bernard and that was all that mattered. She sat back, held Bernard's hand, and enjoyed the view as the train puffed its way across the flat landscape of rural Ireland.

Coming into the railway station at Ballybeg the first person that Bernard saw was Doctor Ryan. He was waiting, no doubt, for his wife who often went on shopping trips to Dublin. Bernard hesitated for a moment and wondered if it would be possible to avoid the doctor. The memory of Mick was still in his mind and, even though it had happened a while ago, things were still a little strained between the Kelly brothers and the Ryans.

It did not however, work out that way as Mrs Ryan, alighting from the next carriage glimpsed Annie with Bernard and nudging her husband to follow, made a bee-line for the newlyweds.

"Why, Bernard Kelly," she gushed, "are ye going to introduce us?" Her sharp eyes fixed on Annie's face.

Bernard, holding cases in both hands, put them down and held out his hand for Annie. At that particular moment, Bernard thought Annie looked beautiful. She was wearing a brown tweed jacket with a flared skirt to match. Her light turquoise silk scarf, twirled casually around her neck, perfectly complemented her blue eyes and short curly brown hair. Most men, in love, think their woman is the most wonderful in all the world and Bernard was no exception, so with a burst of pride and forgetting all the acrimony of Mick towards the doctor, announced:

"This is my wife, Annie," and to Annie he added, "I'd like ye to meet Doctor and Mrs Ryan."

At this announcement, Mrs Ryan positively stopped in her tracks for a split second and then exclaimed:

"Why, Bernard. This is a surprise, isn't it, John?" to her husband, who smiled and extended his hand to Annie. She took it shyly.

Mrs Ryan kept talking incessantly about, "How did it happen? When did it happen? Where did it happen?" She was gabbling so much that no one could follow what she was saying. She was poised to continue in order to gain as much information as she could in as short a time as possible. Mrs Ryan was known to engage in trawling for gossip and could be relied on to know everything, or so she thought, about everybody and everything.

Doctor Ryan was fond of his wife but he was an astute enough judge of character to realise her shortcomings. But he, too, was surprised to see Bernard with Annie. He was wondering if Mick knew anything of this and, if he did, what was his reaction? The doctor felt once again the warning bell go off in his brain but not wishing to speculate on present or future events, he quietly took charge of the situation in part to curtail his wife's verbosity and also to spend a little more time with this new arrival in Ballybeg. His Austin Healey was parked at the station entrance so he kindly offered to drive Bernard and Annie to the farm. Bernard, a little cautious but feeling it would be bad-mannered to refuse the doctor's generosity, agreed meekly. Normally, the Kelly brothers walked back to the farm from Ballybeg, sometimes stopping at Murphy's pub on the way, butBernard reasoned that he had Annie now and it was a dark night. He began to wonder to himself as cases and people were packed into the doctor's car, what would Annie think of the farm? She wouldn't actually see it in daylight until tomorrow. Bernard thought perhaps that might be a good thing.

The Kelly farm was situated about three miles out of Ballybeg on the Galway road. It comprised house, outbuildings and about thirty acres. The solid white stone house had withstood the ravages of a few centuries of wild winter weather partly due to its location in a slight valley. The farmhouse was named 'An Teach Ban' – which meant 'The White House', Bernard explained to Annie. Given that all the various farmhouses clustered around Ballybeg were white, the name was something of a mystery. But Bernard told the story of Grandfather Kelly. Grandfather Kelly was not burdened with the kind of fatalism that affected so many of his neighbours. Within him was something of a building urge and he kept extending the house so that it grew larger as the years went by. For this reason, it became

26

"An Teach Ban" with the emphasis on the "An". Thoughts of an American dwelling were in the minds of all about – the humour of this was not wasted on Grandfather and Grandmother Kelly! An Teach Ban – *the* White House, it was and would be for all time. The trees that grew around the house had evolved to grow in misshapen ways, bent the way the relentless wind blew. In fact, these trees and the grass were the only signs of habitation; a garden being out of the question. Generations of Kellys had left behind generations of things – nothing ever seemed to be thrown away so that the whole place looked untidy, neglected and sad. Grandfather Kelly was long gone. How he would have dismayed had he viewed his beloved An Teach Ban now.

As the doctor drove up the rough road to the farmhouse, Annie knew nothing of this. Her first sight of the farm was pure picture postcard Ireland, so she thought, with a whisk of smoke blowing from the chimney, the smell of turf in the air. The darkness of the night gave enchantment to the view. The doctor stopped the car and he and Bernard got out quickly, leaving Mrs Ryan still gushing to Annie:

"Now, ye must let me introduce ye to a few friends. We'll have a get-together soon..."

And Annie smiled, politely, unsure of all the attention she was receiving.

The doctor and Bernard looked at each other and Bernard hastily said,

"Well, thank ye for the lift, Doctor," he hesitated, "I don't think I can ask ye in with Mick the way he is."

The words hung in the air.

The doctor nodded in his understanding way.

"I'm happy for you, Bernard. You have a lovely girl there. Bernard..." He wasn't too sure of what to say. "If you or your wife ever need me you know where I am." And he held out his hand because at that point, it seemed the right thing to do.

Bernard lowered his eyes but took the doctor's hand.

"Thank you, Doctor Ryan," was all he could say because at that moment, Mrs Ryan leapt out of the car to tell her husband that she had invited Annie to a women's get-together at their house next Tuesday and there she would introduce Annie to all the "right" people in Ballybeg. At that, Doctor Ryan smiled and said goodbye.

"Well, my girl," said Bernard to Annie, "Welcome to An Teach Ban", and he lifted her into his strong arms, pushed the door open and deposited Annie in the front room of her new home.

The front room, mainly a store room for clutter, opened onto a hall, three doors, all closed and a room Annie thought must be the bathroom. That was the farmhouse and certainly a larger building than she had envisioned. Her heart beat faster. At the end of the hall was the kitchen. There was a light. Bernard and Annie, giggling like schoolchildren, headed for the light and warmth.

The sight that greeted them was of Mick bent over the kitchen table, his shadow reflected on the wall opposite, showing his whole body. He was there in the kitchen, his back to the stove, standing now, and as he stood up, he stood, this tall man, completely naked in front of them, not making any attempt to hide his nakedness. Annie gasped and Bernard, astonished too, at the sight of his brother, was lost for words for a second and then spluttered:

"In the name of God, man... put something on...!"

But Mick, recovering his surprise, made no move to do so. Instead, he turned... not acknowledging Annie at all... turned... and, speaking to Bernard, just said, "Yer back then!"

CHAPTER THREE

It took Annie several days to recover from the shock of seeing Mick naked in the kitchen. Her first thought had been one of disgust followed quickly by fascination. Here was a man standing in front of her whose physical appearance mirrored her husband. Mick was slightly taller than Bernard but with the same black curly hair with flecks of grey, blue eyes and thin body. Annie had no experience of men. Bernard, equally reticent in these matters, would hardly undress in front of her and here was his brother, showing his manhood without a trace of embarrassment. Annie had felt her face burn, the hot blush seeming to come upward from her neck and covering her face in a tingly sensation. She was as much repelled as curious at the same time. Bernard had quickly moved in front of her to stop her seeing Mick. Annie would never forget the expression on Bernard's face and later on, would wonder at her husband's acute and painful unease.

Even more puzzling for Annie as the days passed was Mick's complete indifference to her presence in the house as she had hoped for some recognition or acknowledgement from him; but she received neither and was left bewildered and nervous in his presence. When she tried to question her husband later, Bernard changed the subject quickly. Annie began to realise that she was quite alone with this situation, and also here was a problem which would not go away in a hurry.

Her introduction to her new home was like life itself, bitter sweet. Although the house was run down, it was not without its charm and Annie's remembrance of her first sight of it on that cold winter's night, remained. So she set about trying to bring some order into the chaos and busied herself cleaning and removing some of the clutter. She was very careful not to touch anything of Mick's, unsure of how he would react, but certain it would not be in a rational way.

As she scrubbed and tidied, Annie thought back to the years of the war and how one day, a house would be standing, the next day reduced to rubble. Her own home had remained intact throughout the Blitz but the house two doors away had been hit. In the war they all had to stand firm against a ruthless and determined enemy, but they were together against this adversary. Here, in the West of Ireland, alone with her husband and his brother, Annie felt painfully aware of her isolation and keenly yearned for the family and friends she had left behind. Somehow, thinking back, that bombed out house reminded her of her present moment. The outside walls of that house had been blown away, collapsing into a heap of bricks, but one wall at the back, for some reason, had remained standing, defiant, like some silent sentinel that would not be defeated no matter what. Annie sometimes thought she was like that house too and she was the brick wall, alone and isolated! She was no coward and the difficulties she had experienced before perhaps prepared her for what she was now facing. With a kind of silent horror, she perceived the enemy might be her husband's brother and her vulnerability could perhaps weaken her to the point of despair if she allowed it.

Bernard continued to be attentive and kind towards her and for this she was grateful, but he would not be drawn about his brother. He was loyal to Mick and refused to acknowledge that there was a problem. He continued to take directions from his brother and agreed to most of Mick's requests. He was pleased to see Annie changing his environment and the house, in a very short space of time, becoming a home, losing the uncared-for, untended appearance. He was pleased too that Annie had begun to make friends in Ballybeg. Knowing the community's mistrust of outsiders, he was proud of his wife's courage in gaining the confidence of some of the local women, Mrs Ryan in particular.

Annie, in actual fact, found Mrs Ryan quite endearing in her gossipy way and had gained an ally in the saga of

Mick. Mrs Ryan had mentioned at one of their get-togethers that Mick liked a drink; but all the men in Ireland seemed to drink, Annie thought despondently, so Mick wasn't unique in that regard. Since her arrival, he'd hardly touched a drop of the stuff. They had been out, Bernard and herself, to Murphy's Bar a few times, but Mick had absented himself on every occasion. She couldn't understand his strange behaviour on the night she had arrived and modesty prevented her from mentioning the incident to anyone, least of all to Mrs Ryan.

Acutely aware of the tension between Mick and the Ryans, Annie carefully avoided any reciprocal visits to the farm. Mrs Ryan, curious but wise enough not to press the matter, resisted the impulse to question, hoping that Annie would reveal more of the situation as time went by.

"He's a strange one, to be sure," she told Annie again during one of their meetings. "No one has ever been able to fathom him out. He's clever, though, and always has been," she added knowingly. "He's got a lot of books, hasn't he?"

Annie, more relaxed now and confident, was eager to release a little information.

"I know. I wouldn't dare touch them, though. He has them stacked high in his room. I peeped in when he wasn't around," and she giggled, regaining some her mischievous behaviour.

Mrs Ryan laughed with her, too.

"What does he read about?"

"I don't know," replied Annie, happy now to be able to talk freely if only for a moment or two. "There's an Irish history book or two there and I noticed he's always looking at rocks... I noticed a huge blue geology book at his bedside..." She blushed.

Suddenly she was curious to learn about Mick from someone who would have known him for years.

"Has Mick ever had, you know... a woman?" and left the question hanging in the air.

31

"We don't think so," replied Mrs Ryan, a little haughtily but with an air of some importance, "but none of us knows. He certainly wouldn't be able to keep one with all his goings-on," and she smiled thinly, dismissing Mick and the subject of women, with a wave of her hand. Mrs Ryan, at that moment, had the air of the matriarch of Ballybeg and was keen to impress this onto her new-found young friend.

As far as the women of Ballybeg were concerned, Mrs Ryan was the authority who guided them and they relied on her for that guidance. Once Mrs Ryan had accepted Annie, the English girl, into her circle, they followed her lead. Although Annie was easy to talk to, and her ready smile won their hearts, there was a universal curiosity amongst the women regarding the situation at the Kelly farm. The considered opinion was that Annie was a brave girl. They all agreed that Bernard wasn't a bad one and it had certainly improved him finding a wife like Annie. As for Mick, well, that was quite another matter. Annie deserved a medal for having him there, there never being any question that Mick would be asked to leave the family home to make way for the new arrival, all the women acknowledged that truth. And so, in Ballybeg at least, Annie, despite her Englishness, was welcomed into the community. Admiration for her strength of character was to grow over the years and agreed by all, men and women alike. This surely started out from Mrs Ryan as fierce as a terrier in loyalty to Annie as is possible for one human being to be to another.

*****

Flowers on a table signify a woman's presence. When the bluebells first appeared in the woods, Annie gathered a huge bunch and arranged them in an attractive display. She placed them proudly in the centre of the kitchen table. She had just finished the arrangement when she sensed a presence in the room and looking around; she saw Mick standing in the doorway, his eyes fixed on the bluebells.

Annie was unsure of what to say. He had only spoken a few words to her in the whole time she had been living at the farm. It was his complete lack of acknowledgement of her existence that hurt her the most. Daily, almost, she had to remind herself that she was Bernard's wife. She had a right to be here after all she had been through. The war with all the painful memories was behind her and she was as loving a wife as she could be.

Mick walked towards her and then sat down at the table, his long, thin body easing itself into the chair, becoming almost snake-like in his posture. He gently placed his slender fingers on one of the bluebell's petals, stroking it with an intensity that altered his whole being. And as he did so, he spoke, looking at Annie and smiling.

"Bluebells... now, aren't they are so beautiful? So very beautiful, ye know. Delicate. They're the first sign of the spring, they bring the warmth to a frozen world, don't they now? The wee blue flowers..."

Annie was completed and utterly unnerved by his words, unsure of what to say, she found herself gabbling something about flowers brightening a room and could only smile her lovely smile, the whole moment being for her, both unexpected and unsettling.

Mick seemed far away, in some other place or time or both. Dreamily, he continued, his quiet voice filling the room:

"My mammy would pick them for me, ye know. We would walk along the side of the road and gather bunches and bunches... or so it seemed at the time. Sure I must have been about five, I think..." he was serious for a moment. His blue eyes appeared troubled and he frowned slightly. "She died when I was ten..."

Annie, sensing a spark of rationality between them for the first time, sensing a moment that she might be able to use to her advantage, replied, quietly, her heart pounding in her chest as she did so, "Yes, Mick... Bernard told me about your mother..."

But Mick was talking again, back there with his mother and the bluebells, picking them, a little boy again, young again, before time and bluebells wrought the changes. He smiled at Annie and as he did so, a pang of sadness went through her, because it was so like Bernard's smile, even the nose, the eyes, the hands, Bernard's. If they could just be friends, she thought, everything would be all right. Her thoughts tumbled around in her head, it had had to be a shock for Mick, Bernard suddenly appearing with a wife, after they had lived together, the two of them, for so long. He must have felt that she was an intruder into his world, a threat to his place at the farm. She tried to make sense of it all, didn't understand anything of his strange behaviour, and forgave him for his alienation of her. Yes, at that moment she forgave him and her heart beat faster. She didn't want to harbour resentment; she just wanted peace in the house. And for that brief moment her wish was granted, but how a brief a moment it was because Mick suddenly stood up, towering over her, his blue eyes changed, and turned, and walked out of the room without another word, leaving Annie, bewildered, anxious and just the slightest bit afraid.

*****

Over the next few months after the incident with the bluebells, Annie and Bernard settled more comfortably into their life together. She began to feel at ease with her husband, and Bernard relaxed more with her and would tease her in his quiet way. There existed between Bernard, Annie and Mick an invisible barrier, a wall dividing them, and into each compartment the three of them retreated, safe in a kind of strange way, behind the sanctuary that they themselves had erected. It seemed to Bernard and Annie, the safest way to live. Of Mick neither of them would hazard any opinion, as Mick himself had built a permanent home there behind which he hid.

Life is a series of events. The brothers continued their work on the farm leaving Annie to look after the house and she was grateful for this. Bernard was glad to leave the cooking and household tasks to his wife and Mick had never taken any part in these duties anyway. He would eat his meals, silently, his dark head focused on the food on his plate, eat his food and then push his plate to the side, stand up and without a word to the two of them, take himself off to his room for the night. Annie had first felt the strain of these silent mealtimes but gradually grew to accept the situation. In fact, she was relieved when Mick left so promptly, the unease of his presence in the house all so pervasive.

This situation continued for a couple of months until one day, when the leaves began to fall from the trees and the wild winter wind that pushed in from the Atlantic increased in furiosity, Mick disappeared.

Bernard became taciturn, tense, refusing to talk. Annie felt quite at a loss to know what to say, her usual optimism assailed with doubts.

"Where does he go?" she enquired, tentatively, two days after Mick's disappearance.

"How do I know?"

He continued eating his evening meal, slowly, not looking at Annie. For the rest of the night he remained silent, staring into the distance. It seemed to Annie that she was a spectator, that she was being drawn into something she didn't understand, something almost too much to bear, too much suffering for one so young. Her hands trembled slightly as she washed the dishes. Her usual loving husband, morose and distant, and Annie, too became distant and thought of her mother and London and a life before Bernard and Mick and the West of Ireland and this white house, this An Teach Ban. The dishes scrubbed; her tears behind her eyes and the lonely moments of marriage and exile somehow filled with the sadness of death and war and suffering rising up within her. Wondering, wondering if only for a second, but the thought came into her head as she finished her work...were Bernard and Mick one? Had she somehow been duped, swept off her feet with a madness, it couldn't be called a passion, a madness, perhaps, to have met and married and removed herself from all that was familiar? Where was the wretched Mick? How could he just disappear without a trace? Without a word of farewell, taking nothing, just leaving his room the same, his dog sitting disconcertedly at the door, waiting – leaving dog and brother, bereft? Annie felt a savage moment of self-pity that threatened to well up inside her and take over and end in a flood of tears. She was happy enough with Bernard and her life in the West but Mick's shadow was always there. The world of the three of them revolved around Mick and he imparted a kind of control, his silences as much as a problem as his occasional moments of civility. Annie felt trapped between the two men, with no way out.

*****

Bernard knew his brother, or at least he thought he knew his brother, but he was reticent to speak about Mick to Annie, fearful that she would leave him. So he clung to the hope that if he kept quiet about Mick, Annie would stay. He knew Annie had a right to know what had happened but a mixture of fear if he told her and a kind of twisted loyalty to Mick, kept him silent. There was a fierce loyalty in Bernard to Mick that no one, not even Annie, could come between.

So Bernard knew he would have to look for Mick in all the familiar places. He would have to start at Murphy's pub and then the other bars in Ballybeg and finally go to Doctor Ryan and Garda Liam O'Sullivan and then, cap in hand, to Father O'Malley. All three men, doctor, policeman and priest, knew Mick on differing levels; the one constant with the three of them was a strange sort of responsibility for Mick and a pity for Bernard. The three of them would do their best to bring the recalcitrant back to the farm and back to his brother. They would ask around, even search along the shore in case Mick had wandered to the sea.

Garda O'Sullivan had found him there once, wandering along the shore, muttering to himself in Irish, incoherent and distant; unaware it seemed of his surroundings. Mick was stumbling along, with no hint of whiskey on his breath, stumbling along; one foot minus a boot and in the process of walking over the shingle beach, this foot was bleeding. Like Doctor Ryan, Liam O'Sullivan felt compassion. He had, after all, sat next to Mick Kelly as boys when Brother Michael would ridicule him for his slowness in arithmetic and Mick would gently explain how to get the answers right when Brother Michael's back was turned. Big, bumbling Liam, Sergeant of Police, had never forgotten that. So on this occasion, he took Mick by the arm and walked him back to the police house. There his dear wife who looked after him and their five children with self-sacrifice and devotion, took one look at Mick and his bleeding foot and without a second's hesitation, made Mick sit down. She brought warm water and bathed the foot, talking and scolding all the time and Liam watched his wife kneel at the feet of Mick Kelly. He felt a reverence tinged with awe and he thought of Jesus bathing the feet of the disciples and he was overcome momentarily with a feeling of humility. His wife washed and fussed and Mick muttered away, still in Irish, but was as docile as could be, even smiled with gratitude when the foot was dried and a clean sock found. He was grateful that night to lie down at the police house waking, the next morning, not belligerent, but slightly bemused at his surroundings. Because of this incident Mrs O'Sullivan and Liam always found it difficult to picture Mick in the light of Mrs Ryan's account.

But no one had seen Mick this time when Bernard went calling, policeman, priest and doctor all equally puzzled at Mick's whereabouts. So Bernard went home to Annie, still argumentative and withdrawn, his lips set in a hard line, not wishing to speak. Ten days passed and still no Mick and then came a night like no other.

It was Mick's dog, whimpering and anxious, sitting at the back door, that alerted them. Outside, the wild wind and rain combined to lash the windows, so dark and cold that Bernard and Annie were thankful to be inside, the turf fire burning. They were about to retire for the night when the door was thrust open and wind, rain and Mick entered into their cosy togetherness. Mick was as wild as the night. He hadn't shaved for days and his dark blue eyes seemed to be on fire. He stumbled, almost falling into the warmth of the kitchen, tripped over his excited dog as he did so. Annie and Bernard stared transfixed. Mick's cap was wet and nearly covered his eyes. He looked like a caricature of a person, so comic almost in his stumbling although he didn't appear to be drunk.

Time stops at some moments of stress or so it seemed as Mick lurched forward bringing his tall body nearer to Annie and Bernard. Suddenly, without warning, he banged the palm of his hand onto the table and his eyes looking in the direction of Annie, but almost not seeing, cried:

"She'll have to go! She'll have to go!"

And he pulled a chair from the table, sat, his eyes all the time fixed on Annie.

"Bí i do thost, a Mhícheál," (Calm down, Michael), and Bernard tried to restrain his brother.

But again, Mick brought his hand down onto the table, again and again, the noise of the wind outside and the captive soul of Mick Kelly inside.

"Go to bed, Annie. Go to bed, in the name of God, Annie! Go to bed!"

And as he spoke, Bernard half-pushed Annie towards their bedroom door. She stumbled, too, like Mick, in the dark away from the light of the paraffin lamp, stumbled into the safety of her bedroom; all the time she heard the hand of Mick hitting the table with a rhythmic pummelling until it seemed he would destroy his hand.

Annie thrust her face into the pillow and sobbed. She could hear the two men arguing in Irish. Not able to understand a word of it, she felt more and more the pain of loneliness as words and the thud of the hand kept on and on and on. Hours later, or so it seemed to her, all went quiet.

The cruelty of the situation confounded her. She had been so overjoyed today. A visit to Doctor Ryan had confirmed her instinct and she knew she was pregnant. All she had wanted to do was pick the right moment to tell Bernard and she thought he would be happy too. They had talked about starting a family and now it was happening. It seemed doubly painful for Annie that on, what was for her a joyful day, she had had to witness such a horrible verbal attack from her husband's brother. In a short space of time, or so it seemed, she had gone through all the emotions as far as Mick was concerned, fear, alienation, confusion and tonight, absolute despair.

The door to her bedroom remained shut but somehow the noises kept on in her head all through the long night.

CHAPTER FOUR

Annie woke early in the morning to find Mick's collie dog, Paddy, lying fully stretched out along her back. The dog, warm and contented, stirred as Annie did, his brown eyes staring sleepily at her. Annie stretched out her hand to stroke the top of his black head. The dog had never ventured into her room before and she found it surprising that he had that of all nights. Mick, strange in so many ways, was consistently kind to "Paddy-dog" as he called his dog and the dog, for his part, adored Mick. Annie found it slightly odd that Mick, from what she had observed and from what Mrs Ryan had said, was devoted to his dog. After all, he had exhibited on so many occasions, the worst being last night, a complete lack of regard as far as people were concerned. It was as if with this creature he could be at ease, that the dog accepted him for what he was, made no judgements and that the intelligent brown eyes of Paddy-dog held wisdom beyond human understanding. The consistency of this bond between man and dog puzzled Annie and she was surprised that the dog had decided to somehow find his way to her bed on the one night Bernard had not.

During that dark night a change occurred within Annie Kelly, a change perceptible to no-one – not even to herself. Annie was no stranger to either grief or despair. With Bernard she had come to Ireland with all the innocence and excitement of a child. Now with the stirrings of new life within her, she was no longer a girl. There was even a slight change in her relationship with Bernard; he would never again have the magic of before. That was gone forever. She would love him, support him, look out for him but she had seen his weakness, had felt for a moment, betrayed, and known the agony of that moment. She never spoke of this to another living soul, not even her mother, but it was there along with the innocence of her girlhood, gone forever. Welcomed into the world of womankind was Annie and never again would there be any doubt as to who was the strength in the Kelly household.

Bernard changed, too, after that night. He was now a little wary of his wife although proud to know he was to be a father. Proving his manhood to the people of Ballybeg was of importance to him but he would begin to show signs of a melancholy that had always been with him – a melancholy which was hidden with the excitement of meeting and winning Annie. This sadness had been masked in those early months of marriage behind a screen of joviality. But now, he too, would brood, in a silent agony of doubts and fears. The compartments where Annie and Bernard found themselves now widened between them. Although they went about their day-to-day lives, structured, mundane – but filling in their days – with acceptance and a certain amount of resignation, neither one would ever recapture the complete happiness of their early life together.

The only one who seemed totally oblivious to the change in the household was Mick. He never spoke to them of his wild night of emotion. Annie would often ask herself: Did it ever happen? Had he spoken those words to her, were they even directed at her? Had he banged the table for so long? Was it something she had dreamed up? Because the next morning Mick, still silent, had smiled at her in a rational way, disarming her with a smile. He greeted her pregnancy, unexpectedly, with interest and remained working on the farm alongside Bernard. He would read his books in the evenings and didn't go to his room so often but would remain seated, his dark head down, reading. Bernard, tired, and Annie, too, as her pregnancy advanced, would sometimes retire earlier than before, leaving Mick to himself, alone with his thoughts. Life in the Kelly household began at last to have a little meaning, the tedious hours of physical work, during the day, tiring them all.

*****

When Annie was seven months pregnant, Mrs Smith made the long journey from London to be with her daughter. She stayed the night with Mrs Slattery in Dun Laoghaire and travelled the next day to Ballybeg. Although Mrs Smith was born in London and had never been to Ireland, it wasn't a foreign country for her and she was glad to fall under the spell of its charms. Her mother and father were from Cork and had lived out their days in London, never being able to return to their native land. But the longing of the exile was in them and many stories from Ireland were told – stories which wove fascination into both Mrs Smith's and Annie's early lives so that Ireland became a mystical place of leprechauns and fairies and quaint people who spoke in a different way.

Annie waited, pregnant, at the Ballybeg Railway Station, waited with Bernard for her mother whom she missed dearly. She waited, wondering what her mother would make of her new life. She had written letters but she wasn't very good at expressing herself on paper; her letters were brief, full of day-to-day events. Of Bernard, she spoke in glowing terms; of Mick, she said nothing. But all the time she longed to talk about Mick; he caused her such confusion when she thought of him.

She need not have worried about her mother's reaction to her life in the West. Mrs Smith had the verbosity of the people from Cork in her genes – once started, it was hard to get her to stop. Everything was lovely. Mrs Smith was over the moon to see her daughter again and happy to meet Bernard, too. Bernard grinned from ear to ear; he was fond of his mother-in-law. All the suffering of the war and post-war Britain and being away from Annie forgotten, Mrs Smith talked incessantly as though to stop would be to hear silence which would be deathly, a silence she could not bear. It was far better to fill every waking minute with words. It mattered little to her whether the words had any meaning; the silence had to be filled.

One of Mrs Smith's endearing qualities was that she could see no evil in any living soul. This virtue was tested when she lost her husband, Jimmy and then her son in the war...plucky little Jimmy Smith, struggling on the Dunkirk beach to reach the waiting fishing boats, ducking noise and bullets and blood. There to the side of him was his mate, lurching forward and falling. Without a thought for his own survival, Jimmy leapt to save him. That one act of self sacrifice cost Jimmy his life as the next German bullet went through his chest, killing him instantly. Brave Jimmy Smith, who owned the butcher's shop in Camden and thus posthumously decorated for this act of heroism. Mrs Smith kept the medal beside a photo of Jimmy in his uniform... kept the photo, framed on the mantelpiece above the fire. Every day she dusted the shelf and a few years later, the photo of her son, William, framed also and in uniform, too, would be dusted... because William, aged eighteen when his father was killed, couldn't wait to get over the Channel and kill as many Germans as he could to avenge his father's death. For hatred burned into William's heart and who knows how many mother's sons did William kill because he was a fine and determined shot? But Germans were to be killed. Until one fine day as the British Army pushed through Italy, one fine day in the little village of Lapeggio, a German bullet pierced William's heart and there was no more killing. No medals for William, just one of the many "Killed in Action". And Mrs Smith grieved for her husband and her son, grieved and went to Mass daily to make some sense of it, spoke of everything and everyone but never of her Jimmy or her William. And the mantelpiece was dusted as a kind of ritual, unspoken and sad, for she could not understand the meaning of it all. Finally one day, she forgave the German bullets and laid her pain to rest... but the photos and the medal on the mantelpiece still had to be dusted.

All that was behind her now because here was her Annie, looking beautiful with that quiet Irishman, Bernard, beside her and Mrs Smith's heart swelled with motherly pride.

Both Annie and Bernard were a little anxious about introducing Mrs Smith to Mick but they needn't have worried. Mrs Smith chattered enthusiastically from Ballybeg to An Teach Ban and alighted from Bernard's new Baby Ford motor car with surprising alacrity.

"Annie, this is lovely", and truly the white house was on that beautiful summer's day. The house had been whitewashed thanks to Mick and Bernard and it looked cared for, tidy. Annie had achieved wonders. Somehow she had coaxed a motley group of garden plants to grow at the front of the house. Sheltered from the bitter north-west winds, red fuchsia and hydrangea had survived and now in the heat of the summer, were flowering profusely. So there was colour and the green, green of Ireland with the wild and passionate beauty of the West dazzling Mrs Smith who had for so long been amongst all the grey of London's post-war buildings.

She enthused non-stop and Annie and Bernard stood back amused. Mick appeared as if from nowhere. He had been working all day in the vegetable garden and his hands were black with the soil. This was of no consequence to Mrs Smith and she rushed towards him and, without waiting for a formal introduction, spoke as rapidly as she had been doing all afternoon, hand outstretched in greeting:

"So you must be Mick! It's just lovely here. After London... but oh, it's so quiet but I guess you're used to that, aren't you? My mother and father came from Cork, did Annie tell you? But you know, I've never been to Ireland before... it's such a journey, isn't it? I've come to see my Annie and I'm so excited, aren't you? A baby in the house! Well, that's a turn-up for you all, isn't it? What do you think of it? Sleepless nights, but you men sleep through anything, don't you?" and she flirted a bit, and then went on, "But oh, it's good, oh so very good. Isn't this lovely?"

And her eyes took in the kitchen, the yellow linoleum floor, the dark brown cupboards, the range, the chairs, table, yellow walls with a red trim, strange combination of colour, she thought privately, but Annie looked as though she had done wonders, and it was so tidy. Why, Annie was always a tidy girl and with the war and all that, well, you never knew from one moment to the next. She paused for breath and then started again:

"Oh, I must sit down. You'd think I wouldn't want to sit. All those hours on the train... but Dublin is lovely, isn't it? And the people so friendly..."

Annie glanced at Mick to see how he was taking this sudden burst of trivia in what was usually a semi-silent house but he seemed unbothered and was busy drying his hands. He hadn't even appeared surprised at Mrs Smith's constant chatter but greeted her shyly, taking her hand warmly almost, which made Annie for a moment jealous of her mother. Such a different greeting from when I met him, she reminded herself grimly, if not a little amused now; her own shyness was slowly disappearing as she stamped her authority on the house. And being pregnant, that seemed to count a lot. Everyone seemed pleased about it, that's for sure, she thought, even Mick. He had been different somehow.

He had got drunk a few times since that awful night but he hadn't disappeared for days as he previously had. Instead he worked away and spent the evenings reading. Even his drunkenness seemed more akin to confusion, and he had slept it off both times, slumped in his old black reading chair in the kitchen with his faithful Paddy-dog, non-judgemental, at his feet. Not a word about it in the morning, Annie recalled and he had gone silent for a few days but there didn't seem to be the irrational behaviour, so Annie and Bernard, too, could only surmise that perhaps Mick was feeling better.

Annie wondered how they would all cope with her mother in the house for a few months but at least it was summer and the long days made life so much more enjoyable. There would be the excitement of the baby, too. Mrs O'Sullivan, Norah as she insisted on being called, was both policeman's wife and midwife, and she was ready to assist when the time came. Annie's pregnancy was going well, she was tired now at night, but everything else seemed fine and Doctor Ryan kept an eye on her. Annie, over the last seven months, had begun at long last to feel part of An Teach Ban and the community of Ballybeg. She knew she was referred to in some quarters as "Bernard Kelly's English girl" and that Father O'Malley was very cool towards her, which puzzled her somewhat as she had not done anything to antagonise him, except perhaps, be English. But Mrs Ryan was an ally, a mother in the absence of her own, and Annie was eager for her mother to meet the Ryans, hoping that her mother and Mrs Ryan would get on.

She was to be proved right when she was able, a few days later, to introduce the two of them. Mrs Ryan prefixed nearly every sentence with, "And I said to John..." Mrs Smith mirrored this with, "And I told Annie...", so the two of them chattered away, not really taking much notice of each other, but contented, nevertheless. For an outsider, it was hilarious to listen to, as both seemed to be quite unaware of each other's words. It was to be a friendship based on mutual resemblance and a surprising number of other similarities in both their lives. Mrs Ryan was from Cork also and liked fancy hats. She was an attractive woman and was considered a beauty when she first caught the attention of young Doctor Ryan. Her beauty, however, gave her pretensions. She was pleased to accept Doctor Ryan's attentions and to distance herself from her many brothers and sisters who teased her unrelentingly, enjoying the anger which resulted. Mrs Ryan was quite relieved to leave her native Cork and go to live in Ballybeg with Doctor Ryan and become the doctor's wife. In her mind, she was convinced that being from Cork gave her status in Ballybeg over the local women and in the twenty years or so that she had lived in the small community, she had gained power and authority.

There was no trace of bitterness in Mrs Ryan and she never for one moment regretted not having children, fearing the change that this would have made to her figure, but her childless state made her vulnerable in the world of women. She compensated by setting herself up as the leading light of Ballybeg and an invitation to one of her afternoon teas was highly prized by the other women in the town. She liked Annie from the moment she first met her and in truth, as time went on, Annie became like a daughter to her. So it was natural for Mrs Ryan to find a friend in Annie's mother.

Now An Teach Ban became a house of women. For so long, too long, this had been a bachelor's domain; now Annie and Mrs Smith held control and the men spent most of the time outside. One well-remembered day, a few weeks before her baby was born, Annie finally invited Mrs Ryan to tea and that good lady came, enthusing and curious, wearing her pale blue hat with the navy blue silk rose on the side, came and drank tea with her young hostess and was very pleased with herself. She chattered away to Mrs Smith but all the time her eyes were everywhere; there was Mick's tweed jacket hanging at the back of the kitchen door, his extra pair of boots by the range and Mrs Ryan was unsure whether to speak of him or not because Mick's presence was in the room. Invisible, but they were all aware of it somehow. No one sat on his black leather reading chair next to the range. No one spoke of Mick at all but carefully avoided the subject. Bernard was mentioned and Mrs Ryan noted his tweed cap and scarf flung casually on a chair. He wasn't far away. For Annie, having Mrs Ryan in her house was a minor triumph, she had at last asserted her authority and Mrs Ryan was the outward and visible sign of this. She had been careful to invite her when she knew the men would be away cutting turf, and wouldn't be back till after dark. So it was a happy day for the women and further cemented the friendship between the three of them.

* * * * *

It was fine again the next day. Mick was stacking the turf at the side of the shed, rhythmically, seemingly absorbed in his task, mundane but in the nature of him doing it, somehow majestic, and Annie stopped to watch. He was unaware of her presence, she had noticed since she first met him, how he could distance himself quite neatly from day-to-day events, become contained in his own work, seemingly oblivious to things around him. She wondered if this was a positive thing or whether it was a sign of something else in Mick that no one could fathom. She stared, the basket of wet washing balanced on her hip, and admired the physique of the man. Under his blue-striped, collar-less shirt, the sleeves rolled up to above his elbows, she could see his muscles as his arms moved backwards and forwards, backwards and forwards, the hands, those hands that she had noticed so often, taking the turf from the dray and stacking the heap, higher and higher.

Mick paused, stopping for a moment and turned and saw Annie looking at him. They stared at each other and then Annie broke the moment and, almost running, her face burning now, took her basket of washing to the clothes line, her back to Mick. He stretched his long body, still looking in Annie's direction. From the pouch secured always on his leather belt, he took a cigarette paper, tobacco, rolled the tobacco into a cylinder and carefully licked the edge of the paper, spat a strand of tobacco onto the ground, and lit a match, breathing in the smoke. The smoke reached Annie's nostrils and she looked around, saw Mick staring at her, her heart beat in her chest and her hand shook slightly as she pegged out the clothes, men's clothes.

All the time Mick smoked and stared until Annie's work was done. She had to walk past him to get back to the house. Now it was she who was nervous, she kept her head

48

down to avoid his eyes, but all the time he kept staring at her. When she retreated to the safety of the house, she saw that he had resumed his work and was stacking the turf again, seemingly absorbed his task.

*****

On a warm August day when the inhabitants of Ballybeg awoke to think that their part of the world was the most beautiful, in fact the most *perfect* place in the whole world for there wasn't a cloud in the sky and the blue sky and Slieve Geal were etched perfectly against that sky, making this claim almost a certainty. On that day Annie Kelly went into labour and the process of bringing new life into that perfect place, began.

In the bed that she and Bernard shared, his father's and mother's bed, in this bed where she had laughed and cried, too, she felt the indescribable pain and the indescribable joy of childbirth. The small room with wardrobe, chest of drawers and mirror above, held secrets spoken and unspoken and Annie cried out in her pain, her eyes fixed on the Sacred Heart of Jesus on the wall and Jesus on His cross above her head, suffering Jesus, who had cried out too.

Calm Mrs O'Sullivan, prepared and in control, took charge of the situation... and Mrs Smith, there too, feeling for her daughter, loving her. This was a world of women, and Bernard, banished to the kitchen, could only wait and pray until, finally, there was silence.

The cry of a baby. Bernard was summoned to meet his wife, all scrubbed up, with the baby at her breast. Bernard Kelly, quiet Irishman that he was, with warm tears running down his face because this was life, new life at last in An Teach Ban and all thanks to Annie. Bernard and Annie had a son, another male in a house of men, this boy they would call Francis. Francis for Bernard's father and the James was for brave Jimmy Smith and joy was theirs to share.

Bernard did what he always did at moments of great emotion. He took his fiddle out of its battered old leather

49

case and went outside An Teach Ban on that beautiful day, and, leaning against the window ledge, he played as he had never played before. The jigs, the reels, the glad songs, the sad songs, the tension and the release of the music drove him on and on and the sound filled the summer air. He must have played for an hour or so, so great was his joy at the birth of his son. And the only witness to his happiness was an old brown hen who clucked away and looked interested as the notes rose and fell. Annie, weary but joyful, could hear the tunes coming to her as she lay with her baby in her arms, and was humbled and at peace, all at the same time.

*****

Mick disappeared again but this time his disappearance was hardly noticed, so great was the excitement and happiness in the house. For fifteen days he stayed away and no one knew where he was. When he returned, he came back in the early morning and was making a cup of tea for himself when Annie met him there.

Annie surprised as always with Mick but so complete was her joy with her new son that she put her hand on Mick's arm and softly said,

"We have a son, Mick... a little boy... Francis, after your father, Francis James... James, after mine... you're an uncle now, Mick."

And she looked into his eyes, not frightened of him anymore. She wasn't sure of his reaction; she just wanted to tell him the news, herself. And to her relief, Mick smiled.

"Well, well, well...", and he put his hand on hers and his eyes were calm and untroubled.

They stood like this, the two of them, contented somehow for the first time and this was a moment to remember. Mick broke away first and from his pocket he brought forth a carving, carved in bog oak, black and hard, a carving of a spoon, beautifully executed with a Celtic cross at the end. The wood so hard to carve, like stone, it would have taken hours of patient work.

"I made this for yer wee bebee", and he shyly gave the carving to Annie.

Annie was overwhelmed and it was now she, who shyly accepted the gift, at a loss for words.

"It's beautiful, Mick. Thank you... I didn't know you could do work like this..."

She held the wooden spoon in her hand and somehow she was holding Mick because this was part of him and it was his. For her, it became a special moment. She was bewildered by the gift, but glad.

Again, Mick seemed to change and, without another word, he moved away from her and back to his cup of tea. Annie held the wooden spoon in her hand for what seemed an eternity until the crying of Francis James aroused her from her reverie and Mick was forgotten.

*****

Ma and Pa Murphy ran the most popular bar in Ballybeg. No one was sure where they came from. Some said they hailed from Tipperary and others said it was further east in Wexford but no one knew for certain; everyone could remember their arrival and no one knew their names. Ma called Pa, "Pa" and he called her "Ma" so ever after it was Ma and Pa. They took over the sheebeen and Ma sold groceries and such-like at one end. The bar was situated at the other end with a piano in the corner, tables, chairs and a turf fire burning in the winter. The Murphys arrived with their three children and in a very short space of time transformed the place and prospered in so doing.

Ma Murphy exuded sexuality from every pore of her well-endowed body. Red-haired, with strands of grey, and a voluptuous bosom that sent every male heart pounding, she was the perfect businesswoman. Ma had a way of pulling the pints of Guinness, talking and laughing as she did, and leaning ever so close over the counter so that many a Ballybeg man would order more pints just to catch a glimpse, just a hint of that delightful cleavage. Murphy's

51

Bar smelt of Guinness and whiskey and tobacco smoke but come close enough and there would be the heavenly, ever-agreeable waft of Ma's cheap perfume.

Pa kept his eyes on his wife along with all the other men. He was a short man, balding and minus his two front teeth. Rumour had it that he had got into a fight with one of Ma's admirers and in the ensuing battle, lost those teeth. This could not be verified by anyone as no one knew anything about the Murphys, which was difficult for Ballybeg folk, who made up for their lack of knowledge by speculation.

At first the women were jealous of their men going too near Ma but as time wore on, they began to see her as the astute businesswoman that she was and grew to admire her, too. Ma's private thoughts were that men were weak, governed by their sexual desires, and women would always be in control. She was firmly behind her fellow women in the battle of the sexes and this solidarity increased the takings at Murphy's Bar for food and drink and brought in both men and women.

The Murphys had three children who were part of the bar scene. Helen, the eldest, red-haired too, with her mother's ability to disarm men; Dermot who helped his father behind the bar and young Liam who got in everyone's way. Pa always wore a red cravat and red braces. When he thought that Ma had gone far enough, he would stand back and pull the braces out from his body, over and over again. It was a signal that Ma understood and she would discontinue her amorous innuendos until Pa stopped pulling on his braces. There were other bars in Ballybeg and no Irishman would let a bar go dry, but Murphy's was definitely the place to be, especially on Saturday nights when Bernard Kelly played the fiddle and Helen Murphy sang. So it was natural that after the baptism of Francis James, everyone, including Mick, would go to Murphy's. Even the Ryans. Mrs Ryan thought Ma a trifle coarse but she had to laugh sometimes at Ma's ever-present wit which, upon analysis, revealed much about life and the peculiarities of humankind.

"Well, here ye all are!" cried Ma when the Kellys arrived. "And drinks all round, isn't that right, Pa? Now, where's this wee bebee? Oh, Bernard, he looks just like ye", and she winked at Annie but thrust her ample bosom in Bernard's direction.

At this, Bernard, husband and father, but still shy, blushed as Ma flung her body onto him and kissed him on his cheek – twice!

"We'll be havin' that drink, Ma", replied Bernard, trying to hide his embarrassment, "before ye change your mind."

"And I hope ye've brought yer fiddle, Bernard Kelly, to pay for it," retorted Ma with her characteristic quick wit.

"I'll be havin' the drink first, Ma, then ye can have yer music," answered Bernard because he was a proud man that night amongst his family and friends.

At first Annie had been self-conscious at Murphy's but gradually as she got to know them more, she relaxed and enjoyed the banter and gossip. She had grown up listening to her father's humour in the butcher's shop in Camden, so she could give back almost as much as she got. And Ma had proved to be a good customer, too, for Annie's surplus eggs and vegetables. So the two women got on well enough. Ma was straight in her business dealings and Annie admired that; her own father had been the same, and it had paid off for them.

Ma oozed sexual fantasy to all the men, even to Father O'Malley, if the truth be known... all the men but Mick who seemed oblivious to her charms. She served him drinks but she treated him with a certain amount of caution and refrained from leaning too close. She was civil to him but that was all. When he drank too many whiskeys, it was Pa who escorted him to the door and it was Pa who told him he had had enough. Annie noticed Ma's polite behaviour towards Mick and it further puzzled her to the enigma that was Mick.

That night at Murphy's Bar, Bernard played the fiddle, joyfully, freely and Ma Murphy did a little jig in front of him, lifted her skirts, threw her head back and her bosom rose and fell as she danced. Everyone talked at once. Francis James, the new arrival in Ballybeg and the reason for the joyfulness, slept through the evening somehow... and Mick got drunk.

*****

Mrs Smith left for London a few days later. This time she took with her other photographs, Francis James in his christening shawl with Bernard and Annie and one of Mick with his arm around her shoulders and another one of her Annie in her best dress, looking content. And these photographs were framed, too, and placed on the china cabinet in the flat above the butcher's shop and well away from Jimmy and William. These photographs were dusted daily because here at last was a happy memory and the flat didn't seem quite so empty now.

*****

In the late summer of the next year when baby Francis was beginning to take his first tentative steps and Annie's workload increased by the hour, Mick and Bernard had another argument. They were cleaning out the cow shed when Mick announced:

"They were hirin' in town last week. The one from MacArthur's was toting for work. Me and Tommy Flynn have signed up for the season."

Bernard stopped shovelling:

"Have you taken leave of yer senses, man? What are we goin' to do here? Things are lookin' up now..."

But Mick did not seem to hear. His mind was made up.

"The first farm's at Ardrossen, then on to Maybole in Ayrshire. We'll take the ferry from Larne... it's all arranged. They'll be at Stranraer with the lorry. There's a few of us goin'. Ye'll need money for Annie and the bebee," and Mick's face set hard in his determination.

"But, man, we have work here. We'll manage somehow... it's not like father's day. Things are gettin' better here."

But Mick was adamant. "Me mind's made up. There's twenty signed up to go but me and Tommy will stick together... there's work."

Bernard felt unsure. Mick always got his way but Bernard was nervous of Mick going over to Scotland, tattie-hoking. He was reassured a little with Tommy Flynn going with Mick. Tommy and Mick had been to school together and Tommy, simple soul that he was, would see that no harm came to Mick. Tommy lived with his sister in Ballybeg and did odd jobs around the place. He often helped the brothers on the farm when the workload increased with the seasons. A bachelor, too, Mick and he got on well but Bernard always worried about Mick's disappearances and would he be all right away from home?

"Annie needs the money," was all Mick would say and as far as he was concerned, that was the end of the matter.

So Mick packed his case and got ready to go to Scotland. A case, now; his father used to wrap his few possessions in a black cloth, the bundle, and he would carry it under his arm. All the men from the West carried their bundle. In those days it was useful to sit on in the long journeys by train and boat and lorry. His father told stories of the black bundle carried to the market places of England. It was a sign for the farmers looking for Irish labour. But Mick had his small leather case in which he put an extra pair of boots, shirts and his few books. He was reading his way through *Gulliver's Travels* and a book of the poetry of Yeats.

Annie wondered at his going and felt a peculiar twinge of apprehension for Mick. In this she was in agreement with Bernard as there was enough work to be done on the farm. Mick's leaving for six months would mean more work for her as she had learnt to help on the farm. But Mick was determined that he could make more money for them, working ten hours a day, doing farm work and pulling up potatoes in Scotland. He and Tommy would stick together and he would be back in no time.

*****

Annie and Bernard received just one letter from Mick in the six months that he was away in Scotland. He enclosed some bank notes which helped them. And he wrote the letter from a farm in Perthshire. The letter was brief.

Everything fine. Plenty of work. There's money for Annie. Going next to the McNultys in Berwickshire. Then to a farm near Glasgow. Tommy's been with me most of the time. Be home for Christmas.
Mick.

Bernard looked relieved and worried at the same time when he read the note. Annie didn't say a word but placed the letter on the mantelpiece above the range... and waited for Mick.

It was Annie who saw Mick and Tommy Flynn returning home. When she saw Mick, she gasped in surprise because Mick was wearing a black patch over his left eye and he seemed to be finding it hard to walk. Bernard was summoned from his work and Tommy told the story. The two men sat gratefully in the kitchen, Mick in his old black leather reading chair.

"It had been their last night in Scotland and they had had a good time, working from farm to farm. They got lodgings for the night off Argyll Street in Glasgow and decided as it was their last night to have a drink. They were sitting in a bar having a whisky when a big Jock, the worst for the drink, started to pick on Mick and call him all the names under the sun. Mick refused to be provoked

56

and Mick and Tommy left the bar but this big Jock followed them outside and leapt on Mick's back. Mick shook him off and felled him with a blow to the chin. Tommy and Mick were about to beat a hasty retreat when, out of nowhere another even bigger Glaswegian threw a punch straight into Mick's left eye. Blood everywhere. Tommy took Mick's arm and they made off down the street. Mick could hardly see and the pain was excruciating. Somehow, the two of them made their way to the Casualty Department of the hospital and the flesh around Micks eye was sewn up. Tommy had some holy water his sister had brought back from Lourdes and he administered it to the eye and didn't Mick's eye begin to get better straight away but his sight was blurred in that eye and a black patch had to be worn. Doctor Ryan would have to take the stitches out and, please God, it has healed because all the two of them could think of was getting to the boat and the train back to Ballybeg and away from Glasgow. Mick was in pain all the time and Tommy fussed like a mother hen. That's why Tommy brought Mick home but they had the money, thanks be to God, and had avoided it being stolen, and there it is..."

Mick carefully eased a wallet from an inner pocket in his jacket and brought out Scottish bank notes, fivers, tenners and laid them on the table. Everyone was silent because the effort and the work to bring them home had been incalculable. Mick and Tommy laboured for ten hours a day, six days a week, sometimes lifting the potatoes,throwing them into baskets and other times carrying the full load, shaving and roping the barrels, sometimes loading. Back-breaking, constant work. And for all that time, Tommy had made sure that Mick wasn't far away and made sure Mick didn't leave any of the farms. The gaffer was pleased with their work and rewarded them at the end of the season with a bonus, well deserved. It had been worth it, the unfortunate incident of the fight and the damage to Mick's eye souring an otherwise uneventful six months.

But Mick was tired now. Bernard and Annie could see that. Annie cooked a sustaining pork stew with potatoes and turnips and they were all content. Mick sat in his chair and baby Francis climbed onto his lap, much to everyone's surprise and tried to play with the black patch over Mick's eye until Mick gave him his watch chain instead. Paddy-dog, arthritic in all legs now and eyesight diminishing too, curled up at his master's feet and laid his old head on Mick's boot. He was glad to have Mick home. Bernard and Annie were glad as well. Annie could only wonder. She had suffered so much with Mick's changing moods – his indifference, his hostility. But she had witnessed a gentle side, the long silences, the disappearances and the confusion. The night that Mick came home to An Teach Ban, weary and in pain, Annie knew in her deepest being that the barrier which had divided the two of them had softened a little. Mick was safe, praise be to God, and asleep in his own chair beside the range, his dog at his feet and his infant nephew in his arms.

*****

The year that electricity came to the West and lit up the lives of the people of Ballybeg, Annie was pregnant again. The lives of Bernard, Annie and Mick had taken on a kind of routine – a certain inevitability between the three of them, each still in their own place and time. Francis James was a great distraction as young children are, and he was made much of in this house that used to be a house of men. Bernard proved to be what is deemed a good father but it was the relationship between Francis and Mick that puzzled them all. From their first encounter the night Mick came home, there seemed to be a bond between the two of them. Francis would wait for Mick to come in from the fields and jump up and down when he saw him. Mick, usually so withdrawn and silent, responded in a like fashion. Before very long, they would be chattering away in a way only decipherable to them and Annie was convinced that no matter what Mick did to himself, he would never harm her son. This was a comfort to her as she went about her day-to-day activities. She was helping the men more on the farm and there was no more talk of Mick going to Scotland tattie-hoking. Annie worked hard, and the London she knew as a girl gradually dimmed in her memory.

*****

One afternoon the Murphys made a deputation to An Teach Ban with Ma at the head and her children following. Ma was panting by the time she had climbed the gravel road to the house. She mistrusted the outside world, happier within her four walls and the road up to the farm was a rough track. Helen and Liam squabbled all the way. Although Helen was sixteen and could sing like a nightingale, she would often revert to a childlike state with Liam and torment him, too. So the two of them were quite a handful for Ma and she was annoyed with them and told them to stop or they would be sent home.

Annie was surprised to see Ma panting and slightly harassed at the door, her red hair an untidy heap on the top of her head. But she invited them all in for tea and Helen and Liam were dispatched with Francis to see some new born chicks. When Annie and Ma were alone, Ma announced:

"I'm after stealin' yer husband, Annie."

And Annie, knowing Ma's implied reputation, hesitated before answering with a weak, "What do you mean, Ma?"

"Well", said Ma, and she hoisted her ample bosom upwards and forwards as she always did when she wanted to emphasise her words, "I'm fer expandin' the business." And she proceeded to enlighten Annie.

At the side of Murphy's Bar, just a few paces away, was an old outbuilding and Ma had decided to knock a hole in the bar walls and join the bar to this outbuilding. She had plans, you see. Pa and Dermot were busy this very day with Tommy Flynn clearing out the outbuilding and she had organised Seamus Hennegan, the builder, if she could catch him between drinking bouts, to do the work of connecting the two buildings together. She had been thinking of this project for a while, in fact ever since Francis's baptism party, and had come up with this imaginative plan. In the barn, she would have space for various functions as the existing bar was far too small and often people had to be turned away because of the overcrowding. This was anathema to Ma and she had decided to make provisions for progress. The barn would have a bar, too, and a dance floor. She would hire the hall out for weddings, funerals, baptisms, any celebration in fact, and on crowded Saturday nights, it could be used as a second drinking establishment. This new fangled electricity would light up the place and in time Ma would consider providing food for the functions.

Annie could only admire Ma's shrewdness and skill at making money, but wondered what it had to do with the Kellys.

"Well, yer see," retorted Ma, as if it was totally obvious, "yer Bernard brings them in. Him and Helen, well, they're a good combination. I have a proposition for Bernard, ye can tell him from me."

And she breathed out, wriggling her ample body on Annie's kitchen chair, "I've been payin' him in pints for the playin' on Saturday nights but I'm offerin' him a wage and more regular work and the pints, too. I'm a generous woman", she added, laughing. "I'd like Bernard to play for the functions and more work as it comes in. Ye'll tell him, won't ye? He can give me an answer on Saturday night," and at that Ma got up to leave. "Now, where's that wee divil, Liam?" she said. "There's a lot to put up with when we have boys, isn't there? It must be we're doin' penance, I often think to meself. And ye'll have another one, too," and she looked at Annie's expanding form. "I always know. It's

60

the way they lie. Thanks for the tea, I'll be goin' now and see if Pa has managed to do anything while I've been away."

Ma never expected an answer to any of these questions and Annie didn't volunteer any. All she could think of was what Bernard would make of Ma's offer. She knew he loved his music and he was a talented fiddle player. When he played, she saw the happiness in his eyes and the far off other world look that, not being a musician herself, she could only observe.

When she told Bernard of Ma's proposition, he didn't say a word but a surge of excitement went through him. He spoke to Mick and said he would accept Ma's offer. Mick was silent so Bernard took that as approval and was glad. Bernard knew that Ma would succeed in her project and that she would be true to her word as far as the wages were concerned. But in actual fact, Bernard would have played his fiddle for no monetary recompense, so filled with joy was he when he played.

For Bernard hated the farm and the farm work, hated the never-ending daily grind, the hours of physical labour, the struggles with the seasons, the never-ending sameness of the days. Hated it to the very bottom of his being but in his hatred he was trapped. With his fiddle he could escape, his fiddle and he were one, it was a kind of other dimension type of release and he could forget the farm, ever so briefly. When he was younger, he had longed to join the emigrant ships, to escape from the West and from Ireland, to make a new life for himself, somewhere, anywhere. His mother's family, the Reillys, had left in great hoards after the Famine, gone to Canada and then another group left for Boston, a few years later. They now considered themselves Canadians and Americans, respectively, and only thought of Ireland as a place of their ancestors.

The closest he ever came to leaving was just before he met Annie. There was a cousin he had grown up with who lived in Ballybeg, a musician too, who could play the piano accordion and make it dance. This cousin paid the £10 passage to Australia and ended up in Wollongong; even the name was exotic to Bernard's ears. This cousin met up with a few Irish lads and they had formed a band. They called themselves *The Lively Leprechauns*, bought an old bus and spent six months of the year travelling around western New South Wales and sometimes into south-eastern Queensland. They played in shearing sheds, in bars, in returned soldiers' clubs – the RSL clubs – anywhere in fact they could get a gig. The other six months of the year, they stayed round Wollongong playing in miners' clubs and the RSL clubs. It sounded idyllic. They needed a fiddle player and his cousin thought of Bernard. In a letter he wrote of the girls. There were plenty of them. You could lie on the warm sand and watch them. No priests around to warn you of the perils of female flesh. You could watch the girls frolicking and giggling in swimming costumes that clung to their bodies. Wet swimming costumes that sent your imagination rocketing. And the sea was warm and you could swim in the sea and not feel the cold. It sounded like heaven on earth. The Australians were a friendly lot and made much of the Irish lads. They were having the time of their lives and making money.

Bernard almost made up his mind to go. He thought for days about how he would tell Mick but when the time came to speak of it, a kind of fear overtook him and he knew then that he would never leave Mick, that Mick's hold was stronger than freedom and that the farm and the land would hold him, a prisoner, to the end of his days. And he remembered the sadness he went through for the lost opportunity and for his cowardice because he did consider it cowardice, and hated himself for it.

When the melancholy came upon Bernard, even sometimes when he was with Annie, he knew where it came from, and was sad. The release could only be through the fiddle, somehow the fiddle connected him to his missed opportunity, the dream that he could have been playing in shearing sheds in the Outback, in that far distant world, where life was so different and there were no dark days of winter. No one to say he was Mick Kelly's brother, Francis Kelly's son. The farm would have been a memory the way Australia was for him now, a dream. He was a fine musician and he would have done well. At least playing more hours at Murphy's Bar, he would have a momentary release from all those regrets. Bernard took his fiddle out of its case, sat on a kitchen chair, and played to Annie, Mick and Francis. Annie listened and knew that she had lost him to the music and that Ma would indeed, steal her husband away.

*****

Ma Murphy was to be proved right when Annie was delivered of another fine boy. As she held her newborn baby in her arms, Annie thought of William. In her new son's face, there was a remembrance and a similarity to her lost brother. It is a paradox, perhaps, but sometimes great happiness is stolen away by the sadness of another moment. Thus it was for Annie as she cradled her new son in her arms and caressed his tiny head. The tears welled up in her eyes, warm, rolling down her cheeks. She longed at that moment for William and her life before Bernard and Mick, before marriage and Ireland. If there had been a means of returning to the past, to what had been before, Annie would have gladly and freely and without hesitation, taken it. But life goes not backwards, it moves inexorably on. All Annie's longing could not bring any of it back because it was gone now; the sadness buried with William, along with her girlhood. Perhaps God has sent William back to her, she thought as the tears kept flowing, perhaps this little baby held William's soul? She looked into his small face and loved him. Of all her children, this was the one she loved the most.

They called him Declan because she liked the name. She somehow wanted William there, so he was baptised Declan William. She wondered what her mother would make of the "William", that never spoken name. This child

63

had to have her brother's name, of this she was certain and she would face her mother's grief if need be.

When Mrs Smith travelled once again to Ballybeg for another baptism and held her second grandson in her arms, she looked up at Annie, her eyes full of tears, a mother's pain. And quietly, but with a dignity born from suffering, spoke just four words:

"He looks like William."

She had never mentioned William's name since the German bullet had taken her son from her, years ago now.

This was another of those moments in a life, a secret moment between a mother and a daughter and no-one ever knew. Least of all Declan William.

*****

The seasons turned time into years. Francis became Frankie and started school. He was bright, like Mick, but had a temper when things didn't go his way, so Annie despaired, when she had a moment to think about it, which was rare. Bernard played the fiddle more often at Murphy's Bar and, true to her word, Ma paid him well and the Bar, refurbished and expanded with the electric light, flourished. Ma put a few of the other pubs in Ballybeg out of business in the process so she wasn't popular in some quarters. But Ma wasn't in business to be popular, she was in business to make money, and that is what she did. People liked Murphy's and kept coming. Bernard was happy to be part of the prosperity process and he and Helen were indeed a good combination.

The Kelly farm, too, began to show signs of success after so long being a subsistence affair. The Kellys looked to be winning the battle of the rural scene along with some of their neighbours. So it seemed to be that Mick and Annie were together more often. Most times, he was still sombre with her but occasionally he talked of his life, of life in the West of Ireland, of the emigrations, the hardships, the pathos, his mother and father. When he spoke of these things, Annie felt as though she had been granted a privilege, that she had been allowed into the secret parts of his being and she wondered if he had ever talked of these things to another. Had another woman ever heard these words or did his strange behaviour exclude him from female company? He fascinated her and intrigued her. All the things she had witnessed and all the different versions of events as far as Mick was concerned, continued to confuse her. She had tried to talk to Bernard about it, but he still ignored her questions and finally she gave up asking. Now she felt that she had no right to pry. Nor did she want to any more and refused to be drawn into talk of Mick to Mrs Ryan or Ma Murphy.

Mick had to wear his black eye patch most of the time, now, and he got weary when he read too much, which vexed him. But the gentle side remained with him with Annie and he never once raised his voice to her, the way he had done on that wild winter's night when Annie's world changed forever.

Annie loved having her boys with her. At night she would listen to Mick read to Frankie. Bernard was so often at Murphy's those nights, it was a contented little world with Frankie on Mick's lap and Declan trying to compete with his brother to be there too. And precious times between them all especially when Mick would look up and smile at Annie at something Frankie would say.

Was it questions of fate, given the circumstances that prevailed, or did Annie have free will the night that her third child was conceived? Mick perhaps would have thought on this imponderable had he known. But Annie was unaware of such matters. She only knew that on the night she lay with Bernard, she thought of Mick. A different type of passion engulfed Annie that night, a passion she had never known before. It surged over her body in waves of desire but all the time she was with Mick. So intense was the pleasure that night that she nearly called out his name. Her body felt for him and it was Mick she longed for. It was only afterwards that she became aware of what she had done, that the twin swords of shame and guilt soured her brief moment of joy. The innocent child who was conceived that night, was conceived by an adulterous mother, or so she thought. For that thought and that thought alone would so alter Annie's feeling towards this child that it would poison any love that she could have had. She would suffer greatly because of it.

Annie's guilt that she wanted Mick and her shame that she could not love her third child would eat away at her. What thoughts pass through the human mind, known only to God? It was this guilt in Annie's mind alone. This guilty secret would change her life. But could she have altered her thinking, forgiven herself, and in so doing, have loved this child more because for her this was the child of the man she desired above all others... her husband's brother?

CHAPTER FIVE

Annie suffered. Alone, with her thoughts, she suffered. Her inner pain manifested itself in a difficult and, what seemed to her at times, unending pregnancy. She was physically strong. She worked in the fields beside Mick and Bernard. She milked cows, killed chickens, walked the three miles into Ballybeg in all weathers. She struggled along through the wild winter storms that lashed the town and An Teach Ban. She refused to let the weather prevent her from venturing out. It was this determination in Annie that she would not let the wind and the rain and the West defeat her; the same determination that kept her courage as the bombs fell on London and death was in the air. The wild winter's savagery was nothing to what she had been through, she grimly reminded herself. But this third pregnancy, this tested her to an almost unbelievable dimension.

Annie had never questioned her faith even in the darkest days of the war when her father and her brother were taken from her. She accepted that, consoling herself that it was God's will and she was fearful to doubt as she feared her doubts would be judged at her final hour. Annie's God governed all, rewarded the good and punished the bad. Her God was an all-encompassing, all-seeing dispenser of justice.

But this new thing that had come upon her, this longing for Mick and his body, confounded and confused her. She told herself constantly that she had committed a sin, a mortal sin, had disobeyed the 7th commandment *'Do not commit adultery'* or maybe it was the 10th, *'Do not desire another man's wife; do not desire his house, his land, his slaves, his cattle, his donkeys, anything else that he owns.'* Hadn't Jesus said this? Jesus Himself had cautioned, "From the heart comes adultery..." She longed to confess her sin, wanted absolution but she was fearful of Father O'Malley and his judgement. And the miserable thought came to her, that even if she were forgiven by the Church, she would look at Mick again and desire him even more. The whole thing tore her apart and changed her, changed her because where there was once innocence there was now bitterness.

She was nervous around Father O'Malley. She thought if she could just talk to old Father John, back in Camden, he at least would have tried to understand. She remembered his gentleness and his heroism when the bombs fell. Everyone in Camden loved Father John – Catholics, Protestants, Jews, even unbelievers. But Father John was not in Ballybeg and even if he had been, he was now too old. There was just Father O'Malley and the curate and she mistrusted them both. She went to Mass every Sunday without question. She knelt and prayed but all the time she was aware of Mick's dark head, bowed; wondered at his thoughts, wondered at his beliefs because Mick surprised her at every turn, and his seemingly troubled life troubled her even more.

One evening, when Annie was four months pregnant, she and Bernard were sitting quietly in the kitchen. Frankie and Declan had been put to bed and Mick was out somewhere. Annie placed her knitting on her lap – she was knitting a white coat for her new baby – and said to Bernard with some anxiety:

"Why do you think God punishes people? It seems so unfair sometimes."

Bernard looked up, surprised by the question and at a loss as to how to answer. He had been busy reading *The Ballybeg News* and wasn't prepared to discuss a question of such depth. Religion, as far as Bernard was concerned, was best left to the priests and the nuns. He went to Mass weekly and on Holy Days and to confession occasionally if he got drunk or missed a Day of Obligation. He wasn't even sure whether he believed in God but he thought there must be something that held it all together. Sometimes, when he played his fiddle, he felt both peace and elation, especially when the notes sounded right, so he thought if that was what God was like there could be a divine being. But any discussion on the reason for suffering humanity, well, that was best left to Father O'Malley. And why was Annie asking such questions? Pregnant women often acted strange, he thought and, especially this time, Annie's pregnancy wasn't going well. He worried about her tiredness; saw the sorrow in her eyes, but this question...? He hesitated before replying:

"Why, I don't know. Whatever made ye think of that?"

Annie was persistent.

"Well, I've been thinking of this old couple in Camden. She was in a wheelchair. Everyone liked them. One night one of those doodle bugs came over and hit their house. Killed them both and destroyed the house. Why?"

Bernard was dismissive. "That was war, Annie. No one could be blamed. Just the war."

But Annie wouldn't let it go.

"What about... Mick, then?" she asked with some urgency in her voice. "Why did he have to lose the sight in his eye? Why was God punishing him?"

She spoke quickly, lest Bernard notice the slight hesitation when she said the name "Mick".

But Bernard took this as a way out of a theological nightmare and looking at Annie, said:

"Why, that's just Mick. He has things happen to him. Always has. Ye should know that by now. He gets confused or has blackouts... no one knows... but ye can hardly blame God for Mick."

And as far as Bernard was concerned, the subject was closed and he turned once again to *The Ballybeg News* with some relief.

Annie kept thinking of God and Mick and whether she was getting punished for her thoughts towards Mick because certainly she was suffering with this pregnancy. It didn't seem fair, she thought to herself and Bernard hasn't got a clue, she angrily concluded.

69

Annie's conviction that she was somehow being punished for her thoughts about Mick was further tested when, a few days later, an event took place which, although expected, was nevertheless sorrowful, and affecting in different ways all the family, including Frankie and Declan. It was one of those wonderful spring days when the world felt new and waking from the deep slumber of winter, so that the whole family was enjoying being outside on the warm Saturday morning. Mick puffed away on his cigarette, not saying much, as was his nature, when Paddy-dog suddenly rose to his feet, tottering slightly as he did so. The dog was old now – sixteen. There were two other dogs on the farm but only Paddy, because of his intelligence, good nature and loyalty, was allowed into the house. He spent most of his days asleep on the mat in front of the range and Annie had grown used to him being there although as soon as Mick appeared, he would wag his tail and try to get up. No one was sure whether Paddy could see very well as he seemed to have developed a cataract in his left eye but he remained devoted to Mick above anyone else. And it was to Mick now that he tried to walk. He took the few paces to Mick and his tongue licked Mick's hand. His failing vision saw Mick for the last time and he fell, onto his side. His breathing stopped and his body twitched. It was the perfect end for a dear old dog but the effect on his master was dramatic. Mick knelt down and put his hand on Paddy's heart:

"Why, my poor old dog – he's gone."

He was completely taken aback by the abruptness of the death.

Bernard went over and touched Paddy too, tenderly stroking the dog's side.

"Right enough, Mick", he agreed. "It was goin' to happen. He couldn't have gone on much longer, the old fella. He's had a grand life."

It was at that moment that Frankie bounded over to his father and, giving Paddy a slight nudge with his foot, cried out:

"Why won't Paddy move?"

It was the first time Frankie had seen death. There was a hollow silence while Annie, Bernard and Mick wondered with their different experiences, wondered how to answer this eternal question of a child. It was Bernard who knelt down and putting his arm round Frankie, he gently said:

"Old Paddy's dead, Frankie..."

At that, Frankie became inconsolable and shaking himself free from his father's arms, rushed to Paddy and shook him as furiously as a six-year-old could.

"Wake up, Paddy. Wake up", he sobbed, for Paddy was so much part of his world and he didn't want his world to change.

"Now, stop this nonsense, Frankie," his father admonished him, bewildered.

But it was Mick who lifted Frankie in his strong arms, held him tightly and without saying a word, held him until Frankie's tears subsided. Annie was a silent witness to the drama. She, too, was surprised by Paddy's unexpected passing and remembered the old dog's loyalty to her and with that came the memory of that black night when Mick came home.

At the back of the farm steading and up a slight hill, unprotected from the relentless wind, a hawthorn tree had somehow grown. The tree was bent sideways and lost branches every winter but it held on to the ground, a kind of silent reminder of Nature's power to live, to survive against all odds. From here, you could see over to the sea and Ballybeg with the spire of St Peter and St Paul etched against the ever-changing skies. It was to this tree, as a kind of a ritual, that Mick, Frankie and sometimes Declan, would walk Paddy-dog nearly every day in all weathers. It was under this tree that Mick wanted Paddy to lie.

So the next day, after Mass, they buried Paddy-dog. Watching him gently and nobly placing his faithful companion into the grave, Annie noticed a tear roll down Mick's cheek. We have many friends in life, she thought. Is the one with four legs any the lesser than the one with two?

*****

If the entire population of Ballybeg awoke one morning to find that Father O'Malley had gone, not one of them would shed a tear. After thirty years of Father O'Malley, some might even be jubilant but say nothing. Undoubtedly the whole population would experience a sense of loss; the kind of loss that comes once familiarity has gone.

"We'll have to tell Father O'Malley we're wed", Bernard had said to Annie the week they arrived in Ballybeg.

Annie accepted this as normal. She'd only known one priest and that was Father John at St Mary's and, in her opinion and in the opinion of others, Father John's gentleness was akin to holiness. She had known him all her life. He was a welcome visitor to the flat above the butcher's shop. When he called on them through all their troubles, her mother fussed over him, talking all the time. Father John was a cultured man and had been born into a wealthy family. Renouncing his considerable material wealth for a spiritual life of service proved no hardship for him but he still retained the air of a rich man without the encumbrance of possessions.

So Annie was totally unprepared for Father O'Malley. She remembered that afternoon that she and Bernard, very much in love, stood in Father O'Malley's study. Motioning them to sit down he looked at them both without speaking. He was an untidy man in his dress and appearance and his study reflected that trait. Finally, he spoke to Bernard, curtly and as he did he ran his fingers through his thinning hair as if to emphasise what he was saying:

"I have heard ye were wed, Bernard... and that ye were wed in England." And he stared at Bernard who, under the

72

scrutiny of the gaze felt himself colouring to his hair line, his hands moist with perspiration.

"Aye, Father," he muttered, not looking at Annie or the priest but at his feet.

Then, without warning, Father O'Malley turned to Annie:

"Ye're an Englishwoman, I believe."

The words stung Annie like a viper's tongue, directed at her with as much venom. She was completely unprepared for the attack. She had naively thought that she was to meet another Father John. She recalled it had been so different when Bernard met Father John. Father John had beamed at Bernard, shaking his hand vigorously, saying:

"So you're the man from Ireland we've all heard so much about."

And Bernard, visibly relaxed, started talking about Ballybeg and the West. He even mentioned his love of music, much to Annie's surprise. At this, Father John recognised a kindred spirit. As a youth he had studied the piano in Leipzig and, given his background, was all set to embark on a dazzling concert career but a skiing accident in the Swiss Alps had left him paralysed for months. As he lay in the Zurich hospital, he went through all the anger and the pain; bitterly blaming God until one night he became convinced that he should enter the priesthood. He could never explain the how and the why, but certainty came to him at that moment. He became convinced that it was indeed God's work. Something of a miracle, too, because the next morning he found he could move his legs and in a few weeks' time he was able to take tentative steps. Gradually, as the months went by, he regained the use of his legs.

But the love of music remained with him and it was said that he brought in converts at Camden with the heavenly chords he played on the organ reverberating around the silent church. So Father John found it easy to talk to Bernard, and Bernard, for his part, was slightly bemused that he was able to talk to a priest and not feel inadequate.

As Annie recalled past events in a vain hope that she could find a way out of her present predicament, it occurred to her that both she and Bernard had been foolish to try to compare the two priests and that no worthwhile thing could ever come out of such a comparison. In the unlikely event of the two priests ever meeting face to face, they would have no common ground in which to engage in conversation. Father O'Malley's rigid dogmatism would have dismayed Father John and Father O'Malley would have sneered at the urbane Father John's English mannerisms. That they were both ordained priests of a similar age was their only common denominator and would have remained so. Father John could have attained high office in the church hierarchy given his intelligence and his wealth. He chose to spend his life in the service of the people of Camden, a choice he never regretted. Father O'Malley, on the other hand, by virtue of his insular outlook remained rooted in a country parish seen by many as isolated and backward. It was not his choice to be there and he viewed it as a misfortune that he could never see a way out of it.

Father O'Malley was feared by all in Ballybeg and this gave him a certain perverse pleasure as a recompense for being there at all. His control of the town afforded him some measure of satisfaction and the knowledge that a man such as Doctor Ryan, learned man that he was, would not cross him on any point of doctrine, gave him a certain feeling of superiority which he relished. Everyone in the town treated him with caution, even the indomitable Ma Murphy who would whisper to Pa if the priest was too long at the bar:

"Slip him a double, Pa and let's be rid of him."

But she spoke under her breath for fear the priest would hear. So everyone in Ballybeg lived in awe of Father

O'Malley; everyone, that is, except Mick Kelly who saw no reason to fear and would not move off the pavement to allow the priest to pass.

Father O'Malley firmly believed that because of Mick the whole Kelly family were troublemakers and he would use any method in his power to bring them into line. He often thought, too, of his first meeting with Annie and what he had felt that day...for Bernard to have sneaked off to England and brought back a bride showed complete disregard and rebellion in Father O'Malley's opinion. As a member of the church in Ballybeg, Bernard should have told the priest of the proposed marriage. To have found out, second-hand, so-to-speak, irritated Father O'Malley, and to his way of thinking it was just another example of Kelly perversity. The only mitigating circumstance in the whole sorry story was the fact that Annie was a Catholic and they had had a proper Church wedding and Father O'Malley had seen written evidence of such.

Annie being English and the fact that no-one knew anything about her further irritated him, because Father O'Malley held a dark, terrible secret within his psyche which refused to be healed... and in any case, he was reluctant to have it healed, so deep was the wound. Because he loathed the English and all they stood for and that Bernard Kelly had had the temerity to marry an Englishwoman and bring her to live in the Parish of St Peter and St Paul, Father O'Malley's parish, God-given, was to him the greatest insult he could think of. All because Father O'Malley's father had believed passionately in a free Ireland and the hatred of the English was as mother's milk in the household of his childhood. One day, his father's eldest brother had been rounded up, like a dog, and shot for "Incitement of Rebellion". On a rational level, Father O'Malley knew that to hate a whole race for the actions of a few went against every Christian principle that he preached every Sunday but deep, deep down, he could not let go of this anger. It was engraved into his very being and he never

75

forgot those childhood feelings when his father, in murderous tones, told him what had happened. No one in Ballybeg ever knew the story of Father O'Malley's private Hell – *no one* – and it would go with him to his grave. But innocent Annie suffered for it. He addressed her as "Mrs Kelly" and his lip curled slightly when he did. Always Bernard was "Bernard."

Annie was right in her avoidance of Father O'Malley as she struggled with her guilt. To have spoken to the priest would have brought contempt from him and so devastated her gentle soul to the point of despair. And who would know what would have happened afterwards?

*****

Annie considered talking to Mrs Ryan about Mick. She knew that the older woman's opinion of him was different from what her own had become but she wondered if speaking of him would help in her present situation. She was convinced that she would receive no solace from the church in the person of Father O'Malley and thought perhaps that Mrs Ryan would provide understanding or, at the very least, some sympathy. The two women had become quite close and although Annie was aware of Mrs Ryan's propensity to gossip, she had been able to talk to her, without fear, about the war and the deaths of her father and William. It had proved to be a release of sorts for Annie because she hadn't talked much about these events to either Bernard or Mick. Silent, she had kept her sorrow to herself and she was relieved that Mrs Ryan had listened quietly and without judgement. That had meant a lot to Annie. But to talk of Mick would be so difficult, Annie thought, and her secret shame might best be hidden from everyone even – and especially, perhaps – Mrs Ryan.

In lots of ways, life was getting easier for Annie. That summer, Frankie turned seven and in the autumn Declan started school. If Annie had not been so troubled and so ill with this third pregnancy, she would have enjoyed having a little more free time because Mrs Ryan proved to be a great

76

asset in looking after Frankie and Declan who thought going to the big house was wonder itself and regarded Mrs Ryan as a surrogate grandmother, their own being so far away.

Doctor and Mrs Ryan lived in a large grey stone Georgian house just along from the Ballybeg Hotel. An oak panel door, similar in design to the one at the hotel, was sited between two imposing stone Doric columns. This oak door opened onto a spacious vestibule. It was here that patients, visitors and Frankie and Declan would wait and remove their coats and umbrellas before being allowed into the house. An inner frosted glass door separated them from the hall from which various rooms led Frankie and Declan into magic tours. At the end of the hall, a dark oak stair with a polished banister brought them upstairs to a mezzanine floor where the two boys could lean over the railing and watch Doctor Ryan's patients coming and going from above. And at the street side, to complete the wonder, was a huge stained-glass window of Finn McCool brandishing a sword with roses and shamrocks in a semi-circle around the top. Opposite on the garden side of the house was a similar design of window with a stylised Grania O'Maille, the pirate Queen of Connaught, encircled by the same design of roses and shamrocks. Four bedrooms upstairs and a bathroom with a shower of all things... the two little boys were enchanted by it all. Mrs Ryan had sets of rules for everyone who entered her house. Husband, patients, men, women, dogs, cats and small boys all obeyed these rules. Even Father O'Malley had to remember his manners and would not call without prior arrangement.

One rule for small boys was to remove their shoes in the vestibule before entering the house. This was a rule that was never disobeyed. Although Mrs Ryan had no children of her own, her numerous brothers and sisters had given her many nephews and nieces, so there were puzzles and jigsaws, colouring pencils and paper, a wonderful swing seat in the garden and rooms to peep in. The most awesome room of all for Frankie and Declan was the dining room with its large dark mahogany table, high backed chairs to match and a sideboard with its beautiful carving. Frankie loved to run his hand along the wood and feel the indentations and study dragons and birds and all manner of things. And resplendent in the middle of the sideboard sat a silver vase usually holding cut flowers. It was like a palace where wondrous things were sure to happen. But the best room of all, at the end of the long hallway, was a large kitchen where Frankie and Declan could feast on cherry cake and blackcurrant cordial and fresh homemade bread, Mrs Ryan's speciality. No fighting, no spitting, no football, no mud. No cake if the rules weren't obeyed, and who wouldn't obey the rules under those circumstances?

*****

One autumn evening, Father O'Malley came across Mick Kelly slouched on a park bench near the seashore. Father O'Malley often took a stroll along the shore on the pretext that he was going for a walk, but in actual fact he was on the lookout for little boys whom he assumed would be up to mischief. The nervousness of the boys when they saw Father O'Malley approaching gave him a certain pleasure. Control was his. Sometimes he didn't need to say a word, and the boys would scatter. And Father O'Malley considered this a personal victory.

But the sight of Mick, hunched over, his head in his hands, slightly unnerved him. For a second, he hesitated and wondered if he should stop and talk to the unfortunate Mick. A soft rain had started and a fine vapour was sprinkling his face. He had been thinking of his evening meal which Mrs O'Reilly, his housekeeper, would have ready for him. He disliked Mick but his conscience troubled him as thoughts of the Good Samaritan rushed into his head. It would have been quite easy to avoid Mick, and he considered it, because the man seemed oblivious to his surroundings. The priest puzzled how long Mick had been sitting there. Was it another of his absences, he mused, after which his brother would scour the town looking for him? Father O'Malley was irritated. Torn between indifference and duty, he stood back and contemplated his next move. Finally, and a little reluctantly, duty won and he walked around and sat on the bench beside Mick.

"Are ye alright, Mick?" he enquired in a valiant effort to show priestly concern for the one member of his flock whom he did not understand.

"Are ye ill, man?" continued Father O'Malley, becoming more irritated. "Do ye want me to call Doctor Ryan?"

At the mention of the doctor's name, Mick looked up and, seeing the priest sitting beside him, tried to get up but he fell back onto the seat, toppling over as he did, so that he now gave the appearance of a man on a slope. Father O'Malley was unsure whether to reach and push Mick back onto the back of the seat to make him more comfortable. There was no smell of whiskey on Mick's breath and this slightly alarmed him. Somehow, Mick's cap was pushed over onto his forehead and completely covered the eye that wore the eye patch. Still Mick didn't speak but panted slightly as he tried to get his breath.

Father O'Malley, at last, began to look around for help. For once, there was no one along the shore, and the old folk and boys he often encountered were nowhere to be seen. He tried again to rouse Mick:

"Can ye walk, Mick?" and "How long have ye been sittin' here? Ye'll have to get out of the rain or ye'll catch yer death..."

At that the priest wondered if Mick was almost dead because Mick's face had turned an ashen grey and he was now slumped onto the arm of the bench. Father O'Malley was no longer young and to try to get Mick to stand and be supported by him would be almost impossible. Mick was tall and the priest was short, their height differences alone would make any movement difficult. Father O'Malley tried once more, in an effort which he began to think was futile, to get some recognition out of Mick.

"Where's Bernard?" he asked, hoping that mention of his brother's name would spark a response in Mick. But Mick did not answer. He remained slumped on the bench and his good eye was shut now, Father O'Malley noticed with some alarm. He could feel panic well up inside him and his dilemma became more pressing. Should he leave Mick sitting there – it was raining more heavily now – and try to get help or should he try to persuade the Kelly brother to come with him, because, the priest thought, this is surely a case for the doctor?

Then Father O'Malley made the only decision that he could have done given the circumstances. He would leave Mick and fetch Doctor Ryan. If only the boys he used to chase were about, he thought crossly, they could have run the half mile to the doctor's house in a fraction of the time it would take him to walk there. He needed a stick now for support which made life easier for him since he no longer had the agility of youth.

"I'm goin' to have to leave ye, Mick... for a bit." Father O'Malley spoke against the rain, thrusting his lips close to Mick's ear. "I'll have to go and get Doctor Ryan. I don't think I can help ye up the steps by meself."

There were thirty concrete steps up to the grassy bank near the shore. These steps were quite steep and, holding onto the handrail, it usually took Father O'Malley at least five minutes to reach the top on the best of days and it would take longer this late afternoon. The rain was heavier now and a wind had started up, blowing in a north-westerly direction which meant that the priest would have to battle against that as well. The tide was coming in too, he noted, and the waves, breaking on the shingle beach, tossed black seaweed further towards the shoreline so that the water was getting even closer to the bench. If there hadn't been so much urgency with Mick, mused Father O'Malley, it would have been a spectacular scene to watch as everything was turning black under the night sky. But he had to attend to Mick so he tried one last time:

"Do ye think ye can stand, Mick?"

But Mick remained silent. Now his head was lying on his arm which was resting on the arm of the bench. He seemed unaware of the rain and the wind or the priest. Indeed, it looked as if the rain had got through his coat.

So Father O'Malley pulled himself up from beside Mick, and, holding onto his stick for support, began to climb those thirty steps which led up to the playing fields and along North Street to the doctor's house. Half way up the steps Father O'Malley paused for breath and looked back at Mick. He noted that Mick was in the same position, his body still leaning sideways. He could just make out the silhouette against the half dark as the night descended.

It took Father O'Malley about thirty minutes to reach Doctor Ryan's house and he was irritated to see that the oak door was shut so he had to hammer on the lion's head brass door knocker to make himself heard. He hadn't passed a single soul on his way up from the shore and he was getting even more annoyed with himself and with everyone else. Finally, the door opened and Mrs Ryan stood in front of him and he could not help but notice her beauty. The light at the back of her reflected almost halo-like in the half-dark and her greying hair arranged and held high with a tortoiseshell hair clip, made her look even more striking.

"Mrs Ryan", the priest rushed his words because he couldn't get the image out of his mind, "is the doctor in?"

At this, Mrs Ryan replied, somewhat haughtily:

"He is... but he has just this moment started his evening meal."

"He must come. I've just left Mick Kelly on the park bench at the steps near the sea... he's ill. Very ill. I can't get him to talk or to recognise me. And there's no hint of the drink," he added in case Mrs Ryan dismissed Mick as inebriated. He was well aware, along with the rest of the population of Ballybeg, of her views on the matter of alcohol consumption and Mick Kelly. Mrs Ryan allowed Father O'Malley into the vestibule and then she left him, standing there, while she closed the glass door in front of him. He stood there, feeling slightly indignant as pools of water dripped off his boots and coat and left puddles on the black and white chequered tiles. Well, she's from Cork, he thought, and she's always like this. At least, the doctor is here and his car is outside, and Father O'Malley continued standing, feeling very much like an errand boy.

When Mrs Ryan told her husband that the priest was at the door and that Mick Kelly had collapsed, obviously in need of medical help, she added, "Honestly, that man is a menace, John," meaning Mick.

As Doctor Ryan got up from the table and looked at the steak and kidney pie on his plate, uneaten, he wryly agreed with his wife although he didn't say anything. Instead, he just sighed:

"Oh well. I'll find out what's the trouble this time."

But after he heard Father O'Malley's account, there was some urgency in his voice as he instructed his wife:

"Irene, ring the ambulance to come to the steps and also notify the hospital that Mick is on his way. Also..." he paused slightly, "perhaps ring the Garda too and get Liam to come down to help. Those steps will be difficult tonight to bring a stretcher up. Now..." he closed his black bag and, as he reached for his coat, added, "we'll have to tell Bernard... but let's see what's the problem first...?"

Mrs Ryan was many things but above everything else she was calm and reliable. She hadn't been a doctor's wife for twenty years without learning anything. She lifted the receiver of the telephone in the hall even before the two men had left.

When Doctor Ryan and Father O'Malley got to the bench they saw that Mick had moved slightly and was now leaning back, his head down.

"What's wrong, Mick?" asked Doctor Ryan. He was unable to conduct any diagnostic examination in the dark but his first thought was right. Mick would have to be hospitalised. This way, the doctor could treat him and perhaps get a second opinion? Mick still did not speak but when Liam O'Sullivan and Sean the ambulance man arrived, he allowed himself to be lifted onto the stretcher without protest. Almost with relief, Father O'Malley thought. It was indeed a struggle to carry Mick up the thirty steps to the waiting ambulance but they managed despite the horizontal rain and the unforgiving wind.

*****

Ballybeg Hospital with its six beds was small but served the needs of the town. Anything serious went to Galway City. Sister Assumpta was in charge and was somewhat of a disciplinarian. She thought Mick Kelly was a drunk and that his latest episode was the result of this. Even if this had been proved not to be the case, Sister Assumpta would have remained sceptical. Once she had made up her mind, she rigidly adhered to that opinion. And in her opinion, all Mick Kelly's problems were the result of the drink.

But when she saw him on the stretcher, she wondered. In a split second her medical training took over and, in no time at all, Mick was made comfortable in the hospital bed. Colour returned to his cheeks and his temperature stabilised. Doctor Kelly examined him but he was still unsure of the problem. All he could think was that Mick was beginning to recover from whatever had caused him to collapse.

"He won't be needing ye this time, Father," he told the priest, meaning the Last Rites.

Father O'Malley nodded absentmindedly. At that particular moment he had been thinking of Mrs Ryan's figure silhouetted against the hall light... and Mick Kelly was furthest from his mind.

It had been a long night for both priest and doctor. Finally and thankfully, Doctor Ryan opened the oak door of his home. He was tired; very, very tired. He had driven out to An Teach Ban to tell Bernard and Annie the news and to reassure them that Mick was comfortable but would probably need to stay in the hospital for a few days. They reacted to the news in two different ways. Bernard, again, felt responsible and somehow trapped while Annie just felt relieved that Mick was being looked after. She felt responsible for him now, too, but behind her responsibility there hid her secret. Doctor Ryan knew nothing of any of this. He was just glad to be home. As he drifted off to sleep, he thought it was about time he got a junior partner. He didn't think he could cope alone any more with the continuing problems of Mick and the demands of his many patients.

Mick remained in the hospital for three days. At the end of those three days, he decided it was time to leave and Sister Assumpta could only agree. Doctor Ryan advised bed rest for about a week at An Teach Ban and it was now that the women of Ballybeg rallied around Annie. Ma Murphy sent a bottle of whiskey with Helen who was instructed to help Annie clean the house. Mrs Ryan brought Frankie and Declan to her big house much to their delight. Norah O'Sullivan baked bread and pies and looked in at Mick. She was pleased with his recovery. And the men, too, helped in their various ways. Tommy Flynn arrived and said that he would help on the farm for a few weeks. He would not take wages but wouldn't say no to a good meal. Hugh O'Connor, Mick's friend, part time librarian and clerk, brought books for Mick to read from the library and told him to return them "sometime". This was good news for Mick. Doctor Ryan looked in too. Still unsure of the causes of Mick's collapse but he was, nevertheless, pleased with his patient's progress. Father O'Malley would not go to the Kelly house, on principle, and sent Peter, the curate, who arrived on his bike. Peter arrived, pimply-faced and pious and Annie was glad to see the back of him. Mick was, too; he shut his one eye and pretended to be asleep. But it was Annie who looked after Mick.

And in the caring for him, she sensed his vulnerability. That he had to submit to the attentions of others was difficult for him but his weakness made protest impossible. A few days after he came home to An Teach Ban he was able to move from his bed to his chair in the kitchen and he would sit there, forlornly, missing Paddy-dog and watching Annie. For a few days, she fed him broth from a spoon, like a baby, and daily he regained his strength. Sister Assumpta came in to check on him regularly. Full of importance she said to Annie that Mick would have to have a shave, as though Mick wasn't there. But Mick overhead and, in a voice like thunder, retorted:

"I'll have no woman near me with a razor, do ye hear?"

And the two of them glared at each other like caged animals. This time it was Sister Assumpta who retreated and crossly said to Annie: "Well, maybe he would let Bernard...?" and let the subject drop.

So Bernard shaved his brother's face, tenderly almost, and Mick certainly looked the better for it and didn't offer a word of protest.

He started to read the library books that Hugh O'Connor had brought him and began, at last, to take an interest in his surroundings. Frankie and Declan returned home full of tales of the big house and both feeling very grown-up for their week's holiday. Mick was glad to have the two of them home and Bernard started playing the fiddle again at Ma Murphy's.

One afternoon, three weeks after he was discharged from the hospital, Mick put down his book and watched Annie as she busied herself in the kitchen. As she passed close to him, he reached out his hand and took hold of hers in a firm grasp, and looked at her, speaking in Irish:

"*Go raibh maith agat, Annie, a chailín'...*"(Thank you, Annie my girl).

She knew no Irish except she heard the word "Annie". Her baby fluttered inside her. The gentle kicks reassured her of the life that was there, within. She longed to take the hand that held hers, Mick's hand, and place it over her rounded belly so he, too, could feel the baby's movement.

Mick spoke again, softly:

"Thank you, Annie my girl".

She turned her head so she didn't have to look into his eye. She could not bear to look at him. She felt the tears welling up behind her eyes and she pulled her hand away from his grasp, to be free. She fled from him... outside.

Their Large White sow had just given birth to twelve pink piglets. The mother was lying on her side, her babies clambering over her. The pig grunted contentedly as her babies suckled. Annie leaned her head against the door of the shed and, looking at the mother pig, she wept.

*****

One evening a few months later, Ballybeg was hit by the first storm of the winter. The wind and the rain gathered strength out in the Atlantic and their combined force struck Ballybeg in the late dark afternoon. The lights in the town flickered ominously, threatening to plunge the town and its inhabitants into the darkness they used to know. A total fragility settled on the population in the face of Mother Nature's fury and, as the hours went by, the storm refused to yield to anything approaching calm.

Doctor Ryan was already in bed, and Mrs Ryan was about to join him, when above the roar of the wind and rain she heard the knocker on the oak door, loud and insistent. She sighed. When she opened the door to see who was knocking with such persistence, Mick Kelly thrust past her and through the frosted glass door and, in a wild voice, as wild, she thought, as the night itself, cried out:

"Where's the doctor? Holy Mother of God, where is he?"

And he pushed Mrs Ryan aside as he strode up and down the hallway like a man possessed. Mrs Ryan was completely unprepared for this confrontation and she noted with a kind of surreal vexation that Mick was dripping water onto the floor carpet, completely unaware of what he was doing.

Doctor Ryan heard the commotion downstairs and he quickly dressed, guessing his services were needed. As he came down the stairs, Mick rushed at him. He grabbed the doctor's jacket, shaking the doctor as he did.

"It's Annie," Mick cried in a panic.

The hall light flickered again, threatening to go out. Mrs Ryan looked anxiously at the light as her husband tried to calm the distraught Mick. Then, in a flood of words, Mick told them the story.

Annie had felt contractions in the late afternoon and Bernard had driven into Ballybeg to fetch Norah O'Sullivan, leaving Mick pacing the floor and Frankie and Declan frightened. All seemed to be going well; after all, this was Annie's third baby but she hasn't been well, Mick cried out. All this time she's been tired and sick, but everyone thought all would be well with this birth but Norah said something was wrong, something was going dreadfully, dreadfully wrong and the doctor was needed and it was urgent. If the doctor didn't come, Annie might die and as he said these words, Mick stopped talking. He whipped his cap from his head and stood in an almost catatonic state, his one eye staring at the doctor. No more words came out of him.

Now the doctor was alarmed for both Mick and Annie. Why, he thought, I saw Annie yesterday and she seemed fine. Why, oh why, can't they all have their babies in the spring like the lambs? What a night to be born, he thought. They can still die. Infant mortality was reducing but it still happened with depressing frequency and if Norah, who had delivered more babies than anyone he knew, if Norah was calling out for him on a night like this, it was serious. All these thoughts were rushing around Doctor Ryan's head as he prepared to go to Annie.

Mick still stood, motionless and silent and the doctor thought suddenly of Mick's mother, all those years ago. His predecessor had told him how he and the midwife had struggled to save her but there was nothing they could do for either of them and Mick's mother and baby sister died together. Then there was emptiness at An Teach Ban and Mick's father turned to the drink which finished him in the end. Mick left school at ten to work on the farm and look after both his father and Bernard. Mick must have heard his mother's cries all those years ago, the doctor thought. Now he would think history is repeating itself. Oh, the irony of life.

Doctor Ryan knew he must get to Annie and quickly. By the sound of it, he wondered, there will have be a Caesarean and that means getting her to the County Hospital in Galway City. There might be hope, he thought, as fear took hold of him, there just might be hope. There was a fine Scottish surgeon in Galway who might be available. If he could just get through to the hospital to prepare them, there could just be a chance to save Annie and the baby. He lifted the receiver and prayed as he did, that the girl at the exchange was there and that the phones weren't down. It was with relief that he heard her voice and miraculously he got through to Galway and also to Sean, the ambulance man in Ballybeg. Twenty miles to Galway on this wild, wild night. There was no way that Doctor Ryan could perform the operation. Ballybeg Hospital was just too small and hadn't the facilities of Galway. He had to get Annie to Galway to save her life.

"I'll take Mick back in the car. The ambulance is on the way."

And Doctor Ryan patted his wife's arm to comfort her. She was fixed to the spot in the hall, staring at Mick... frightened. The doctor coaxed an almost unresponsive Mick to come with him. As the two men left the house, the light flickered off in the hall and the street lights outside did the same. Ballybeg was in darkness.

When Doctor Ryan examined Annie he knew his decision to try to get her to the hospital was correct. She was in great distress and even greater pain. He administered nitrous oxide and oxygen to calm her and together he and Norah reassured her but Doctor Ryan felt powerless for once in the face of such human suffering. All his experience and his knowledge seemed useless and he thanked God out aloud when the ambulance arrived. If the wind and the rain were causing havoc in Ballybeg, it was even worse at An Teach Ban and there was a struggle to get Annie to the ambulance. They left a dazed Mick and two very scared little boys but there was nothing else they could do.

The twenty mile journey was terrible and Norah held Annie's hand as the ambulance shook with the force of the wind and rain hitting onto the side of it. Annie's cries could be heard above the noise of the ambulance and the relentless sound of the rain. Doctor Ryan drove with a stunned Bernard beside him, following the ambulance on its perilous journey until the lights of Galway came into view. Thank God they still have power, the doctor thought as Annie was rushed into the operating theatre. All went quiet as Doctor Ryan, Bernard and Norah, waited exhausted and thankful to be relieved of responsibility at last. Nothing left but prayer and the Scottish surgeon. Doctor Ryan was thankful for that. If anyone could save Annie, the Scot could.

And save Annie he did and delivered her of a tiny baby boy, her third son. But Annie had been close to death and was weary with the effort of coming back from its doorway. Her baby son was brought to her. She turned her head away. This is my punishment, she thought. I should be dead. I should be dead.

When Bernard came to her offering words of comfort, the tears rolled down her cheeks and the well from which they came, seemed to never end.

PART TWO

CHAPTER SIX

An awesome mystery of inexplicable probabilities decrees that a person is born at a certain time, in a certain place, into a particular family and even in that family, a particular place within it. What is this mystery that decides that a person lives out his life in a situation, sometimes with wealth or health or both, sometimes without? The homeless beggar in the streets of Mumbai or the dissolute philanderer sunning himself on his yacht in the South of France; the woman, near penniless and fading in a city tenement or the vain woman with too many shoes – all these millions of souls, throughout the ages, through time and place and circumstance – each one unique, each one with his or her own peculiar problems. The one with a life of comfort and ease is no less beset with anxieties and joys than the one who scrubs the floors of public buildings, ignored by all.

When Bernard and Annie returned to An Teach Ban with their new baby they, too, were beset with problems. The childAnnie held in her arms had almost been the death of her.It was only by the skill of a surgeon and the faith of a hardworking, kindly doctor that her life had been saved. Annie was so, so weary – almost to the point of exhaustion. When Frankie saw his new brother, he was dismissive.

"He looks like a frog," was all he said.

And the tiny baby did indeed look amphibian-like with eyes sunk into his head and a flat nose that seemed to half cover his face. He had virtually no hair and his ears stuck out, seemingly huge, on each side of his face; somehow, he didn't seem to be in proportion. Even Annie had a fanciful notion, and she knew it to be foolish, but it came into her head and wouldn't go away. Was this strange little child her own or had there been a dreadful mistake and was some other woman now holding her own baby? It was absurd, she knew, but the thought had come to her and she had allowed it to stay in her mind, briefly, but it was there if only for that fleeting second. Because the baby she held in her arms bore little resemblance as far as she could see, to either her family or to Bernard's.

The frost was hard and white on the ground the morning that Bernard took his fiddle in its case to play a tune for his new son. He climbed from the farmhouse to the hawthorn tree under which old Paddy-dog lay buried and sat on the bench he had made. The sky was a clear blue and not a cloud to be seen. Icicles hung in an uneven line along the guttering of the house and the outbuildings and Bernard could see his tracks over the frozen ground. Earlier in the day, he and Mick had had to break the ice on the water troughs as they gave feed to the pigs, cows and hens. It was a cold day but perfect for thoughts, Bernard decided.

He sat on the bench and recalled how he had made it. After Paddy died Bernard thought that a seat under the tree as a kind of a memorial to the old dog would be appropriate. Also, he loved the view from this vantage point, especially on cold, crisp mornings. He enjoyed carpentry and had a workbench in one of the outbuildings. There his saws, chisels and planes were arranged neatly. A vice was attached to the bench and this is where Mick did his carving, too. The shed got cold in winter but the brothers threw off-cuts of wood into a wood stove which warmed them. It was a refuge for them both but rarely were they there together. At the back of the shed, Bernard had found about five teak wood planks, gathering dust. He could just remember the excitement of the teak wood. When he was a boy, a violent winter storm blew a ship off course resulting in the vessel keeling over on the beach at Ballybeg. A major rescue operation had saved lives but some of the cargo, including wood from the Far East, had drifted onto the beach. This unexpected bounty was too much for the locals and there was a desperate attempt to salvage as much as they could before the authorities intervened. Bernard's father had managed to acquire five heavy boards of teak. Given the satisfaction of acquiring something for nothing, the wood had remained, unused, at the back of the shed from that day.

So Bernard used this wood for his bench. He carved out mortice and tenon joints, of which he was justifiably proud, and attached a rail to the back legs so he could lean backwards to relax. The bench was of simple construction but comfortable. As he sat on the seat admiring his craftsmanship, he recalled the eventful day that the bench was sited and the differences between his two sons became apparent. He and Mick had carried the frame to the tree and then nailed the seat down. Frankie, as always, was enthusiastic at the beginning and insisted on carrying the hammer. He argued with Declan who was given a few nails to hold. Frankie was full of importance for a short time but then just as quickly he lost interest in the whole procedure and ran off. But Declan – and Bernard smiled as he remembered – Declan studied the whole operation so very carefully, absorbed as he handed his father the nails and it was with a solemnity which was enchanting to Bernard. Somehow, this absorption in the practical things of life was a comfort to his father. When the two of them finished their work and sat on the bench for the very first time, Declan suddenly smiled. With childlike simplicity, he had thought of something that was momentous to him.

"We can sit and talk to Paddy now, Pappy," and he clapped his hands. Bernard looked at the unturned face and just said, "Aye, that we can, son," his heart full of fatherly pride.

Bernard sat on the bench. His fiddle case lay on his knees, unopened. When Frankie was born, he was so proud and full of joy, he had played for hours. Even when Declan came, he had played at Murphy's and it was special too, but this time, for his third son, he wondered. He thought of the terror that had gone through him the night he feared he would lose Annie... his Annie... the girl with the lovely smile who had won his heart and the hearts of the people of Ballybeg. But the smile that so disarmed wasn't as evident as it used to be and somehow this baby had contributed to this but Bernard didn't know how or why. All he knew was the fear that had gone through him the night she nearly died.

And he thought if he had lost Annie he couldn't have gone on. Not even for his boys or for Mick or for the farm. He knew he would be like his father. The light would just go out inside and in a short space of time, it would be extinguished forever. Bernard Kelly, farmer, would be no more; just a few names written in the records and, if lucky, his name on a stone in the cemetery.

Annie seemed almost indifferent to her new baby. She went about the tasks of caring for him in a mechanical way as though it was a duty, but there was no feeling there. She was weary and weak and seemed to have retreated into a shell from which it appeared she didn't wish to emerge.

There was a problem with the name.

"You can give him a name this time, Bernard," she said wearily.

So Bernard pondered over a name as he sat on his bench. He recalled male names in his family but nothing even remotely suitable came into his head for this tiny, frog-like creature who was his third son. It had been a struggle for this child to be born, to survive against all the odds. Despite his physical appearance, Bernard thought, this one must be a fighter, a survivor at the beginning of life. Then suddenly as if from nowhere and almost as a divine message, a name came into his head and wouldn't leave him. It took hold of him. This was the name for his son. Oisin. It had to be Oisin. The warrior! The poet!

Whether it was a conscious deliberate act, given the circumstances of Oisin's conception and subsequent birth, or whether it was something less portentous, everything connected to the first few weeks of his life seemed to be unlike anything that had been before. In fact, this very difference set him apart. His place in the family as the third brother and his unusual physical appearance almost precluded him from the attentions that new babies normally receive. When he was out in his pram, sometimes asleep, sometimes not, women would stop to talk to Annie. Once they had given a perfunctory glance at the diminutive figure almost hidden with shawls and blankets and knitted bonnet, they would say something to the effect that he was very small. That observation completed, they would move quickly on to other more interesting topics. Ma Murphy's antics or Mrs Ryan's latest afternoon tea would be infinitely more appealing than talk of tiny, insignificant Oisin Kelly.

In fact, even amongst his own family, once the initial excitement of a new baby in the house had waned, no one took much notice of him. If he had been able to discern his mother's thoughts as she cared for him, he would have further doubted his welcome into the world. For it was as if Annie had arrived at a conclusion that her life now had no future, that she had suffered in so many ways and the thought that she would just go on for years with nothing but loneliness as a companion, filled her with sadness.

She knew she was sharp with her boys and distant with Bernard. She hardly dare look at Mick in case others became aware of her secret. This control that she kept tight over her emotions hindered her and made her appear different from the girl she used to be.

It was not that she rejected tiny Oisin. It was just that she was weary and the hours hung heavy over her. She kept herself busy as she always had because she knew if she stopped, the weariness would deepen within her and defeat would loom ever closer. She was fearful of the kind of immobility that this state would allow. But the loneliness came like a mantle which engulfed her in her waking hours.

She was surprised too, like Bernard, at the differences between their children. Even Oisin's welcome into the church proved to be non-eventful. There was nothing of the celebrations that had marked Frankie's arrival or even Declan's. He was baptised "Oisin Kelly" because no one could think of a second name. Oisin became a member of the church of St Peter and St Paul, Parish of Ballybeg that cold January morning in front of a congregation who seemed more mindful of the temperature in the church than what was happening at the altar. Annie held her little son in her arms and was thankful that she didn't have to look at Father O'Malley. He was in bed with an attack of pleurisy and the priest from the next parish was in a hurry to be gone. Oisin's baptism was over as soon as it was possible to be. Doctor and Mrs Ryan stood as godparents and Oisin, wrapped securely in his shawl, motionless, until he felt the water on his brow and then he opened one eye, promptly closing it again just as quickly. It was hardly an auspicious occasion and a complete contrast from the dramatic events which had heralded his birth.

It snowed a few days later. The soft, silent flakes fell like powdery confetti onto the frozen ground and the Kelly family woke to find their familiar world had turned white. Into this world so transformed, ran Frankie and Declan, full of boyish fun and excitement. Outside the air was crisp and cold but the sky was blue and it was perfect snow for snowballs and snowmen.

Annie watched her boys from the kitchen window and she thought of Mick and Bernard as brothers, too, and how they would have played in the snow. She could almost hear Frankie instructing his younger brother, "Ye do it this way!" and she could see Declan, watching as Bernard would have watched Mick, watching, not too sure, but going along with the preferred plan. Frankie always got his way, always. She wondered how frail little Oisin would cope with Frankie and she was certain there would be difficulties between them. She sighed.

"Look at our boys, Bernard," and she summoned Bernard to watch with parental pride and amusement at the antics of their sons.

"Just like Mick and me," he chuckled good-naturedly, and gave Annie a little squeeze around her waist.

"Wonder what they'll make of the baby?"

"Sure, our Frankie will set him right," replied Bernard. He was feeling a wonderful sense of well-being as he looked out onto his world, white with snow. He was proud of his boys at that moment and of his Annie. This scene had been his scene since his first memories and all the life that had gone on through that time but the land remained the same. The land would be here after he was gone. The farm would go on, without him. He put his arms around Annie's waist and rested his head onto her shoulder.

"I love ye, Annie," he said softly, "Love ye, my girl, always have and always will. I couldn't go on without ye."

Annie twisted herself around to look at Bernard.

"Don't be silly, Bernard," she spoke as a mother would to a child. "Life goes on." But in her heart, she knew he spoke the truth and she was sad.

They remained holding each other for a few minutes more until they both were distracted with the scene outside in the snow. Mick had arrived to examine the snowman and Frankie giggled uncontrollably. He scooped up a handful of snow and, with a precision that little boys can sometimes muster, threw a perfectly shaped snowball at Mick. It hit Mick on the shoulder and, as Annie watched, Mick turned and with a swift movement brought Frankie down onto the snow. He was laughing too and heaped snow over the boy. Declan danced around with delight, wondering, no doubt, if his turn was to come.

"Mick's a big kid, sometimes," said Bernard, fondly.

It surprised Annie to hear Bernard speak of his brother in such a way. He must be feeling happy today, she thought and for a second, she remembered how she had felt when she first saw Bernard, walking along the street, all those years ago now, beside Pete Nolan. It had been exciting to meet him and love him. If only life had remained as simple as it had been, as it had promised to be, all those years ago. She raised her head towards him and gently kissed him on the lips. Their eyes met and they were young again.

*****

"Do ye think I could hold the bebee?"

Mick and Annie were sitting peacefully in the kitchen and the house was quiet. Oisin had just been fed and was cradled in Annie's arms. Modesty prevented her from feeding the baby in front of Mick. The intimacy of the act caused a measure of embarrassment within her when he was around so she would take Oisin into her bedroom, shutting the door behind her. There the two of them were secure and away from the eyes of men. Her bedroom had become her private space, a haven from others.

She was surprised by Mick's question as it seemed so out-of-keeping with his character, or how his character was perceived to be. But something in his eye ensured that she would agree because to refuse would be to insult him and might provoke an outburst. So she carefully positioned the sleepy Oisin into Mick's waiting arms, conscious as she did so that a button was loosened at the top of her blouse and Mick's eye ever fleetingly rested on the curve of her breast. As she bent over him in an intimate fashion, she felt herself reddening as she did, aware of his eye and the eye patch and the smell of tobacco and the nearness of him.

Mick's long arms cradled Oisin securely. His thin fingers joined together so the baby lay nestled in those arms, safe and contented, without a murmur. All Annie could see was the top of Oisin's head, surrounded by those arms of Mick's. Annie had knitted a dark blue sweater for Mick at Christmas and Oisin seemed to be covered in blue.

"Well, ye know, Annie, Bernard was right with the name."

At these words, Annie was astonished. Although Mick and Bernard never spoke against each other, the two of them hardly talked and when they did, it often ended in argument and for Mick to praise Bernard was puzzling enough. Annie wanted to know more, so she prompted Mick to continue. He smiled.

"Oisin. Our Irish hero. Do ye know anythin' about him, Annie?"

Annie shook her head.

"Well, now, this is the way it's told. First Oisin is a hero, a warrior and some reports say the word means "little deer". Oisin was the son of Finn and went off to the "Land of the Young" for three hundred years. He was King there, of Tirnan-og. He met a beautiful woman in the woods but alas, she had the head of a pig. She told him that the head was the result of a spell but it would vanish if he married her. And true enough, it did and they lived happily in the "Land of Youth" for many years. Oisin had a harkening for the green of Ireland and his wife told him, if he must go, he must ride on a white horse and not dismount. But didn't he slip and his marvellous white horse dead and there on the ground was Oisin, a blind old man."

"That's so sad... but what do you mean, Mick? Why was Bernard right in the name? I'd never heard the name before..."

"Because I see it this way. This little man will travel far and conquer worlds. Just because he is small, it doesn't mean he isn't mighty."

Annie was silent. The words were spoken with such certainty and the presumption that baby Oisin would achieve some measure of influence in the world surprised Annie. She hadn't taken much account of her new baby and when she thought on Mick's words, coming to her in an almost prophetic way, she was puzzled. A stab of guilt shot through her and she looked at the top of Oisin's head, wondering now. She longed to ask Mick more. What on earth had possessed him to say such things? But when she looked again at Mick, he had shut his eye and appeared to have fallen asleep.

*****

In the spring of that year, Annie received a welcome letter from her mother. Mrs Smith had made up her mind to come once again to Ireland. Even though she found the long journey from London tiring, she was anxious to meet her new grandson and be reacquainted with Frankie and

99

Declan. Although when she spoke words flowed from her like a river in full flood, she found it hard to put those words onto paper. From what Annie could make out, her mother hadn't been well but she was getting better now. Because of her ill-health, Mrs Smith had asked her brother, George, to accompany her and he was delighted to accept. He had never visited Ireland and he was fond of Annie.

"My favourite niece," he would tell others. He hadn't seen her since the day she left for Ireland with Bernard by her side and he was delighted to think he would meet up with her again. Mrs Smith spoke constantly of the welcome she always received in Ireland, of Mrs Slattery at Dun Laoghaire, of Mrs Ryan and the Murphys. Her grandsons were a source of pride for her and she missed seeing them growing up. Over the years, because of the family connection, she had become quite close to Sinéad Nolan and often wrote to Annie about the Nolans' affairs and their grown up children.

Annie read her mother's letters with interest but in truth, London and Camden and her life back there had gradually receded in her mind, so preoccupied had she become with her own problems. Life in Ballybeg was closeted and insular; the outside seemed not to penetrate. Now she understood what Bernard had told her on their honeymoon. Ballybeg was indeed removed from the world. They could almost be a lost tribe, she decided, undiscovered by the world beyond. Once upon a time, Annie had been a city girl. Now, the thought of life in the city and London, in particular, seemed a far distant memory. It existed for her as another time and could even be another life, she decided. So the visit of her mother and Uncle George would bring that outside world into her life again and no doubt, would cause a vague unsettling feeling to invade her soul. She waited for the visit with a mixture of happiness tinged with slight apprehension. She wondered if her mother would see through the new Annie... the Annie who kept longing for Mick to be closer to her. No-one was aware. She was certain of this. No one knew, except perhaps Mick, a thought she pushed to the back of her mind, terrified that it might be so. But a tiny nervous notion entered into her waking hours. Perhaps her mother would suspect that all was not well. She hoped that the situation might be disguised by the excitement of the new arrival and that any tension in the house would be defused by the combined mischief of Frankie and Declan. That is what she hoped for. It was not to be. How others see us can often cut close to the bone, and what we try so valiantly to hide becomes visible to eyes that are not our own.

*****

When Annie and Bernard arrived at the Ballybeg Railway Station to await the arrival of Mrs Smith and Uncle George, they were already ten minutes late. Recorded time and actual time were different in Ballybeg, Annie had discovered, so it was no surprise to either of them that the Dublin train was not at the platform. In all the years that Annie had now lived in the West of Ireland, the Dublin train had neither left on time nor arrived on time. At first, she found this irritating but gradually as the years passed she, too, sank into the kind of torpor to which the locals had adapted and she now found it easier to talk or to spend time in talking about the time than actually worrying about it. Recorded time mattered only for Masses, and Father O'Malley would glare from the pulpit at any latecomers who slunk into the pews, wishing no doubt for a cover of invisibility to descend upon them.

So Bernard and Annie and baby Oisin waited for the Dublin train. Waited and waited. Finally the stationmaster appeared. He spoke first to two nuns who were also waiting and then hurried along to Bernard and Annie, stepping over a brown dog, curled up and fast asleep in the sun, as he came towards them. He was a neat man and everyone liked him in Ballybeg. His great love was for plants and he tended geraniums in pots along the station platform in the summer and lovingly cared for ten tomato plants every year. He grew them in the waiting room and no one took umbrage at tomato plants growing in a public place. People would just say to one other, "Oh, that's Daniel O'Connor, was there ever a man for his garden?" and leave it at that. Daniel was a brother to Hugh, librarian and clerk and friend of Mick's. Both Daniel and Hugh were ideal servants of the public, respected and conscientious. Daniel was full of importance as befitted his position in life.

"Bernard, now we have a situation here," he said to them both, politely raising his cap to Annie as he spoke, " I've just this minute had a call from my colleague in Roscommon and the Dublin train is delayed. Be Jesus, a cow has died on the line and the train can't get past. The train didn't hit it, ye know, but there are two farmers now claiming the cow is theirs."

When Annie looked puzzled, he explained it to her as though it was the most obvious thing in the world. Bernard nodded sagely all the while.

"Well, ye see, they'll be wantin' some recompense. If the line wasn't there, the cow wouldn't have died on it, now would she? My colleague says it will take King Solomon to sort this one out! So, Bernard, now why don't ye take yer good lady and the wee one along to the Railway Hotel for tea and sandwiches and I'll send the boy along when the train gets in." He paused, and then asked inquisitively, "Who would it be that yer waiting for?"

"My mother and uncle from London," replied Annie with resignation, for it was all getting beyond her.

"Holy Mother, now what will they think of Ireland! But I'll tell ye mother, Mrs Kelly, aye, she's a grand woman and to come all this way. What a welcome..." and he shook his head in disbelief that such an occurrence could have happened. "Off ye both go now and enjoy yerselves. It'll be an hour or two by my reckoning."

It was now half past ten. So Bernard, Annie and baby Oisin made their way along to the Railway Hotel, just a few minutes walk away, on the corner of what was grandly referred to as The Esplanade. Ballybeg boasted two fine hotels. The Ballybeg Hotel in North Street, two doors along from Doctor and Mrs Ryan's house, was by far the most pretentious. In times past, it had been the favoured accommodation of the English gentry but as times changed, so did its clientele. The well-to-do from Dublin and Cork now stayed there in the summer months. It shut its doors for the winter and the owners left for the south of Spain much to the envy of the locals.

The Railway Hotel, on the other hand, was far less grand and more serviceable with a fine view across to the sea. It was the preferred hotel for businessmen and visitors passing through. When Annie and Bernard arrived at the entrance, Bernard suggested that they have their tea in the conservatory area at the front of the hotel. As the hotel faced the sea, this was an ideal position to enjoy the view on sunny days. And the sun was indeed shining and Annie and Bernard, despite having a long wait for the Dublin train, were both in good spirits. Baby Oisin sat cradled in Annie's arms looking for the entire world like a white bonnet with attached ears.

"Well, this is a fine day to be sure, Annie girl," announced Bernard as he, too, sat down on one of the cane wicker chairs and waited to be served. There were about ten cane tables with glass tops in the conservatory area. Between these tables, aspidistras in brass-embossed pots sat on high oak stands neatly dividing the tables and chairs and giving the place a look of faded Edwardian splendour. This division allowed the guests some measure of privacy but it could be difficult sometimes to be seen in order to be served. Annie relaxed and looked around at the few people enjoying their morning teas and conversation. One or two women, recognizing her, smiled and nodded in greeting and Annie felt the warm glow of belonging.

The waitress arrived to take their order from Bernard, bobbing up and down as she did so. She had been trained at The Ballybeg Hotel and was used to showing deference to the gentry. As Annie's eyes moved around the room she thought that she saw a hand she knew behind the leaves of the aspidistra at the far end of the room. The hand that was connected to the body moved and Annie became acutely aware of a familiar tweed coat loosely fitting a thin frame.

"Bernard?"

Bernard, in the middle of ordering, stopped. Annie blushed, embarrassed. The order was quickly taken, the waitress still bobbing up and down as she left the table.

"What is it, Annie?"

"Bernard... is that Mick over there?"

And Bernard twisted his head to get a better view. He frowned. Annie was in a better position to see who was sitting with Mick. Why, she thought? When she left Mick this morning he was busy fixing a tractor and here he was, in The Railway Hotel, with a stranger because the man sitting facing Mick was most certainly a stranger to Ballybeg. Annie's eyes followed the line of his face. The first thing she noticed was his swarthy complexion which suggested someone of a southern European origin. His greased black hair was neatly parted on the left with a strand of hair over his forehead. A thin black pencil line of a moustache adorned his upper lip making him appear somewhat theatrical, Annie decided. The men in Ballybeg all wore dull jackets and trousers, usually tweed. There was nothing that remotely resembled fashion in their dress. They moved around the town wearing their brown jackets, well-worn and functional. Annie had become used to the conformity of the men-folk. But this man with Mick was so totally out of place both in dress and manner. He sported a well-cut brown pin-striped suit over a colourful light cream shirt with a red and orange silk tie, or at least Annie decided it was silk.

"Who is that man, Bernard?" she questioned her husband again.

enchanting, don't you, Bernard, but guess you've lived here all your life so it mightn't be enchanting to you, is it Bernard?"

She paused for breath not expecting a reply and even if one was forthcoming she would have started up again, regardless. Neither the long journey nor the increasing number of years had in any way diminished her verbal capacity.

"How's Mrs Ryan, Annie? You'll like the Ryans, George. Why, he's a wonderful doctor, goes out at all hours, day or night. Wish we had him in Camden. It's all change, Annie... you wouldn't know the place. You'll have to come back and see it again... that is when he's a bit bigger... he's such a wee lamb, isn't he?" And she glanced briefly at Oisin who returned her gaze, unblinking, snuggled tight in his mother's arms. Having been thought of firstly as a frog and now a lamb, he must surely have wondered at his membership into the human race but he didn't understand a word and continued staring at his grandmother whose eyes darted from left to right, anxious not to miss anything.

"Now, how's everyone in Ballybeg? Do you still go to Murphy's? What a woman that is, George, wait till you meet her! And what about Mick, Annie? I hear he hasn't been well..."

At this, Annie turned her head away because she knew she would stammer a reply; a reply that would be noticed. Her mother seemed determined to speak non-stop from Ballybeg to An Teach Ban and beyond. It was possible though that she would note the hesitation in Annie's reply. Loquacious though Mrs Smith was, she could also be perceptive, especially where her daughter was concerned. Annie had to enlist the aid of Bernard so she broke into her mother's tidal wave of words and thankfully Bernard explained that Mick had been having a few blackouts which resulted in him having to go to the hospital but latterly he seemed to be better. At that moment, the car arrived at th farmhouse and talk of Mick was forgotten in the excitement of seeing the farmhouse and getting out of the rain.

That evening Frankie insisted that his father play the fiddle. He was anxious to impress on his grandmother and uncle how clever his father was. This was important to him and it gave him an opportunity to exhibit his organisational skills which were developing with each passing day. And of course, Bernard was only too willing to get out his fiddle. He perched on a stool in the crowded kitchen and, with a twinkle in his eye that always came with the music, drew the bow across the strings and awoke the magic. Talking ceased as Bernard's wonderful renditions of the old Irish songs brought tears to eyes and kept feet tapping.

At first, Frankie and Declan were shy of their grandmother and uncle but Mrs Smith and Uncle George were kind and in no time at all, Declan had climbed onto his grandmother's knee and Frankie had positioned himself next to his Uncle George. Baby Oisin, propped up in his pram, soon fell asleep. His father's playing seemed to induce a soporific state to descend upon him and no one bothered him.

Mick remained seated, as always, in his black leather armchair, slouched over a little with his hand under his chin, resting, seemingly far away. He had greeted Mrs Smith warmly enough and it was impossible for anyone not to like Uncle George but there was a barrier between him and the rest of the family that night. The music and the chatter and the noise went around him and he was untouched by any of it. Annie surmised that his silence had to have something to do with the stranger in The Railway Hotel. The whole curious event was intriguing to say the least, Annie thought.

"Aye, pleased to meet with ye," Mick had greeted Uncle George, taking the proffered hand. These were the only words he spoke all night.When Bernard put down his fiddle and Frankie and Declan went to bed, Mick still did not speak. It was only when Annie handed him a cup of tea that he looked up and, taking the cup from her, smiled slightly.

That night in bed, Annie played out the whole day in her mind. The stranger's face as he appeared at The Railway Hotel took over the space in her head and his image would not go away. Although she did not view the man as sinister, there was something deeply troubling about the whole incident. Not for the first time did she drift off to sleep with thoughts of Mick in her mind but this night there was another man in her thoughts as well.

*****

Mrs Smith was determined to be busy every waking moment of her three weeks in Ireland. The one person she wanted to see once she had talked herself to a slight stop was Mrs Ryan. In due course, a day was arranged for an outing for the two of them to Galway City. The bus to Galway now passed a little more regularly half a mile from An Teach Ban and, one sunny day, Mrs Smith boarded it complete with handbag and shopping basket. Mrs Ryan was already seated in the front of the bus and she had carefully placed her bag so that her friend could sit beside her. As usual, Mrs Ryan had the appearance of a colourful, tropical bird in rather a dull setting. A kingfisher blue beret was set on her head at an angle. On the side of the beret a silver clasp with a brown feather completed the picture. Around her neck, in a manner of casual elegance, she wore a black and gold silk scarf. Her light blue beautifully-tailored woollen coat completed her outfit. Women behind and at the side of her noted Mrs Ryan looking for all the world the Dowager Queen of Ballybeg and whispered to each other. They resembled her subjects arranged in neat rows around her.

"I've saved ye a seat beside me," greeted Mrs Ryan as Mrs Smith sat gratefully down, drabber to be sure, but pleased to be seen in the company of the doctor's wife.

Most of the people on the bus were known to Mrs Ryan including the curate, Peter, who sat at the back of the bus, his hands clasped together in a gesture of piety.

"I don't know how that one is getting into the church," sniffed Mrs Ryan, disapprovingly. She disliked the curate and hoped he wouldn't replace Father O'Malley, who had his shortcomings, but at least he was familiar.

"And now ye must tell me what ye think of Ballybeg... all the changes?"

Mrs Ryan didn't wait for a reply but brought out a photograph from her black leather handbag and started to enthral Mrs Smith who, amazingly, stopped talking to listen, about her brother in Australia. Mrs Ryan's brother, Gerard, her favourite brother, ye know, had emigrated twenty years ago now – how the time flies. He married an Australian and they had a daughter. Well, Gerard, had done well for himself. In western Queensland, he had gone into the building trade and now had ten men working for him and here's his photograph just come in the post today – well, he's just become Mayor of this town with an unpronounceable name and doesn't he look smart, with the gold chain around his neck? Why, Gerard is the first one in the family to attain high office and what do ye think of that?

And Mrs Smith could not fail to be impressed with Gerard because he was indeed handsome, the male equivalent of Mrs Ryan with the same lift of the chin. But Mrs Smith could not contain herself any longer and with a look to her friend which meant, 'Please be quiet, just for one moment, please...' said,

"What has happened to my Annie?"

At this, Mrs Ryan did indeed stop talking of Gerard and paused, biting her lip slightly as she did.

"Why, she's had a hard time of it. Poor girl. She nearly died with this last one, ye know. It was touch and go, John said... but ye knew this, didn't ye?"

Mrs Smith nodded.

"I'd heard from Annie."

But she was determined to go on as the bus bumped over the uneven road and the noise level increased with each bump.

"She seems so tired. Won't talk of it. But a mother knows." And Mrs Smith looked worried. She rubbed her hands together in an anxious motion.

"It's a lot for her out there on the farm with the two of them... and now she has her boys..." Mrs Ryan chose her words carefully.

"What about Mick?" asked Mrs Smith directly, expecting an honest reply. Mrs Ryan was cautious.

"He was ill, too, ye know. It's the drink, perhaps, but no one knows. John never talks about his patients but... I can tell ye, Mick was beside himself the night Annie had to go to hospital. Why, he dripped water all over my carpet and never a word of apology."

Mrs Smith was unsure of what reply she expected but this was not the one. She tried again.

"Annie seems to get on with him and Frankie adores him. It's just he doesn't say much, does he? And the eye patch... has he lost the sight in that eye, do you think? Annie just changes the subject any time I ask. What's happened to her? I thought you might know. She thinks the world of you," she added as an afterthought.

Mrs Ryan was flattered.

"I like her too. Why, she's like a daughter to me and those two boys... were there ever a pair of rascals?" and she smiled thinking of Frankie and Declan.

Mrs Smith sighed. Galway City was coming into view. She tried once more. "Mick seems to sit in that black chair of his, most of the time... why, it looks like Bernard's running the farm, that is, when he's not at Murphys'..."

Mrs Ryan changed the subject.

"We'll get off at the next stop before the bus station," she said.

It was when the two women got off the bus that Mrs Smith said to Mrs Ryan:

"I'd like to go to the church. I want to say a prayer."

Mrs Ryan, though surprised by the sudden request, was unperturbed. Going to church for Mrs Ryan was just something you did, like brushing your teeth.

So the two of them walked to the church and entered into its dark sanctuary. Peter, the curate followed them in, much to Mrs Ryan's slight annoyance. Inside was the smell of incense, the candles burning at the back, the holy altar before them, the rose window reflecting a beautiful light above and Mrs Smith knelt and bowed her head. Mrs Ryan did likewise.

When the two women left the church, Mrs Smith said to Mrs Ryan as she blessed herself, "I needed that," as if she had been handed a glass of water. Given their conversation in the bus, Mrs Ryan could only agree and taking her friend's arm she gleefully announced,

"Now, let's go shopping!"

*****

Uncle George was considered an affable man. Certainly his affability helped him in his pursuit of the ladies. Although Uncle George had married young and widowed early, he always found the company of women preferable to that of men and indeed, women related to him in a comfortable manner. Uncle George was very fond of Annie and always had been ever since he bounced her upon his knee. "My favourite niece", he would say and, "My best girl," as she proved to be. Uncle George had fathered one son with his wife – a son whom he loved. This son, who was a few years older than Annie, enlisted in the R.A.F. and was one of Churchill's heroes. To have a son a fighter pilot to defend Britain in her hour of need was for Uncle George the greatest source of paternal pride imaginable. Alas, and sadly, his beloved son paid the hero's price when his plane came down in Northern France and he was never seen again.

112

The effect on Uncle George's wife was sudden and dramatic. From the moment she heard the terrible news, she lost the will to live and nothing could bring her back and in a very short space of time, or so it seemed, she gratefully and almost eagerly crept through Death's door leaving Uncle George alone in the world except for his sister and Annie. A lesser man might have succumbed to the grief as well but Uncle George was made of stronger stuff. He rallied around and, after a respectable few months, resumed his acquaintance with the ladies. There were many widows now in Camden and Uncle George was popular and welcomed into their houses. In fact, he had women to cook for him and bake cakes for him and his sister to do his washing and ironing. All his working life had been spent in the soft furnishing section of a large department store and he knew everything there was to know about curtains and drapes. It was no wonder that women found him appealing and responded happily to his amorous innuendos.

When he arrived in Ballybeg for his three weeks holiday he announced to Bernard, in all seriousness but the humour was behind his eyes, "Now, Bernard," he said, "I must tell you this. I know an awful lot about fabrics but nothing about farming... so just you watch where you point me?"

This was to prove prophetic. Both Bernard and Mick, too, warmed to Uncle George but he was certainly and without a doubt useless around the farm. Why, Bernard mused, Declan knew more about farming at eight than Uncle George would ever know in a lifetime! But whatever his failings in farm life, he made up for it with his affability and generosity of nature so in no time at all, the two brothers were eager to take Uncle George to Murphy's Bar and Uncle George, for his part, developed an abiding taste for the Guinness to say nothing of a never-to-be-forgotten attraction to the delights of Ma Murphy.

"That's some woman there," he remarked to Mick on one such occasion as the two men were sitting, perched at the bar.

"Aye," replied Mick, dryly. He didn't talk of anyone much and had never been heard to comment about Ma Murphy which made him somewhat unique amongst the male population of Ballybeg.

Bernard sat on his stool in the corner, playing away on the fiddle with Hugh O'Connor, Mick's friend, keeping in time and banging furiously on the piano keys at such an ever increasing tempo that the noise level in the bar was considerable and speaking over the din, difficult. Uncle George was back to his old flirtatious behaviour and Ma Murphy was quick to respond.

"Sure," she laughed, "if all the men in London are like ye, how can the girls cope?"

"Well, now you'll have to come over to check it out, won't you, Ma?" replied Uncle George and he grinned somewhat lecherously as he downed another pint. "Give us another one, Ma... and one for Mick as well, while you're at it!"

And Ma leaned over close to Uncle George much to his delight.

"I might just stay in Ballybeg if you keep pouring like that, Ma," he murmured with a look on his face that suggested that he was about to ascend into Heaven.

At this, Pa pulled on his braces and Ma hurried off to serve another eager male who was in the process of getting drunk.

Uncle George was about to comment further about Ma when, out of the corner of his eye, he noticed a different sort of man open the door and walk into Murphy's Bar. Bernard, playing on the fiddle and tapping his foot as he did, noticed the man, too, recognised him as the stranger who had been with Mick in the Railway Hotel, and frowned but continued playing. However, he was aware of every move the stranger made. Uncle George, too, kept his eyes

114

on the stranger and was as fascinated as Annie had been at The Railway Hotel. The stranger, his appearance so different from the men around him, pushed his way to the bar. His well-cut camel coat stood out amongst all the brown tweeds and he carefully positioned his elbow on the surface of the bar so that two hefty Ballybeg men had to move to allow him to stand. Uncle George's observation was such that as the stranger looked and saw Mick, he moved from his position at the bar and elbowed his way towards them. Mick seemed not to notice any of this. He was busy staring at his half empty glass, deep in thought and, at that moment, not wishing to disturbed.

"Michael... I did not see you there!" which was untrue because the stranger had come looking for Mick at Murphy's Bar having been told that it was Mick's preferred drinking establishment. When Mick looked up and saw the man before him, his expression darkened and Uncle George noticed that Mick's hand gripped his glass so firmly that the knuckles turned white and Uncle George feared the glass might break.

The stranger nodded to Uncle George but kept his eyes on Mick. He did not remove his hat. All around and about, the noise and the music reverberated but it seemed to Uncle George that he and Mick and this stranger had been removed physically from Murphy's Bar, that there only existed the three of them at that particular moment in time. Finally, the man spoke in a heavy accent, leaning in front of Uncle George as though he wasn't there.

"Ah, Michael... I have the thirst," and he moved his right hand towards his lips in a gesture that implied that he would like a drink.

Mick nodded and beckoned Pa who came over, looking harassed and red in the cheeks.

"Give this man whatever he wants, Pa," was all Mick said.

"Ah, Michael," replied the stranger. He parted his lips in a smile but his eyes were as hard it seemed to Uncle

115

George, as hard as the diamond in the signet ring on the little finger of his left hand. "I think... a whiskey, *grazie... sì*, a whiskey," and he indicated that his preference was for a large glass.

All this time, Mick's hand gripped his own glass. The stranger took a sip of the whiskey and, turning to Uncle George, said in a low voice, his accent a little hard to follow:

"This man, Michael... he is a good man, *sì*?"

Uncle George, surprised by the question, could only nod his head.

"*Sì*, Michael. I stay in The Ballybeg Hotel. It is... how you say in English...?"

He rubbed the fingers of his left hand together. "It is a lot of money... a lot of money, Michael...?"

At this, Mick stared at the man and answered the question with a kind of resignation, with almost a look of inevitability on his face.

"How much?"

"You are a good man, Michael... I think we will say... twenty?"

And then to Uncle George's utter amazement, Mick opened his well-worn battered old wallet and handed the man fifteen punts.

"That's all I have," he said wearily.

And the stranger took the notes, carefully arranging them in his own seemingly brand new wallet which, Uncle George noticed with some consternation, already held quite a few punts.

"*Grazie*, Michael... I will go now," and he finished his drink in one gulp. Turning to Uncle George, he said, "The Irish... they are friendly, *sì*?" but there was mockery in his voice.

Then he moved away from them, pushing past some men at the bar without a word of apology. The room was heavy with smoke and, as he reached the door, he turned back towards Mick and Uncle George and touched his hat in a gesture of farewell. Bernard, playing at the far end, saw

116

the stranger leave and, glancing towards his brother, noted the expression on Mick's face. He stopped playing and rested his fiddle on his knees. Mick did not speak. He sat, immobile, and Uncle George, his usual affability completely disappearing by the minute, remained silent as well. Finally, Uncle George aided no doubt by four pints of Guinness, gained the courage to ask the question that consumed him with curiosity:

"Mick," he hesitated, "Mick... who is that man?"

Mick gazed at Uncle George in a kind of a daze. Uncle George began to doubt that he would get an answer but finally the words came from Mick in a mechanical way, quietly, and he pronounced every syllable clearly.

"His name is Silvio Luchetta," he answered. "He will go now... but he will be back."

Then, suddenly and without warning, Mick turned his face towards Uncle George and, with a voice so completely different cried out:

"They think I'm mad in Ballybeg... what do ye think?"

Any words that Uncle George might have had, disappeared from his head but mercifully, at that precise moment, Pa bellowed out "Time," glowering with a face as dark as the winter clouds over Ballybeg. An inebriated and over amorous-youth was intent on positioning a one punt note between Ma's ample cleavage.

"Time!"

But all Uncle George could think about was Mick's question and the name, Silvio Luchetta. Silvio Luchetta and madness. He wondered if he had been witness to something it was better not to know. The Italian's name, because he was most certainly Italian, kept circling around in Uncle George's head as he steered an unsteady Mick out of Murphy's Bar.

CHAPTER SEVEN

Summer came and with it change. The lives of Mick, Bernard and Annie settled once more into the unending routine of work and more work broken only by the seasons. The memory of Silvio Luchetta and the unexpectedness of the encounter between himself and Mick often came into the minds of both Annie and Bernard. That this person could bring such mystery to the world they inhabited caused endless questions for which they received no answers. Mick refused to speak of Silvio; went silent as soon as the Italian's name was mentioned and so in the end, exasperated, Bernard and Annie also kept quiet. Letters came for Mick from Silvio, postmarked Edinburgh; thick letters in brown envelopes, and once there was a parcel which looked as if it contained books. Still Mick said not a word but would take the letters and books to his room to open in secret – never once explaining 'who or what', so barriers went up between them all.

One late summer's evening Bernard climbed up the slight hill to the hawthorn tree, now in full foliage, and sat on his bench. He was tired and there was just the silence of the land around him. It covered him like a protective coat and he felt the security of his environment. His thoughts were dark and troubled for he felt himself growing old, old before his time, and with all the tension within the house ever present in his mind. He longed for understanding. He longed for reassurance. The church promised him eternal life if he could only just believe, but his doubts brought fears and he was mindful of death's approach. He sensed his own mortality and knew his days were numbered. For the years went by with their relentless certainty. If he could only have the assurance of faith, he thought sadly.

To the rest of the world, he presented a joviality expected of him but underneath was a melancholy... like Ireland herself. Here lay sad regrets, loneliness and feelings for lost opportunities. The one constant in his life was the love he felt for Annie. To Bernard, Annie was something pure, a gift to him he didn't deserve. Or so he perceived her to be. She was so elevated in his mind that she sat above him sometimes, the eternal woman. He was uncomfortable with the sexual act somehow. He had fathered three children and now there was another one on the way. This has to be the last, Doctor Ryan warned him and, in the deepness of his soul, he was relieved. He hated the demands his body put upon him and was ashamed of his nakedness before Annie.

His shyness when they had first met had been acute. It took him months to relax in her presence. Her warm body beside him at night did nothing to prevent his natural modesty. She was pure and chaste and the fact that she was his wife in no way changed his feeling towards her. He knew this adoration exasperated her but he could not stop himself.

"I'm not perfect, Bernard," she would snap when he hinted that she was.

It still seemed a miracle that she was his, that this London girl had consented to be his wife and come all the way to the West of Ireland to look after him and be a mother to his children because she was a good wife to him and she loved her boys, except possibly Oisin. He had noticed she disciplined him more than the other two and compared him unfavourably to Declan in particular. Not that it seemed to bother frail little Oisin. Bernard guessed the boy was intelligent, far cleverer than any of them, he thought, even Mick, and it was perhaps his intelligence and sensitivity that kept him apart from the others. Hard to believe, thought Bernard, that the lad is four and off to school soon to join his brothers in the playground.

And with the thought of Oisin came the thought of his birth and the whole fearsome drama went through Bernard again. Back, back into the recesses of his memory went his thoughts and he remembered his mother on her last

119

terrible night. How Mick had held him, tight, and covered his ears to try to block out the screams. He played it out in his mind. He remembered praying that night. A child's prayer to God to stop the cries and then suddenly there was silence, an eerie, deathly silence... because God had answered his prayers. The noise stopped. There was silence. There was silence...only there was no mother. God had taken her from him and God could never quite be trusted after that. No one would answer his questions, not even Mick. But Mick had tried. Bernard remembered Mick had tried.

When Annie nearly died, too, on that winter's night, Bernard dared not pray for fear God would take her from him, just as He had taken his mother away. There would be nothing but grief at An Teach Ban, grief in a house of men as it was before. The sadness cut into his soul, it seemed. God had betrayed him, so how could he trust the priests again with all their talk of salvation, the end to suffering and eternal life? Bernard thought of Mick and how his brother had looked after them all after their mother's passing. Mick was just a boy, too. Bernard knew he would always be loyal to Mick, no matter what. If it ever came to a point of deciding between Annie and Mick, it would be Mick he would choose and he hated himself for it but that was just the way it was. He thought of Annie and the sex act and his nakedness before her. With that thought, he remembered the night he brought her home; remembered her face at the sight of Mick's nakedness because Mick had none of Bernard's shyness about his body... revelled in his nakedness, even. Once Bernard had found his brother stretched out on the wet green grass with the soft rain falling like a vapour over his body, stretched out, naked, his arms outstretched in the manner of the crucified Christ, not aware of where he was, it seemed. Bernard could not speak but had stood, fascinated and horrified, too, as the droplets of rain lay on Mick's white skin.

Bernard crept away; tried to understand. That night Mick was his usual taciturn self, dressed in his old brown tweeds, as if nothing had happened in the afternoon. Bernard knew that certain Ballybeg folk called his brother "Mad Mick Kelly" and he always felt the shame of it. But he said not a word to anyone, even kept silent with Annie and tried to hide his embarrassment. Only Tommy Flynn and Hugh O'Connor refused to say a word against Mick. Both were loyal to him because he was their friend. But the shame Bernard buried deep within himself because he, too, was loyal to Mick, no matter what.

His thoughts grew darker. In his mind he was seven again, walking home from school, with Mick beside him. He felt the stone hit his shoulder and it was Fergus Hennegan who had thrown it with unexpected precision. The two of them had been arguing all afternoon and Fergus had waited. Seizing his opportunity as Mick and Bernard passed by, he had aimed the stone at Bernard, not meaning to wound him, just to warn him. Bernard cried out and Mick, looking backward, saw Fergus dancing around, ready to send another stone in Bernard's direction. With one giant leap, or so it seemed, Mick caught hold of Fergus and pushed him to the ground. The whole incident would have been forgotten by the next day no doubt had not Father O'Malley been lurking, as was his nature, behind the privet hedge at the side of presbytery. Father O'Malley was younger then, and more severe. He appeared as if from nowhere and grabbed hold of Mick's collar.

"I'll teach ye to pick on those smaller than ye, Kelly," and he shook Mick in the manner of a dog with a rat. He dragged Mick through the hole in the privet hedge, into the presbytery, into his office with Bernard and Fergus creeping behind at a safe distance. They could see through the window the fury of the priest. He held Mick who had stopped struggling at this point and he reached for his strap which lay on his desk. Bernard and Fergus watched in a kind of silent motion because the whole event seemed to

121

them both terrifying and unreal. Watched and saw Mick extend his right hand, palm upwards as Father O'Malley brought the strap down hard onto the boy's outstretched hand. Mick didn't flinch but looked at Father O'Malley without emotion and it seemed that this lack of fear in one so young, incensed the priest even more because the strap kept coming down again and again until it was thrown back onto the desk and Father O'Malley bellowed:

"Get out of my sight, Kelly. Ye'll rot in Hell so ye will and none of the saints will be there to help ye, ye despicable boy."

And Bernard and Fergus watched in wonder as Mick quietly left the room, his right hand clenched at his side. When he got back to them he carefully covered his bleeding hand with his handkerchief and said not a word.

"I didn't mean it," said Fergus to Bernard.

"I know ye didn't," replied Bernard and from that moment on they were best friends and remained so. Both of them were in awe of Mick but neither told anyone else about the incident. The fear of Father O'Malley remained with them but admiration for Mick's courage was stronger.

Bernard sighed. The memories were a long time back now, he thought and they were no longer boys. Fergus had emigrated. Father O'Malley was still there but his physical power had weakened. Bernard feared him even now and avoided him if he could. As he got up from the bench, he felt himself grow dizzy and he sat down again. He felt it was a warning.

"The good Lord is thinkin' of takin' me up," he said to himself, "or maybe, down?" and he chuckled as the dizziness subsided in his head. But he felt the inevitability of his passing, an awareness of it coming, suddenly. Perhaps, he thought wryly, perhaps not long now...but not today.

He made his way back to the house and the comfort that was there for him.

That night, at Murphy's, Bernard played his fiddle. He played the sad songs, of emigrant ships, and exile, of lost loves and other people's wars.

"Ye have the longin' in ye tonight, Bernard!"

Ma gently placed her hand on Bernard's arm. There was no hint of sexual advance. Her keen eyes saw another Bernard, hidden from the world. He had brought customers to her. Sometimes at night, after they had cleared the bar, he would play again, just a few songs, just for her. She liked him and that was enough for Ma.

"Aye that I have, Ma," replied Bernard, sadly, "that I have."

Ma watched as Bernard gently and lovingly placed his fiddle into its well worn case. He looked into her eyes and Ma saw the tears behind them and she, too, had the longing.

*****

At the end of the summer, when approaching autumn days brought rain and darker evenings, Annie thought she saw Silvio Luchetta. As she walked along North Street having just seen Doctor Ryan, she noticed an unusual-looking figure of a man smoking a cigarette and leaning on the railings at the corner. His figure and manner suggested the Italian she remembered but she wasn't sure. It had been four years since she had seen him last at the Railway Hotel with Mick and the memory of him was slightly blurred in her mind. She hesitated but her curiosity compelled her and, in an almost a mechanical way, she walked towards him. As she came closer, he looked up and she was able, in that split second of time to study his face and assure herself that he did seem to be the mysterious stranger. He noticed Annie and smiled at her.

"Ah, signora," he said, raising his hat as he spoke, "it is beautiful here, this Ballybeg, sì?"

Annie now had a chance to study the man more closely and she decided to do just that. She was weary and pregnant and her feet hurt but the Italian was such a different sight in the drab community she now inhabited that her usual reticence to speak to strangers disappeared and, with a lightness of tone, she agreed with his remark.

"Ah", replied the Italian with a spark of recognition, "I see, signora, you are not from Ballybeg. Your voice, it is different. I have lived in London after the war and you are perhaps from London?" he finished somewhat theatrically, gesticulating in the manner of those of a Latin temperament.

"Why, yes," said Annie, surprised at the perspicacity of the man, "yes, I am from London but I have lived here now for many years and not been back," she concluded somewhat sadly.

"Ah, signora. You miss the bright lights... Piccadilly, Oxford Street?" and he smiled at her.

Annie decided at that moment that he wasn't as sinister as she had first thought. In fact, there was an attractiveness about him which would be quite appealing to members of the female sex. And she blushed slightly at the thought.

"Well, you see, I have my husband and children here and my mother has visited a few times but yes," and she looked into his brown eyes with a candour that surprised herself, "I do miss London sometimes, especially in the winter," she concluded somewhat lamely.

"Ah, the winters!" replied the Italian, throwing his arms around in a Gallic gesture of disapproval. "Sì. Sì. Too cold. Too wet. Signora, perhaps you might know of a person?" he said, changing the subject of the weather which he found immensely boring, "Signora, a person... a man. Michael Kelly, he is known to you?"

Annie reddened and looked away before answering. She was unsure whether to tell him of Mick or not, remembering Mick's behaviour at the Railway Hotel. But the Italian looked at her in such a way that she would have found it difficult to lie and she weakly replied, trying her best to be nonchalant as she spoke:

124

"Why, yes. He... he is my brother-in-law in fact. My husband is Bernard, Mick's brother."

"Ah, signora, signora! This is good news. You will take me to Michael?"

At this Annie began to wonder what to do next. If she were to arrive home with the Italian, goodness knows what state Mick would be in. She concluded somewhat irrationally that the best course of action was no action at all.

"I'm sorry but I'm not able to take you there. What is your name?" Because she thought the time was now right for introductions.

"My name is Silvio Luchetta," he answered. So it *is* him, Annie thought and her heart beat faster. "And you are Signora Kelly."

He smiled, taking her hand and kissing it softly. She felt the roughness of his moustache on her skin. He held her hand for what Annie thought was a little too long until she pulled away. But he kept his eyes on her, studying her, so that she began to feel embarrassed.

He was so well-dressed and Annie remembered the spivs in London she used to see about. He reminded her of them. He was still awaiting her answer so she cautiously said:

"I can give you our telephone number."

They now had the telephone at An Teach Ban which had already proved a godsend. She was wary of using it but Frankie and Declan seemed to have no hesitation in talking to their friends.

"Ah, signora, that is good. Perhaps you will tell Michael that I must see him. You see, I write to him and I know his address... but where does he live?" and he shrugged his shoulders.

Annie told him the number and Silvio, much to her surprise, wrote this down on the back of his hand.

"So I not forget," and he smiled at her. "Please, signora, you tell Michael that Silvio Luchetta is here and he wishes to see him. *Grazie*. Ah..." and he raised his index finger, "I stay in Ballybeg one week and then I go, you tell Michael."

And with that, he raised his hat to her once more and turned on his heel, walking quite rapidly away and along North Street towards the church of St Peter and St Paul. He did not look back and Annie watched him go, puzzled by the encounter but also just a little excited about Silvio. He brought mystery and colour into the bleak autumnal setting of Ballybeg. He came from a world beyond and, for that reason, was welcomed, Annie thought. But she wondered how she was going to tell Mick.

As Annie pondered the best course of action, her thoughts turned to her life in the West of Ireland and what she had learned over the years. She had made the observation very early on that there appeared to be two subjects that an outsider, or a "blow-in", as she knew the term to be, would be well advised to avoid. Politics and poteen. And she smiled at the thought of the poteen. It was one of those secrets in the West that everyone knew but no one talked about. She was sure that Ma kept a few bottles under the counter for her regulars and once, early in their acquaintance, Ma had proudly offered Annie a piece of poteen cake.

"It is the best fruit cake ye'll ever eat, Annie girl," she had announced with a devilish twinkle in her eyes as she handed Annie a generous slice. "Why, it is the cake of the Gods, I'll be tellin' ye. And this here is me mammy's recipe she got from her mammy. And I'll be passin' it on to Helen, too. 'Tis a secret, ye know. Now what do ye think of it?"

And she leaned towards Annie expectantly, waiting to hear words of approval.

Indeed, Annie liked it and would have quite easily asked for more but she was too polite and a little in awe of Ma at that stage, so she just replied with a smile of satisfaction on her face.

"It's lovely, Ma. But what is poteen?"

"Ah", cried Ma aghast, "the drink of Ireland to be sure. But..." she added, darkly, "we don't speak of it... 'specially to the Gards or the priest. So remember that. But aye, it makes a lovely cake." And she chuckled to herself that she was able to enlighten this shy London girl on a subject dear to her heart.

"Now, ye go away and ask Bernard all about it. I don't care for the stuff meself," she added as an afterthought.

So Annie had asked Bernard and he, too, had a bottle he kept hidden in the shed at the back of the house. But Annie decided once she took a sip, that she, like Ma, didn't fancy the stuff. After that she was loath to mention poteen... but politics, however, now that was another matter entirely. It was here that she thought Mick might be involved. It would explain his absences, she reasoned. Annie, herself, was distrustful of politics. She had seen dozens of lives ruined and the millions who had died in the war, she reminded herself, all down to politics and power. So she carefully avoided any references to the political situation in Ireland. She thought she was wise too but, in truth, she had no opinion about a united Ireland. There was a small company of IRA in Ballybeg, she gathered that could be active but she wasn't sure. Again, it was like the poteen, something that everyone knew but no one spoke about. She wondered if Mick was somehow involved. Bernard, it appeared, was a bit like herself regarding politics. At Murphy's he tactfully avoided an opinion and Annie, being a woman and English was thankfully excluded from having any meaningful political debate. But Mick was different. Mick was an unknown. Could this explain his disappearances and his wild behaviour? She wondered. He reads a lot and had such passion, and she reached the conclusion that Mick might even be the leader.

But when she tentatively asked Mick, years ago now, when they had one of their quiet evenings together whether or not he agreed with a united Ireland, he answered her with almost a riddle.

127

"It is men and their governments that put up barriers," he replied enigmatically. "In the hearts of men there are none."

After that, Annie could only surmise that Mick, too, left politics alone. But now there was Silvio Luchetta. Where on earth had Mick met him, and perhaps it was to the Italian that he went when he disappeared for days? Annie grew excited at the thought that she had possibly solved the mystery. All these thoughts of politics and poteen, Ireland, Mick and now Silvio Luchetta tumbled around in her head until finally she mentioned to Mick that the Italian had asked to see him and might ring, but Mick just stared at Annie with his one eye visible, just nodding his head. And the lack of finding out more annoyed Annie a little so she didn't speak to Mick all evening.

She didn't have long to wait, however, until she saw Silvio Luchetta once again. One evening, a few days later, after they had finished their evening meal, there was a loud knock on the door and Frankie, excited, rushed to see who it was. On the doorstep stood Silvio Luchetta, dressed as elegantly as a peacock and with as much conceit.

"Is this the house of Michael Kelly?"

Annie heard Frankie reply and suddenly Silvio was in her small kitchen. He was almost incandescent; the whole room shrunk because Silvio's body seemed to take up so much space such was the force of his personality.

Silvio swept his hat from his head as was his custom. He looked around the small room and with his usual flair, spoke in his heavy accent:

"Ah, la famiglia Kelly... and Michael..." and he looked at Mick who remained seated in his black leather chair. Annie noticed that Mick's hands clenched the arms of his chair but he did not speak.

"Ah, signora," and Silvio turned with a flourish to Annie. "Introduce, *grazie*..."

"I'm Frankie," announced Frankie. He extended his hand much to Annie's surprise. The Italian shook it politely.

"I'm Declan," said Declan and he shook hands too because he always did what Frankie did.

"And you?" asked Silvio, smiling at Oisin.

"That's frog," said Frankie rudely.

"Frankie!" admonished his mother sharply and she said to Silvio, "This is Oisin."

She pronounced "Oh-sheen" the English way with the emphasis on the "O".

"It's Oisin," corrected Frankie. He was annoyed at his mother.

"Ah, Oisin," and Silvio's pronunciation of the name was even more amusing. "Do you think I'm funny?"

And Oisin, shy, nodded his head.

"Ah, ah! This is an honest man, *sì*? What do you say, Michael?" and he turned once more to Mick who still didn't answer.

Bernard extended his hand. This was Bernard's way.

"Now what is yer name, sir?" he asked politely although he knew it was Silvio.

"You are the brother of Michael," answered Silvio. "I am Silvio Luchetta, signor. *Amico!*" And he shook Bernard's hand. His eyes, it seemed, were everywhere.

Still Mick did not move from his chair. His very posture was tense but he remained quiet.

"You have a fine *famiglia*, signora," Silvio said to Annie and he smiled. Annie reddened and Bernard frowned. Suddenly Silvio looked completely at ease in the small kitchen, unaware of the effect that his presence was having on the family. He removed his coat and laid his hat next to it. He sat down, uninvited. Now Annie had a better chance to study his face. She noticed that his hair was greying at the temples and not as greased as she remembered. His moustache was still neatly trimmed and everything about his appearance was impeccable. He had style and charisma, a powerful combination. As he spoke, his words seemed to take control of the room and his hands moved as fast as his tongue. Silvio spoke of Italy and about his home, a little village outside Bologna, of barmy nights and constant music but never once did he mention his family, his business, his place of abode or why he was in Ballybeg. No one in the Kelly family dared enquire further because there was a trace of sadness present in his conversation until finally and abruptly he looked at Mick and said:

"Ah, Michael! I see the hour is late. Perhaps we talk now?"

Everyone looked at Mick. He shrugged his shoulders slightly and obediently got to his feet without a word of protest.

"And now, good people," continued Silvio, "I go now with Michael. Perhaps we meet again, *sì*? You, my man," and he turned his brown eyes to Oisin, "I will meet because I am funny, *sì*?"

He took Annie's hand, pressing it to his lips, not holding it for quite as long as before but enough to cause her heart to beat faster, "Signora. I thank you. And Signor Kelly, *arriverderci!*"

He extended his hand once more to Bernard who took it cautiously.

Mick was already in his coat and waiting at the door for Silvio. It seemed to Annie that he was wary but relieved that Silvio was going. When the two men left the room not one member of the Kelly family spoke for a few minutes. Each one, even Oisin, was thinking of the strange encounter with this man who brought unanswered questions and fascination, too, into their lives. Lives, which a few hours before, had seemed so mundane.

*****

Although the physical presence of Silvio Luchetta disappeared from view, the memory of him remained in the minds of all the Kelly family for a long time after. Lesser mortals are forgotten almost as soon as introductions are made. Not Silvio. If he had not been seen for one month or one year or even ten years, he would have been remembered because Silvio was unlike anyone they had ever met before. It was not just his obvious Italian nationality that set him apart. Had he been Irish with pale blue eyes and red hair but with the same force of character, he would have been noted because there are certain individuals who captivate others and indeed, inspire. They move around and take control of whatever situation in which they find themselves. Even if silent, people are drawn to them, not knowing why. When they speak, those they are with hang on to every word, hoping to gain recognition from them, wanting to be part of their world, wondering at the secret that sets them apart.

It appeared that Silvio was one of these people. He had enthralled Annie with his stories and his thick accent made him even more appealing. Uncle George, Annie remembered, had recounted the story of Silvio and Mick at Murphy's, and so embroidered it that the Italian had appeared almost Machiavellian and posed a threat to all. Uncle George was convinced that Mick was being blackmailed for some mysterious reason although this was implied rather than proven. Annie doubted that now. After all, she mused, Uncle George was prone to exaggeration. Indeed, her mother often remarked anything George said could be divided in half but this in no way diminished her mother's fondness for her younger brother. It was just George, so his opinion could not be altogether trusted, however well-meaning his motives for recounting the story had been, Annie concluded.

She was puzzled as was Bernard, though, about Mick's reaction to Silvio and she recalled once again the incident at the Railway Hotel. Silvio appeared as vain in his appearance and dress as it was possible to be but he was not a threat, at least not a physical threat, she was sure of that now. And whatever his relationship was to Mick, which

131

remained a secret, Annie would have wanted to meet Silvio again. With that thought came a feeling within her that this would happen and the possibilities of meeting him and in what circumstances they would be brought a tingle of excitement. She did not know how long she would have to wait for such an event and, in the meantime, the letters and the parcels continued to arrive addressed to Mick and bearing Scottish stamps. Annie's curiosity was continually aroused and she longed to know what words and messages were contained inside. Mick remained silent and the tantalising mystery deepened with every letter received.

*****

"Ye have a wee angel there, my dear," gently spoke the midwife into Annie's ear.

Joy came at last to Annie and Bernard, fleeting though it was, and it came in the form of Mary Louise. All the tensions, hidden suffering and unspoken longings that stood between them, all this, was taken away from them as they gazed at their beautiful baby girl... because Mary Louise was a beautiful baby with Annie's light brown hair and clear blue eyes and long lashes. Six months after Silvio Luchetta's departure from An Teach Ban and, on a near-perfect day in the spring, this little person came into their world, quietly, unhurried and safe. Perfect, it seemed to them, in every way. Doctor Ryan took no chances this time and Annie gave birth at Galway City Hospital with the minimum of suffering and no complications.

Bernard, too, was relieved that it was all over. As he held his baby daughter in his arms thoughts passed through him, unspoken, because he couldn't put words to them. Words were inadequate, clumsy somehow, and would not be able to describe such a perfect gift as this baby seemed to be. He held her in his arms and was conscious of the reality of holding her. This was reality and at that precious moment in time, nothing else mattered but the reality of this child in his arms. He was conscious of his farmer's hands, huge they seemed to him to be, with the dirt under his nails and wee Mary Louise, so small and so beautiful being held by those hands and in his arms. She was his. This was the reality. He smiled at Annie but still he couldn't speak. Thought of his three sons, how different the three of them were... Frankie, so clever, so dogmatic, so taking command at every opportunity. Then there was Declan, who, pleased to help, followed with not so much as a murmur. The farm would be his, one day. Then Oisin, the unknown. Somehow he was in the family but not part of it. And Bernard wasn't quite sure why. Oisin was intelligent. There was a gravity about him which was so unlike any of the others and Bernard wondered what he would become in his life. He sighed for the uncertainty that he felt for his son. But now here was his daughter and the spell had been broken at An Teach Ban and there would be women in the house at last. Annie had changed their world and brought him sons and a daughter and there would be no more children. Bernard could not take the risk of losing Annie. That part of his life was finished. The needs of his own body were as nothing to him. He would not put Annie at risk ever again although he loved her. They were blessed.

Mick's reaction to the arrival of Mary Louise was much the same as Bernard's, or so it appeared to Annie. She was tired but there was contentment within her because she knew she had achieved a victory of sorts, to bring another female into the house that had so long been dominated by men. Somehow the ghost of her long-dead and unknown mother-in-law was there, in the house, however briefly, but she was there. There was a healing for all, a mystical healing that night which could not be explained in human terms. They all felt it but no one spoke of it. These matters were best left unsaid because they are private matters and not for ridicule. When Bernard played his fiddle for them, he played fast up-tempo jigs and the boys jumped around the small kitchen, trying to keep in time, but failing and collapsing in a heap in front of the adults who laughed too. The night Mary Louise came to An Teach Ban was a joyous

133

night. It is a precious moment in life to never forget the arrival of a long-awaited child and it seemed to be, and not fanciful in the slightest, that angels were present that night.

The next morning Mick presented Annie with a gift for Mary Louise. Once again he had spent hours carving because he loved to carve when he could, when the dark moments weren't with him. He loved the creative energy that flowed from him as he transformed a piece of humble wood into something in his own mind's eye. This time he had worked on a relief carving of bluebells because he had wanted so much to make something beautiful for Annie and her new baby. Bluebells. His mother's favourite flower. And he had made the incisions sharp and clear and was pleased with his work.

"I'll carve her name there, if ye like," and he pointed to a space at the bottom of the wood, just waiting for a name.

Annie took the gift, loving it too because it had been Mick's hands that had been on the wood and the gentle side of Mick had brought beauty out of something that others would have ignored.

"She would like that, I'm sure. You be sure to tell her that you made it for her on her first day home."

Annie longed to take Mick's hands and hold them the way he had held his chisels, and the wood, the way he had carved the bluebells. No matter how hard she tried not to allow the longing for Mick into her mind, it came at unexpected moments and at moments she wished it would not. She always tried not to look at him closely because to look at him might give away her desire, but this time she couldn't help herself. She looked at his face, a face that was furrowed with lines from an outdoor life, a farmer's life, and smiled. For she was at peace with herself at that moment and with him and there was just the two of them, together, once again.

"I'll do that for ye then, Annie, *mo chailín* (my girl)... and for this wee Mary. For two women. Aye, I'll do that. I'll do that right now."

134

And he took the carving back, holding it carefully, too, because this was a gift of love.

*****

There came now to the Kelly household a wonderful sense of calm and wellbeing as though the tensions of the past were laid to rest and suffering had somehow and miraculously ceased. It was all due, it appeared, to Mary Louise. From her first moment of arrival in the house, she was the centre of attention, and her presence brought visitors and gifts. Annie was suddenly beset with kind words and cooing and much discussion because hadn't that English girl had to struggle along for so long with all those boys and the brothers, especially that Mick, but now she had a daughter, praise be, to provide female solidarity, all in good time and wasn't it just the most beautiful baby, this Mary Kelly? Until Annie had to say to Mrs Ryan, with some exasperation:

"Why, Mary is getting so much attention. No one looked at Oisin when he arrived. Such a difference, you wouldn't believe!"

To which Mrs Ryan retorted with words to the effect that after all Mary is such a beautiful baby and well... poor Oisin... and left further comments hanging in the air.

Even Father O'Malley announced from the pulpit the safe arrival of Bernard Kelly's daughter and the date of her baptism.

"Sounds like I didn't have any part in it!" whispered Annie to Bernard and he grinned at her, giving her hand a little squeeze of affection.

So Mary Louise became a welcome diversion for the Kelly family and she somehow joined the fragmented group together for a short time. It would have been possible to hope that this state of affairs could have remained and that Mary would have brought with her, from infancy on, a healing, and that all the unspoken tensions, desires and mysteries would have been forgotten. In fact, Annie began to wonder with a kind of wild hope that perhaps she would

135

find some happiness at last and that all the longing she had for Mick and the disappointment she felt with Bernard, could be resolved by the arrival in the house of her beautiful little daughter. She hoped for this. She prayed for this. She felt she would have given anything for this.

But the illusion of happiness, for that was what it was, proved to be fleeting and a new baby, however beautiful and however welcomed, could not stay a baby forever. Mary, surveying the world from the safety of her mother's arms, could not give to that mother or to those around her, the happiness that they craved. It was not possible, nor could it ever be possible however much they desired it. For life is joy mixed with sorrow and it was Mick who once again shattered the fragile happiness, such as it was, that had rested for such a brief moment upon the Kelly household.

Annie was surprised to see Mick in a somewhat distracted state on the morning he went away. He was dressed for travelling and he had already put on his well-worn tweed overcoat when she saw him. It was just another ordinary day; she had thought having already planned out her work routine, so to see Mick in such a state in the small kitchen unsettled her. Bernard had risen early as was his nature and was already at work. He normally didn't return to the house until about mid-morning. Mick's cap was pulled over his eye patch and his cigarette was resting on his bottom lip giving him a rather rakish appearance.

"Why, Mick, what are you doing?"

By now, Annie was able to speak to Mick freely. He no longer frightened her or worried her to the extent he used to when she had first come to An Teach Ban. Indeed, the two of them had been growing closer at least in their conversations and Annie was beginning to sense that there was a Mick there whom no one knew. His dark moods and irrational behaviour masked perhaps a gentler side and this was the Mick that Annie longed for and dreamed of at night. But Mick was distracted and Annie noticed with some consternation that his old brown leather suitcase was sitting quite prominently in the middle of the floor. Somehow this suitcase was a symbol of all the suitcases that had been packed for all those souls who had left Ireland, more often than not, never to return. It was a sad sentinel, this old suitcase of Mick's, sitting on the brown linoleum floor and Annie nearly fell over it.

"Mick," she said again, distracted, too, "are you going somewhere?" This seemed the obvious thing and the words were somehow trite but she couldn't think of anything else to say.

Mick didn't answer but looked down at his boots and not at Annie which worried her. He normally looked at her. In fact, in his looking at her sometimes, she had felt embarrassed and nervous and worried that he, too, felt something for her and that was a concern. But he hesitated as if unsure of what to say and, when he spoke, he mumbled the words so Annie could hardly understand them.

"Aye, I have to go away."

She cried out, "Mick... why?" because she feared his leaving almost more than his staying. He turned and looked at her the way he used to, the way she had grown to love. It was as if he formulated the words in his head and then he spoke deliberately and there was no trace of a mumble. His diction was clear, his words precise:

"Ye see, I have to go. Ye know that, Annie *a chara*". (my dear).

He took hold of her hand, then, and wouldn't let it go. He held it as if his life depended upon it.

"I have to go," repeated Mick and all the time he looked at Annie and she could not know what he was thinking or what he wanted to say but all the time she was conscious of his hand holding hers. His strong farmer's hand, rough, but his fingers were the fingers of a craftsman, long and slender. It brought back the memory of the day when they had started to perhaps become friends, all those years ago now. The day he talked for the first time of his mother and the bluebells he loved. That was the day she lost the fear of him.

"Annie," he said, in a rush of words. "Ye see, how can I say? It's Silvio. He's in Dublin now and I have to meet him. Aye, I have to see him, Annie. He can't come to Ballybeg this time so I must see him. I'll catch the Dublin train at midday. I'd better be off. Ye man O'Connor won't hold the train forever and I must go today. Aye. I must go today. Tell Bernard, I'll be back. Don't worry, *mo chailín*, I'll come back but Silvio wants to see me and I must go."

That seemed to end the matter as far as Mick was concerned. He put his head down but he still held on to Annie's hand, tight. And then he did a surprising thing. He leaned over close to her, leaning now because he was so tall and she was just a little woman. He kissed her quickly on the lips. So quickly that it almost didn't happen and then quickly, before Annie could speak, he pulled his hand away. He reached down and picked up his suitcase. Without another word, he turned and left the room, not looking back.

Annie watched him go. Her heart beat like a drum in her chest. In the silence of the room, she cried out his name, to herself, alone for there was no one to hear. The only sound was the ticking of the clock on the wall as it measured time and it seemed to Annie, as she stood there silent, that the measurement of time was happening somewhere else. The ticking intruded into her thoughts, unwanted, because at the present moment in time she felt so very much alone... so very much alone.

CHAPTER EIGHT

There was a mist on Slieve Geal the day Mick arrived back at An Teach Ban. Slieve Geal was just visible from the farm. Its conical peak provided a barometer of the seasons. Sometimes it hid its shape under a heavy mist or rain and then it was mysterious, undisturbed. Other times, it showed off its beauty, etching its silhouette against a blue sky but its real majesty was most evident on those clear, crisp winter mornings when the top was bathed in white contrasting so dramatically to the sky behind. Annie had grown fond of the mountain and the ever changing patterns of the seasons it displayed. The mountain, or perhaps in more rugged landscapes it would have been a large hill, was part of their environment and loved by all inhabitants of Ballybeg. So that when they were away from their homeland, it would be to Slieve Geal that they would give their fondest memories and their poignant longings.

Annie and Bernard had climbed to the top many times over the years. Its steep, shingle slope did not yield easily to even the most determined of climbers and it took a sure step and a steady heart to reach its summit. But once conquered, it gave of itself and the panoramic view from the top over to the sea and town surrounded by green fields with their rugged granite rock walls was reward enough for the effort. Annie knew that Mick climbed to the top as well. He, too, loved the mountain. So Annie was thinking of the mist on the mountain when she saw Mick appear, carrying his brown leather suitcase and looking for all the world as if he had never been away. He stopped when he saw her. Thoughts rose in each but Mick didn't say a word and, still holding his suitcase, brushed past Annie and went into the house. She followed him because she wanted so much to speak to him, to find out about his meeting with Silvio, to make him engage in some sort of conversation – offer an explanation. Instead of silence, she wanted to hear his voice.

"Mick...," was all she said. Lamely, weakly, still unsure of him.

But then he smiled and all her annoyance vanished because he was back with her, once again. And her heart missed a beat, or so it seemed.

"Silvio wishes ye well, Annie *mo chailín*. He says he will come again, that he wants to meet ye again and young Oisin. 'My man', he calls the lad, he said as much. But that's Silvio." He paused slightly, thinking, it seemed of the Italian. "Now, I'll be wantin' a cup of tea. For sure, that's a long journey sometimes and today, beJesus, it seemed to take forever."

And he sunk gratefully down onto his black leather chair, tired.

"How's Bernard been managin'?"

Annie did not want to talk about Bernard. Her desire to know about Silvio and now Mick's reticence to speak of the Italian, annoyed her so she brought the subject around to Silvio again in a hope that more might be forthcoming. But still Mick was evasive, changing the subject deftly so that Annie knew she couldn't learn more but the knowledge that Silvio spoke of her and of Oisin, quickened the desire in her to know what had happened. Mick took the cup of tea when it was handed to him and that, as far as he was concerned, was the end of the matter.

"That's Silvio," was all he said as though those two words told it all. The image of Silvio was once again in the small kitchen. The larger-than-life figure taking command and he somehow entered the space, invisible to the eye but visible, it appeared, to the mind.

That Silvio wielded a mysterious power over Mick became evident to both Annie and Bernard as the months slipped by. What this power was they could not be sure. It did not in any way appear that the influence of the Italian on Mick was malevolent or threatening. Rather the contrary as Mick grew more and more pensive. Always a man of few words, his words became fewer and fewer and certainly this was the case after letters came from Silvio; letters that Mick read eagerly with a kind of unexplainable joy. He would read his letters and then take them to his room after which his manner would become more thoughtful. How the receiving of a letter could cause such profound happiness in another human being was an enigma to both Bernard and Annie. Indeed, Mick's expression on some occasions bordered on elation. Neither Bernard nor Annie had much affinity with the printed word. It was puzzling to say the least and neither ventured to guess to what extent Mick replied to the letters. It was a mystery also as to how the Italian, whose English was punctuated with words of his native tongue, could write in such a way as to affect such a change in another being. It did not occur to either Bernard or Annie that sometimes it is possible to write more easily than speak to another and this certainly appeared to be the case between Silvio and Mick.

The letters contained many pages in Silvio's surprisingly neat handwriting which in itself was the subject of conjecture. His manner had been flamboyant to say the least and his appearance bordered on vanity so that whatever he wrote to Mick seemed not to be in keeping with the character that he outwardly portrayed. The possibility that Silvio was able to communicate on a deeper level seemed to be the only probable answer, or was that supposition on Annie's part? She wasn't sure. Bernard and Annie could sense that the letters had to contain something more than news of events and other people's stories which was the usual form of letter writing to which they were accustomed. Letters to have such an effect on Mick who appeared to look forward to receiving them with such an anticipation that neither had ever witnessed before, further added to the mystery.

Until one day Mick announced in a voice which could not be argued with that it was his intention not to attend Mass on a Sunday or any other day, for that matter. He spoke with conviction. It was his desire to sever all ties with the church in any form and he would notify Father O'Malley of his decision at the earliest opportunity. Indeed, he had spent many hours pondering and questioning his faith until he finally reached the conclusion that this was the course of action he had to take and he would not be persuaded by anyone, least of all Father O'Malley, to change his mind. He had made a decision, the consequences of which he would live with. If it meant eternal damnation, so be it.

If Mick had taken a knife and drawn blood across her hand it would have felt the same to Annie, so sudden and so unprepared was she, for his words cut through her to the bone. Never for one moment had she thought he would renounce his faith. He had seemed so settled in it – going to Mass every Sunday with the rest of them, bowing his head and kneeling along with everyone else. The two of them had never discussed religion. It was part of their daily life, accepted without question because this was the way of it. Had always been the way of it. Doubts, sometimes, yes, but never a thought to give it up without any explanation. Just that he had decided. How could he do this? It seemed to Annie so very selfish because it would cast a shadow over them all and her children would suffer, Father O'Malley would see to that. And the fear of the priest rose within her and she trembled at the thought of his reaction. She looked at Bernard who was looking as apprehensive as she felt, biting his fingernails as he did at moments of stress.

"What do ye mean, man?" Bernard frowned, fearful now. It would be "Mad Mick" again in Ballybeg and people would whisper as they passed by. And the children would feel it and Annie would suffer as well. Bernard knew because this had been his life. Mick's drinking and his absences could somehow be explained but how do you explain not going to church? Bernard's heart went cold with the fear of it. Mick wouldn't answer. Refused to

142

answer. Refused to give them *any* answers. Would not explain.

"Ye can't do this to us, Mick! Ye'll have Father O'Malley out here. What in the name of God are ye thinkin' of? What about us? Have ye ever given us a thought, man... ye might as well end it all now for what it will do to ye when Father O'Malley hears of it."

He was bitter now. All the years of silence and all the unspoken words coming into his mind and he could have hit his brother hard for that's how he felt.

"Is it that Italian?" he suddenly asked. "Has he got to ye? All the letters that come to ye... it must be something. It has to be the Italian," he said to Annie.

Still Mick was silent. He sat in his chair, unmoved. His mind was made up. He would not change no matter what. If he had decided not to attend the church and it had been Silvio Luchetta who had influenced that decision, they would not know, at least not today. Mick set his mouth hard the way he did when he did not want to change. And they all knew that look. Annie didn't say a word. Deep inside her she loved him a little bit more and didn't know why. She disagreed totally with his action and wondered if she would be damned along with the rest of them. But still, the admiration for Mick grew. She held Mary Louise in her arms and cradled her tight. She worried if her thoughts escaped and Bernard captured them, he would know the truth and this she couldn't bear. She looked into the face of her sweet angel of a baby and tried not to think.

*****

"I haven't seen ye at Mass, Mick," said Father O'Malley and there was a hint of a threat in his tone.

"No, ye haven't."

"I'll be seein' ye this Sunday, then?" replied the priest, expecting obedience because that was his way. He moved from Mick, turning his back on him and was about to continue walking when Mick's reply forced him to turn around again.

"Ye won't see me there, not on Sunday nor any other Sunday."

"What are ye sayin'? Am I hearin' ye right? I'll see ye on Sunday."

Father O'Malley breathed heavily, leaning on his stick for support. He was not used to being answered back and was unprepared for what he assumed was perverse behaviour. No one spoke to him like this and it bewildered him. For thirty years, he had been under the impression that his word was law in Ballybeg. He might be a little fish outside his parish but here he was King and no one crossed him. Least of all Mick Kelly. He felt his heart pounding in his chest. He clenched the top of the stick and glowered at Mick who returned his gaze, without flinching. Father O'Malley's memory went back to another time when Mick didn't cry out but had stood as the strap hit his hand, unmoved then as he appeared to be now. Mick always wore his eye patch these days and his good eye fixed on the priest.

"I'll see ye in Mass on Sunday," repeated the priest and he shook his stick, trying to control the anger that arose within him. But Mick showed no reaction to the words and, shaking his head ever so slightly, walked away leaving Father O'Malley standing, a solitary figure on the pavement, unnerved by the encounter and contemplating his next move.

Then he hurried as fast as he could to the safety of the presbytery. Built in the same grey brick as the church of St Peter and Paul next door, it had been his home for thirty years. His manner as he walked was somewhat distracted and, as he made his way along the street, his thoughts were elsewhere so he hardly noticed two of his parishioners who stepped aside to let him pass. He paused as he reached the front door and he was out of breath. Meeting Mick had unsettled him and he was grateful, indeed, to get off the street and away from people. He wanted to get into his own space and think. He went into his study and closed the door

144

behind him. Around him in various heaps lay thirty years of accumulated life – books, papers, garments, all the trappings of a religious life. Father O'Malley sank gratefully into his worn brown leather armchair and surveyed his life as it appeared in the material form of possessions. Not that he had need of possessions. That was a vow he had eagerly renounced knowing, believing, that the Lord would provide for his every need. He sighed. He was once again a young priest, newly ordained and travelling to Ballybeg full of zeal and enthusiasm in his youthful heart. He was old now and in his mind the present sometimes became his past. But he remembered. How well he remembered. Getting to know his flock. Taking over the upkeep of their souls. Fighting over his own inner demons and how he had fought those wretched temptations.

He would lust after Mrs Ryan. Oh, she was such a beauty. He had longed to clasp her to him, to kiss her neck, her breasts, her body, to conquer her... to remove every item of her exquisite, so expensive clothing, one by one, until she stood naked in front of him. Then he would take her. Conquer that aloofness until she begged for more. And the demon of desire tried to crush him. Not for a moment did she guess. He was her priest and forever the doctor's wife but how he desired her. Sometimes with such urgency that he would leave her abruptly, rushing back to the security of the altar to fall on his knees, to plead with God to take the temptation away for he was weak. Weak! He would tremble at the altar to quell the lust that rose within him. All for that woman from Cork. Women! They take away your power. They tempt you with their bodies and taunt you with their eyes. Ah, Mrs Ryan. Now, Ma Murphy was different. If he hadn't been a priest he would have taken her casually, without a thought of the consequence, enjoyed her and forgotten her till the next time. He had been weak but never once had he given in to his desires. That must count for something. For the celibate life had been hard for him to follow. He sighed once again.

In his youth, he had channelled his frustrations into physical pursuits. He was stockily built and strong and a good athlete. He could run for miles and he did. Early after he had said first Mass, he would leave the presbytery and run along North Street, down the Galway Road, past the Kelly farm and upwards to Slieve Geal. As he ran, he forgot and the motion of running took over until he got near to the top and the rocks and the shingles made speed impossible. He would clamber over the stones till he reached the summit and then breathing deeply and triumphant, view the scene below. Ah, Slieve Geal held many secrets of the people of Ballybeg and Father O'Malley left them there too. On the top, in the silence, in all weathers, he would take breaths that went to the very bottom of his lungs and sometimes, he cried out, to release the frailties of his human body. Father O'Malley cried at the top of Slieve Geal, alone but for his God and the mountain was a giant, a silent witness, holding secrets there, a confessional no priest could match, or so it seemed, even now. But that was then. Now Father O'Malley could hardly walk. He had to hold his stick firmly for balance and the arthritis was in his hands and legs.

They were retiring him. His days were numbered. Father Byrne was ready to take over and Peter, the curate, itching for his own parish. Peter wanted his own souls to save and he was anxious to begin proselytizing. He was an intense youth, thought Father O'Malley. So Peter would go and there would be a new priest and a new curate in Ballybeg. They would let Father O'Malley stay because this was his home. This study would be his to the end and they would let him say the occasional Mass until he grew too weak for even that.

A savage pride took over. He did not want Father Byrne to know he had lost a soul in Mick Kelly. Obey the rules. Follow the ritual. He watched over them all to make sure rules were obeyed because he obeyed them to the letter, without question. His certainty was in his obedience and he was victim to his own piety somehow but that thought never occurred to him. His reward would come at the end of all this time on earth. He was sure of this and this belief gave him conviction. So Mick Kelly had no right to rebel. He was keeper of the wretched man's soul. He was his priest, after all, and the image of Mrs Ryan faded as Mick came into his head... would not go away... Mick Kelly, with his eye patch and tweed cap and no fear of the priest... calm, untroubled and unafraid. The man's a drunk, thought Father O'Malley. But there had been no hint of the drink on him as the two of them stood in the street, facing each other. The Divil is in him and Father O'Malley swept his hand through his thinning grey hair. The Kellys have always been trouble, he thought. Right from the start. Mick would not be subdued, even as a lad and Father O'Malley remembered again the strap pounding down on the boy's hand. And then that London girl Bernard had found. What a situation... out there on the farm... two men and one woman. Father O'Malley's imagination took over. Things might be better now with the children there but he had noticed how Annie looked at Mick and he wondered. But what to do about Mick? Because something had to be done and soon, too, or he would have to explain to Father Byrne and he did not want to do that. The Divil is in Mick Kelly, the priest thought again. Of course, he knew that his flock sometimes left the church and went off to England and beyond. He knew some fell away but that wasn't his problem. They weren't his responsibility because they weren't in Ballybeg. But Mick was. Never once did Father O'Malley question the teachings of the church. He was God's representative on earth. The souls of the people of Ballybeg, every man, woman and child, were his to watch over and the rules had to be obeyed because that was the way to Heaven away from this mortal trial. And Mick Kelly was his responsibility, God help him, for that was the way it was. For thirty years, that was the way it was.

When Francis Kelly's wife had died all those years ago now, Father O'Malley had gone out to An Teach Ban to comfort the man. Francis had wanted the priest to take a drink with him and that was the beginning of the end for Mick's father, God rest his soul. Mick had looked at the priest without emotion, even then. Aye, Mick Kelly had always been a problem. Father O'Malley had only once set foot in An Teach Ban since then but now he knew what he had to do. He would get Peter to drive him out to An Teach Ban and plead, if he had to, for Mick to come back to the church for the sake of his eternal soul. It was the only course of action and Mick might just agree, especially if Bernard was present, he might just agree, before it was too late and Father Byrne took over. And for Father O'Malley, the problem was resolved... or so it seemed.

With a feeling of relief, he opened the drawer at his desk and brought out a bottle of the finest single malt Scotch whisky and a glass. He half filled the glass and felt the warmth of the drink slide down his throat. This whisky was for special occasions. He had met a young priest, years ago now, from the Western Isles in Scotland, who espoused with some eloquence the virtues of single malt whisky and ever after that, he sent over at Christmas a bottle for his friend, Father O'Malley. Father O'Malley would reciprocate and travel to Dublin to buy the finest Irish whiskey in return to send to Scotland. The bottle would be carefully wrapped and taken to the GPO in O'Connell Street and sent off. It became a tradition between the two of them. Even the Luftwaffe could not destroy the exchange and all through the war the bottles changed countries, every Christmas. Father O'Malley took a drink when he had something to celebrate and today he felt he had resolved the problem of Mick. So a drink was in order. The special drink, not the cheap whiskey Ma Murphy served up and Father O'Malley's mind was at rest. He would drive out to An Teach Ban tomorrow, in the late afternoon, and confront Mick.

*****

When Father O'Malley and Peter arrived at An Teach Ban, the sky was already darkening. The full moon rose from behind the black outline of Slieve Geal and hung there in the sky, casting a silvery reflection in ribbons through the dark, ever-moving clouds. It had rained during the day and, as Father O'Malley eased himself slowly out of the car, his foot stepped into a large puddle, wetting both his shoe and his sock. He uttered a profanity under his breath and wondered, somewhat irrationally, if Peter had parked the car where the puddle was in order that Father O'Malley might step into it. Peter, he decided, could be quite perverse and difficult, too, and his sanctimonious behaviour often covered up for a certain lack of character. Father O'Malley was already feeling nervous about his pending visit to the Kelly farm and the discomfort of the wet foot did not help him to regain his composure. So he was quite frustrated by the time he reached the front door and let Peter hammer on it noisily.

The farmhouse, Father O'Malley observed as he stood waiting, had certainly improved in appearance since the arrival of that English girl and he noted with some degree of approval that the door was now painted pillar box red. Things looked well kept which was a change from his last visit quite a few years ago now. The fuschias on either side of the door appeared to have taken over and he could make out their profusion of flowers in the dark. There were never a sight of a flower here before, thought Father O'Malley as Peter knocked once again. Finally, it was Bernard who opened it and, seeing the two priests standing there in the half dark, stepped back to allow them to enter.

"We have come to see Mick," announced Father O'Malley with his usual air of importance. "Is he in?"

Peter stood behind his superior in his accustomed manner of deference to the older man but all the time, his eyes were everywhere and he kept moving his body

149

sideways so his head appeared to swivel around in a peculiar manner.

"Aye, that he is," replied Bernard. His heart beat faster. He had been expecting the visit.

When Father O'Malley and Peter entered the kitchen, the sight of contented domesticity greeted them and both felt a tinge of envy at the warmth, companionship and the smell of the just eaten evening meal. So different, Father O'Malley thought, to the last time he had set foot in this kitchen and tried to reason, unsuccessfully with a drunken Francis Kelly. The man had been totally drunk and full of self pity, blaming God for the loss of his wife, cursing and condemning all and sundry. Ever so often he would stop and cry to the priest, "This is nothin' personal towards ye, Father," and then continue so there was no reasoning with him. Father O'Malley had done no good that night. But tonight the kitchen was warm and Father O'Malley, once seated, leapt straight into the reasons for his being there.

"Ah, now, Mick, I have looked out for ye, aye, that I have now... for two Sundays now but I haven't seen ye in the Lord's house. Will ye be givin' me a word of explanation for it's a dark night, to be sure, and I will be needin' to be gettin' back? Will I be seein' ye next Sunday? Bernard and the family have not missed a Sunday so I would be waitin' for a reason from ye for this is indeed a sorry state of affairs when a man does not give thanks to the Lord but goes on wilfully without a thought for his eternal soul or indeed..." he hesitated, catching his breath, "or indeed for those about him."

Mick did not reply but looked the priest in the eye. He sat on his leather armchair and appeared not to have much reaction to the visit of either the priest or his curate. Father O'Malley tried again.

"Ye know this is a serious matter, Mick Kelly. It's a serious matter. I have not set foot in this place since ye father, God rest his soul, since yer father passed away. So

150

do ye not think that I am aware of the seriousness of this situation?"

Still Mick did not answer and Bernard butted in, attempting a reconciliation.

"He has not been at all well, Father. So he has. Maybe he will be there next Sunday."

At that, Mick turned to Bernard.

"Ye'll not answer for me, brother. My decision is mine and mine alone. It does not in any way have anything to do with ye or anyone else in this family," and he looked at Annie as he spoke.

"There, there, man," retorted the priest, "haven't I heard all this from yer own lips that afternoon in North Street and haven't I been on my knees ever since prayin' for ye?"

"There would be no need for that."

"Aye. Aye. Ye sit there and say that but what about Judgement Day? Have ye a wish to burn in Hell?"

"I have seen enough of Hell on this earth."

"And what do ye mean by that, man? Life's a trial but we have the promise of eternal life not eternal damnation," and Father O'Malley spluttered. He had no wish to argue semantics with Mick. His purpose was to bring Mick back to the Mass before Father Byrne arrived.

Still Mick kept his eye fixed on the priest. There was no trace of discomfort or fear in his gaze.

"I have no wish to argue with ye. Ye have yer work to do and I am one less for ye to worry about."

At this, Father O'Malley seized a theological opportunity.

"Ah, but there ye are wrong. Why, if one repenteth, the angels in Heaven celebrate."

"That they do. But I have no wish to..."

"Now, ye admit it, Mick Kelly. Sinner that ye are."

"I admit nothing."

"What?"

"I have nothing more to say. The matter is closed."

151

"The matter is *not* closed. Ye will be at Mass on Sunday. Ye are out of yer mind, Mick Kelly. I will see ye on Sunday."

"We've all said what we have to say on the matter. There is nothin' more to be said. Ye have yer beliefs. And so have I."

"Yer beliefs!" cried Father O'Malley, aghast. "Why, yer beliefs! Yer belief in havin' yer own way that's yer belief... with no thought of yer brother or his children. How do I explain to Father Byrne that ye have set yer mind against the teachings of the church? For ye will need the comfort of the church, Mick Kelly, so ye will. None of us are immortal. If yer sainted mother could hear ye speak to a priest this way in front of yer brother's children, God rest her soul!" and the priest shook his stick at Mick.

At this, Mick rose from his chair and, with a sound in his voice that seemed to come from the very depth of his being, cried out:

"Ye'll leave my house now. Now, I tell ye."

He made a movement to hit the priest who flinched slightly but remained seated.

Suddenly without warning, Oisin jumped down from the stool he had been sitting on all evening and ran to Mick, grabbing hold of his uncle's legs.

"There ye are," retorted the priest because he was just a little fearful for his own personal safety. Mick was tall and threatening and again, there was the question of his mental state. The priest noted that the frail little lad clung to Mick and this gave him some ammunition or so he thought.

"There ye are," he repeated. "Look what ye've done to the boy."

But Mick seemed unaware of Oisin. He stood, rigid in the room. All eyes were on him and his good eye was on the priest.

"Ye are not welcome here. Be gone."

This sounded like a dismissal for Father O'Malley and a fury rose within him. Turning to Bernard, he spat the words out.

"As far as I'm concerned, this is finished now. Ye brother is finished now and forever. Did ye hear what was said to me, Peter?" and he turned for support to the curate who nodded furiously, sliding backwards and forwards on his chair as he did so.

"Ye will hear from me again," the priest continued, "or Father Byrne when he comes. This is not the end of the matter, whatever ye may think. We will go now. When ye have time to reflect on yer actions, I will see ye, Mick Kelly. I will see ye in Confession, so I will."

For Father O'Malley could not believe that he had been the object of such words. Never once had his authority been in question, never once in thirty years. He could not believe that a man whom the whole of Ballybeg thought was mad or a drunk, or both, would dare speak to him like that or question the authority of the cloth? And he trembled within himself. At this time in his life, he could do without all this.

The atmosphere in the room had changed from warm domesticity to a cruel tension and the children looked on in fear. Slowly, Father O'Malley pulled himself up from the chair. The water had made his foot wet and cold but such was his state of mind at that moment, he was unaware of his discomfort. Peter took hold of his superior's arm and the two of them made their way to the door. Father O'Malley did not say goodbye.

"We will make our own way out," he announced sarcastically, but Bernard and Annie were in such a state of shock that neither made any effort to move to the door. Mick stood, immobile, in the centre of the room and Oisin clung to his uncle's legs, not speaking a word whilst the world of adults changed his own world forever.

*****

The news that Mick had threatened Father O'Malley travelled round Ballybeg with a rapidity which suggested

153

that the population had little to do and even less to keep them interested. In the repeating of the tale, the story became exaggerated so that it ended with Mick physically assaulting poor Father O'Malley who had to fight for his life as Bernard and the curate tried to restrain mad Mick. Though Father O'Malley was feared by all, he was still their ordained priest. Mick Kelly, on the other hand, was of unsound mind and wouldn't he have to be to hit a priest, a poor defenceless old man at that, and wouldn't you know because Mick had a temper on him, everyone agreed. And the stories grew in exaggeration. Finally, it became for Mick much the same as it had been and memories of his almost forgotten altercation with Doctor and Mrs Ryan all those years ago, surfaced once again. There was ever such a slight, almost imperceptible change in the way people greeted Annie. Even Mrs Ryan who was Annie's great friend kept her distance and was in agreement with the rest of the Ballybeg folk. When Annie told the truth about the incident and that Mick had not laid a finger on the priest, Mrs Ryan just shook her head and remarked that Mick, "and you have to admit it, Annie", was considered unstable. It was a shocking thing for him to suddenly renounce the church and threaten the priest because didn't it bring shame on the whole Kelly family? Poor Bernard, having to cope with such a brother. Annie thought if she sprung to the defence of Mick, which she longed to do, that her attraction to him would be noticed so she kept her silence, biting her lip to prevent the words coming out. She was glad now that she hadn't unburdened her soul to Mrs Ryan. The barrier went up ever so slightly between the two women and they were never again quite the friends they had been before. Annie once again felt the cruel isolation of the outsider. It served only to deepen her attraction towards Mick and she defended him in her heart and refused to be part of the conspiracy of words that now surrounded him and was, by default, directed to the whole of the Kelly family.

154

It was only Ma Murphy who refused to be swayed by the majority.

"Here's a drink on me, Mick," she told Mick when he entered the pub a few days later.

"I'll not be doin' with gossip," she said to him as she poured a Guinness, "whatever happened, that is between ye and himself," for she rarely called Father O'Malley by his name.

Mick looked a little bemused by the generosity of such a woman but he took the drink, nevertheless, downing it in a few gulps. The other men at the bar turned away and started to talk amongst themselves. It was only simple Tommy Flynn who sat beside Mick as loyal as ever and with as much concern as he had shown when the two of them were in Scotland. Tommy passed no judgement and Mick sat as implacable as ever, perched on the bar stool where he always sat.

Bernard was there too, that night, and he played his fiddle and wished once again that he was somewhere else far away from all of it. His pain rang through the notes as he played and he tapped in time with his boot. No point in arguing with Mick or pleading with him to come with them on Sundays. Once Mick's mind was made up, there would be no change in him. He knew that.

"It *has* to be the Italian," he remarked to Annie a few days later. "Why else?"

"Has he spoken to you about it?"

"Mick never speaks to me about anythin' like that. Aye, it has to be that Italian."

And Bernard shook his head as if to shake the image of Silvio Luchetta out of his mind.

The knives were out for Mick Kelly and although it would only be a matter of time before something new would occur which would stop the tongues wagging, Annie never forgot how isolated she had felt at that time. The memory of the incident would dim, but trust in those about her was lost forever. She knew her boys suffered because of

155

it, especially Oisin. She was unprepared. For the first time in her life, she had been the victim of words directed at someone she now knew she loved. Although she did not understand any of Mick's actions and her own faith remained resolute to the end of her days, she had reached a point in her life where the love of another was greater than the opinions of the many.

*****

Over the next few months changes came to Ballybeg. Changes came but Mick Kelly did not change but remained resolute in his decision to stay away from the church. Father O'Malley refused to talk about his encounter with Mick and preferred to talk of other, less sensitive, things. He had failed in his duty but he rationalised his failure by dismissing Mick as obdurate, drunken and a lost soul. These labels he inflicted on poor Mick with varying degrees of intensity but to newly arrived Father Bryne he said nothing, such was his sense of inadequacy.

Father Byrne came to take up his pastoral duties with an almost evangelical zeal. It did not take him long to realize that the Parish of St Peter and St Paul had sunk into a kind of inertia as Father O'Malley aged. Father Byrne was in his early forties and he set about getting to know his flock with vigour and a certain degree of humour. Such was Father O'Malley's sense of failure as far as Mick was concerned that he did not even mention the recalcitrant. Just said there was a farmer, a Bernard Kelly by name with an English girl for a wife and four children. He had decided that Father Byrne could find out in the fullness of time about Mick and to allude to him beforehand would be foolhardy. I might even be dead by then, he reasoned to himself, and be finished with the lot of it. It was to be many months before the cheerful Father Byrne discovered the existence of Mick Kelly.

In the meantime, the new priest effected changes. One of his first moves was to take himself across the Owenbeg and make the acquaintance of the Protestant Reverend

Williamson and his wife. Never in thirty years had Father O'Malley made any signs of recognition or reconciliation to the church across the river. The Protestant congregation was small and insignificant. Father Byrne with his ecumenical enthusiasm thought the very least he could do, was to make himself known. This he considered to be his Christian duty in such a small community. To Father O'Malley, had he known, it would have been a betrayal.

It was Mrs Euphemia Williamson, "Effie" to her friends, who opened the door to Father Byrne. The priest was confronted with a tall woman whose coloured auburn hair was swept back off a face heavy with powder. She was inclined to cover her lips in bright red lipstick often unevenly and hastily applied. The overall effect was theatrical which indeed she was. Flummoxed by the sight of a Roman Catholic priest on her doorstep, Mrs Williamson could only utter the usual polite civilities as she beckoned him inside. It would be difficult to imagine who was the most surprised by the sight of each other. Father Byrne, for his part, was totally unprepared for the image of Mrs Williamson or for her living room. His first problem was to try to subdue two gigantic Irish wolfhounds that proceeded to lollop and leap around the room, barking incessantly.

"Down, Sophocles and Aristotle," admonished Mrs Williamson but the boisterous creatures took no notice. "My husband is immersed in the Ancient Greeks," she added as a way of explanation. "Now, would you care for a cup of tea?"

Poor Father Byrne tried valiantly to maintain his composure as the ever increasing crescendo of barking and leaping threatened to topple him onto one of the lounge chairs. The living room resembled just the sort of room in which you would expect two enthusiastic dogs to reside. Not one part of the room held space. The whole area it seemed was filled with faded rugs and ornaments, books and magazines. Even the walls were covered with framed watercolours of seascapes, hills and valleys. The wall that

157

wasn't covered with paintings was fully furnished with various sepia photographs of weddings and moustached gentlemen in uniform. The culmination of all this was an ornate gilded frame at the end of the room outshining everything else. Here was an oil painting of a woman, scantily clad, holding onto a harp between her legs. Father Byrne could only wonder. Through all this Mrs Williamson waded and, with a wave of her arm which was adorned with bracelets that jingled as she walked, she advised the priest to sit where he could. Whereupon he sat on one of the rugs draped untidily over a sofa and as he did so, he almost descended onto a plate with the remains of an uneaten meal which had somehow escaped the attention of the dogs. As Father Byrne perched awkwardly there, Mrs Williamson announced in a well modulated English voice with just the trace of a Scottish accent that she would summon Leslie who no doubt would wish to make the acquaintance of the new priest and wasn't it just a lovely day? Perhaps he would care for some cake along with his tea? At that, one of the dogs leapt onto the sofa and proceeded to try to lick Father Byrne's ear. Neither the behaviour of the dogs nor the awkwardness of the priest had any effect on Mrs Williamson as she boomed: "Leslie. Someone to see you!" and left the room leaving Father Byrne who tried unsuccessfully to get one huge dog to get down and the other to stop licking his hand.

What seemed an eternity later, Leslie appeared. He was shorter than his wife and his grey beard stretched half way down his chest making him appear like a little goblin. He was about the same age as Doctor Ryan, but that was where the physical similarity ended. The Ryans and the Williamsons had arrived in Ballybeg about the same time. Mrs Ryan, given her penchant for entertaining and holding court, was at first a little jealous of the minister's wife but it soon became evident to her and to the other women in Ballybeg that Mrs Williamson was no threat, despite her theatrical ways, and that the Protestants would keep

158

themselves to themselves and things would remain as they always had been. Thanks be to God.

Effie Williamson adored her husband and it was apparent to all who made their acquaintance that the two of them were sublimely happy in each other's company. They were as poor as the proverbial church mice but this didn't bother either of them. Effie was a widow when she first met shy, absentminded Reverend Williamson and it proved to be a match made in Heaven. Life in the West of Ireland suited them both fine. The Reverend spent most of his time painting watercolours. He was often observed overlooking the sea or near Slieve Geal with his easel in front of him, completely unaware of anything or anyone. He held a First in Classics from Oxford and wrote obscure poetry that was never published. His pastoral duties took third place in his life and indeed, with a congregation of just twenty, he could hardly be pushed.

The Reverend and Mrs Williamson were considered slightly dotty by the good folk of Ballybeg. They were, after all, the minority and would remain so in Catholic Ireland. Mrs Williamson had received some measure of fame earlier on and her photo had appeared on the front page of *TheBallybeg News*. It was a surprise to all, that such a dramatic-looking woman who wore brightly coloured scarves and hats and was regarded by all and sundry as an eccentric, was also a keen fisherwoman. She landed a twenty-two pound pike from Lough Dibh. The photograph showed her, grinning triumphantly and holding a fish which was nearly as tall as she. The record had not been broken to this day and Effie remained the champion, the men in Ballybeg grudgingly giving their approval and just a little admiration to the minister's wife. No one, least of all Father O'Malley, had bothered to fill Father Byrne in with any of these facts.

When Effie finally appeared with tea in a silver pot, bone china tea cups and saucers, sugar cubes and Victoria sponge, Father Byrne was even more bemused and balancing tea, plate and cake precariously on his knee, all the time elbowing the gigantic hairy dog beside him, remarked:

"I thought I would make yer acquaintance as I was wanting to meet all of Ballybeg's folk."

At this, Leslie leapt from his chair and pointing his finger at Father Byrne, answered:

"What do you read, young man?"

Father Byrne's reading was sparse to say the least. He read the Bishop's letters and occasionally books about the Saints. Latterly, however he had been struggling through *The Definitive History of Ballybeg*. It was heavy going and he was only half way through but he thought that was his best bet.

"Ah," cried the Reverend, aghast, "written by a charlatan... completely inaccurate, my boy... the chapter about the naming of North Bridge, complete poppycock. Now, you must read a much better version... written by my predecessor... where is it, I wonder?" and he started to rummage through the piles of books, magazines and various items of clothing that were heaped rather precariously on the table, muttering as he did so.

"It might be in the Library," directed Mrs Williamson rather grandly.

You mean, there's more, thought Father Byrne, weakly.

"Yes. Yes. You are right, my love. I will find it for you, my boy and send it to you. What did you say your name was again?"

"I didn't... but it's Joe. Joe Bryne."

"That's a good strong name, my boy. Don't read any more of that wretched book and I will locate Geoffrey's version. Why, Geoffrey devoted his whole life to research of the subject and he was a meticulous researcher... came down from Cambridge but won't hold that against him," he paused. "Well, my boy, who have you met in Ballybeg?"

160

"Have you met Mrs Ryan?" enquired Effie before Father Byrne could answer. Although the two women bore no rancour, each saw in the other her mirror image.

"Mrs Ryan. The illimitable Mrs Ryan," interrupted the Reverend. "Would that I was a portrait painter she would be the divine subject. The lift of the head, the sweep of the hair, the straight nose... ah, but alas, I am but a humble watercolourist and must content myself with sea and sky. Do you paint, my boy?"

Father Byrne shook his head.

"We have an artist set around us, don't we, Effie? You're most welcome to join. My wife has theatrical connections. Indeed, the last production of *The Importance of Being Earnest* was well received in Ballybeg, wasn't it, my sweet?"

Effie nodded. "My husband writes poetry," she said.

"Too kind... too kind... I have been known to dabble... the odd villanelle or two. Do you write, my boy?"

Father Byrne was beginning to think amongst all this creative talent, he was something of a simpleton.

"The man you *must* meet when you can is the Italian."

At this, Mrs Williamson laid her hand on her heart and looked upwards with a rapturous glance at the ceiling.

"Silvio," she pronounced each syllable as if she was rolling an exotic fruit around in her mouth.

"My wife goes quite weak at the knees at the mention of the name, don't you, my sweet?" and he chuckled. "Silvio. Now there's a man of knowledge but sadly he doesn't come to Ballybeg as before. But when he does, my boy, I will introduce you. Yes. You must meet Silvio."

Father Byrne was beginning to think it was time for him to depart. Sophocles and Aristotle had neatly pinned him to the sofa and were hypnotising him with their eyes as he tried to valiantly eat the last of the cake. He had been with the Williamsons for two hours. Quietly, he gave Sophocles a tiny portion of cake and patted the head of Aristotle as he got up to leave.

"You must come again, my boy," said the Reverend warmly and he extended his hand to the priest.

"Yes, do," reiterated his wife with as much warmth.

Father Byrne felt pleased with himself for crossing the doctrinal divide and he thought with interest, given his evangelical persuasion, that no word of theology or church duties or any talk at all about religion had taken place. The Reverend and Mrs Williamson, he decided, were a wonderful eccentric pair, highly intelligent but no harm to anyone. He was glad to have met them and it was his intention to continue the acquaintance. The Presbytery was austere and living with an old priest difficult, he concluded. Besides, the new curate was no company. Peter had gone. A small under-populated parish had been found for him in Donegal and his replacement, although not as sanctimonious, was of a nervous disposition. He wrung his hands together and said, 'Oh, dear', all the time. His name was Matthew, but because of this habit he had been nicknamed 'Oh Dear,' and the name would stick for his time in Ballybeg. What with a difficult old priest with his intractable thinking and blatant bigotry and a nervous 'Oh Dear', Father Byrne mused that the two hours he spent with the Williamsons had been a welcome relief. It was pure amusement even if the dogs were uncontrollable, the cake inedible and the room indescribable. He would certainly call again.

As he crossed over North Bridge on his way back to the Presbytery, he noticed a tall figure of a man leaning on the iron railings. The winter clouds were dark and dramatic in the early evening sky and the man was dark, too. His cap was drawn down over his eyes and Father Byrne noticed the eye patch as the man turned to stare at the priest. Father Byrne was about to remark on the cool air of the early winter when the man walked quickly away without a word. His head was down and the collar of his worn tweed jacket was pulled up about his ears. There must be more to Ballybeg that I first thought, wondered the priest as he

162

entered the dark Presbytery. I think I'm going to enjoy living here. The place is awash with characters.

Back at the Manse, Mrs Williamson was feeding the last of the cake into the eager jaws of Sophocles and Aristotle.

"That's a fine young man," her husband remarked. "That mass of red hair and freckles... there's another one I would like to paint if I only had the gift of portraiture."

"Yes, he is," agreed his wife, and then with some irony in her voice, she concluded, "for a Roman Catholic priest..."

CHAPTER NINE

Father Byrne, red-haired and lively, changed Ballybeg. Father O'Malley, tired, old and irritated, retreated and was rarely seen. The homilies improved. Suddenly, going to Mass became more than a duty. It became interesting. Everyone agreed you could talk to the new priest which had to be a good thing, even if a little strange.

Father Byrne set about getting to know his parishioners, one by one. On rare occasions, he would consult Father O'Malley but mostly he went his own way, sometimes by himself, sometimes with 'Oh Dear' in tow. Father Byrne had a mischievous sense of humour and he, too, found himself calling Matthew 'Oh Dear' along with everyone else. But there was one place that Father Byrne went to that he kept secret. He went alone and was careful not to be seen. Ever since his first meeting with the Williamsons, he had ventured forth, warily at first but gradually gaining more confidence as time passed. The Williamsons were happy to see Joe, as they now called him, and any doctrinal differences between them were never mentioned. In fact, they saw one another as friends and felt no need to speak of the established religious practices in their two communities. The closest they ever came in their discussions to anything religious was the state of the roof of St Michael's. Indeed, Reverend Williamson despaired on the frequent rainy days as various buckets had to be placed in strategic places to capture the drips. His sermons were conducted with difficulty over a cacophony of plopping, and often not heard at all as the elderly congregation spent most of their time coughing. Father Byrne could only sympathise as the roof of St Peter and St Paul was in perfect condition.

The Manse stood in its own ground and was considered a grand building, but sadly years of neglect had taken their toll. Various tall trees and shrubs hid the front entrance from public view and Father Byrne was able to enter the Manse without being noticed which suited all parties well. He became a regular visitor to such an extent that, after a few months, Sophocles and Aristotle hardly stirred from the sofa when the priest entered the room. "A fine young man," the Reverend would say to his wife. "Indeed!" was her reply. As time went by, Father Byrne was introduced to more rooms until one day the Reverend insisted on showing his young friend his accumulated art work. Underneath a heap of sketches, the preferred version of *The History of Ballybeg* was found.

"Aha!" cried Leslie, with glee. "Found at last, you renegade. Hiding! Here, take it, Joe. Take it before it goes missing again." And he handed a well worn copy of the book to an amused Father Byrne who, obediently, had not read another word of the much belittled *Definitive History*.

It would be fair to say that whatever the priest had thought of the Williamsons' living room paled into insignificance at the sight of the library-cum-art-room. In this room, paintings, books and paper competed uneasily for space. Even the threadbare carpet was barely visible because of paint and paper. At the end of the room, facing the window, a large easel was situated and on it, an almost completed watercolour of Slieve Geal. It was surprisingly good. "Why, Leslie..." because it was now 'Leslie', "You have quite a talent there. Do you sell your paintings?"

Although Father Byrne had renounced materialism, he was comfortable with buying and selling. His family were in business so capitalism was in his genes. However, instead of being flattered, the Reverend looked aggrieved. He peered at Father Byrne over the top of his rimless glasses.

"What a thought, my boy! Sell them? Why on earth should I sell them? These are my babies. Take one. Pick any one. Please do."

Father Byrne looked around, hesitant. His eyes focused on one particular painting and would not leave it, no matter how hard he tried.

165

"Ah," said the Reverend, noticing. "You like this one? It's yours, my boy."

It was indeed a beautifully executed work of art. Leslie had captured the blue-black changing clouds over Ballybeg with almost photographic precision. The houses along North Street and the Owenbeg were meticulously represented. It was easy to identify the Ballybeg Hotel and the doctor's house beside it. Further along, the church of St Peter and St Paul stood out dramatically against the dark sky. It was a brooding painting, full of feeling. But Father Byrne was cautious at being the recipient of such a gift. What would Father O'Malley have to say about it given that "Leslie Williamson" was boldly written along the side of the painting? Still, Father Byrne longed to accept. The painting seduced him. He grew weak at the knees. Finally, he made up his mind and all the dragons of material possession were sent packing.

"Delighted, Joe. Delighted. It's yours," and Leslie looked as pleased as a boy winning a race.

As he carefully rolled the watercolour in order not to damage it, he said thoughtfully:

"You must always come to see us, my boy. Effie is quite enchanted with you. We both are. In these troubled times of man against man, creed against creed, we all need to support one another... for who knows what lies ahead?"

The two men looked at each other as friends do. Then Leslie continued in a somewhat abstracted voice as was his way:

"This is an unusual place, this Ballybeg. You will do well here. We will help if we can, Effie and I. Silvio... now you must meet him when he comes back but there is another man, Joe. Another man... much maligned and misunderstood. His name is Mick Kelly out at An Teach Ban... a farmer and a free thinker. Whatever is said against him, use your own judgement. There is no man in the whole of the West like Mick Kelly, mark my words."

This was the first time that Father Byrne had heard mention of Mick Kelly. Later, he would recall that the day he received a gift from the Protestant minister he also received the gift of a name.

*****

Annie, struggling along at An Teach Bán, was pleased, too, with the new priest and with the changes in Ballybeg. Even Doctor Ryan had finally taken on a partner, a handsome young fellow who had all the young girls developing all manner of illnesses in a very short space of time! What with Doctor Flannery and Father Byrne, Ballybeg seemed to be awakening from a deep sleep.

"You would like Father Byrne, Mick," Annie said to Mick one day when the two of them were alone except for Mary who was happily engaged with her toys.

Ever since Mick had given Annie that fleeting kiss, they had been a little less at ease with each other but Mick's decision not to go to Mass worried Annie even more than the thought that she committed adultery every day in her head. She feared what the decision would do to him. She longed for him to change his mind and come once again with them on Sundays. She longed for him to sit with them and see his head bowed. This, she felt, would save him. She had strengthened her resolve to be above the gossip but it was Mick and his spiritual life that worried her more. But he remained silent. He never mentioned his decision or even seemed to bother when they all packed into Bernard's car on Sundays. It was a closed subject.

She was baffled by the barrier of ideas that had come between them. She tried again.

"He's a good man, Mick," she continued hopefully that the thought of a good man at the altar might bring the wayward one back but Mick just smiled; his expression sad.

"I daresay he is, Annie, *mo chailín...* but I have my doubts that any of us, priest or not, are good."

"I mean, he's..." Annie spluttered, searching for the right word. "He's friendly. Why, you can talk to him. He's

167

just like that old priest I knew at Camden, Father John. Well, not perhaps as clever, for Father John had such a brain on him... but Father Byrne is kind. Yes, he's kind and he's got a wicked sense of humour. Why, the other day he was joking about the number of babies that Norah O'Sullivan had delivered, well, you would never hear Father O'Malley saying anything like that, now, would you?"

And that, as far as Annie was concerned, was conclusive proof that Father Byrne was indeed a good man.

Mick smiled again at Annie.

"No, ye would not," he replied and as far as he was concerned, that was the end of the conversation.

*****

One day, Father Byrne with 'Oh Dear' lolloping behind like one of the Williamsons' giant dogs, arrived, unexpected and unannounced at the Kelly farmhouse. Father Byrne believed with complete sincerity that it was his duty to meet and listen to each and every one of his parishioners and that it should be a regular thing. In this, his motives were pure. He was puzzled about the mysterious Mick Kelly. Various versions had been given to the priest and his curiosity was aroused. Experience had taught Father Byrne that the best time to call on his flock was early evening as often times there would be a chance of being invited to share in the evening meal. Father Bryne came from a large family and missed the companionship of mealtimes. He was in luck this time as the Kellys were about to sit down to eat. It gave him a chance to observe them all. Bernard and Annie, he recognised. The children, too, he had seen around. There was Frankie, now sixteen, quite polite with Declan beside him, a little on the shy side. The odd-looking one had to be Oisin and Mary, sweet wee girl that she was with her brown curls and blue eyes and her mother's smile. Then the priest studied the other Kelly, the one he had not met, Mick.

It looked like a scene of domestic harmony but Father Byrne was astute enough to observe that this would not always be so. He had the gift of putting people at their ease. He did this unconsciously and for this reason he was thought of as a likeable man by all who had benefited from his easy presence. It was Mick who spoke first much to everyone's surprise.

"I hear tell yer a good man," to the priest. Annie coloured.

"Well, now, that's not something I've heard..."

"Even so, it's been said."

"You must be Mick. I haven't had the pleasure of yer coming...?"

There was an embarrassing silence. The priest continued, speaking slowly, unsure of what to say.

"I've heard a lot about ye, Mick, from various quarters."

"No doubt."

"Have ye lost the sight in yer eye?" It was 'Oh Dear' who spoke, unexpected, and everyone looked at him. "It's... it's just the eye patch..." and his voice trailed off. Mick smiled at the discomfiture of the curate.

"Well, no," he replied, "but I get some amount of awful headaches, right behind my eyes."

No one knew anything of this. So *this* is why he mightn't go to Mass, Annie thought and her heart beat faster. Perhaps that's all it is. Perhaps he hasn't lost his faith after all – just gets headaches. And she suddenly felt pleased at the thought of Mick's pain.

Father Byrne murmured a word of sympathy. He spoke again to Mick.

"I think I saw ye one evening now... in the early winter, aye. On North Bridge. Aye, it was most definitely yerself. Don't suppose ye can recall the meeting?"

"Can't say that I can. I would have remembered yerself, that I would. A good man is always remembered."

Father Bryne reddened. He wasn't sure if Mick was sincere or sarcastic. Either way, it was awkward to say the least.

169

"There ye go again, Mick. Do ye consider yerself a good man?" and he turned the question round.

"Doubt very much if there's any here present who would call me that."

"Oh, come now, Mick. Ye are with yer family... and friends," he added, hopefully including himself.

"I stand by what I said."

And the look came into Mick's face again. He was silent for the remainder of the evening. Father Byrne's usual joviality deserted him and, he too, spoke less. When he got up to leave, he extended his hand to Mick who took it firmly, looking all the time at the priest with his good eye.

"We'll have to have a talk sometime," said the priest because there was something in Mick's expression that he couldn't discern. There was something about Mick.

"Ye know where I am," replied Mick. "I'm not goin' away." And he looked at Annie.

*****

The next morning Bernard met Father Byrne in North Street, outside the Post Office.

"Father," he was nervous, "me brother means no harm. It's just him. He's always got his head in some book or other, so he has. Now, he's taken up with this Italian..." Father Byrne pricked up his ears, "and there's more books comin' in and letters, too... but he means well, so he does. Annie and me, we'll be at Mass on Sunday with the children. And Mick, he'll come again. It's just Mick," and he shook his head, shuffling his feet nervously as he did. "Why, I think our young Frankie might enter the priesthood, he said as much the other day. Why, with Frankie's brains, he'll be a Bishop... not meanin' anything against yerself, Father, just..." He stumbled over his words. "Anyway, pay no heed to me brother, all that about a good man. Never know what he's thinkin' of, that's the trouble. I'll be off now, Father," and he touched his cap in farewell.

170

Father Bryne watched Bernard walk away. Aye, he thought to himself. Leslie was right. I'll make up my own mind about Mick Kelly, so I will.

Over the next few days the image of Mick Kelly took up permanent residence in Father Bryne's head or so it seemed. The priest was no fool. As he pondered Mick's words, a kind of uneasiness came in to his thoughts. Mick with his few words had opened up a debate in Father Byrne's mind. What was 'a good man'? Am I a good man? He wondered. He had assumed he was, up to that point. He bore no malice towards anyone. He had faithfully, and with no thought of self, served the spiritual and sometimes secular needs of the communities he had been involved with, or so he had thought. Being seen by others and assumptions made that your actions are good, does this constitute 'a good man?' He wondered. Mick Kelly had made no such assumptions about his goodness, quite the opposite in fact. But he had not labelled himself a bad man either. Could it be possible that Mick, by virtue of his few words have more understanding of human nature than all the learned tomes written or all the words spoken on the subject? That, after all, none of us are 'good men' but show off our goodness, in fact, to hide our darker and baser side? Father Byrne was acutely aware that the majority of the people of Ballybeg were convinced that Mick Kelly was mad as a way of explaining his sometimes irrational behaviour. In fact, the only one who had hinted that this might not be so, had been Reverend Williamson whose judgement Father Byrne now respected. After all, the Williamsons were viewed as totally eccentric and it was only on deeper analysis and acquaintance, that they had revealed themselves as having an awareness not readily found in others. Could this be the case with Mick? Was it more expedient to label him of unsound mind than to search for a deeper reason for his actions? Father Byrne began to wonder if this was perhaps so. If this was the case, Mick's refusal to go to the church could not be judged by the

171

acceptable standards of the day. It occurred to the priest, somewhat uneasily, that Mick might have tapped into something deeper and his outer actions hid a sublime self, not understood by those around him, including his own brother with his clumsy attempt at exoneration. Yes, Mick Kelly is not your usual type of man and the Kelly situation is not at all that it seems, the priest concluded soberly, if not a little warily. He would take his time before he ventured back to An Teach Ban. His next visit would have to be prepared. It was not just a matter of comradeship and a free meal, a visit to the Kellys would be certain to bring surprises, of this he was certain.

*****

The changes that came to Ballybeg brought other changes as well. True to his word, Father Bryne stayed away from An Teach Ban. He busied himself with his pastoral duties and put Mick to the back of his mind. It was safer that way, he reasoned. Mick continued to avoid the church and refused to listen to any attempt at persuasion. But it was in Annie's life that a change occurred. Often she despaired that she would remain in Ballybeg to the end of her days – almost in a state of suspended animation; just growing older and watching those around her do the same. Sometimes on her sad days this place was her prison, holding her captive with its gentle beauty and seductive charms. I am always 'that English girl' she would think miserably... forever the outsider. Part of it but not part of it at all. Then the loneliness would bring despair and the despair would lead to the painful conclusion that a life away from Ballybeg was unimaginable... and a life without Mick, impossible.

But change came to Annie and it came in the form of a summons from her Uncle George in Camden. Mrs Smith was very, very ill. Annie had to go to her, go to her quickly before it was too late and bring Mary Louise, her granddaughter. After all, Louise was Mrs Smith's name too.

172

"I'll have to go," Annie said to Bernard. "I'll have to go back to London with Mary and yes, I'll take Oisin as well. I want my mother to see Oisin, almost grown up. It's been so long..." And the tears welled up behind her eyes for love of her mother and for what had become of herself in the West, in this Ballybeg so far from what was once 'home'.

Arrangements were quickly made because there was urgency now and delay might mean it would be too late. It would be the same journey in reverse that she had made all those years ago with Bernard beside her but oh, the changes. She said goodbye to an anxious Bernard, kissing him softly. As she did she thought of Mick and closed her eyes briefly. Mick was always there in her mind somewhere. With a sigh she hugged Frankie and Declan, as a mother would, reassuringly. Then thought of her mother and London... there was no way out of it but through.

*****

Dun Laoghaire was warm and sunny. Along the Promenade people wandered in groups of twos or threes or more eating ice creams while others sat on benches overlooking the sea. It was a carnival atmosphere almost and, had the circumstances in Annie's life not been so anxious, she would have enjoyed it too. The place was tidier than she remembered and noisier. Arrangements had been made for her and the children to stay with Mrs Slattery and take the ferry to Holyhead in the morning. Mrs Slattery was older, of course, and took in fewer guests but she remembered Annie. She greeted her warmly.

"Oh my," she said, "isn't it grand to see ye again... all those years. How time flies. And these are yer children?" And she smiled at Oisin and Mary.

When Annie told her of the circumstances surrounding her visit, Mrs Slattery sympathised in her businesslike way.

"Oh, my dear. I'm sorry to hear that. Why, yer mother's a grand woman just like yerself."

Mrs Smith had stayed with Mrs Slattery on her few trips to Ireland and the two women had got on well. There

173

was a change in Annie, though, Mrs Slattery observed. The years take their toll, she thought to herself philosophically. A sadness there now that wasn't there before. Why, she had been so much in love back then... and such an innocent, too. Aye, the girl has changed. She's a woman now and she's weary. Life's been difficult for her but her children are grand and she said so.

Mary always got attention but it was Oisin who captivated. Usually grave and quiet, he responded to Mrs Slattery in a lively manner and chatted to her as if he had known her all his life. Why, there's such a change in him, thought Annie. It was as if the boy, released from the restraints placed on him by his elder brothers and by the restrictions that living in Ballybeg imposed, changed personality. He had never been further than the West of Ireland. He was exhilarated by the crowds of Dublin. They energised him. He was lively and entertaining. He smiled and his appearance changed. The restricting labels that had been placed on him had been torn away, it seemed, and with their departure he blossomed. He was only ten years old but his conversation sparkled with humour and intelligence. He kept his mother and Mrs Slattery entertained until he was instructed to go to bed.

"What a grand wee lad ye've got there," said Mrs Slattery when Oisin left. "Ye must be so proud of him."

Guilt hit Annie hard. Her son had never been so elated, it seemed. Mick's prediction about the boy came into her head. Perhaps Oisin would travel and conquer worlds? The son she always thought of as Mick's might one day be a hero. She wondered what he would make of London. If he was the way he was tonight, she concluded as she fell asleep, my mother will be glad.

*****

London was a land of ghosts. The familiar world Annie had imagined so fondly from afar had vanished and the remembrance of what had been danced through her mind. Memories were there, everywhere but it was all so changed, so different. She was a stranger in her own home. As she walked along the High Street where the butcher's shop once was, people pushed past her; everyone seemingly wrapped in their own world, unfriendly, uncaring, their faces set hard and unseeing. The butcher's shop had gone, replaced by a second-hand furniture shop. Chairs and tables spilled untidily onto the pavement. Annie searched faces for the familiar but saw none. Even Uncle George was old and frail. His tiny house set amongst all the others appeared just the same with its green door but, on closer inspection, the years of neglect exposed the changes that had taken place within its walls. Uncle George was no longer the jovial man he used to be. He fussed. Oisin and Mary perched awkwardly on chairs that were dusty and uncomfortable. Suddenly shy, the world of London with its crowds and noise frightened them. So far from their familiar green fields and sea and Slieve Geal, they were uneasy and tongue-tied.

"She's finished, Annie," said Uncle George as he poured tea from a china pot into a cup that perfectly matched it. "You were right to come... poor Lulu."

That was his name for his sister... always had been. He shook his head sadly and his hand trembled as he poured the tea. He had faced death before but it didn't make the present moment any easier for he loved his big sister and feared the gap in his life after she had gone. The doctors had told him it was just a matter of days, not weeks. Annie was right to come, dear girl, and to bring her children. At least Lulu would meet Mary Louise, this sweet little angel, and know she would live on. It must be hard for Annie, he thought, so far away but she had made her own life and it was better that way... nothing here for her. He could have wept when he thought of it all but he had to be brave.

"Oh, Annie," he continued sorrowfully, "she's been suffering so. But she'll recognise you... she's been waiting for you. She loved going to Ireland, was so full of it... wouldn't stop talking about it and all the people over there.

It was the highlight of her life, I think, and her grandchildren... so proud, so proud... poor Lulu."

He shook his head sadly and Annie thought life had defeated him at last. The Uncle George she knew was gone, replaced by an older, tired man. But he suddenly seemed to brighten up, as much to her surprise he asked, unexpectedly:

"How's Mick?"

Not Bernard but Mick. It was all too much for Annie and she shook her head. She didn't want to talk about Mick, not now, not when her mother was dying in a hospital bed. Uncle George always rattled on, she thought to herself crossly. How do I talk about Mick because I never know about Mick? No one does. Mick's a mystery. How can Mick suddenly arrive in Uncle George's house in Camden and unsettle things? As if things weren't unsettled enough as it is. Uncle George's words brought the presence of Mick into this faded room with its faded carpet and faded wallpaper and dusty ornaments and the clock on the wall where Time had stopped at half past four. Mick came into the room, unannounced. He sat on one of the uncomfortable chairs and swept his cap off his head. Then as he always did, he ran his hand through his black hair peppered now with grey. He would either not utter a word or utter too many. You never knew with Mick... and Annie, cross with Uncle George, snapped at Oisin for no reason. The tension rose slightly in the faded room.

Until Annie, annoyed, answered Uncle George.

"Oh, Mick... he does seem ill... somehow. But then he won't speak..." She paused, unsure, and then her words burst from her in a flood almost. "You know, he won't go to Mass. We had an awful night of it with Father O'Malley awhile back. Mick was so rude... ordered him and Peter out of the house. Why, it's my house too, you know. But Mick just threatened Father O'Malley and after that... well, I can tell you, Uncle George, you knew who your friends were after that. And Bernard never talks about it... won't say a

176

word against his brother. Only thing he ever says to me is to blame it all on that Italian. Remember him? Silvio Luchetta. But no one knows what's going on in Mick's head. He just clams up and won't speak. Gets all these letters and books, too, from the Italian and no one knows what's happening."

Uncle George shook his head. Oisin, listening, frowned slightly.

"Did I tell you that Father O'Malley is retired and there's a new priest there now. Father Byrne. He's such a nice man, Uncle George. You can talk to him. If you had a problem, well, I think you could talk it over with him." She hesitated slightly. Perhaps not *every* problem. "But he came out to see us all with the new curate. Peter's gone. Well, the new curate's a funny one... they've all called him 'Oh Dear' because he worries a lot and wrings his hands and says "Oh, dear, oh dear," all the time. I must confess I call him that as well. But anyhow, Father Byrne was so nice to Mick but Mick talked a lot of rubbish and poor Father Byrne didn't know what to say to it all... well, you know what Mick's like... and he hasn't been back to see us and it's months now and still Mick keeps away from the church. Half the time he doesn't do the work on the farm and it's left to Bernard. Just as well we have Declan – he's a great help, thank God – but you asked how Mick was and that's all I can say..."

But that's not all, thought Annie. You don't know the half of it, Uncle George. You had a holiday there once and sat in Murphy's Bar and took walks along the beach and it was lovely but you don't have to live there. You think Ballybeg is all good humour and music and soft voices. Little do you know. I lie in bed half the night thinking of Mick as if I am possessed by him and no one knows. It's too cruel. I even feel he's sitting here now, over there in that chair, listening to all of this and I don't know if he's laughing at me or if he wants me too. You ask me about Mick Kelly, she concluded bitterly? I am drowning in desire

177

for him and no one knows. She stood up abruptly taking the tray with the teapot and cups.

"I'll help you clean up, Uncle George," she said. This place needs some cleaning up, she thought. It will give me something to do while I'm here... something to take my mind off Mick.

The next day the small, sorrowing family group stood beside Mrs Smith's bedside in a crowded deafening hospital ward where distracted nurses rushed around in a frenzy of activity, pushing trolleys and clattering trays while bells sounded incessantly as patient demands increased. Noise and silence. Mrs Smith lay propped up on pillows. Her face, grey; her eyes closed, her hands by her side, still. She half-opened her eyes and, seeing Annie's face so near to hers, murmured in her throat a word, just a word that Annie could not understand. But her mother's hand gripped Annie's, just slightly, but enough.

"Is that William?" and she slowly turned her head on the pillow to look at Oisin.

Around about the noisiness and the din increased. It was mealtime. At Mrs Smith's bed, removed from all movement on all sides and about, Annie, Uncle George, Oisin and Mary, stood silent watching as Mrs Smith closed her eyes.

*****

No sun shone for Mrs Smith's funeral; only a light drizzle wet the faces of the few who came to pay their last respects. No Father John but a younger priest, in a hurry. Uncle George cried like a baby and Annie took hold of his hand. She stood as rigid as a statue at her mother's grave. Only when the coffin was lowered into the ground did she allow a tear to trickle down her cheek, to be quickly wiped away.

Dust to dust. Ashes to ashes.
And goodbye...

*****

Annie delayed making arrangements to return to Ballybeg but made excuses to herself to stay on with Uncle George. Their relationship had always been kindly, built as it was on a long term liking for each other, so it was easy enough for Annie to settle quite happily amongst the faded memories of her uncle's house. Uncle George still managed to endear himself to the fairer sex and hot meals and cakes arrived regularly on his doorstep. A kiss on the cheek and a hug was duly given to the provider of such generosity and all parties seemed perfectly happy with the arrangement much to the amusement of Annie and her children. Given that he had just buried his last remaining sibling, more cakes and sympathy arrived. At times there was a steady stream of visitors into Uncle George's modest dwelling. It's almost the way it always was, said Annie to her uncle on a morning when a particularly delicious apple pie had arrived. Life in London was beginning to weave its old magic charm over Annie; the nostalgia of the past giving a poignant reminder to the present moment. She was surprised by her feelings now that she was away from Ballybeg. It was refreshing to be amongst people again. At first, she had felt uneasy with the changes around her and the sorrow of her visit further intensified this feeling but as the days slipped by, she began to fit comfortably into the urban landscape of her girlhood and her old optimism reappeared. She remembered, and accepted as the truth, Silvio Luchetta's summing up of her character and that she did, indeed, "miss the bright lights of Oxford Street and Piccadilly". In the rebuilding of London, Annie thought that she, too, was being rebuilt. History was in the buildings and the streets and the parks. History was on the faces of the people who hurried along the crowded pavements. Here was life, throbbing, intense, passionate... but *life*. And Annie decided that, after all and despite everything, she was still a London girl.

She soberly concluded to herself that return to Ballybeg and the West of Ireland was inevitable and that the longer she stayed on, the harder it would be to leave. She accepted this as inevitable but her emotions, those impassioned, unpredictable and uncontrollable feelings, weakened her resolve and she persuaded herself to stay rationalising the delay with protestations about disposal of her mother's possessions and concern about leaving Uncle George in his frailer state.

A few days after her mother's funeral Bernard's cousin, Sinéad Nolan arrived at Uncle's George's doorstep. Sinéad was now a widow – Pete having fallen to his death from some badly erected scaffolding on the building site ten years previously. Sinéad was anxious to talk. In the manner of many people who find themselves living on their own, she was quite talkative amongst company and spoke non-stop to Annie before she was ushered into Uncle George's sitting room.

"Now, Annie, how is Ballybeg? You must give me all the news," she asked with all the eagerness of the exile, for that was how she viewed herself. She settled with some difficulty into one of the uncomfortable chairs and took a sip of the tea that was offered.

What paradox dwells in the human heart that causes such restlessness? One's life might be comfortable and secure but the conviction grows that another time and another place would be infinitely more desirable. The peculiar connection between Annie and Sinéad was that Sinéad, having lived in London for most of her life, was totally convinced that Ballybeg and the West of Ireland held the eternal promise of her happiness which could not be found in her present situation and that the green grass of Ireland was somehow more pleasant than the green grass of England. The reasons behind the absolute belief that life would be better somewhere else contributed to both women's restlessness, but neither Annie nor Sinéad would ever concede that both lived under the same illusion and that the geographical differences were, in fact, part of that same illusion. If it had been pointed out to either woman the similarities in both their lives, they would have denied it vehemently, even laughed at the notion. After all, was life not better in Ballybeg than London and vice versa?

The two women were alone. Oisin and Mary had persuaded their uncle to take them on a visit to see the changing of the Guard at Buckingham Palace and there was just enough of the old affable Uncle George to enjoy the company of children. You'll be able to get on, he said to Annie as he ushered the excited pair out the door and Annie, sifting through all the bits and pieces of her mother's life, agreed readily enough. She was finding the task daunting to say the least. Old photographs particularly brought a lump to her throat and the reading of the letters not addressed to her, she viewed almost as an intrusion. She accepted the irrationality of the feeling but it persisted nevertheless. Decisions as to retain or destroy accentuated the whole painful process, and in so doing, Annie's thoughts of her own mortality came into her mind. She was quite pleased to allow Sinéad to distract her from her solemn task.

Sinéad was still lively and her eyes darted around Uncle George's living room taking in the faded curtains that had once been his pride and joy. Even the wallpaper had turned a sallow yellow. The china ornaments on the mantelpiece above the coal fire were the only reminder of a happier time in his life when he had been under the care of his wife. Not much had changed in the intervening years, except that Uncle George, like the curtains he once knew so much about, had just got older and greyer, too.

"He's an old rascal still," said Sinéad affectionately. "But no one dares move anything..." And as she spoke, her hands itched to rearrange the ornaments on the mantelpiece. To take the china carthorse with its load of beer barrels and place it at the other end of the room. Annie nodded her head in total agreement and the two women paused momentarily and surveyed the room with

181

critical eyes, each thinking what they could do to the room if only Uncle George would allow it.

"He'll be alright, Annie. We'll keep an eye on him," because Uncle George still had his entourage of willing widows to watch out for him. "He'll miss your mother though."

And she was quiet for a few moments.

"Now, how's that Bernard? You've fed him up, I hope. What a thing it was to get him into his wedding suit!" She sighed, remembered Bernard, her shy and awkward cousin and the trouble they had fitting him into his wedding jacket.

But Annie did not reply. Bernard had been put into a compartment in her head along with the other Ballybeg folk and she wanted him to stay there. Fortunately, Sinéad didn't stop to find out but continued asking all manner of questions about Father O'Malley and Doctor Ryan and her poor sister, Doreen, married to that drunk, until she paused slightly and Annie brought up the subject of the priests as a safer option.

"There's a new priest there now, Sinéad," she said. "Such a nice chap, too. Father Byrne. Well, Father O'Malley can't do the work anymore. In fact, he rarely leaves the Presbytery and when he does, why, he's on two sticks now and it's painful to watch."

"I was frightened of him and I was in my teens when he arrived," replied Sinéad. "I can tell you Annie, I never liked him. I know you shouldn't say that about a priest but he scared the living daylights out of me. So Father O'Malley can't walk now. What a shame. He was such a runner too... used to run for miles... could run right to the top of Slieve Geal. Now that was something, wasn't it? But we all get old. The children want me to go into a Nursing Home but I'm like your Uncle George and I'll stay on. Well, it's my home. We survived the Blitz, didn't we, and our homes stood up to Hitler? Don't think it's right to leave. They can carry me out. But Annie, I didn't ask... how's Mick?"

Suddenly Mick had been taken out of the spot in the back of Annie's mind where she thought she had carefully arranged all the Ballybeg folk. She hesitated before answering and Mick's face danced once again in front of her eyes.

"He's not well, Sinéad." Then a kind of wild curiosity took hold of her and she wanted to know more. "What was he like as a boy?"

"Oh, Mick," replied Sinéad, eager to enlighten. "Well, Mick's different. I can tell you that now, Annie, well, you're family. We all think he's clever. Well, he is. Always read a lot. Too much, if you ask me... but whatever, let me put it to you this way. You got the better brother. Mick's unstable, always has been. The mind, ye know. Never know with Mick. But that Bernard of yours, never says a word against his brother. That's the Kellys for ye!"

It was getting time for Sinéad to leave. As she stood up, she had one more thing to say about Mick.

"Did ye know that Mick once stood up to Father O'Malley? Stood up in the class and questioned the story of the Creation! What do ye think of that? Father O'Malley nearly had a heart attack. Why, Mick left school early... about the time his mother died... he must have been about ten when I think on it, aye, about young Oisin's age... well, didn't Father O'Malley give him some hammering. He was a bit of a hero after that with all us kids because none of the kids liked Father O'Malley but none of us knew what Mick was about. Fancy asking questions like that! When I think on it now, aye, Mick Kelly's always been an odd one if ye ask me. Mark my words, ye got the best brother. Imagine Bernard doing that! Wouldn't say boo to a goose that one. Still plays his fiddle, does he? I used to love to hear him play. He was just five and he could get a tune out of that thing. Well, his father could play, too, before the drink got to him. I can tell ye a lot about the Kellys... the Kelly Saga... could fill a book about the Kellys, so I could. Tell ye, Annie, Bernard was lucky to get ye. We all thought the two of them

183

would be just old bachelors. Ye were a brave woman to take them on. Oh, what I could tell ye about Ballybeg... I'd be here all day. No place like it in the world, I used to say to Pete and he would agree. He liked it too. We both missed it, ye know." And she sighed. The years of widowhood and exile cast a shadow over her face.

"Ah, Annie... I envy ye... living there... all that clean air. It's a wonderful place for sure and the Kellys, well, Ballybeg wouldn't be the same without them, I guess. After all, I'm related to them! Bernard and Mick. What a pair!"

Annie decided that it was not the time to continue to ask about Mick and wondered what Sinéad would make of Mick's refusal to have anything to do with the church. It apparently started at an early age, she thought to herself as she saw Sinéad out the door.

"Goodness me," Sinéad was saying to herself. "Is that the time? I was due at the Hall about half an hour ago."

Since her widowhood, Sinéad had become addicted to good works and was usually to be found in the Hall, ladling out plates of soup or in the church, arranging flowers. She kissed Annie on the cheek.

"It's lovely to see ye, Annie. We'll meet up again before ye leave..."

*****

Finally, Annie could delay no longer. Bernard rang nearly every day, anxious and forlorn. With a heavy heart, she got ready to leave. She carefully packed her mother's few treasures, well loved pieces of jewellery, her watch. The old sepia photographs of her father and William arranged neatly along with her father's medal into her suitcase. There was a sense of finality in the packing, she knew that and wondered when or if she would ever see London again. She compared herself to a moth attracted to the light for life. Once that light was taken away, darkness descended and, like the moth, she would die.

She wanted to say goodbye to her mother one last time so she went alone and, as she placed the wildflowers she had carefully gathered onto the grave, the tears ran down her cheeks and would not stop. She wept. Her future appeared in front of her eyes. She would go back to Bernard knowing she loved Mick. She would live out her days far from her mother's grave until she, too, lay beneath the earth, silent but for the wind and the rain. She dried her eyes with her mother's lace handkerchief and, with sorrowing steps, turned away. Uncle George, Oisin and Mary were waiting at the gate. Oisin took hold of his mother's hand and the little group made their way slowly along the pavement.

"I don't want to go back to Ballybeg either," Oisin suddenly said. Annie never forgot his look or that moment. No one spoke until they were back in the safety of Uncle George's living room and talked of other things.

CHAPTER TEN

There seemed to be no end to the journey from Dublin to Ballybeg. They were half an hour late leaving Dublin Heuston Station. When the train stopped somewhere between Mullingar and Longford, Annie could sense within herself that she was slipping into the old inertia of Irish time. She tried to resist. She had no wish to be dragged back after only a month away. But the steady, hypnotic movement of the train made resistance impossible and somewhere near Castlebar, her eyes grew heavy. She was awakened at Ballybeg by Oisin pulling on her arm. She opened her eyes and seeing Slieve Geal with her scarf on, she knew she was nearly there. The scarf's on today. She won't be takin' it off, meant that they would be in for a misty wet day and to make the most of it. So today is wet, thought Annie.

"Oh dear," she sighed.

"There he is... on the platform," said Oisin and sure enough the young curate was there, stamping his feet up and down in the manner of a soldier on parade, rubbing his hands as he did so.

"I didn't mean...?" and Annie giggled.

Oisin laughed too and then Mary joined in, although she didn't know what was going on, and the three of them were still giggling when they got off the train, trying not to go too close to 'Oh Dear' and thus bring about more merriment.

Bernard was there for them. He was slightly bemused at the sight of his little family, all giggling uncontrollably, but gave each one a hug nevertheless.

"It's grand to see ye all," he said and to Annie, he whispered, "I've missed ye, love."

Now Annie had a chance to study Bernard and she thought with some alarm that he didn't look at all well. There was a grey pallor to his face and weariness behind his blue eyes. But he was so glad to have them home that she put thoughts about his health to the back of her mind. He allowed Mary to sit in the front of the car beside him. She sat upright and proud, chattering all the time. As they drove along North Bridge, Annie noticed Father Byrne and Doctor Ryan engaged in animated conversation and she sighed. She didn't feel as if she was home. Her thoughts were still in Camden and London. Out of Ballybeg they went, past the line of assorted painted stone houses with strings of smoke spiralling from their chimneys and along the Galway Road until they reached Murphy's Bar and were nearly home.

"Whatever's happened to Murphy's?" asked Annie with some surprise. Murphy's Bar, through the mist and the rain, was different. When she left Ballybeg just a month ago, the building was the colour it had always been, yellow ochre with grey shutters. Bernard told the story with just a little touch of importance and a little exaggeration, if the truth be told. It seemed that Pa had taken Ma to Paris for their twenty-fifth wedding anniversary.

"He kept it all to himself, so he did... and off they went," Bernard grew more talkative. "Well, it was only for four days but on their return, Ma went all French!"

He told Annie how Ma set about converting both the Bar and the extension into her idea of what a Parisian bistro should be; even to hanging bunches of onions up at the Bar and adorning the walls with prints of Parisian scenes. She had plans to rename "Murphy's" to "Murphy's-sur-la-Mer," but Pa put his foot down at that. She has become quite affected: "When Pa and I were in Paris..." waving her hands around in the way of a Parisian. Her appearance changed, too, and she now dressed the way she thought a Parisian woman did but Ma being Ma it wasn't quite working and the old buxom Ma was ever there under the surface. She insisted on Pa wearing a black beret and she now revealed even more of her ample bosom. She wore clothes a few sizes too small because *that's what they wear in Paris*, but alas, every ring of fat was highlighted and the proportions weren't quite right. She got them all working to change the outside of the building. Even Frankie and Declan earned a few punts because it all had to be done quickly as there had been a good spell of weather. The outside walls of both the Bar and the extension were whitened. Ma has become quite obsessed with colour now, particularly red. New red shutters, in the style of the apartments where they stayed – off the Boulevard Montparnasse – were fixed to the windows and the old grey ones flung away. Overnight, red doors, black guttering and six wooden planters, also painted red, appeared. The six planters stood in a perfect line at either side of the gravel path leading up to the front door. Somehow, Ma managed to plant small ornamental evergreen conifers in each of them, quite an achievement given the prevailing wind from the sea. And heaven help anyone who dared to touch Ma's planters!

"She's got all these ideas," continued Bernard as they stared with amazement at the new-look Murphy's Bar. "In the summer, she's talkin' about outside dining, 'à la fresco' she calls it, like they do in Paris, and she's havin' chairs and tables with umbrellas bolted down... 'cause she's got to have the umbrellas bolted down... this is Ballybeg not Paris!" And he chuckled. Murphy's Bar was a road away from the shore and the rain and wind were relentless but even so, it was an ingenious plan and no doubt, in time, it would bring in more custom and tourists. In the meantime everyone was enjoying the new Ma but waiting for the old one to reappear.

"She's not gettin' me to play them French songs," Bernard grumbled. He never read music and French songs weren't there in his head!

All this in a month... there's no-one else in the whole world like Ma, thought Annie and, at the thought of Ma, her spirits lifted slightly to be dashed somewhat as she neared An Teach Ban. Her home, yes, but how dismal and remote it looked under a sheet of rain. Apparently, it had rained constantly for the last few days. Slieve Geal was now completely hidden. The scarf wrapped right down tight and only the outline of the outbuildings and the farmhouse could be seen through the mist. When Annie put her foot out of the car she trod into a puddle of water. The thick squelch of mud stuck to her shoes newly bought from a shop in Oxford Street a week ago, and she was vexed. Water streamed down from the hill past the farm outbuildings and onto the road swamping the path up to the front door. Progress was problematic. In an effort to avoid the numerous water holes Annie found herself stepping into more and more mud so she was not in a good humour by the time she reached the front door and the shelter of her home. Wet, tired and not wanting to be back, she sank gratefully into a chair in the kitchen and let Bernard fuss. Annie's mind, at that precise moment, was focused on the mud and her new shoes and the patches of drying dirt now visible on her stockings but she was also thinking of being in the kitchen at An Teach Ban again and right at the bottom layer of her thoughts, was Mick. Anxious to know where he was, she ventured to ask in a voice that trembled slightly as she spoke, as to his whereabouts?

"Ah, Mick," replied Bernard as he set about stoking the range with some dry sticks, "He'll be back."

He seemed more intent on Mary's chatter and getting the fire going than talking about his brother. Oisin, perched on his stool, watched thoughtfully as his mother attempted somewhat unsuccessfully to remove the mud from her shoes. Ballybeg and the farmhouse had suddenly become small and oppressive somehow. London was a long way away and people, streets and noise even further.

Mick returned to the farmhouse in the late evening but he was withdrawn and non-committal. He hardly spoke to any of them but remained sitting in his black leather chair. There was a far off look in his good eye and a feeling of sadness in his posture. Annie despaired.

189

Finally, it was Declan, not Bernard, who told her a few days later what had happened. Gentle, like his father, Declan saw beauty in a blade of grass. The changing seasons and the land held mystery for him and he was as secure of his place in the universe as it was possible to be at his young age. His acceptance of his world made him the anchor of the family and his words could be relied upon. Although he was just fourteen, he saw no reason to embellish the tale and the account would be as near to the actual event, as it was possible to be. It seemed that two weeks after Annie, Oisin and Mary had left for London Mick had had a 'turn' at Murphy's. Word about Ma's French decorations had got around so that the Bar was even more crowded than was usual for a Saturday night.

"Da was busy in the big room playin' away," recounted Declan, "Frankie and me were runnin' around, clearin' tables. Ye couldn't move in the place. Ma's arm must have been almost pulled from its sockets, she was so busy pourin' pints and ye know Ma, she never stops! Well, Mick got himself to his perch at the Bar – ye know where he sits – when...well, I don't know what happened, but the next thing, his head's down on the bar counter an' Ma was shoutin' for Pa to get a doctor. Seamus Hennegan as drunk as a Lord started to shout that Mick should be locked up but didn't Ma lay into him at that! Told him to get out... that Mick had only had one small whiskey. Me and Frankie didn't know what to do. I managed to get over to Mick and his face was all grey and he was a lather of sweat. I can tell ye, I got a fright. Ma and me got hold of him and we managed to get him out of the Bar to the room at the back. Ye know... where they keep the stores? Mick was trembling all over and cold. His hands were like ice. Ma got a blanket and covered him and Pa rang for Doctor Ryan or Doctor Flannery, I don't know who he got, but it didn't matter."

Declan paused. He always took his time. That was his way. Annie's heart beat faster.

"Well, it seemed forever but finally Doctor Flannery arrived and took a look at Mick. 'He'll have to go to the hospital,' he said. So Mick was taken off in the ambulance and was in the hospital for two days. Doc seemed to think he might have had a fit. What's a fit, Mammy?"

Numbed by her son's account, Annie had no words to explain epilepsy. She was annoyed that it had been left to Declan not Bernard to tell her any of this and she listened, tight-lipped to the rest of the story. She had no medical background but she doubted the doctor's diagnosis. It was too simplistic, she thought, and, after all, Doctor Flannery did not have Doctor Ryan's expertise or his knowledge. With regard to Doctor Flannery, she was in agreement with the rest of the Ballybeg folk... Doctor Flannery was not old enough to have proved himself.

"Anyhow," Declan continued, "Mick's been better this last fortnight... even been doin' a bit of work around the place. Tell ye though, I was glad to see him come home. What do ye think's wrong?"

Declan was a child again. His puzzled young face expected an answer but Annie had nothing to give. She mumbled a reassurance but she was far from reassured. The love for Mick grew within her once again. The misery that that love caused seemed to cover her soul. Like the mist that came down over Slieve Geal, she hid her feelings but they were still there, behind the clouds.

The next day Mick was back with them again. Somehow he balanced on the edge of an abyss, almost sinking into its dark, hidden recesses. The dark moods and the pain that they brought to him and to the others around him, imprisoned him on this fragile edge. Then something or someone would draw him back, and he was safe again.

"Well, Annie *mo chailín*," he would say to her when they were talking again, "do ye think I'm a better man if I'm sittin' here in yer warm kitchen or if I'm sittin' in the cold of St Peter and St Paul's?"

For at these times Annie used a kind of emotional blackmail in an effort to get Mick to come back to the church even to enlisting the aid of Frankie, Mick's favourite.

"Now, Annie," and Mick's voice was as gentle as the autumn leaves falling on silent ground, "the truth now. Frankie is his own man and ye know it. If the boy decides on the priesthood, well, he'll be a priest. It won't make the slightest bit of difference to Frankie if you go to Mass and I don't... Frankie will do what he always has done... please Frankie."

Annie, annoyed, turned away for she knew he spoke the truth.

*****

In the months that followed, Frankie was seen around Ballybeg in earnest conversation with 'Oh Dear', their heads down, walking slowly along North Street, looking for all the world as if they were unaware of their surroundings, somehow in an another dimension. On occasions, they would be observed ambling along the shore with the same contemplative demeanour. Frankie spent more and more time on his knees in front of the altar and, when he rose to his feet, his face held the same 'other world' look. In fact, he spent more time at the church than ever before and Declan was left on his own to make his way home from school with Oisin and Mary tagging behind in a somewhat straggly fashion. It could only be surmised that Frankie was serious about his entry into the priesthood and given time he would make his intention known to his family. He was a lean youth, accustomed to having his opinion listened to and his intelligence assured that most times this was so. To argue with Frankie Kelly was a course of action that was not recommended as he invariably had a way of proving himself right. Only Mick could not be drawn into any argument. Attempts by Frankie to engage his uncle in discussion, the favourite topics being religion and politics, fell on deaf ears and Frankie was left, hanging, thwarted and feeling frustrated.

"Aye, now young Frankie," Mick would mutter, "ye have yer opinion."

This lack of opinion was a continuing source of irritation to young Frankie as he was curious about his uncle. Mick's opinion, thought Frankie, would be worth knowing. His father and mother were absorbed in day to day living. To elicit an opinion from either of them on any deeper issues would be well-nigh impossible and the usual outcome, if an attempt was made, was a reassuring murmur about religion and a frown of disapproval if politics came into the discussion. Politicians and priests according to his mother and father were much the same. Both represented authority and for that reason should be left well alone. But Mick? Now, Mick had to have an opinion. Mick was different.

Since as long as he could remember, Frankie had been fond of his uncle. He refused to speak against him to anyone. Often it was difficult. Mad Mick was the usual name for Mick Kelly and all the Kelly family were aware of the pain of these taunting words. But no-one in the school would be heard speaking derogatively about Mick in front of Frankie. Once Tim O'Sullivan had been the recipient of Frankie's wrath. An ill-advised remark that questioned Mick's parentage and the resulting blow to his nose from Frankie had left Tim in pain for weeks. After that, no one ventured opinions about Mick or any other Kelly for that matter. Frankie was not to be trifled with.

Father Byrne was thinking about Frankie as he strolled over to the Manse one cold December evening. Frankie, the priest judged, was an interesting lad and likely to be of some importance in whatever field he chose. It appeared to Father Byrne that Frankie, now aged sixteen, was destined for a religious life. He had been pleased to witness the friendship that had flourished between Frankie and the young curate. He remembered his own youth and the

193

fervour that had taken hold of him then. Frankie's earnestness was akin to that but Frankie had another string that Father Byrne wryly accepted he lacked and that was a high intelligence tempered to an analytical mind. Frankie Kelly would go far. Bernard was right, Father Byrne mused. Frankie was definitely Bishop material or higher.

As Father Byrne knocked loudly on the door of the Manse, he could hear through the thin winter air the sound of a joyful jazz band playing the blues, so it was a few minutes before the door opened. Effie was in theatrical mode. A stout woman, she had a liking for colourful chiffon caftans that flowed around her body and swept down to the floor, so that when she moved she looked much like a skater, gliding across the ice. Father Byrne, whose knowledge of women's fashions being non-existent was, however, impressed. The sight of Effie in her bright orange and red outfit which she complemented so well with her red beads and red bangles, made him feel somewhat of a dull nondescript dressed as he was in his clerical clothes. He couldn't take his eyes off her hair. Three ebony sticks similar to those worn by a Japanese geisha were stuck somewhat randomly at the back of her head in a vain attempt to hold up her hair which still managed to fall over her forehead. The light and Effie and the music invited him in to the cosy, warm comfort of the living room.

"Joe. We're having a jazz night. Don't you just love the blues?" and with that, Effie told hold of the priest's arm and escorted him in. For some reason, newspapers were laid out across the carpet floor and Father Byrne stepped gingerly over them, wondering what was underneath. Finding a seat was difficult. There was even more disarray than normal in the room. Armchairs that had once been able to be used for the purpose for which they were designed were now covered with rugs, cushions and piles of magazines. Father Byrne was so intent on finding an available seat that he didn't immediately notice that Sophocles and Aristotle were lying flat out on the large sofa

194

both with their heads sitting comfortably on a man's knees. Sophocles managed to open one eye and give an obligatory wag of his tail while all Aristotle could manage was a yawn. Neither dog made any move to get up. This was not unusual as Father Byrne was such a familiar figure at the Manse that neither dog thought it necessary to expend any energy to greet him. It was easier to leave their enthusiasm for a stranger. The music filled the crowded room. The beat bounced off the walls and all the time Effie moved in time, shaking her shoulders and swinging her hips. Leslie leapt to his feet as he always did. He found it difficult to be still and would sit for a moment, think of something and then immediately jump up. The only time his body was without perpetual motion was when he sat at his easel. His art stilled him. Even when he conducted his services, he moved around in front of his congregation in a bewildering way so that they were never quite sure where he would pop up next. He rushed over to Father Byrne and swept magazines, books and cushions off an armchair which appeared to have the least amount of clutter.

"Sit. Sit. We're in the mood tonight. Effie, my sweet, some mulled wine for our guest... not a guest now, goodness me, no... our friend, dear boy."

At that, Father Byrne sank gratefully into the chair. It was now that he was able to observe the Williamson's other guest. When he saw who it was, his astonishment was profound.

"Why, Mick... it's you!"

For Father Byrne was surprised beyond belief that the man who was sitting so comfortably on the sofa, stroking the heads of the two gigantic dogs, was indeed Mick Kelly. Father Byrne had not spoken to Mick since that night at An Teach Ban. Mick's words had unsettled him then and the sight of him again in such unexpected surroundings, unsettled the priest now.

"And it is indeed yeself, the good man."

"Now, Mick... I think we'll move on from that. Sure, ye have given me some food for thought, so ye have. Well, now, bless me, I didn't know you knew Leslie and Effie?"

"The same could be said about ye."

Father Byrne reddened. The saxophone sounded mournfully in the background and Father Byrne sipped his mulled wine, glad of the musical distraction.

Mick was perfectly relaxed. His hands rhythmically stroked the sleeping dogs and his eye fixed on the priest. Father Byrne was nervous. He was usually so relaxed at the Manse but tonight the surprise of seeing Mick unnerved him and he was glad of the saxophone and of Effie who floated in with a plate of mince pies. She offered them to Mick first and then to Father Byrne. He took a mouthful and immediately wished he hadn't.

"This is Mick. The farmer from An Teach Ban." And Leslie bounced up to capture a mince pie.

"Aye," said Mick, "I'm the farmer from An Teach Ban. And ye're Father Byrne, Parish Priest of Ballybeg."

"That's correct."

"Are ye finding any comfort in the fact of being the Parish Priest of Ballybeg? Is the experience to yer likin'?"

Father Byrne laughed. But it was not an easy laugh. There was tension behind it. Mick caused tension.

"I'm enjoying the experience. Aye. I am. There's a lot of good people here."

"There ye go again... ye and yer good people. Is the Reverend a good man, would ye say?"

Father Byrne hesitated. It was difficult to speak over the saxophone and he was wondering if the mince pie had taken out one of his fillings but he pushed on, regardless.

"Leslie's my friend... and Effie, too. I would say that they are good people but ye would have to ask them. I no longer consider myself a good man," he concluded, sorrowfully.

Hearing his words, Effie put her arm around his shoulders, hugging him. He was suddenly slightly

196

overcome with her proximity and the eau-de-cologne. Mick's eye never moved from the priest's face. It appeared that he was unaware of the effect of his words upon the group. The saxophone finished and the room was silent. At that moment, Sophocles decided to finally get up and his enormous shape stood unsteadily at first on four legs and then slowly and carefully eased himself from the sofa to the floor, his long nose hovering close to the mince pies as he did. The dog was a welcome diversion. It meant that Father Byrne could now engage himself in making conversation with his canine friend. And all the time, Mick did not move but continued to stroke the other dog, all the while his eye on the priest.

Leslie popped up again.

"I agree with Mick," he said. "I am not a good man. Didn't our Lord say that no man is good except God? All I can hope for is that I am a better man today than I was yesterday."

Father Byrne looked gratefully at Leslie. He nodded his head.

"Aye. Aye. Ye are right indeed, Mick Kelly. We are all sinners, that's for sure and Leslie... aye, I would hope that I am a better man for knowing ye... and a better man today than yesterday."

And he was relieved and thankful at the same time. Lightness filled his body and he didn't know why. Effie replenished his glass again and the warm liquid slipped down his throat combining with the glow of lightness in his spirit.

"Aye," he said again. "It is indeed a joyful occasion to be amongst friends."

He lifted his glass to Mick and this time, he was able to look into the eye of the farmer from An Teach Ban. Mick continued to stare but there was softness in his eye. Aristotle snored. Leslie had replaced the saxophone with a Christmas carol. *Hark the herald angels* descended like a

197

soothing balm over them and they were all silent listening to the words. All four thinking their own thoughts.

It was just ten days to Christmas.

*****

Frankie left his announcement until Christmas Day. For years now, Doctor and Mrs Ryan had been guests of the Kellys at Christmas and it suited Frankie fine for them to hear his news. Sometimes Mick was there. Sometimes not. Whatever was between him and the Ryans had softened over time. It was an uneasy truce between the three of them but it was a truce nevertheless and the Ryans were comfortable at An Teach Ban although you could never be sure of Mick.

"I have an announcement to make," and Frankie's posture and demeanour was already suggestive that a sermon was about to take place.

Oisin giggled.

"I have decided," continued Frankie somewhat grandly and he waved his hand at Oisin with what was almost a papal gesture, "that I have the calling and I have been accepted at Maynooth to start at the end of summer."

And he sat down.

He had carefully thought out his words to make the most dramatic effect as possible and was certain that leaving the announcement until Christmas Day, after the hearty meal and the opening of the presents, he would be assured of that. It worked. The first to speak was Mrs Ryan as verbose as ever. Mary balanced contentedly on her knee.

"Why now, Frankie. That is indeed the most wonderful news. I'm sure ye have thought all this out... why what a wonderful thing! Isn't it just a wonderful thing, John? Frankie a priest. Well, I never. Annie, ye must be so proud. Why, it just seems like yesterday that we were at yer baptism, young Frankie... and ye eating cherry cake and leaning over the banister... it's grand news..." she was about to go on but was stopped in mid-sentence by Oisin.

"What do ye want to do that for?" the boy asked.

198

Everyone laughed. Frog-like Oisin with his diminutive features was the least likely to have an opinion and if he had, it didn't count.

"Don't interrupt, Oisin," cautioned his mother and she frowned. She rose and kissed Frankie on his cheek... her Frankie... her first born. They were so proud of him and there would be more pride now. And her heart was glad. She turned to Bernard, her eyes shining... her son... a priest. Now there would be no snide remarks behind her back. No one would dare for the Kellys had a priest in the family... the very first ever... and Frankie, so clever.

The would-be priest sat back in his chair, satisfied. His words rolled around the room until Bernard spoke:

"Now. This calls for a celebration. A drink all around and a toast to ye, Frankie, my lad... can't say it's a surprise though."

Frankie managed a small pout but said nothing.

"A drink and we'll have some music. I'll get me fiddle out and play a tune. Why, it's not every day we get to have a priest in the family, is it now?"

He bustled around. He was the father of the chosen one. From the cupboard he produced glasses and a bottle of whiskey.

"We should be havin' the poteen," he winked at Annie, his eyes twinkling.

This was the cue for Mrs Ryan to start a discourse about the demon drink until she was cut short by Bernard who raised his glass.

"Here's to our son, Frankie Kelly. And I can say now, there'll never be a priest like him, I'm sure. It'll be Rome for ye, my boy... I can feel it in my bones... it's a grand Christmas Day at An Teach Ban. Let's all drink to Father Kelly. And may the saints watch over ye."

They raised their glasses. The adults, whiskey; the children, lemonade... all drank but Mick. He did not say a word.

An hour later, the Kelly boys were alone in the kitchen.

"If yer a priest, ye can't call me 'Frog' anymore!"

"What's that, Frog?" and Frankie's right hand ruffled Oisin's curly black hair. Oisin flapped his arms about but Frankie was too agile and neatly avoided his young brother's lively blows.

"Leave off, Frankie." It was Declan, the peacemaker.

But Oisin, a seething mass of fury, waited on his stool and when Frankie's back was turned, pounced. He landed neatly on his brother's back and took hold of his collar. Frankie, turned, and with a shrug, for that was all it took, released Oisin's grip. The unfortunate Oisin landed on the floor, red-faced and furious.

"What are ye doin' down there?" asked Frankie, good-naturedly as he placed his foot, very carefully but enough to hold the squirming furious Oisin who lay on his back while out of his mouth there poured a variety of profanities.

"Now, what am I goin' to do with ye, Frog? Tis not the language ye should be sayin' to yer elder brother. Just as well our mother is out of the room for she'd have the belt to ye, ye young rascal."

Frankie swept Oisin up in his arms and neatly deposited him back onto the stool; all the time avoiding his furious young brother's legs and feet. He carefully and firmly pinned Oisin's arms.

"Now look here, Frog. Ye just stay in yer pond till ye cool off," and with that, he once again ruffled Oisin's black curly hair.

"I hate ye, Frankie! Hate ye... hate ye... hate ye! Yer only bein' a priest so ye can boss everyone about... I know... an' wear those funny clothes and everyone will think yer great..."

Frankie clenched his fists. The two brothers glared at each other. Neither noticed that Mick was standing at the kitchen door. His arms were rigid at his side and his good eye was focused on Oisin. The boy was beside himself with fury and for a moment it looked as if he would attack his brother once again but Frankie turned away, pushed past the silent Mick and out into the yard beyond the farmhouse.

*****

Frankie's news was no surprise to Father Byrne given the boy's predilection of late to almost take up permanent residence within the sanctified walls of St Peter and St Paul's. Father Byrne was pleased. He considered the news to be something along the lines of a divine intervention given all the mystery surrounding Mick. He rather hoped that Frankie's vocation might be part of this same divine plan and influence the wayward Mick. Then he would return to the sanctuary of the church and in so doing, all would be forgiven. For this reason, the priest was eager to relay the news to Father O'Malley. The older priest, however, was not impressed.

"The Lord be praised," was all he said.

Father O'Malley was now almost completely bed-ridden and arrangements were in the process of being made. Nothing else for it. The old priest would have to go to the Ballybeg Hospital and be under the care of Sister Assumpta. This meant becoming helpless under female authority. Sister Assumpta was authority and to be subjected to that was something that Father O'Malley would have dreaded in his younger days. But now he was too old and too weak to care. Assumpta could have the last word as far as he was concerned. He would obey her. He no longer had the will to argue. He was done with the lot of them and he would meet Mick on the other side for he had had no success in this. If Mick's nephew wanted to be a priest, so be it. Father Byrne and the curate could have the glory. All Father O'Malley wanted to do was shut his eyes. Assumpta's face would be the last face he would see.

Once the priests had been informed of Frankie's vocation, it was left to Mrs Ryan to pass the news to the laity. The rapidity that this indomitable woman could relay information around Ballybeg and beyond had not diminished over the years. In fact, some were even certain

201

that her ability had progressed to such an extent that, if the recipients of the news heard it in the morning, it would be old news by the afternoon for Mrs Ryan would have found more to relay by then. It wasn't long, therefore, before Frankie's calling reached Ma Murphy's ears on a crowded Friday night. And once Ma got wind of it, everyone knew.

"'Tis a grand day for the Kellys, sure it is."

Ma's layers of flesh swamped Bernard with an exuberant display of affection when he arrived to play his fiddle.

"Sure, Ma... it wasn't a surprise at all. Not at all. He's been spendin' a fierce amount of time at the church and walkin' around with 'Oh Dear' till all hours... ye must have seen them around?"

"Now, Bernard, ye know that I rarely leave me post," chuckled Ma with a wink, "but Pa was on about young Frankie walkin' along the shore the other day, I recall it now. He said the two of them were lookin' for all the world as if they were away in another place... and maybe they was?" she concluded, thoughtfully. "Now what do ye think of all this, Mick?"

Mick was in the bar, too, perched on his stool at the counter, the glass of Guinness in front of him, the cigarette between his long, slender fingers. He looked up at Ma's words.

"Ye'll be speakin' about me nephew, Frankie, I suppose. As has been said, it's no surprise. He'll enjoy himself no doubt... but who of us will call him Father?"

Ma laughed.

"Ye have a point there, Mick, so ye do. 'Twas only yesterday we was havin' the party and he such a wee beebee... come on, father Bernard... get out that fiddle of yers and play one for the new priest!"

At that, Ma did a turn around almost colliding with a string of onions and, as she did, she narrowly missed knocking over a regular's glass.

"Steady on, Ma. Ye'll have yer onions on top o' ye!"

"Yer right enough there... that wouldn't do, now would it? When Pa takes me back to gay Paree," she winked, "ye knows what them Parisians get up to and it's nothin' to do with onions... least I hope not!"

"Come on, Ma. Another drink over here. Ye'll wear poor Pa out, so ye will. Isn't it about time ye had a feed o' them onions? And give a man a drink for I have the thirst on me something terrible-like with all this talk of onions!"

With a deft movement for someone with such an expanded form, Ma was once again behind the bar and the black Guinness flowed. Her sides rollicked. She chortled happily as pints and punts disappeared into their respective positions with an alacrity which came from years of experience.

"Aye," she agreed, "yer right enough. Guess we'll jist have to eat them onions. French Onion Soup on the menu tomorrow... and there's nothin' like onions for creatin' a thirst, is there now? So drink up, ye miserable lot and help a poor woman make a decent livin' out of ye!"

It was the best night of the week for trade and with the passing of the hours, Ma's wit quickened. The laughter and the banter became so outrageous no one noticed that Mick had downed three pints of Guinness in quick succession. Then he left the bar with as much speed. Bernard did not notice either. He had played happily all night but as he drew the bow across the strings, a shooting pain seemed to come out of nowhere. Right along his right arm it travelled. He gasped and laid fiddle and bow onto his knees. Such was the din surrounding him he was able to sit quietly on his stool, unnoticed. A few seconds later, he took up his fiddle again but this time, he played a slower tune. No one was aware that Bernard's music had changed. It was just another Friday night. And Murphy's was the place to be.

*****

At the end of the summer, a few days before he left for his new life, Frankie went searching for Mick. He found his uncle on his knees in the vegetable garden. Mick was most particular in his garden and cabbages, kale, carrots and parsnips grew in perfect straight lines. He took extra care with his potatoes and sprayed them regularly with copper sulphate and washing soda. The washing soda was used to make the copper sulphate stick to stem and leaves. He loved his potatoes for in his mind was the collective consciousness of a time long ago and often present in the souls of Ireland when there were no potatoes to eat. He watched over his garden as a mother with a child. On his good days, he was at peace in his garden. He and his vegetables were friends. Years ago, the garden produced so much that the brothers were able to sell the surplus. Even Annie was able to sell vegetables and eggs to Ma Murphy but, as the Kelly family increased in number, the surplus dwindled and it became even more imperative that the garden produce.

The sun was bright in the summer sky. White, wispy clouds stretched across the rarely seen blue and Mick was dressed for the weather. His faded blue striped shirt, unbuttoned to the waist exposed his chest and arms. His thin frame meant that he needed black braces to hold his trousers up securely. Over the last few months he had lost weight and aged, and Frankie noted Mick's hair had become greyer. For a moment, Frankie was unsure of Mick and wondered whether to disturb his uncle. Mick was so in tune with his repetitive work that to speak might disturb him and thus prevent the exacting task from reaching completion. There was a tin beside Mick and he was carefully picking over the cabbage leaves. He studied each leaf, holding it between the fingers of his left hand and, with his right hand he squashed the caterpillars, squeezing them tightly so that these fingers were covered with the colours of the dying caterpillars. Then he dropped each broken body into his tin and soon the tin was almost full with the green oozing innards of the half dead. Mick's concentration was hypnotic. He was unaware of Frankie, as caterpillar after caterpillar met their speedy end. Finally, he looked up and stretched his back in the manner of a cat that, awakening from a deep sleep and seeing the cause of its disturbance, immediately shuts its eyes again. Mick did the same and returned to his merciless task.

"Yer caterpillars have been havin' a grand old time of it, so," said Frankie as his uncle despatched another into the tin.

"Aye! Here's life and death and it's death yer seein'. The leaf is life for me and the caterpillar, so it is. But I am Death and I need to eat. I'm more powerful, it seems to me, in this than the caterpillar... but we both need the cabbage leaf... and the cabbage leaf needs us both!"

He sank back onto his legs. The relentless devourers of the leaves were now consigned to the tin; the only evidence of their insatiable appetites was misshapen and no longer perfect leaves.

"The only difference now, it seems to me, is that there'll be a day of mournin' for them caterpillars till they regroup and it all happens again. But it has to be. Yer mother makes a lovely colcannen, so she does – for an English girl."

"Aye," replied Frankie and he sat down beside Mick on the warm, slightly damp earth. "Ye're a great man for the philosophy, my Uncle Mick," he continued, fondly. "I'll miss ye in Maynooth... aye, I'll miss ye killin' caterpillars in yer garden. But I would be hopin' that when I come back at Christmas, ye will be in the church as well as yer garden because God is there too, ye know."

Mick smiled.

"Aye. So He is. Now, why would ye be wantin' me to be back in the church, young Frankie... is it the beginnin' of yer preachin'? Here we are, the two of us, sittin' in the warm sun in God's world after despatchin' a few dozen caterpillars to the next and ye be tellin' me what I should be doin' next... I ask meself, why would ye be wantin' to disturb the moment?"

Frankie frowned.

"A lot of people would welcome ye back to the Mass. Father Byrne for one."

"Oh, that's a good man. So he is. Well now, there seems to be an awful amount of people spendin' an awful amount of their time thinkin' of me... when there's caterpillars to be killed."

Frankie was vexed.

"Maybe they're right in Ballybeg. Maybe they're right... maybe, ye are not quite... oh, forget it..." he said, crossly.

"Yer father says for sure ye'll go to Rome... a Bishop, no less. What do ye think of that? And yer mother would be able to wear her best hat, now, wouldn't she?"

"Oh, Mick... we were talkin' about ye, not me!"

"It seems to me that yer goin' off to be a Bishop would be more to talk about than me killin' caterpillars and not goin' to Mass, now, wouldn't it? Am I right in sayin' this?"

Frankie stood up, angry.

"I'll never make ye out, Mick. Never, for as long as I live... whatever or wherever I end up, priest or Bishop! But I'll pray for ye, whether ye like it or not," he added, piously.

He wanted the last word and Mick could not argue with that. But Mick stood up, too, holding the tin of dying caterpillars so that Frankie could not avoid looking at it.

"Aye, Frankie, me lad," he said. "Here's to Life and Death and the mystery of it all. Say a prayer for them poor dead caterpillars and yeself as well for we're all part of the same."

"I'll never understand ye, Mick. I just came to say goodbye... so goodbye it is..."

And Frankie turned away. His mind was confused and he wished it wasn't. He had been so certain a moment ago. But Mick did that to you. Tension and confusion that is my Uncle Mick. I'll be glad to be away from it and not have to live with it ever again. But I'll still pray for you, he concluded as he and Mick made their way back to the farmhouse. You're in need of everyone's prayers, so you are, Mick Kelly!

*****

What a day it was, the day that Frankie Kelly went off to be a priest. Would ye never forget the send-off young Frankie got! Why, Stationmaster O'Connor kept the Dublin train waiting for half an hour so every one could have their farewells... such tears... such pride. For it was a long year since that a priest had been called from Ballybeg and wouldn't ye know it, it had to be a Kelly from out An Teach Ban, now that was something, wasn't it? Ah, the Lord works in mysterious ways...

Red-haired Father Byrne was there with the curate. 'Oh Dear' would see that Frankie got safely to Maynooth and already the curate was in a state, rubbing his hands and worrying about getting across Dublin and would they miss their connection with all this delay? 'Oh Dear' panicked and Father Byrne pondered. Human life, Father Bryne thought to himself, human life is akin to a railway station – all those arrivals and departures, the comings and the goings, all the sorrows, all the joys and the leaving and the returning. Why, he thought as he shook an excited Frankie's hand, I could use the railway station as an analogy in Sunday's sermon. Shall have a word with Leslie – wonder whether he could use it too? Father Bryne was forever a generous man.

He took Frankie's hand in his firm grasp.

"God be with ye, young Frankie my lad," he said warmly as the throng of well wishers pushed forward.

Oisin, at the back, spied a loose stone on the platform and gave it a slight kick with the toe of his boot. The stone moved a few paces away and Oisin, interested, kicked it further. It rolled across the platform gathering speed and travelled right through Mrs Ryan's legs to hit Frankie on the ankle just as he was about to say goodbye to Sister Assumpta. The stone caused pain. Frankie gave a yelp and fell slightly forwards. Assumpta, startled, took hold of Frankie's arm and thus avoided embarrassment. She pressed a small leather bound book into his hand.

"Something for you, Frankie. Such a comfort to me, so," and left as abruptly as she had arrived, for Assumpta very rarely left her hospital.

Frankie's ankle throbbed but at the next moment, he had to contend with an effusive Mrs Ryan for she took hold of him, clasping him to her bosom.

"Ye'll make us all proud, so ye will."

"Ye're a good lad," said Dr Ryan.

"Here's a wee bit of spirit for ye body Frankie, me lad," and Ma Murphy thrust a brown paper bag into Frankie's outstretched hand.

"I'll miss ye," said Declan.

"You take care and write," said Annie, through tears. And she asked Bernard, "Where's Mick?"

"I've said farewell to my Uncle Mick," answered Frankie.

Bernard shook his head. He was overcome and his side hurt. Then Frankie and 'Oh Dear' clambered aboard the train and positioned themselves with their heads out the window. They looked like two excited spaniels about to be taken on a long walk. Daniel O'Connor could hold the train no longer. He held up his hand, waved his flag, blew his whistle and the Dublin train from Ballybeg pulled away from the station taking Annie and Bernard Kelly's eldest son off to the priestly life.

Oisin, still apart from the group, suddenly spied the troublesome stone and, with a movement of his foot that would have give pride to a champion footballer, kicked it yet again. Such was the propulsion this time that the stone turned into a missile and with speed and deadly accuracy, shot across the platform to hit one of the end buffers of the departing train... unnoticed by all.

*****

There was a space now at An Teach Ban where Frankie had been and it was a deep space. The family went about their day to day living. They spoke briefly about Frankie and all looked forward to his letters. Frankie's letters were

208

well-written and entertaining. He was succeeding, of course. Success, it appeared, came natural to Frankie. He had already established himself as a formidable goalie in the hurling team. His strong body was a wall that made penetration difficult. In six months he had become a hero. He approached his lessons and religious study with the same assurance and enthusiasm. Learning was effortless and it would be no time at all before his ordination would take place. Frankie Kelly would make a fine priest and be a credit to the family. No question about it. If he had chosen a professional career or a business one, the same success would have been his, Frankie was a favoured one. No one doubted that he would make a determined and zealous priest and his voice would be heard. Soon the Kellys and Ballybeg would be able to bask in the glory of their priestly son.

At home, Declan was now the elder brother. He left school without a backward glance and he lived for the farm. His was perhaps the easiest path of them all... or so it seemed. Mick was as unpredictable and unreliable as ever and Annie busied herself, suffered more and spoke less. Now it was time for Oisin to go on to the big school and meet Baldy Lawrence, a man without hair or compassion. Brother Lawrence saw an easy target in the frail, diminutive new boy, and pounced.

"Ye have an older brother, Kelly," he said to Oisin the first time he saw him. "An elder brother of whom this school is proud. Will ye be making us proud too?"

He took hold of Oisin's arm and shook the boy roughly enough to make Oisin's teeth chatter slightly.

"Well, speak, boy! Ye have a brother, have ye no, top of the school and off to be a priest and fine reports we're hearin' from him, so... are ye followin' in his footsteps, or no?"

Still Oisin did not speak but rubbed his arm with his hand. His silence vexed Baldy. He pushed him once again, harder. This time Oisin tripped and fell to the ground.

Above him, fat Baldy glowered like an avenging devil, for never could he be thought of as an angel, and fear ran through the supine body of Oisin Kelly. Frankie's footsteps before him were far too meritorious to even attempt to emulate. His rose shakily to his feet expecting another blow but Brother Lawrence, the keeper of the many innocent souls was already away. Out of the corner of his eye, he spied two older lads pushing each other. It looked as though they were about to engage in a battle and frail Oisin was too faint an adversary to bother with any longer. With a roar, Baldy descended upon the two pugilists and left the shaken Oisin to contemplate his first day at the big school. He would remember it as a miserable day with only the thought of being the big brother to Mary, his only solace as the day wore on.

*****

Bernard felt the pain once again in his chest and it frightened him. He gasped and steadied himself on the stone wall at the back of the farm where the pigs were housed. His breath came in short, sharp pants. A moment before he had hauled a bale of hay over the wall. The next moment, his arms were numb at his side. The remorseless moment. The pitiless moment. He fell onto the wall. Far off in some distant land, he could hear the lonesome call of a seagull. High above, the bird cruised in perfect circular motions; all the time its shrill call rang down through the air, without pause. Bernard felt his legs grow weak and he toppled like a rag doll, almost, onto the damp soil. He sank to his knees. Through a haze he saw Oisin approaching. The boy was running, it seemed, jumping up and down, trying to avoid puddles and occasionally the muddy water splashed onto his bare legs.

When Oisin saw his father, he stopped. His legs grew weak and his feet refused to move. They no longer functioned as feet. He was just a few paces away from Bernard near the heap of neatly stacked turf, but he could not make himself move. He watched as Bernard sank

210

further down, holding his chest with his right hand, his left arm out from his side. Then he landed face down in the mud and was still. It was all an event that happened slow motion... and Oisin, the onlooker was not part of it. A moment before, he had been contemplating the length of step required to clear a larger than ever puddle and now, in front of him, lying in that very puddle was his father. Bernard's cap had fallen from his head as he came down and it now lay beside him, apart from him. His cap and he were no longer connected. Above the seagull swooped, no longer calling. No sound above. No sound below.

And then Oisin could move. Somehow the silence moved him. He ran to his father. Knelt down into the soft brown mud and called his father's name. But Bernard did not answer. He lay with his face half submerged in the puddle. Oisin took off his jumper and carefully eased his father's head out of the water and gently onto the woollen garment. Bernard groaned. His right hand still gripped his chest and everything about him was the same. Only Bernard was losing his battle with life. There was his son beside him, but that was all. And high above the seagull was joined by another and the two birds flew together, round and round in the blue sky, calling to each other. Bernard tried to speak but the words stuck in his throat. He tried vainly to lift his head. Here was his warrior son, his poet son.

"Get yer mother."

Oisin had been stroking his father's black hair, the hair with all the grey coming through. Stroking this hair and as he did, the tears ran from his eyes and would not stop. What could he do? He heard his father's words and he knew then. Run. Run. So he did. Past the outbuildings, through the puddles and the water splashed his legs but he did not stop. Past the vegetable garden and the green where his mother dried their clothes, to the back door, to the kitchen where he knew she would be. There was no Frankie or Declan or Mick, not even Mary. No-one but his mother and she would be there and she would know what to do.

She was making bread. Squeezing the sticky mixture together in her hands and shaping the dough roughly. All the while, she hummed an old World War Two tune from her girlhood and the rhythm of kneading and singing induced a kind of contentment within her. She was so absorbed with the tune and the making of the bread that she hardly noticed Oisin until she felt his hand pulling her arm and his urgency.

"Mammy... it's Da... he's... he's...!!!"

She knew. She wiped her sticky hands on her apron. She was to remember that moment for the rest of her life – the apron, the bread, the song. She followed Oisin and the two of them ran back through the puddles, scattering three brown hens that cackled with indignation. One flapped onto the wall and feathers flew. But Annie and Oisin ran on to where Bernard lay. Anne fell to his side and cried out:

"Run back to the house! Ring Doctor Flannery... hurry! Find Mick..."

And little Oisin, still bewildered, still afraid, stood looking on, confused and scared... he could feel his heart pounding. It was as if he had a drummer in his chest and the pounding would push his heart out from his body.

"Go on, Oisin... hurry! The exchange will know the number... just ring... but hurry...!"

At last Oisin could move. For the third time he ran through the puddles. His father's life depended on his speed. He must not panic. He would ring. Get the doctor. Get the doctor. That was what he had to do. And he ran and this time he didn't look back.

Annie fell upon Bernard and cradled him in her arms. Now her apron was covered in wet dough and flour and mud and water. Tears ran down her cheeks and mingled with her sweat. Bernard tried to lift his head. Annie. His Annie. She was there. He must tell her something. She must hear but when he tried to move his lips, no sound came from them. The words stuck in his throat and would not come out. He only had five words he wanted to say to her. God, please let me speak. Please God. He opened his eyes and saw his beautiful Annie's face so close. Her breath was upon him. His face was buried in the wool of Oisin's jumper but now he somehow eased his right hand from his heart to hold, to try to hold his Annie's hand. Through her tears she was aware of what he was trying to do. She took his hand and squeezed it. And all the time he was trying to get the words out. They came from his lips finally but they were just a whisper and hardly a sound. But Annie heard them. For a momentary second, her hand holding Bernard's, loosened its grip.

"Mick... ye've always had Mick."

And Bernard shut his eyes.

*****

They managed to get Bernard into the ambulance. Sean, the ambulance man and Doctor Flannery and all the while Oisin stood, and watched as his mother tried to comfort Bernard. It started to rain, the soft rain of Ireland and it fell like dew onto Oisin's face and wet his hair. He shivered without his jumper but he could not move. His shoes were glued into the mud and his legs were weak. No one thought to speak to him but left him standing as the droplets of rain ran down his cheeks and mixed with the salt of his tears. They drove Bernard to the Ballybeg Hospital, to Doctor Ryan and Sister Assumpta but it was too late.

Annie was distraught. She had to hear from someone of her own. Through a crackling line, she told Uncle George.

"I'll be over," he said, "I'll bring Sinéad."

And Annie wept.

*****

At the funeral Mass for his father, Frankie stood beside Father Byrne at the altar. He was handsome in his clerical clothes and many a girl thought wistfully to herself, "Such a

213

waste!" but then there was Declan, almost as handsome and now with a farm of his own. And the girls turned and looked in Declan's direction as he sat, head bowed, beside Oisin and Mary. There was Mick beside Annie. Their hands so near to each others but apart. Mick had not been inside St Peter and St Paul's for five years. He stared without emotion as he looked on his brother's coffin. People wondered and shook their heads. Behind the family sat frail Uncle George, now totally dependant on his stick for support. And Sinéad Nolan, that loyal cousin of Bernard's, fussed and dried her eyes with a white linen handkerchief.

But it was a grand funeral and the shopkeepers shut their shops for an hour as a mark of respect. Bernard's sudden passing had shocked the people of Ballybeg but they knew how to have a good funeral and Bernard was one of their own. Ma Murphy refused to open the Bar.

"I'll not have the place open," she said, "Bernard was my friend. It is the least I can do."

And she would not be moved. Murphy's Bar, for the first time in living memory, closed for twenty-four hours on that Friday, the day they laid Bernard Kelly to rest.

On Bernard's gravestone there would be carved a dash between two dates. This is the dash for Everyman... such a brief span, the beginning and the end, this dash between. Bernard's dash was a quiet dash for his life was quietly lived and just as quietly did he die.

*****

One late evening, just as the twilight descended, Mick and Annie sat on Bernard's bench on the hill under the hawthorn tree. The sun sank, a golden orb over the sea and through the clouds of grey and red, the day ended. Behind them Slieve Geal was lit from the reflected rays and the world was at peace. But under the hawthorn tree the presence of Bernard was everywhere. Any minute now they would hear his fiddle play or hear his voice.

"What will become of me?" Annie moaned. "What *will* become of me?"

214

She leaned her head on Mick's shoulder and his arms held her, his lips kissing her hair. But she hardly noticed. She clung to him as she had clung to him in her dream all those years ago.

They sat there, the two of them, holding each other as the dark descended over the farm and the streetlights in Ballybeg flickered into view.

PART THREE

CHAPTER ELEVEN

In some narrow compartment, deep down and hidden in the very depth of his being, Oisin placed the memory of his father's death. Within his heart and unknown to all, he kept the fear of that moment, that all-pervading, helpless moment, when he had seen his father weakened. And this fear he locked away and told no one for he had witnessed the bewilderment of the adult world at such moments. He felt alone and yet part of all humanity. The paradox troubled him deeply but he remained silent as the world around him tried to adjust to life without Bernard. It was a difficult and a sad time for them all for Bernard was often in their thoughts. His personal possessions had been swept away so as not to intrude into the visible world but his spirit remained about them. Any moment now he would walk through the door and be with them once more.

Annie grieved but could not weep. She clung to Bernard's memory and built a shrine for him in her mind. Now she spent time in the church, on her knees before the altar and looked on a judgemental God, distressed. She was shamed for her guilt but she could not let it go. If she did, she would be even more alone. And that she could not bear, not for one moment. She tried to keep busy. Rising early, she worked through the day in a wild hope that the constant repetition of her work would drive away her guilt. Since Mick had held her to him that evening and stroked her hair and kissed the top of her head, she had tried to avoid him. She had no idea of his feelings for his brother. She had no idea of his feelings for her. The combination of the two was such an unknown and, for that, she would keep away from him. He was silent most of the time, enclosed in his own thoughts and he would sit for hours in his chair, reading or watching her as she busied herself. Now she was uneasy in his presence but the longing for him was still there and would not go away. Her prayers were to be released from the desire for Mick but no amount of prayer brought peace. Annie hated herself for her perceived weakness. She would have given anything to have Bernard back with her and to have his forgiveness. She looked at his photograph or held his jacket to her cheek and cried for him, but she shed no tears. And so the days slipped by.

Annie had hidden Bernard's fiddle away in its case. No one had dared look at it for it contained the very soul of their loss, or so it seemed. It lay for months, gathering dust on the top of the wardrobe in Annie's bedroom. She had carefully wrapped it in a tartan travelling rug in order to obscure it from view and to hide it. No one spoke of the fiddle until one day Declan took it down, unknown to anyone. He carried it to the bench on top of the hill under the hawthorn tree and sat with the case on his knees. It was a quiet day, that day with just his collie dog for company. The dog sat on the bench beside Declan and the silence was around them. Then Declan opened the case and brought out his father's fiddle. He stroked it, caressed it as you would a baby, and just as tenderly, ran his fingers along the strings. He placed the instrument under his chin and drew the bow across the strings and brought a sound out of it for it had been silent for many, many months. The air was still about him and the tune was one of his father's favourites. He was nervous at first but gradually, confidence grew in him and he played with a wild, glad abandon and the dog jumped down from the bench and wagged his tail in appreciation, it seemed. The notes rose and fell and Declan tapped his foot on the ground and then stood up, still playing and joyous as the music brought Bernard back. Declan could not stop. He grew wild with wonder at his own playing. Back and forth over the strings, the bow moved in his hand as if it had a mind of its own until finally, he sat back down, exhausted. The sweat was on his brow and his hands were wet too but he wanted to laugh and to cry at the same time so great was his joy. The dog rested his head on Declan's knee and the two of them looked at each other. Then Declan returned the fiddle and

218

the bow to its case and locked down the metal clips securely. This time he carried the precious possession to his own room and said nothing.

*****

Declan stood on the flagstones in front of Murphy's Bar and pulled his coat collar up around his neck. He hugged the worn leather case containing his father's fiddle closer to his body. Droplets of rain fell like mist onto his black curly hair and the water ran softly down his face. He was nervous and had forgotten his cap. When he had left the farm, it had been dry and, in the short space of time it had taken to walk to Murphy's, just a short distance away, the rain had come on. Soft. He was wet through and his hair now resembled dew on early morning grass. It was a year since he had first taken the fiddle from on top of the wardrobe and he had practised all the time. In all weathers, when his work was done, he would take the fiddle and play. On summer days, he played outdoors and sometimes he would climb to the top of Slieve Geal, a pilgrimage almost, and the music would cascade out into the clear air. This was a special time. When the days grew dark and cold, he would retire to the outbuilding where his father used to do his woodwork and, in the silent room, play. Annie heard the music and knew what he was doing but said nothing. A tiny resentment rose in her heart but she dismissed it as foolishness and went about her business.

Now Declan thought he was ready. It was early afternoon and he knew that it would be a quiet time at Murphy's and Ma might have time to talk. It had been a good summer and the conifers had grown slightly in their red planters. 'Murphy's' had been repainted in black uncial letters on a board above the entrance and the place was inviting, prosperous-looking. A few weeks after Bernard's funeral, Ma took down the onions and the prints of Paris off the walls. She replaced the red and white chequered tablecloths in the big room and threw out her Parisian dresses. "I'm an Irishwoman till I die," she told everyone, ruefully but with a little pride, too. The old Ma had returned to them and they were glad. Now she and Pa were finding it harder to manage the running of the Bar. Only their youngest son, Liam, who refused steadfastly to marry, was there to help. Helen had caught the eye of a Dublin businessman and went to live in the city. Perpetually pregnant, it seemed, she returned to Ballybeg occasionally with her ever-increasing brood and no longer sang. Dermot, the second one, escaped to England and set about making a name for himself in the building trade. Soon he had made enough money to marry a girl from Manchester who had pretensions and they both kept away from Ballybeg while Dermot did his best to forget his Irish roots. So there was just Ma and Pa and Liam at Murphy's now with Declan and Oisin to help clear tables on weekends. The music wasn't there. Sometimes, a drunken patron would burst into song, without accompaniment and the Bar would fall silent. "'Tis not the same without Bernard," they would mutter amongst themselves and try not to look in Mick's direction, nervous of his reaction. But Mick, if he was there, said nothing and people shook their heads as they always did when they thought of Mick and talked of other things.

Declan opened the door into the Bar and true to his plan, the place was quiet. Ma was wiping the bar counter and getting ready for the evening trade.

"I've come to play my father's fiddle... if ye'll let me play, Ma?" blurted Declan, somewhat clumsily.

Ma looked up, surprised.

"Well now. Let's be hearin' ye... just one song... ye've picked the right time to call."

Declan nodded. His hand was shaking. He brought Bernard's fiddle out and ran his hand over it lovingly. A month ago, he had driven with Oisin to Galway City to the Music Shop. An old string needed replacing. Now the old fiddle sounded like new after that. Oisin had chattered all the way. Once he was away from Ballybeg it seemed, he developed a verbosity that wearied the listener. Declan half wished he hadn't taken him but he wasn't thinking of his little brother. He was intent on making a good impression because Ma was shrewd. If he could pull it off, he would have a job but he would have to earn it. He started to play and the fire leapt in his belly and the song, a favourite his father loved to play, took hold of him and the pure, sweet notes filled the air. Pa heard the music from the big room and he came into the bar, wiping his hands on a cloth as he did. He stood beside Ma and he smiled his toothless smile.

"Play another song, lad," he said when Declan finished.

So Declan played and played again. His face was wet from rain and sweat but he couldn't stop. The music controlled him and he was just an instrument, playing out the tunes. Finally, he had to stop and he sat down on a chair near the piano and wiped his face with his handkerchief. Then Ma took a glass and poured a Guinness. As she handed the full glass to Declan, she smiled.

"Here, lad," she said, "Here's a half. When ye can play like yer Da, ye'll have a pint."

Declan blushed, unsure.

"Ye've got a job, if ye like... on weekends and maybe other times. We'll get Hugh back to play the piano."

Her brown eyes softened.

"Aye, Declan. Yer a grand lad, so. And 'tis a wondrous thing to hear the old fiddle play again, isn't it now, Pa?"

And Pa nodded sagely because he always agreed with Ma on such matters for this was indeed a wondrous thing, to have Bernard's son playing his father's fiddle once again in Murphy's Bar.

*****

When Declan told Annie he had a job at Murphy's, playing the fiddle, she did not reply. Instead, she continued slicing the potatoes for the evening meal. Declan never spoke to her about it again but from then on he went gladly to Murphy's until one evening, six months later, Ma handed him a pint!

At An Teach Ban there was a restlessness which now grew in Annie as the months went by and it was a terrible anxious restlessness. She was unable to subdue it no matter how hard she tried. She felt wasted. Her energy sapped. No amount of prayers filled the emptiness within her and her restlessness grew. She thought if she took a trip to London, she would be refreshed and the anxiety would go away. But the more she thought about going, a kind of ennui descended upon her and she talked herself out of the journey. It was too long... too far. Only Uncle George was there now. She couldn't bear to think of the gap where her mother had been and now there was a gap here, too, in Ballybeg, without Bernard. In the end, the courage which had been so admired when she dodged the bombs in London, that courage deserted her and she fell back, defeated.

Sometimes she thought of her children, one by one... her four children. They no longer needed her. She sighed. There was her Frankie, soon to be a priest. He would not come back to Ballybeg but would make a name for himself, somewhere else. She was proud of him and delighted in reporting to others his successes but sadness would come over her when she thought of him, too. And then there was Declan with the eyes of William and the soul of the Kellys, how she watched over him. He ran the farm now and was kind. He could play the fiddle as well as his father almost, Ma Murphy said as much. And Declan was settled. Soon he would bring a girl home and Annie would be pushed aside, gently but firmly. No longer needed. Like some worn out old shoe that had been thrown into a corner and forgotten about. And as the years slipped by, they would think of her less and less.

She despaired of Oisin... so different from the rest of them... not only in appearance but in attitude too. Perhaps, she wondered... perhaps? Then she would grow guilty once again as she always did, when she thought of *that* night. Quickly, then her mind would turn to Mary because Mary was a lovely girl. Much better than her mother, Annie decided. Mary would marry and be happy. She would never have to live through the burden of a perceived adultery or suffer through the longing for a man who was not her husband. Mary would care for her mother for that was her duty. But it would be duty, Annie concluded, nothing more. And Annie, restless once more would think of that old shoe.

She tried to avoid Mick. At times, they had been friends. At times, they had been deadly foes. Now she dared not look at him. But he watched her always and she grew uneasy in his presence. Until one day he took hold of her hand and held it tight. His good eye was upon her and she knew she could not resist, did not want to resist anymore, just let him hold her hand; let her hand be captive in his.

She grew brave.

"What is it, Mick?" she cried... although she knew.

His face was close to hers. His arms were around her body. She could feel his heart pumping in his chest. With a gentle hand, he placed his fingers under her chin. Her heart beat faster. Her body, so long reluctant to abandon itself, slowly, cautiously and then with urgency, relaxed. Her left hand stroked his face. She had never looked at him before with such intensity. Her mind took in every feature; the line of furrows on his brow, the straight proud nose, the black patch over his eye. She ran her fingers down his cheek. He hadn't shaved for two days. The stubble was on his chin. She felt the tiny hairs under her touch. Now, now she wanted so much, so much, to kiss him. They studied each other. They were artists studying each other. Every line and every feature had to be remembered for this was their moment. No other moment existed for them. No past, it was gone, forgotten. No future to fear, nothing. Nor could there ever be another moment like this ever, ever again. They existed for this moment; this one perfect moment and everything else, what had been and what was before was but a dream.

Then his lips were on hers and her body gave up its fight. His hands, those rough farmer's hands she had studied for so long, those hands explored her body, skilfully and tenderly. Desire rose within her. She kissed him now and ran her hands along his back. Felt his thin, strong frame and loved him. He was so like Bernard, but not Bernard. There was urgency now. She wanted him for she had cried for so long in silence, for almost twenty long years, she had wanted him. There were tears behind her eyes but her eyes shone. It had always been Mick. He kissed her neck, her cheek, her ears. He surprised her with his gentleness for Bernard had been a clumsy lover and Annie had only known one man. She thought if she were to die tomorrow, at least she had had this moment. She gave herself up to the moment. She could not believe it was her own body making such demands. She was on fire with desire, a savage keen desire and Mick's hands were on her breasts. There was no one but Mick. Could never have been anyone but Mick.

Afterwards, they wanted to hold each other. Not let each other go ever, ever again. But the moment had to pass for that precious moment had already gone and they were Mick and Annie once again, separate. She dressed herself awkwardly for Oisin and Mary would soon be in from the school and Declan in from the fields. Once again she was Annie Kelly, Bernard's widow and mother of four. The Englishwoman. But the restlessness within her had passed for she had the memory now. She took Mick's hand and kissed it tenderly as a mother would a child. Now tears rolled down her cheeks and would not stop. Outside, a cock crowed; then came the steady beat of rain upon the roof.

*****

When Annie awoke the next morning there was a tenderness that had never been there before. Even in her innocence, she had held tightness within herself blaming her lack of emotion on outer circumstances and justifying the barriers she had erected around her on the cruelty of war. After all, her father and brother had been taken from her. She could not forget. Even the excitement of meeting Bernard had done little to unlock the deep sorrow within but now there was Mick and her eyes softened when she looked at him. Paradoxically, they were strangers and lovers at the same time observing each other shyly but with the powerful knowledge and this was exhilaration...that between them was now a newly discovered familiarity. This was a delirious mixture and likely to rebound on them if their secret were ever to be revealed. Their love was too new and they both were too vulnerable to allow their feelings for each other to be made public. It would be a betrayal to the almost sacred memory of Bernard and Annie had no desire to become the object of conjecture or, if her love was ever discovered, to be the victim of idle gossip. She had suffered too much in the small community and had no wish to have the opinions of others spoil her happiness. No, her love for Mick would remain hidden but how she longed to touch him, to hold his hand and to lay her head upon his shoulder. Out of the years of married life, of struggle and toil, Annie had discovered her lost innocence and it had softened her and she could smile again. Sometimes, when Mick sat in his chair, he too seemed to soften and when he glanced towards Annie it was the gaze of a lover. Theirs was a quiet love, a quiet love indeed. They were certain that no one would uncover their secret and that their love was made even more precious because of this. After all, Annie reasoned, she had loved Mick for nearly twenty years. Whatever remaining years were given to them should be viewed as a joyful gift to be enjoyed and cherished for that alone. Annie smiled to herself and hummed a tune as she thought on her secret and was glad.

They were comfortable with each other now. At times, when they were alone, Annie would sit on Mick's knee and

225

lean her head onto his shoulder. It was joy for her to study his face; every line seemed to her to be precious. He never said he loved her but one day while she sat near him, he took his black eye patch off his eye. Exposed were the ugly scars and the uneven stitches, still evident, across the wound. She gently placed her hand over his poor eye.

"Ah, Annie," he sighed, "ye are so dim... just a wee blur out of that eye. I can tell you, *mo chailín*... I would always be wishin' to see ye with my good eye... but I just wanted ye to see, just once... now, we'll hide this poor unfortunate eye once again."

Then she knew he loved her. She took his hand in hers and gently rubbed hand and eye patch to her cheek. Neither spoke, for words can sometimes seem intrusive and this was one of those times.

*****

Summer came at last to Ballybeg. Behind the farm, Slieve Geal put on her cloak of green and grey and often, now, Annie and Mick would climb to the top and look over to the sea. Once they kissed on the top, holding each other tightly against the slight breeze and they blessed the moment. It was always special on top of Slieve Geal. The farm below looked well kept and prosperous as indeed it was as Declan, with his youthful enthusiasm, brought changes. The Kellys were reclaiming their place in the district. Declan was sensitive to Mick's authority with regard to farm matters but if the truth be ever told, Mick had little interest now in farming and its problems.

"He's just like me grandfather, God rest his soul," he would say to Annie, "a farmer through and through. Ye'll not want for anything while yer Declan's in charge, mark my words. The lad's shrewd, there's no doubt about it. Looks like he's got the best of both sides of the family runnin' through him, wouldn't ye say?"

And Annie would agree readily enough. Declan certainly had combined the business acumen of her father

with the pragmatism of Bernard. It was no wonder that Declan was her favourite.

"I've never told anyone this, Mick...," she said one day and she hesitated, speaking the words slowly, "but I've always thought Declan has my brother's eyes... my young brother... my only brother, William... killed in the war." And a small burden lifted from Annie as she spoke.

"Aye. Ye wonder how it all comes around again, don't ye now? What do ye think?"

But Annie had no wish to think on such matters. She had spoken of William. That was enough. Enough that Mick was with her and Declan was running the farm. And after all it was summer and the days were long. She no longer thought of returning to London or going anywhere else but An Teach Ban. This was her home and she would stay.

And it was in that summer, too, when the people of Ballybeg buried their priest. Old Father O'Malley, that obdurate and rigid keeper of their souls, fell asleep for the last time, aged ninety-two, sometime during the night of the fifth of June. Sister Assumpta had looked in at him that early evening and said to Father Byrne, who happened to be there:

"He's comfortable at least... and looks so peaceful, doesn't he just?"

She had grown fond of the old priest in his weakened state.

"Any day now, God rest his soul," she added, with what was a prophetic word.

So the sun shone bright and the sky was blue on the day of Father O'Malley's funeral. The Bishop came to say the Mass and Frankie returned from Maynooth for two days to be there. At An Teach Ban, Annie dressed in her best black tailored suit, 'my funeral clothes', she thought sombrely. She seemed to be wearing them a lot latterly. Father O'Malley had disliked her, she knew, but he had

suffered at the end and well, he was a priest after all, and worthy of respect.

"Are you coming to the funeral, Mick?" she asked for she felt he should.

"Now, Annie. Do ye really think that old O'Malley would want to see me there? No, I'll not go."

Annie's lips set hard. She tried again.

"I know what he was like. Everyone knew but everyone is going."

"Well, Annie. Ye should know by now, what everyone does isn't always what everyone wants. No, ye go along and pay yer respects if ye must but I'll not be there!"

And he turned away as he always did when his mind was made up.

There was nothing left for it but that Annie and her children should crowd into the church along with everyone else. Everyone it seemed, but Mick Kelly. It was such a turn out that people spilled out of the church onto North Street. Two American tourists were annoyed.

"Why aren't the shops open?" they said, petulantly.

"We're burying our priest, God rest his soul," was the reply.

And the Americans went away, shaking their heads that commerce could grind to a halt for such a reason.

As the procession made its way from the church it was noted that even the Reverend Williamson, looking from across the Owenbeg, took off his white panama hat and Mrs Williamson was beside him, too. Everyone was there, it seemed and as the sun shone brightly in the sky, the funeral took on an almost carnival air. The procession slowly moved along North Street, across South Bridge and into the cemetery grounds. Everyone had a memory.

"Wonder what the old rogue would make of this?" Mrs Ryan whispered to her husband as people stood on tiptoe to see what was happening at the graveside.

Doctor Ryan smiled. There was ever such a twinkle in his eye as he answered:

"Aye. I wonder. He'll be up there counting the heads as we speak," for he had often thought to himself that Father O'Malley had had a more than pastoral interest in his wife but he kept it to himself. He chuckled at the thought.

"John," she said, "remember where ye are!"

It was eleven o'clock in the morning and everyone was in a jovial mood. It was a rare send-off they were giving old Father O'Malley and he would have expected nothing less.

As the crowd shuffled out of the cemetery grounds, Oisin thought he saw a man he recognised. Puzzled, he nudged his mother's arm.

"Isn't that the man... the Italian man, remember... he came out to see Uncle Mick?"

For he thought it looked a lot like the memory of Silvio Luchetta, that enigmatic and charismatic personage who had caused such speculation in the Kelly household years ago. Could it be? Annie tried to see through the crowd but the sea of heads and hats made it impossible. She was about to ask Oisin in which direction to look but her concentration was distracted for at that particular moment, Ma Murphy pushed through the throng to speak to Annie.

"Well, Annie," she panted, out of breath for there were so many people around, "that's the end of an era, so. He's at peace now, so he is. Ballybeg won't be the same without him, will it now? He did his best for us, now, didn't he? And us such a gang of sinners... he had his work cut out for him... but the other one..." She paused meaning Father Byrne. "Well, he'll see us right with all that red hair! And how's yer Frankie doin'? Where do ye think he will go first? Doubt if he'll want to come back to the West... he'll be startin' out in Dublin or Cork, that one. Ye must be proud of him?"

Ma hardly paused for breath and she had to shout to make herself heard. Annie couldn't help laughing. The whole world was laughing that day, the day of Father O'Malley's funeral. Ma hooked her arm in Annie's and the two women pushed their way through the crowd. Annie

229

quickly forgot to look any more for the Italian man for surely Oisin was mistaken. Why would Silvio Luchetta, who hadn't been seen in Ballybeg for years, why would he be at Father O'Malley's funeral? He didn't even belong here. Mick still got letters from Silvio, Annie recognised the writing, but not as many as before and Mick never talked about it. No, Silvio's never mentioned. She allowed herself to be caught up with Ma's chatter and didn't look any further.

But Oisin was convinced. It *is* him, he thought. Older. Grey hair now. And no moustache but he was wearing an elegant summer suit with a black tie. He craned his neck again to try to see the stranger but there was no sign. He put the matter out of his mind as he caught sight of Baldy Lawrence who looked for all the world as if he was searching for any miscreants and Oisin was always one of them. Who cares, he thought? It's a grand day and no school. Soon school, too, will be over for good.

*****

Annie was in a good mood when she returned to An Teach Ban after the funeral. The sun was still high in the sky and she went looking for Mick. He was nowhere to be seen. Distracted, she wandered around the farm searching in the outbuildings and even climbed to Bernard's bench to get a better view... but no Mick. She peeped into his bedroom but all was as it had been. She ran her hand along the colourful blue and red patchwork cover of the made-up bed, half-smiling as she did. Everything was Mick but no Mick. He didn't return in the evening. Annie said nothing. She was so preoccupied that Frankie's constant tales of life at the Seminary passed unheeded. She listened, nodding appropriately but took little part in the conversation until he said, noticing:

"What's up, Ma?" and gave her a little pat on the top of her head. To which she brushed him aside with a "That's enough, Frankie!" but her mind was elsewhere.

Just as the family were about to retire for the night, Mick opened the kitchen door and sank heavily into his chair. His face was grey and he looked old and tired. Annie fussed.

"I'm alright, woman," he said, wearily. "Just let me be."

The next morning Frankie left for his last few weeks at Maynooth and An Teach Ban was quiet again. Mick came back to Annie. Annie now worried for she feared his illness and grew anxious for his safety.

"Let me look after you, Mick," she said to him one morning. "You mean the world to me."

She turned her face to look at him. When she saw the greyness there and the weariness, too, she would have given anything to take the pain away... if she only had the power. Surely, surely, love can conquer all? Please God, she thought, please God, don't let me lose him too. And she trembled.

"Ah, now Annie... yer such a woman, so ye are... for the sun's out and it's a grand day, isn't it now?"

And Annie had to smile. He always ended up making her smile.

"You're so right, Mick Kelly," she answered gaily, "Why, the sun's up and there's work to do. Declan has been up for hours..."

Declan had indeed been busy outside and would be soon in for something to eat and here I am, thought Annie, getting myself into a state. But I can't help caring for him, my Mick, and she smiled. My Mick, she thought again. It was after all a grand day and too glorious a day for worrying about the future. No. She put thought of Mick's illness out of her mind. Better that way. Why, there were other matters to attend to. The continuing problem of Oisin, for one and what was to be done with him?

Oisin was becoming even more difficult to place into the neat order that Frankie and Declan and even Mary, had been arranged. Why, he had finally had a showdown with

Brother Lawrence and the teacher had called Annie in to intervene.

"Mrs Kelly," Baldy intoned when she sat in front of him in his office. He waved his fat hands in the air. "Your son refuses to cooperate. Such a pity, too, why yer Frankie would be an example for the boy to follow, ye would think it now, wouldn't ye?"

Annie nodded.

"Well, Oisin is clever but do ye think he extends himself? Not one bit. I cannot fault his work, ye understand Mrs Kelly. Cannot fault it at all but it's his attitude. He has the most ungodly attitude," and Baldy's tiny eyes set in his fleshy, rounded face fixed on Annie. "Aye," he continued, "I would say that is what it is. I find it most distressing, aye, it is distressing for me to see for he has a brain on him but he refuses to cooperate. 'Tis a mystery, indeed, with an elder brother whom ye would think the boy would want to follow... such a role model to follow, but no, he is wilful, aye, I'm sorry to have to say this, but that's the word... wilful and ungodly and what will become of him, I ask myself? He has the brain but the attitude, aye, he has the attitude and I'm sorry to say that I can't see any future for him unless he can get rid of the attitude and look to his elder brother. I'm sorry, indeed, to have to say this to ye, Mrs Kelly. Ye have yer worries now ye no longer have yer good husband, I know... I *know*!"

At this, Baldy's countenance took on a solemn look and he clasped his fat hands together again.

"I have known the Kellys now for many a long year," he continued and his expression changed to one of omnipotence as befitted his station in life, "And I must say to ye now, yer two boys have been no trouble at all to the school. No trouble at all. Indeed, I often tell the boys that Frankie Kelly is a fine example for them. We have had a few boys now anxious to follow in his footsteps. The Lord be praised. Aye, we have indeed, ye'll be pleased to know. And even young Declan, not academic but a fine sportsman and a good example, too... but I am sorry to say Oisin is neither a good example nor a good sportsman. It's his attitude, ye see."

He sighed once more as if the weight of Oisin Kelly on his shoulders was too much to bear and he was getting too old to concern himself with a boy with an attitude.

And Annie who was always nervous of anyone in authority was even more nervous at the thought that Oisin now had an attitude. When she tackled Oisin later and told him the story, the boy was completely indifferent and just shrugged his shoulders, dismissively.

"I despair of your brother," Annie said to Declan and to Mick she said, "Brother Lawrence says that Oisin has an attitude."

"An attitude," replied Mick, "Well, well, well... whatever next?"

Oisin, it seemed was destined to be left with an attitude. For his immediate future, it was decided that he was to leave school after the summer and help Declan on the farm. Hopefully, that experience might somehow get rid of the attitude.

*****

It was now two years since Bernard's untimely passing and the world moved on. If Bernard in death was remembered as more worthy than perhaps he had been in life, this is human rationality at work and could be forgiven. Memories of the dead are often given sweetness as time goes by and, if it were possible for the departed to return, often they would be surprised, even amused, at the sanctity they now received from the living. 'Do not speak ill of the dead' still resounds in many a human heart. Bernard's character, in the Kelly household at least, was now one of high moral strength and his virtuousness extolled, increasing as the memory of him faded.

Indeed, Annie loving Mick as she did would still not allow him into her bed. When she could, she spent nights beside him in his narrow bed only to depart at early light.

233

Guilt still dwelt in Annie's mind and although she dismissed her thoughts as irrational she could not forget Bernard's last words to her. They troubled her and would come into her mind at least expected times. She could not speak of them to anyone, least of all to Mick. She had been adulterous, she concluded and the fact that she now was free did little to assuage those feelings within. She had been disloyal then and, she fearfully decided, now. But she would look at Mick and soften and dismiss her thoughts as unwanted for no way did she wish anything to undermine her present happiness. Hers had sometimes been a struggle against insurmountable odds. It seemed totally unfair that her happiness should be spoiled by the uncompromising speck of guilt and she busied herself even more in an attempt to prevent these thoughts from surfacing. But the thought she tried to exclude refused to depart and lurked there in her mind, taunting her.

In the household though there was routine and it was perhaps that relentless routine of daily life that kept them all busy and in some way, gave to each a sense of security. There was always work to do and with Declan at the head, the work had to be done and done well. Mick was now assigned to a corner. His ill-health prevented him from managing to do a full day's manual work. He appeared to accept the change in the family circumstances without so much as a murmur and was happy enough in his vegetable garden or sitting in his chair reading or looking at Annie. He would put down his book sometimes and smile at her. This was enough for at these times, she would answer with a smile, too. Their secret was contained between their smiles and they were glad.

The daily running of the farm was thankfully left to Declan with Oisin giving unenthusiastic assistance. Oisin's mind, it seemed, was forever somewhere else and Declan was known to grumble.

"That brother of yours...?" he would mutter to Mary for at times like these, he preferred not to think of Oisin as his sibling. Mary, for her part, never took sides. All her life she had been the centre of her three brother's attentions and one word from her, she knew, would have the three of them running.

*****

The hot summer of that year gave way to autumn and on a dark November afternoon at four o'clock, a furious storm hit the town and its surroundings. Ballybeg, positioned where it was facing the Atlantic, had known many storms but this one was the worst in living memory. For Annie and for Oisin, too, this storm would later prove to be one which neither would ever be able to forget. For forty-eight hours the town was battered. Such was its power that two small fishing boats smashed against the stone walls of the Quay sending planks of wood in all directions. A surge of water, as spectacular as a tidal bore, swept up the Owenbeg and flooded both North and South Streets. The combination of the incoming tide and the heavy rain caused the water to flood, unstoppable, closer and closer to the houses and shops. There were five steps up to the Church of St Peter and St Paul and the water lapped at the door. The water would have found its way in but for the valiant efforts of Father Bryne and 'Oh Dear' who, along with two other men, managed to position hastily-filled sandbags at the door and, mercifully, stopped the flow. All along the two streets it looked possible that houses and shops would be awash but somehow the sandbags held.

It was even worse along the Promenade. Two beautiful much-admired old windows of the Railway Hotel were smashed. Water and glass mixed with dirt from the pot plants in the conservatory area as the cane tables and chairs toppled one upon the other in the small area. The owners, nervous, locked the main door to the hotel and peered out through the upstairs windows as the grey sea swells crashed onto rocks below. Further along the grassy Promenade, near the steps where Mick had had his turn all

235

those years ago, wooden benches tumbled over. Trees, bent double through the years of pounding weather, weakened, some uprooted; others had their branches snapped as effortlessly as breaking a twig would be for a child. The wind howled and people stayed indoors, fearful and captive, as Nature's fury controlled their world. Communication with the outside world ceased. Power lines came down and electric lights went out. No trains to Dublin. No buses to Galway. The place was isolated, cut off. The indomitable Ma Murphy, ever mindful of her precious conifers and their red planters, carried the six of them inside for safety. Murphy's, just a road width away from the sea, bore the brunt of the storm. Ma and Pa dismally surveyed their empty bar as they watched the sea blow spray over the road and the water sweep in sheets towards the front door. Not even the most dedicated drinker ventured out for the road was flooded and scattered with debris. For forty-eight hours, Murphy's was silent but for the sound of the wind and the rain.

At An Teach Ban, the Kellys were spared some of the storm's fury. The farmhouse was situated half a mile from the main road and sheltered in a slight valley. The force of the wind pushed Bernard's bench onto the hawthorn tree. This proved to be a barrier and it remained there. Some of the slates from the byre lifted and were found later about a hundred yards up the hill towards Slieve Geal. Mercifully, this was the only damage. But their neighbours, two miles along the road and closer to the sea, were not so fortunate. In a two-roomed cottage with a thatched roof, lived old Mother Fahy and her simple son. The old lady, now in her eighties, managed as best she could but with a son who was almost completely dependent upon her, the situation was difficult. The consequence of the combination of age and helplessness meant that the farm, once well cared for, was now run down and neglected. The Kellys and the Fahys had been neighbours for generations and, as far as anyone knew, not one word of discord had ever passed between the

236

two families. In fact, Annie was fond of the old lady and visited her regularly and for the children, too, it had always been a place to go. Old Mother Fahy, a generous and kindly woman, kept a jar of boiled sweets in the cupboard, just for the Kelly children.

It was Oisin who first thought of old Mother Fahy and her son and it was he who said he would saddle up Bess and go along. It was the third day and the wind had dropped. The rain fell as a light shower but the sun was trying its best to shine through the ever moving winter clouds. Oisin was happy to take Bess out for a ride. All the Kellys could ride. They kept five strong Connemara ponies and were considered honest as far as horse-dealing was concerned and the buying and selling of the ponies provided a handy little income for the family.

"The horse," Bernard always said philosophically, "'tis more faithful by far than the motor car and will have served mankind far, far longer, ye mark my words!"

For although he had been proud of his new motor, his love for his horse had been much greater. All his four children had their ponies and had inherited his love of them too. It had been a wonderful day for Oisin when his father had given him, Bess, his very own pony. Oisin's Bess stood thirteen hands high. She was even tempered, lively and intelligent. Bess was a sturdy, attractive little pony, now ten years old. Dark brown, with a black mane and tail, she had the most engaging white triangle between her large bright eyes. She and Oisin were the best of friends and she trusted him as you would a friend but even Bess was nervous of the road after the storm. She was unsure of her footing. She trod cautiously and hesitated before stepping over the branches and stones strewn in front of her. In some places the road was still flooded and Bess refused to advance until she heard the reassuring voice of Oisin and his gentle stroke on her neck and then she went forward, gingerly picking her way through the rushing water and debris.

They were both glad to get to the Fahy cottage or what was left of the Fahy cottage. The tough grasses used to thatch the roof had lifted and as a result the ropes which tied them down had given way. There was now a large opening in the roof exposing the cottage to the wind and the rain. As the ropes weakened and broke, the stones tied round these ropes to secure the roof, loosened and fell to the ground so now there were stones of various sizes scattered in front of the cottage. As far as Oisin could ascertain, the timber lath just above the eaves, which prevented the ropes from cutting into the grasses, had snapped and it was this that had caused the damage. Years of neglect had allowed the wind and the rain to destroy in just forty-eight hours a roof which had stood for centuries. The hole had exposed the second room, the bedroom where both the old woman and her son slept, to the elements. The two of them, it appeared, had huddled together for two days beside the range as they were unable to sleep in their beds.

The second room was awash but the kitchen, also, had not escaped the damage. Oisin had spent many hours in the kitchen of this humble dwelling. The blue and white dresser with the lines of plates was as familiar to him as the dresser at An Teach Ban. Mary and Baby Jesus looked down from the white wall above the range as they had always done but now a brown line of water ran over the faded print. Somehow, the water has got in through the gable, Oisin thought. Nothing had changed in the room in all his life except the pile of newspapers in the corner had just got higher. It was from this pile that the old woman had taken some of them and strewn them across the floor. She had placed pails in strategic places to contain some of the water but as some of these pails had holes in their sides, there appeared to be more water out than in. There she was, poor old Mother Fahy, bent over at right angles almost, trying unsuccessfully to mop up some of the water while her fifty-year-old son looked on, his arms rigid at his side, staring at his mother, uncomprehendingly. Oisin was alarmed for their safety. Something had to be done and done quickly; the pair were in danger of hypothermia. Oisin reasoned he would have to work fast and the best course of action was to get help from Declan and Mick. Mick would know what to do. Although Declan now almost ran the farm, it was Mick who had the experience.

This time Bess cantered a little more confidently back to An Teach Ban as if she, too, realized the seriousness of the situation. Oisin was right. Mick did know what to do. It was decided to take the tractor along the flooded road as it was the most practical solution. So there was quite a deputation of Kellys who set off from An Teach Ban to secure the roof of their neighbours, the Fahys. Declan drove carefully over the branches that threatened to stop progress while the others jolted around in the trailer, hanging nervously onto the sides. A light rain was falling and the whole day took on a kind of adventure. Annie and Mary had brought soup and newly baked bread for their midday meal. This, from Oisin's account, would be an all day affair. In the trailer, the men had flung ladders, ropes, strips of wood, saws, hammers, nails and a strong white waterproof tarpaulin which hopefully would cover the roof. There was a story about the tarpaulin, too, and Mick recounted it as they bounced along. His father, ever on the look out for something for nothing, had won the tarpaulin in a bet with a local fisherman. A drinking bet, no doubt, Mick said somewhat dryly but they had made good use of it over the years and once, it had been needed to cover the roof of the byre where the pigs lived. The canvas would do the job for the Fahys as there was no way their roof could be thatched before the spring. Mick was in a jovial mood and they all were in high spirits by the time they got to the Fahys. The old mother was delighted to see them.

"Why, 'tis the Kellys!" she cried, wiping her hands on her apron as she spoke. "May all the saints preserve ye. And it's young Mick there, too!"

Annie smiled. Mick was now fifty-two.

"What a time we've had," the old lady continued, "I can tell ye all, I've never been through a storm like that before. Why, I said to meself, 'This is it... St Peter better be openin' them pearly gates for sure, for we're goin' to see them', but not yet, we got through the night, thanks be to God. But the roof? Why, bless ye all," she said when she saw what was in the trailer, "ye're goin' to fix me roof! And Mick, it just seems like yesteryear, ye were up there with me old man, God rest him."

She watched with a grateful look as the ladders were placed at either end of the roof. Mick climbed up to inspect the damage. The hole was about two feet across. Sods of dirt had been packed in under the grasses and they had fallen into the room below but the hole could be patched and the roof made watertight. As Mick balanced at the top of the ladder, he started to cough and had to hold on tight for a few moments until he regained his strength.

"We'll have it fixed in no time, Mother," he said to the old lady when he was safely on the ground again. "I'll get these two young bucks to do the climbin'."

And with that, work started. The most critical thing was to ensure that the ropes held tight and the stones heavy enough not to come adrift again. There would be more bad weather before the spring. Everyone lent a hand to get the heavy tarpaulin over the roof. This proved difficult and Declan and Oisin had to climb to the apex of the roof to hold it down. They looked like two monkeys clinging to a tree while below, everyone else, including the simple son, took hold of corners of the flapping tarpaulin. Finally, the ropes were repositioned with their stones to tie them down. Declan and Oisin nailed the strips of wood horizontally across the roof to prevent the ropes from moving. It had been a long morning and the soup warming on the range was welcome indeed.

Old Mother Fahy kept blessing them and blessing herself as she spoke. She kept her best blessings for Mick.

"Ye know, Annie," she said as she shuffled around her kitchen getting plates down from the blue and white dresser, "they all talk about that Mick Kelly in Ballybeg. Some say he's mad. Some say he's a drunk... but I say... all the men have to have a drink. Why, my old man went every Friday night to the sheebeen... it's Murphy's now... well, I know they can have too much an' that's the harm for the wife and the wee ones but Mick, well, I've never listened to all that about him. And there's been a lot said by them that should know better, sittin' in the church every Sunday. That's people! But Mick, well, he's helped us always. Just because he doesn't go along with them all, what's that to them?"

She set a crazed white soup plate onto the table and then moved slowly back to look for another one.

"Mick looked after them all after his mother passed away, God rest her, and it wasn't easy. Yer Bernard... bless him and may he rest in peace... was only a wee lad, so. Yer a good woman, too, Annie, an' bless ye for the soup. My boy loves his soup. Here, Mary, will ye get that plate down for me, bless ye, child? Now, let's get them men in for their soup and I can tell ye, all the saints be praised, I'll be sleepin' like one of them tonight, thanks to ye all...!"

It had been a successful day for the Kellys and the Fahys and boiled sweets were offered at the end of the meal. It would have been impolite to refuse. Now the rain was heavier. Oisin noticed the brown water line no longer dripped over Jesus and Mary onto the blue mantelpiece above the range. He was pleased. Old Mother Fahy would not want Jesus and Mary to be ruined. They had, after all, sat there for as long as anyone could remember. It was dry in the bedroom too and everyone was satisfied with their day's work. All being well, the tarpaulin would hold till the spring when the roof could be re-thatched. Mick would see to that.

He started to cough again when he climbed into the trailer. He pulled his collar up around his ears and hunched

241

into a corner away from them all as the cold rain washed their faces. Everyone was glad to get home to An Teach Ban and the warmth that was there. During the night, it seemed that Mick's cough would never end. Annie spent the night beside him. She slept fitfully in a chair and woke to find he was coughing blood. It was distressing to see him.

"You shouldn't have gone to the Fahys," she said, angrily. She was alarmed. "Oisin had no right to ask you to go."

"Ah, Annie," Mick said between wheezes, "ye couldn't see poor old Mother Fahy without a roof over her head, could ye now? Who else has she got?"

He laid his head back onto the pillow, weakened, exhausted with the effort of coughing. He took the black eye patch from his eye exposing the scars. The eye patch annoyed him, it seemed. His face was wet with sweat but he shivered and asked for another blanket.

"We'll have to send for Doctor Flannery," Annie said to him for the fear was in her heart.

"I'll not go to the hospital. Not this time. No Assumpta and no priest."

Annie put her cool hand onto his forehead. It was wet and clammy. Mick closed his eyes, grateful to shut them.

"I'll have to ring for Doctor Flannery," Annie said to Declan. "He's coughing up blood... he's got a fever..."

She wrung her hands together. Distracted, she walked backwards and forwards.

"He should never have gone to the Fahys. Oisin, you shouldn't have allowed it." She wanted someone to blame.

Mick's coughing brought her back to his side.

"I've sent for the doctor," she said and held his hand. It was cold and she tried to warm it with both her hands. She looked at him and was afraid for she loved him more than she could ever have believed possible. Mick opened his good eye and the lid of his damaged eye flickered uneasily.

"Annie... Annie, *mo chailín*... no priests. No priests. Promise me, Annie. No priests... not even yer good man."

242

He was intent. He meant her to obey him. She started to protest but he fixed her with a look from his good eye which made any argument futile and she nodded.

Mick smiled but then he had to cough again. This time a trickle of blood and saliva oozed from the side of his mouth onto the pillow. Annie wiped his mouth with her handkerchief. Suddenly, Mick started up. He wanted to speak.

"Tell Oisin. I must see that warrior. That poet," and he smiled again but the effort of speaking exhausted him. He shut his eyes and didn't open them again until the doctor came.

"He says he won't go to the hospital," Annie said to the doctor. "He won't be reasoned with."

"It's pneumonia," said Doctor Flannery as he closed his bag. "With complications."

"Will he be alright?" asked Declan. The whole family were frightened.

The doctor, who could be quite brusque, answered briefly. He had seen enough. But he had years of training and had been taught to reassure.

"We'll have to monitor him closely. The next twenty-four hours are critical."

He looked at Annie. This was not her husband but her whole manner suggested otherwise. He had seen a lot of life and Doctor Ryan had filled in the gaps. He had heard a lot about Mick Kelly and could only surmise.

"I'll call back after my rounds," he said. "Then we'll make a decision whether to move him."

"He won't go. He's stubborn."

"Aye. So I've heard."

They heard Mick cough again.

"Keep him warm. If he asks for food, give him broth. Make sure he has plenty of liquid." And the doctor left, his job done.

Annie was exhausted. She had hardly slept through the night. She lay on her own bed and pulled the blanket round her ears so she couldn't hear Mick cough. Somehow, she knew she must sleep a little even if it was the afternoon. They would wake her if Mick got worse but she must rest for he would need her in the night. She woke a few hours later to Mary's anxious voice.

"It's the doctor again... back from his rounds. He's in with Mick now. You've been asleep for two hours."

"Is he any better?"

"He's coughed all the time you've been asleep. Hear him now?"

Annie could hear the painful cough and the voice of the doctor.

"I've made you a cup of tea," said Mary, kindly. "But Mick won't take anything."

"Thank you. We'd better offer the doctor a cup too."

But Doctor Flannery would not have tea.

"There's no change," he said to Annie. "Ring me tonight if he gets worse, won't you?" He looked at her worried face. "Try not to worry," was all he said.

Annie once again sat by Mick's bedside. There was a kind of nobility about her being with him. She tried to get him to drink and he obediently took a sip of water but the effort of raising himself from the pillow, weakened him. He had climbed the ladder at Fahys and carried stones and look at him now, thought Annie. It didn't seem possible. The whole time since leaving the Fahys and now was a lifetime. Surely a whole lifetime was contained in twenty-four hours. With the tenderness of love, Annie wiped Mick's brow once more. His dear face, still moist, grey and cold, turned towards her. A little saliva mixed with blood dribbled from his mouth and Annie took his hand in both of hers but his hand was so cold... icy cold. She would stay with him till dawn. She settled herself once more in a chair beside his bed and pulled a blanket over her body to keep herself warm. Outside, the wind picked up again and she could hear the rain beating against the window pane. She closed her eyes and tried to get some sleep.

She woke at precisely two minutes to three in the morning to the sound of the wheezing and the coughing. Mick was awake.

"Annie."

She took hold of his hand.

"Annie."

She turned on the bedside light. He face glowed in the half dark.

"Annie," he said again and this time he raised himself slightly so he could see her. He reached out to stroke her hair, gently, the way he had done these last few months, these last few months of love.

"I have to tell ye," he said. "Aye. I owe it to ye, my dear girl, for ye have always been my dear girl, right from the start... Oisin must take the key."

She didn't know what he was talking about. Maybe he's delirious, she thought with alarm but there was determination within him and he wanted to continue. She had to put her ear closer to his mouth to catch the words. He wheezed and it was hard to hear.

"Annie... I must tell ye... I have a daughter. A beautiful colleen... I can't keep it from ye any longer, it's not fair to ye... for the truth has to be told. Ye must tell Oisin... please Annie, promise me. He has to meet my beautiful daughter. Tell her that I'm gone but I loved her. I've always loved my girl... my Concetta."

Annie gasped. Her breath came in sort bursts. She panted like a dog that had run too fast, too long. Mick smiled and closed his eyes.

"My Concetta... Concetta Luchetta."

CHAPTER TWELVE

Through that long night, Annie sat, her blue and grey tartan travelling rug clutched tightly around her for she felt the cold light of morning and she shivered. The bedside light remained on and in its muted glow she could see Mick's face turned towards her. He coughed and she reached out her hand only to withdraw it. He was weakened, she knew, and every cough that came out of him echoed within her for she loved him still. In her mind she heard the name, 'Concetta Luchetta', over and over again. That name belonged to a person and that person belonged to Mick... her Mick. He loved this person for he had smiled such a tender smile and she had never seen such a look on his face before. Mick was thinking of Concetta, loving her, as he grew weaker and weaker and it was in his weakened state that he had confessed. Numbed with the knowledge of his secret, Annie sat, huddled in her chair, safe there but still she could not speak. Mick stirred and opened his eyes.

"Annie," he whispered.

But she did not answer nor move. She wanted to be cold. So cold. She wanted to hurt him for he had a daughter – an unknown beautiful daughter he loved whose name was Luchetta and Silvio leapt in front of her for the first time. Annie shut her eyes. Tight.

"Annie," Mick said again and he coughed. This time he was unable to move his head from the pillow but still Annie sat.

"I have hurt ye, my dear."

Still she wouldn't answer but she opened her eyes. When she saw his face turned towards her and, in the grey light of dawn, she could see the pain there in his eyes. She nodded her head for she was frightened of what she might say in anger and later regret.

"I want ye to let me talk to Oisin," he said, "for it's that warrior who must venture forth to conquer the world... the world I didn't do much good in... but he will be better than any of us, praise be, for ye have a great son there, Annie..."

The effort of speaking weakened him and he was silent once again.

"Why did you wait so long to tell me about your daughter? Why? I loved you... didn't you know? I *loved* you!"

"Ah, Annie..."

He reached out to hold her hand. His hand was cold. The life was leaving him. Now she couldn't be angry anymore and she clasped her small hand into his. She so wanted him to talk about Concetta, about a life she didn't know, but in her heart of hearts, she knew it was too late. Too late.

"Oisin will tell ye, my dear girl. It's left to him but ye must let me speak to him... I'm finished... I know."

"You shouldn't have gone to the Fahy's. You shouldn't have climbed up that ladder...you stupid man," and she managed a smile through her tears.

"That's my Annie," and he squeezed her hand so, so gently. "What a pair we are, ye and I... what a damn fool pair..."

*****

That evening Annie called a family conference. They sat around the kitchen table and relaxed in the warmth of the fire but the sadness was in all their minds. Doctor Flannery had called that afternoon.

"We won't move him," he said, "There's no point in distressing him. Just keep him comfortable. I'll call again tomorrow and bring Doctor Ryan."

And he shook his head. Although Doctor Ryan was now retired he would want to see Mick.

"We'll have to fetch Frankie." Annie said as they sat there and from the bedroom they heard the coughing. "Frankie must know what's happened."

But Frankie did not want to know. He was already establishing himself as a curate in a Parish south of Dublin

247

and didn't want to be reminded of his Uncle Mick, his strange Uncle Mick who was lying at death's door in the West. No, he wasn't sure if he ever wanted to see him again. He felt he had said goodbye to his uncle that day in the vegetable garden and even though he had seen Mick since, the farewell had been said then. That was the end of it. There were more deserving cases where he was and his sights were already set on England. So he made an excuse and just said, "I'll come if I can. Tell him I'll come if I can."

"Ah, Annie," said Mick when she relayed the news, "what did I tell ye about that lad? It'll always be Frankie... now ye know."

He shook his fist slightly. "No priests. Annie. No priests."

Annie, alarmed at his intransigence, shook her head as if to shake the thought away and wondered what she was going to say to Father Byrne for surely he would want to call. All of Ballybeg must know by now that Mick Kelly was dying and she bit her lip.

It was nearly two weeks since Mick's collapse. Doctor Flannery came every day and once he brought Doctor Ryan.

"Well, Mick," said Doctor Ryan, "what have you been doing to yourself?"

"Ah... it's the good Doctor Ryan himself, so it is. I've no breath left in me but I'm at peace with ye now... and yer good wife."

"Ah, Mick," sighed the good doctor, "did any of us ever try to follow you, man?"

At his words, the eyes of Mick Kelly looked directly at him.

"Ye did yer best," said Mick, "a grand job ye did on me eye all those years ago. Look how it's healed."

Ever since his collapse he had refused to put on his black eye patch. He was stubborn.

248

"I'll see ye all from both me eyes from now on," he had said and no one dared argue for no one ever did, when Mick had that look.

"Aye," answered Doctor Ryan gently, "It healed right enough."

The old doctor sighed as he looked at the grey face below him.

"You're at peace now, Mick Kelly. I can see that in both your eyes."

Mick smiled.

"Aye. That I am... that I am."

*****

He insisted on seeing Oisin alone but Annie kept making excuses. She feared what he would say so she made sure that Oisin was always with someone else when he looked in on Mick. But Mick grew more and more agitated which brought on painful coughing spells. Finally she had to agree but she still kept putting it off. Oisin was now eighteen and kept his thoughts to himself. Annie worried that Mick would tell him about Concetta or perhaps even worse, about herself and if Oisin was to discover the secrets. She grew anxious and a tiny frown settled onto her forehead as she thought on these matters, but Mick was insistent. She needn't have worried, for afterwards Oisin just said:

"He kept on about a key. He wants me to have a key and he's told me where it is. I'm to get it after he's gone. I had to repeat it to him... to tell him I knew where it was. I had to say it three times and then he seemed satisfied. I don't know what he's on about... just some old key!"

*****

Annie was right. The people of Ballybeg were aware of the decline of Mick Kelly and it was now that those same people exacted a kind of brief revenge on the one they had done their best to malign. It had been more expedient to pin judgmental labels onto the unfortunate Kelly brother for he was a man few could understand and even fewer

249

could befriend. Unsure always of both his manner and his words, now they could withdraw from any enquiries about his failing health and this, to the majority, was the day of reckoning for Mick. He had never fitted into the various compartments that a man of his background should have done. His intelligence was evident to all but that intelligence could manifest itself into irrationality. That was the accepted view. His refusal to attend church or to have anything to do with the life of the community fuelled speculation about his mental condition. Sympathy was reserved for Annie, even if she was an Englishwoman and a stranger in their midst. After all, she had produced four children and wasn't her Frankie, now almost a priest, a fine young man and a credit to her and Bernard, God rest him and Declan, too, his father's son and a farmer through and through. Of Oisin and Mary, little was said. Neither two had made any impact on the people of Ballybeg. It was unfortunate for the young ones that they were now fatherless but at least with two fine elder brothers, they would be provided for should the need arise. It was a comforting thought that provision would be both spiritual and temporal – and the family would soon be released from the shadow of an unstable uncle. They kept away from An Teach Ban and only Tommy Flynn and Hugh O'Connor, Mick's faithful friends, showed any concern. They came, the two of them, on separate occasions and both went away shaking their heads. Old Mother Fahy surprised them all. She caught the bus along the road and climbed the half mile to the Kelly farmhouse. Bent almost double, using two sticks for support and with her handbag slung around her neck, she fought the bitter November wind and rain to see Mick.

"Bless him," she murmured sadly, "and to think a few weeks ago he was fixin' me roof, thinkin' of me and me boy... an' look at the poor soul now. Tell him, I'll pray for him, for Mick Kelly is one deserverin' of a prayer, so."

She blew her nose on her crumpled handkerchief and thanked Annie for the tea. Sometimes it is the most unlikely of people who show themselves true at times of another's need.

Given the seriousness of Mick's condition, it was inevitable that Father Byrne would make contact. He did...by telephone and Annie answered the call.

"Will Mick be needin' to see me, Annie?" he asked.

Annie's heart beat faster. She remembered her promise to Mick and she hesitated before replying.

"I... I think he's quite comfortable now, Father," she said, stumbling a little over her words, "but Doctor Flannery has given him morphine for the pain so... he's... well, a little confused sometimes but..."

"I could come out though, Annie... there might be something he needs."

"Ah..." Annie bit her lip as she always did when she was nervous, "I think he's getting better though, Father."

She lied and her heart beat faster.

"Well now, that's great news, to be sure. Now, Annie, ye keep well yourself, won't ye? And ye know where I am."

Annie put the phone down and thought: I've lied to a priest. What am I to do?

But she stayed every night with Mick. She huddled into her chair beside his bed and watched over him as each day and night, he grew weaker. The morphine made him drowsy and sometimes he would try to sit up and once he called out her name. He grew confused and agitated at times. Other times, the constant coughing exhausted him.

"Ah, Annie *mo chailín*," he would whisper to her when he was able to stop, "it's a wonder yer still here."

They would hold hands until his lids grew heavy once more and he fell asleep. There are many forms of love but surely as Annie Kelly remained faithful at her lover's bedside, this was one of the purest kinds, made purer perhaps because no one ever knew.

*****

251

Day by day Mick grew weaker, but on the eighth day he seemed to rally and asked Annie for something to eat. He had barely eaten for all that time. Annie, joyful, fed him bacon and vegetable broth and Mick was able to sip the liquid slowly only to sink back onto his pillow, exhausted. There was hope in Annie's heart and she thought to herself, maybe I haven't lied to a priest. Maybe, just maybe, he will get better and everyone, including the doctors, will be proved wrong. With that thought in her mind, she decided not to sit beside him all night but would try to get some sleep in her own bed. She would be stronger in the morning for this rest, she concluded happily.

"Goodnight, my love," she whispered to him and kissed him gently on his forehead. It felt normal. He opened both his eyes and smiled at her only to lower his lids immediately. He coughed less and the fever had gone but he was so, so weak and there was no strength left in him. He had been a strong man just a little while ago. He was aware that Annie was still beside him and he opened his eyes and took hold of her hand.

"Ah, Annie," he murmured, "What a woman ye are! What a brave wee woman, indeed!"

"Have a good sleep, love. I'll just be across the hall. God bless you, Mick Kelly... and what a man you are!"

And with those words, Annie crept away to fall into a deep sleep and didn't wake until the morning.

From the kitchen she heard voices and the radio and the comforting sounds of the morning. She dressed quickly and her first thought was of Mick. She peeped in at him from the doorway. He lay on his back with the patchwork quilt drawn up to his chin. On the wall above his head the straw cross of Saint Brighaid kept watch. Although he had renounced the church, the symbols remained, thought Annie, and she was glad for Saint Brighaid watching over him, keeping him safe.

"I'll be in to see you soon," she called softly from the doorway.

Mick was asleep and she would have all day to be with him. Doctor Flannery and Sister Assumpta were due to call late morning. Time to give him a wash and something to eat; they'll be surprised at the change in him, she thought happily and concluded somewhat smugly that doctors could be wrong. Her thoughts took wind on the cold November day as her mind dwelt on how best to care for Mick.

There was porridge warming on the range and tea in the pot. Annie was in no hurry to see Mick. She didn't want to wake him until she could spend time with him so she slowly enjoyed her breakfast. Mary was in the room, getting ready for school and mother and daughter chatted away, contently. Outside the day was cold but the sky was a pale winter blue and a white frost lay on the ground. Maybe Mick will be able to sit up and look out, thought Annie happily, for it was a grand day in the West of Ireland and the perfect place to be. Surely Heaven is something like this.

"On days like this, it's wonderful to be alive," proclaimed Annie cheerfully as she tidied up.

"I just love the cold, crisp days of winter," she added for today she felt on top of the world. The years of toil swept away, she thought, and now there's a future with Mick, and Annie wanted to break into song, the way she always did when she was at peace with herself. She prepared a plate of porridge for Mick and carefully placed it on the tray along with a cup of tea and a glass of water. He has to have liquid, she insisted on that, that's what Doctor Flannery had said. Wonder what the doctor will say when he sees him today? She mused for she had such a good sleep she felt certain Mick must have had the same.

Mindful not to suddenly awaken Mick and thus cause him undue anxiety, Annie crept quietly into his darkened room. She placed the tray with the plate of porridge onto his bedside table. Still he did not stir but lay on his back as before. She cautiously opened the curtains and the shaft of light, shadow and light, lightened the room. Mick's room faced the west and Annie, looking out, noted with a feeling of well-being that the sky was still clear. The rays of the morning sun rising from the back of Slieve Geal shone onto the grey silhouette of St Peter and St Paul's so enhancing the spire that it seemed closer than it really was. Even the grey slates on the rooftops of Ballybeg shimmered against the blue of sea and sky and contrasted dramatically with the white frost on the ground. All around the bare black branches of the various trees further added to the still, silent beauty of the clear morning. As Annie gazed onto the beauty of the day there rose within her soul thankfulness for her life and for the day and for Mick. Without a doubt, the view from the window was sublime, dazzling even in its magnificence and Annie was humbled. Under her breath she whispered a silent prayer of gratitude and made the sign of the Cross over herself before she turned towards Mick to wake him but still he did not move.

"Mick... wake up... it's morning... and it's the most beautiful glorious day you could ever imagine. Cold though... but not a cloud in the sky... we'll try to get you up today..." she spoke as a mother would to a small child and all the time she nudged him to open his eyes. Her mind, focused on waking him, could not understand why he did not move. Her body and her mind existed on two levels. One level was trying to rouse him and the other deeper level began to wonder why he did not stir, why he did not open his eyes to greet her, why he did not smile, why that hand, lying so peacefully would not reach out to hold hers... why he did not speak? The light from outside extended further into the room and shone onto his face so that Annie could see his features more clearly. He was so still and quiet, he appeared contained within his quietness and encased in a peacefulness she had never seen before. Now the deeper level of her mind thrust up from the inner part of her being and her heart beat faster. She shook him again and this time with an urgency as her mind began to focus on the physical appearance before her. His right hand stretched across the top of the patchwork quilt and Annie touched it but still there was no movement. Thin black hairs – white skin – clean nails, Annie photographed his hand in her mind. She gripped his hand. It was cold.

"Wake up, Mick! Wake up! Why don't you wake? Speak to me! Oh, please God, speak to me!"

But Mick made no movement. She struggled to find his pulse but there was none. Again the upper level of her thinking tried to reassure but deeper down, the lower level knew it was of no use. She cried out. Sound came from her lips but faraway and not connected to her. Mick and the room and the day lay before her. She thrust her body over his chest and held him to her. She kissed him... on his cheeks, his forehead, his mouth, his chest. Her kisses travelled over his body. If she could kiss him, she might wake him for surely he was only in a deep sleep and her kisses grew more and more frantic as her panic increased. Finally, she had to stop but she continued to lie over his body for she could not move. The sun rose higher in the sky but still she stayed, holding him. The porridge grew cold in the bowl. She did not know how long she held him. Apart from that one cry, she could not weep. Her heart beat against her lover's chest but she felt no answering beat. She could not let him go.

Oisin stood at the doorway for he was in from his work and ready for his morning break. He saw the intimacy of his mother's posture and felt the silence of the room. Expressionless, he turned his head away for he was intruding and he did not want to know nor did he want to see or be burdened by the sight before his eyes. With a dignity that Mick always said he had, he quietly left the room, closing the door gently behind him. He walked outside into the cool winter air and stood at the gate that separated house from outbuildings. Here he rested his left hand on to the rusty ironwork. All about the scene was tranquil, calm with the beauty of the cold sunlit day but within Oisin emotions welled as turbulent as he had ever felt before. They swept over his body seeming to start at the top of his head and flood through him in waves to finally reach the ground. He remained rigid but later when he examined the palm of his left hand, lines of brown crossed over it in a dark line against the white skin.

*****

And so there came the time to bury Mick Kelly in the stony ground of Ballybeg. There came a time to mourn and a time to wonder once more upon the imponderables of life for Mick Kelly's life had seen to be one of differing extremes, of higher peaks and lower depths. In Ballybeg his lows were intensified for few ever saw his highs. The lows were visible. The highs, unseen by few but one person glimpsed them, and that was Annie for, she too, had known some of his joys. Mick Kelly found beauty in an unseen world. After all, many a soul cannot fit into the pre-conditioned spot and our lives are often very different from what others expect of us at our birth. Whatever Mick had suffered in his life, it was Annie, and she alone, who knew that in death, he triumphed. In the manner of his dying, he had found his peace, she was certain of that and it was this conviction which was to sustain her until the end of her days. Mercifully, it also enabled her to cope with the days following his death. She kept the image of him uppermost in her mind but hid the intimacy and love she had felt for him. This she did by casually not talking of Mick or deftly changing the subject. Others must not be allowed to judge or worse, realise that she and Mick were more than just relatives by marriage. So she distanced herself as much as she could from funeral arrangements so not to arouse suspicion. Only Oisin knew otherwise but he kept silent, unsure how to use his newly acquired knowledge as he observed his mother's clumsy attempts at camouflage.

And how she worried... she worried about burying Mick for his words echoed in her mind over and over. Even when she tried to sleep at night, the words bore into her and she tossed and turned, willing them to go. But they remained resolute: "No priests. No priests." He had gripped her hand when he spoke and his eyes had lit up with intensity as he repeated: "No priests. No priests."

For he had been adamant that he wanted to lie at An Teach Ban, away from his Kelly ancestors, away from mother, father, brother and all the Kellys who had gone before. He had not wanted to lie in the family plot. He had wished to be separate from the family as he had perceived himself to be in life.

"In my vegetable garden, Annie," he pleaded and she had weakly nodded her head in agreement, for what else could she say when his eyes were so intense?

And now, how could she convince the priests? Stumbling over her words, she tried to hint to Frankie. Maybe he would understand. He had arrived back the next day after he heard the news and was already taking control. But he was aghast at his mother's words.

"What are you saying, Mother? What are you thinking of now? We will make the arrangements, Father Byrne and I."

He now considered himself closer to God than those around him and as such, it was his duty to go about things the right way. The right way was certainly not to allow Mad Mick to lie in unholy ground and, most decidedly, the vegetable garden was unholy!

"You know Mick wasn't right in the head most times, Mother," he continued, "we all knew this and I'm surprised that you even mentioned it. Of course, he can't be buried in his vegetable garden... I've never in all my days heard such nonsense. What would people think? It's been enough for all of us to live with Mick's behaviour in life... he's not going to cause our family embarrassment in death... to say nothing of his eternal soul, God rest him. No, Mick has to have a proper burial whatever... there's a place beside my father for him and I'll hear no more arguments about it... enough of this nonsense! Well, he thought he could be apart from the church and go his own ways, wilfully and not suffer the consequences, this will bring him home and God will judge him for his intransigence. He will rest beside my father, in the Kelly plot and that's the end of it!"

Frankie's face set hard with the same determined look, it seemed, as had been observed so many times on Mick's. Frankie found the whole idea preposterous and wondered what had got into his mother to entertain such a thought? Surely Mick was not capable of deciding at the end? Doctor Flannery had said as much. But to his amazement, his mother persisted in her argument.

"But he wanted it... he said to me... over and over again... that's what he wanted... he seemed so set on it. Shouldn't we respect his last wishes... for he was clear on so many things, even at the end?" She finished weakly.

"I don't know how you can even talk like this, Mother? He had no right to burden you with such a notion. After all," he concluded somewhat loftily, "you weren't his wife, were you?"

Annie reddened. She turned her head away so Frankie could not see but she needn't have bothered because he was already discussing practical arrangements for his uncle's funeral.

"I will," he insisted, "of course be in charge. Father Byrne will say the Mass but I will take control of all the arrangements so you needn't worry about anything. It's all taken care of. The sooner we lay Uncle Mick to rest, the better for all of us, wouldn't you agree, Mother?"

Annie nodded her head weakly but still she heard Mick's voice in her ear, clearly and doggedly, "No priests. No priests."

Oh, Mick, she thought fearfully, I've let you down. But what would you have me do? Isn't it better you have the church for I couldn't bear to think of you as a lost soul? Forgive me? Can you ever forgive me?

So it was thanks to Frankie's undoubted organisational skills that the funeral of Mick Kelly went off without a

258

hitch. There were fewer mourners than usual but he was laid to rest beside his brother, Bernard in the cold earth of the Ballybeg Cemetery. Annie wore her black felt hat with a black veil. She stitched the veil onto the hat and covered her face with it. This, she thought, kept her eyes hidden so no one could see her tears.

*****

Two days later, Annie sat beside Mick's black leather reading chair and the sorrow of his not being there weighed heavily upon her. Outwardly, she appeared calm but in her silent moments, she feared that uncontrollable emotions would pour out of her and dismay those around her. If I could just weep, she thought – if I could just weep. But her tears refused to come. She gazed at his chair and thought no-one shall sit there. It remained where it had always been, beside the range, an empty space without its occupant, a gap there in the silent room. The chair without Mick was a lonely hole. She sighed. Life must go on. No one must know, least of all Frankie.

"Keep the door to Mick's room closed," he had admonished his mother. "I'll be back in two weeks to clear his things. Don't fuss yourself."

It appeared to all that Frankie had his mother's best interests in mind and she sighed. She should be grateful. He was a fine boy but how he went on and on sometimes. But what use was there to argue with him? And the image of Annie as that old shoe came into her mind once more. She sat in the silence of her kitchen where her life was, where her life had been for so long, but her eyes remained fixed on the black leather chair and in her mind she saw Mick, reading. He looked up and smiled. Strange feelings swept like a wave through Annie. He *is* really there, she thought. This is not a foolish notion. Of course, Frankie would dismiss this as nonsense but it's real, she thought.

"I know what I'll do for you, Mick, " she said out aloud, "I'll make a little place in your vegetable garden, beside the wall, and I'll plant your favourite flowers there in the spring and it will be our place, too, and no one will ever know, but us two. This way you'll be with me always. Don't you worry, you'll be in your vegetable garden watching things grow... and in your chair, too... and in my bed at night..."

With that Annie giggled. If people could hear me, she thought, they would think I'm talking a lot of rubbish but little do they know, she concluded defiantly. Yes, she thought, I'll plant some red roses there in the spring and get Declan to bring a garden bench to sit beside the wall, so I can talk to you at those times when I miss you the most. I'll not look for you at your grave because you didn't want to be there and after all, Bernard's there. No, you wanted to be in your vegetable garden and that's where you'll be! "Truly Mick," she murmured to herself, "I really did... do... love you. Always."

With a lift of her head, the old Annie reappeared. She placed her hand tenderly onto Mick's old chair and as she did, a tiny salty tear ran down her cheek and plopped onto the arm. She wiped the tear away with her hand for at that very moment she heard the noise of a car and the barking of dogs.

Outside, pandemonium raged. Surprised, she watched as the Reverend and Mrs Williamson tried to climb out of their navy blue Morris Minor and shouted to the dogs to be quiet. Sophocles and Aristotle leapt backwards and forwards in the confined space. Somehow, Sophocles managed to get himself pinned onto the driver's seat. All the time, Aristotle barked furiously from the rear, his saliva quickly covering the windows. Around them the two farm collies circled, hackles raised and barking at a higher pitch. They both leapt at the car, hitting it with some force as, inside, the two wolfhounds grew more and more agitated. Leslie and Effie tried without success to restore calm while the collies, it seemed, were determined to expel the captive interlopers. It was a kind of canine mayhem. Many minutes later, the barking ceased and the collies trotted off, tails in the air, pleased that the two wolfhounds had not been allowed to intrude. Sophocles and Aristotle, defeated, lay back down onto the car seats and shut their eyes.

"They wanted to come," explained Effie while Leslie raised his eyes to the heavens and cried, "Peace at last!"

Effie wore a waxed brown coat which trailed onto the ground. Her bright orange woollen scarf twirled around her neck and she contrasted rather dramatically to her rather drab husband, clothed as he was in his clerical collar and tweed jacket.

Leslie bobbed up and down and shook Annie's hand with unexpected vigour.

"We've only just heard," he said, not letting her hand go.

"We've been away... we always go to Edinburgh this time of the year... before Christmas... we've missed a great storm, I've heard..." and Effie tried to grab Annie's hand too which was rather difficult because she was clutching a large box under her arm.

"We only just heard," she repeated her husband's words. "We happened to bump into Father Byrne yesterday..."

"In the street," emphasized Leslie.

"Yes... in the street."

"We had to come and see you, Mrs Kelly... may we come in? We're sorry to call without notice but we had to come, post haste, didn't we Effie?"

"It *is* important," said Effie.

"Yes. Yes. As my wife says, it's very important."

Annie knew the Protestant minister and his wife by sight that was all. Never had she seen either of them close-up nor spoken to them. They were part of Ballybeg but she viewed them in much the same way as everyone else... a bit dotty, but no harm to anyone. With this thought in mind, she ushered them into the kitchen of An Teach Ban and asked would they like a cup of tea? That would be nice, said Leslie and sat down at the table, looking very much at home. Effie positioned her large frame onto a chair beside him and placed the wooden box on the table.

"So this is Mick's house," she said to her husband.

Puzzled, Annie turned around to look at Effie.

"Did you know Mick?" she asked.

"Oh... did we know Mick!" exclaimed Leslie and both he and Effie laughed. "Mick Kelly, the most misunderstood man in the whole of the West of Ireland!"

"What do you mean?"

"Oh, my dear Mrs Kelly, Mick was a most interesting man. We're sorry to think he's gone. To a better place, of course... and at peace at last. He found little peace while he was here. Except..." Leslie paused as if to emphasize his next words and they took on the tone of one of his sermons, "except... in the last year... we thought, he had found some peace, didn't we, Effie?"

"Yes, we did. We did indeed. He was a lot happier, wasn't he, dear? He was such a clever man, Mrs Kelly. Such a clever man."

"You are right there, my dear. A clever man but alas...," and Leslie sighed. He ran his thin fingers through his long grey beard. "It is often the cleverest amongst us who suffer the most and poor Mick was one of those. But I hear he didn't suffer too much at the end... or so we heard?"

"We've been away, you see or we would have come. We certainly would have gone to his funeral, wouldn't we, Leslie?"

"Yes. Yes. Of course. But we must explain to you why we are here now."

He tapped his index finger on the top of the box.

"There's a genie in here," he said. "This is Mick's box, Mrs Kelly. That's why we've brought it to you... for he wanted you to have it once he was gone. He always told us that didn't he, Effie? 'Take it to Annie, he would say'."

"That's right. You see, he kept the box at the Manse for safe keeping, he said. That's right, isn't it, Leslie? We do not know the contents. It has no key."

262

"Locked," said Leslie.

And the three of them looked at the box. It was the most unusual of boxes and Annie had never seen anything quite like it before. The first feature she noticed was the structure. With a domed lid and brass hinges covered with highly polished ebony marquetry, the large box could have found its way to the auction room of a famous antique dealer, so curious was its appearance. Fine lines of stringers made of white holly inlay were set perfectly around the top and sides and they contrasted elegantly against the black, but the most beautiful feature of all was reserved for the top. Over the shape of the dome a stylised design of a dragon made with mother-of-pearl, iridescent against the black shine of the ebony, was beautiful in its simplicity. The box stood on four tiny solid ebony legs and, as Annie examined them closer, she realised that the same stylised dragons had been carved into the wood. These dragons had to be Chinese, she thought.

"It's absolutely beautiful," she said, and she ran her hand over the smooth top and along the slight ridges of the mother-of-pearl dragon to rest for a second at the key hole, surrounded by brass, at the side. A tiny fragment of wood had come adrift near the key hole but this was the only blemish and somehow added to the beauty of the box. This was an old box, lovingly cared for and mysterious in its origins.

"We've never seen it open," sighed Effie, in her theatrical way. "We've kept it safe for Mick... all those years... on the top of the bookcase in the living room," she added as if this added authenticity to the whole story.

"It is quite definitely Chinese," said the Reverend, "although, alas, I am not an authority on things Oriental. My learning is quite decidedly with the Ancient Greeks... but my persuasion has always been to beauty, be it scenes or sunsets or things made by the human hand. I would agree this is a box of beauty... but its origins, I know not. Mick was a complex man and he never spoke as to his

263

manner of acquiring such a precious object. More's the pity, for we are curious creatures, aren't we, Effie?"

Effie nodded. She would have liked to see inside the box. Its mystery and its contents conjured up secrets in her head. It had sat on the top shelf of the bookcase for nearly fifteen years. Sometimes Mick would ask for it to be taken down and he would hold it on his knee while he drank his tea. Occasionally, he took it with him only to return it a few days later, or weeks sometimes. Once she remembered that Mick had taken the box away for a whole month only to bring it back with a few curt words which offered no explanation. And the box, gleaming and mysterious, was restored to the spot from whence it came to sit comfortably once again beside the dusty leather bound volumes of *The Rise and Fall of the Roman Empire*.

Leslie continued, tapping his fingers once again on the box lid:

"Mick was insistent that you should have it, Mrs Kelly. In fact, the last time we saw him... just a week before we went to Edinburgh, wasn't it Effie? He seemed even more emphatic. One only has to wonder that he perhaps knew his time had come. Wasn't a well man, you know. But it was to go to you. He was quite definite about it... but where he kept the key to unlock its mysteries, one does not know. The box, its contents and its origins, full of mystery... a Pandora's box indeed, my dear," and he shrugged his thin shoulders and gave Annie a half smile, barely discernible behind his bushy grey moustache and beard.

"Where have you laid the dear man to rest?" he asked suddenly and unexpectedly.

Annie paused.

"Next to my husband," she replied puzzled, "in the Kelly plot... but why do you ask?"

"Nothing to worry about, my dear," said Leslie and at that, he rose from his chair and waved his hands in the air, "but Mick wasn't finding solace amongst buildings or things clerical, for that matter. We found it prudent to avoid the subject of organised religion and he was somewhat reticent to discuss the preferred place of his burial, but no matter, he's at peace now."

Annie grew defensive.

"Did he change his religion? I mean..."

The Reverend chuckled. His light blue eyes twinkled behind his glasses.

"Oh, my dear... he made no intention of coming over to us," and he shook his head from side to side. He found the notion of Mick's possible conversion to Protestantism amusing.

"No. No. Mick was beginning to ponder... quite sensibly, I might add... on his origins and his place in the Universe and regrettably, the church of any persuasion had no place in his notions. Hence my enquiry concerning his last resting place."

"Dear man," murmured Effie. Annie wasn't sure whether the sentiment was directed to Mick or to her husband.

Leslie continued. "He was at peace with himself, I would most emphatically say that, when we saw him last. So whatever he had found, it was working in his favour. He was quite witty that day, wasn't he, Effie?"

"Yes. Very. Remember he took the box away and brought it back an hour later?"

"Ah, yes. I remember now. You're right. And he thanked us for looking after it for so long, didn't he? Well, at least we didn't misplace it. Rather, kept it out of harm's way, on the top shelf!"

Leslie glanced at his watch.

"Goodness me, is that the time? We'd better be going. Come, my dear," he said, "and leave Mrs Kelly with the box." And his bright eyes swept around the kitchen as if to conjure up the key. Perhaps it was hanging on a nail on the wall or on a shelf or even hidden under the grain bin?

"Thank you for bringing it. Please call me Annie, everyone else does." And Annie's next words spilled out, unbidden and surprised her: "Would you come to see me again? Please..."

Leslie and Effie both beamed and Effie positioned her huge frame around Annie, hugging her slightly. Lily-of-the-Valley and face powder filled Annie's nostrils.

"Why of course, we'll come again. We'd be delighted. We're curious about the box, too," she said.

Leslie chortled. It wasn't a human-like chortle but sounded more akin to the bray of a donkey.

"Curiosity thy name is Woman! Come, Effie."

He took hold of Annie's hand firmly and his clear intelligent blue eyes seemed to reach right inside her head.

"Yes. We'll come out to see you, Annie. We leave you with the contents of Pandora's Box. We two humble mortals are but the go-betweens in this fascinating saga. No, it was what Mick wanted... and I can see why now," he added knowingly. "We have returned his mysterious box to where it should be. It's in safe keeping now, our duty done. Farewell, my dear. I can hear the sound of the hounds. They wake!"

At this, he bounded across the room and out of the door followed slowly by Effie whose eyes still searched in vain for the key which would unlock the secrets of the box. After all, fifteen years is a long time to keep a secret!

The Williamsons left and silence returned to An Teach Ban. Annie stood quietly in her kitchen and tried to understand what had just occurred. She viewed the visit of the Williamsons as exciting and she was surprised how she had quickly warmed to them. They're lovely, she thought to herself. Nothing like Mrs Ryan's report. Mrs Ryan's opinion of the Williamsons had been less than flattering.

"She fancies herself," Mrs Ryan had told Annie, and sniffed, "and he's an eccentric... although...," she admitted somewhat grudgingly, "his watercolours have to be admired."

As a consequence, Annie had never given the Williamsons a second thought until today when they sat in her kitchen and drank tea. It surprised her that she had been so quick to ask to see them again, too. Normally, she was reserved about strangers and took awhile to trust. But it was impossible not to like the Williamsons and she wanted to hear more. The fact that Mick had been so admired by them puzzled her further and, thinking of Mick, she picked up the box and looked underneath it. In the very centre, etched into the wood, was a small inscription. It was difficult to read the words. She turned on the light and examined it closer. "ITALIA," she read. She placed the box back onto the table and bit her lip. Then she looked at Mick's black leather chair but he wasn't there. All was still and the black box with its tantalising secrets inside remained undisturbed. The problem was the key, she thought. I need the key. What sort of riddle is this? The Williamsons were certain that Mick wanted me to have it and with that thought, she smiled. I'm so glad I met them and so glad I have something special that belonged to Mick. She took the box and hid it under a rug at the bottom of her wardrobe. She didn't want to talk about it to anyone just yet... least of all to Frankie when he came to clear out Mick's room in two weeks time.

*****

True to his word, Frankie came and true to his nature, he organised. All Mick's possessions, his clothes and his books, were to be bundled up and swept away. This was a kind of cathartic approach for Frankie. He had never totally forgiven Mick for his bewildering conversation in the vegetable garden. His uncle's words that day had gone a long way to convince Frankie that he was indeed doing the right thing in entering the priesthood, that his destiny did lie behind the dog collar and there he would be able to apply a certain sweet solace and reassurance to those in his care. In fact, at times he had viewed his uncle as one of those who might be in need of his direction. Mick's behaviour had baffled Frankie throughout his life. It was Mick from whom he had wanted approval when he made

267

his announcement on that Christmas Day, and his uncle's perceived indifference deeply wounded him. In a way, he found it hard to forgive him for that. It cast a burden upon his shoulders. So, having control of the disposal of Mick's meagre possessions somehow released Frankie from the unforgiving demon and he set about the task of organising his mother, brothers and sister with his characteristic fervour.

Mick's dearest possessions were his books, well read and treasured, they sat in neat lines on the shelves of the bookcase that Bernard had made. Annie packed the books into boxes and her eldest son directed. She was relieved in a way to fall into line with Frankie. He had, after all, always been dogmatic and determined and it seemed to her now, as then, that his will was law and the rest of them would meekly obey his directions without so much as a murmur. Everyone, that is, except Oisin whose expression took on an appearance as black as a cloud that hung heavily outside in the winter sky. Annie noticed Oisin's unease around his elder brother but said nothing. Her heart was still heavy with her loss and her mind kept thinking of the Williamsons, the box and Oisin's place in all of this. Mick had been so insistent that Oisin must be the one to lead. He had hardly mentioned Frankie. The saddest part of all for Annie was that Mick had left her nothing of himself; no trinket or letter or anything tangible to remember him. Maybe something would be contained in the precious box, she thought as she watched as Frankie packed Mick's hairbrush, comb and the intimate items of his life, into a small cardboard box. Mick's whole life was there amongst the few possessions and there was nothing for Annie. Maybe it's for the best, she thought. I could not explain this to any of them, especially Frankie. What would he say? No, Mick is with me still, she concluded, and will always be with me in my heart. Material things decay but love never dies.

She had not entered Mick's room since his funeral. She insisted that the door be kept locked until Frankie arrived. Now, as the room was cleared she was able, for the last time to see herself and Mick in the room, loving each other. She folded the patchwork cover from his bed and held it to her lips, quietly so no-one would notice.

"I'll take the bedding to the church," she said to Frankie, "Father Byrne will know what to do. We don't need it now. You're all leaving the nest!"

"Oh, wee mother," said Frankie, affectionately, "you can come and visit me now in England."

For Frankie had already been given a Parish in England, in the Midlands, near Coventry and was set to leave in the next few months. His life appeared to be shaping up to exactly how he wished it to be and his progress within the church hierarchy was already being noticed. He expected that his new Parish would lead him on to bigger things. Frankie did not view his ambition as being contrary to his calling. It was rather a part of it as he felt he had the ability and it was his duty almost, to gain recognition and quickly elevate himself to a higher station. Once elevated, he would effect change and this would be remembered.

*****

And so Mick Kelly's room was emptied and the space was there and the silence in there was empty, too. Dead men leave behind hollowness in the hearts of those left to mourn. It would be many days before Annie could live beyond that state but in the following weeks, she began to accept her loss, even to feel blessed sometimes that she had had such a precious love. Time had not gone on with Mick so long that the passion might have been replaced by the mundane. Standing in his empty room, with its bare walls and empty wardrobe, she sometimes spoke to Mick as if he was still there. In fantasy, she could hear his voice. Or was it fantasy? She did not know. All she knew was she loved him and for Annie that was enough. She decided that his

269

books should be given to the Williamsons. Something within her urged her to do this for Mick. She knew in her heart this was what he would have wanted. She was certain of this. And Oisin would help and the Reverend would be delighted.

One day, a few weeks after Frankie had left and the family were slowly beginning to adjust to the absence of both father and uncle, Oisin came to her and held out his hand.

"I've found the key," he said and lying in the palm of his hand was a brass key with an ornate filigree bow.

"It's the key to Mick's box!" and Annie's hand shook slightly as she examined the key closer.

"He was on about it to me... and just where he said... tucked away in the small drawer on his dressing table... managed to get hold of it before Frankie. What's the box?"

Annie frowned. The time has come, she thought, when Pandora's box had to be opened. No longer could she keep the box hidden under the rug at the bottom of her wardrobe but Oisin must be sworn to secrecy for what might be hidden there? Mick had guarded it for so long.

"Come with me," she said. "There is something I want you to see. Something that is between ourselves, you know."

Now it was Oisin's turn to frown but he followed behind his mother into her room and sat on her bed. From the bottom of the wardrobe she uncovered the box and laid it beside him. He ran his hand over it, gently and murmured,

"Why, this is the grandest thing I've ever seen. Did it belong to Mick?" although he knew the answer already.

Annie nodded and hesitated.

"This has to be the key that opens the box. Shall we open it?"

And her stomach churned. Pandora's box was causing her to be cautious. She nervously inserted the brass key

270

into the lock and turned it. She felt the box open with a click. Slowly she lifted the lid. It was full to the top.

"Wow!!" cried Oisin.

"I never expected all this..." began Annie.

Within the box, its secrets revealed, was Mick. Sepia photographs of long lost relatives were laid neatly on top.

"That's his mother," said Annie and her heart beat faster. She was a child again and wanted to fling everything out to get to the bottom. A weary woman stared out at them. Unsmiling, she held Bernard on her knee and Mick stood beside her, holding onto her skirt. Bernard looked like a girl, dressed up in a pinafore and Oisin giggled. Annie laid the photographs in a line on the bed. There was a youthful Mick standing in a field of potatoes with a laughing group of young men and women surrounding him and Bernard, too, beside a bothy with his hands in his pockets and a rakish look on his thin face.

"That's in Scotland," said Annie for the next photograph revealed Mick, dressed in a brown double-breasted pin-stripe suit beside the Scott Memorial in Princes Street.

The sepia photographs gave way to others, clearer black and white images of Bernard and Annie and baby Francis in his mother's arms. Then there was one of Annie, herself, standing at An Teach Ban in front of the vegetable garden. It was summer and the sky was cloudless. She turned the photograph over and in the corner; Mick had drawn a cross, a kiss. Annie's heart quickened and she quickly turned it back again for the next photograph was of them all. There was Bernard and Annie with the family, all in their Sunday clothes, packed into his new car and off to Mass. Oisin giggled as he recognised himself but then there was another photograph of a young girl about sixteen years of age with jet black hair and laughing black eyes. Her eyes shone and her head lifted defiantly as if she demanded the photographer to obey her and give to her the most beautiful of images.

271

"Who's this?" asked Oisin.

His mother did not answer. The girl in the photograph was smiling, in control and all about her, including the photographer, were held captive before her. Here was excitement and youth and beauty.

"Wow!!" said Oisin. He had just begun to notice girls and this was one to notice.

Annie arranged the bundle of photographs neatly beside her on the bed. Revealed next in this magic black box was jewellery – a pearl necklace, a diamond ring, the gold band of an Irish wedding ring, a brooch encrusted with sapphires and gold. Annie's nimble fingers sifted through. She, too, was excited now. How Effie Williamson would have liked to be here, she thought. Amongst the jewellery was a set of rosary beads, a small wooden cross with Jesus in agony, his face contorted in pain.

"Look, Oisin, he hadn't given up his faith. Why, here's his *Book of Prayers.*"

She carefully opened the well-worn book to reveal on the flyleaf the name, "Mick Kelly" written in blue ink.

But Oisin wasn't interested. At the very bottom of the box were three envelopes, their backs sealed with new tape and the names printed in capital letters on the front. He read the names out to his mother:

"SILVIO LUCHETTA..."

"CONCETTA LUCHETTA..."

"OISIN KELLY..."

"There's one for me!" he cried, delighted. Then he frowned, puzzled as he examined the other two envelopes.

"Why... that's the man," he said, "I told you I saw him at Father O'Malley's funeral... Silvio, the Italian man."

He thrust the two envelopes aside and, trembling, he stared at his mother.

"This has to be what Mick was about. It has to be. He said there was a key... and something for me," he added proudly. "Wonder why me? Not Frankie or Declan but me. Can I open it?"

His mother nodded. She, too, felt her heart beating harder in her chest.

"Open it... open it... see what's inside?"

They were like children at Christmas, but wary, the two of them, for they did not know what secrets would be revealed. Oisin carefully peeled the tape and took Mick's penknife from the box. He carefully slit the envelope across the top and, just as carefully, drew a piece of lined paper out and unfolded it. There was a letter written in Mick's uneven hand. It was brief. Although Mick's reading had been considerable, his writing was often difficult to understand but this was clear. It looked as if he had thought about the words a lot and committed them to paper with much care. Oisin, his voice trembling slightly, read out the words:

"It hasn't a date," he said, "just Ballybeg..."

"Dear Oisin,

I want you to take the box, the key and all the contents contained therein, except the photographs, to Silvio Luchetta. His address is:

42 Willow Crescent
Edinburgh
He will know what to do.
Thank you.
Your loving uncle,
Mick
P.S. Remember you are a warrior and a poet."

Oisin handed the letter to Annie. She read the words and smiled. Mick wanted her to have the photographs. There *was* something for her after all.

Oisin frowned, his blue eyes looked puzzled.

"Who is Concetta?" he asked.

CHAPTER THIRTEEN

"Take me with you," said Mary. She balanced on the top of the iron gate with her long legs hanging over one side. Her feet, clad in tough leather walking boots, rested on one of the rungs for support. It was the end of summer and the days were growing shorter. Oisin looked up and smiled. He was busy rubbing Bess with the rough brush used for the horses. The pony loved the attention and, if Oisin paused for any reason, Bess would nudge him to continue. Oisin stretched upwards and patted Bess on her shoulder and as he did, he studied Mary's face. Sixteen now, she was already a beauty with a mass of curly brown hair and a face full of freckles after the summer sun. The sun was behind her and all around her head was the glow, almost like a halo, Oisin thought.

"Well, now," answered Oisin, "this is something I have to do myself... you know that."

"I do not," replied his sister, pouting, "I could come... I'm finished with the school anyway and Aunty Ryan said that I'd like Edinburgh."

"Did she now? When was all this discussed?"

"Oh, the other day. Please, Sheenie... I'd help with your bags," she added, her voice softening and pleading.

'Sheenie' was her pet name for her older brother. As a toddler, learning to speak, Oisin was a difficult name to pronounce and she had softened it successfully. Although on this occasion, she sensed the pleading wouldn't work. Oisin was intent on leaving. It had something to do with Uncle Mick. Ever since Oisin and her mother had discovered the contents of Mick's box, there had been discussion in the house. There were things between them and Mary was not part of it. She was not used to this and it annoyed her.

"I'd really love to come with you, Sheenie," she said again, "I'm fed up with Ballybeg. You're lucky to be leaving! Who'll look after Bess when you're gone?"

She knew the bond that existed between her brother and his horse and used a bit of emotional blackmail in one last attempt to dissuade him. But he laughed and got to work on Bess's mane. The horse whinnied with delight.

"This tough wee Bess... why, she'll be grand. Declan will keep an eye on her and brush her when he can. She'll be fine. I'll be back to see her..."

"You won't," cried Mary, "You'll go away and won't come back. You can't wait to go. It's not fair!"

At that, she jumped down from the gate. She was angry and Oisin deserved to know, she thought.

*****

The more Oisin thought of leaving, the more he thought of staying. The two opposing forces, resembling performing clowns, taunted each other, playing out their conflicting images and trying to influence Oisin's decision so that his poor mind was unable to advance either forwards or backwards. Often a permanent knot fixed itself at the bottom of his stomach and refused to go away. The clowns played out their gleeful game and he hesitated, fearing to make the decision. He had dreamed of leaving Ballybeg but now the reality was with him, he kept making excuses. He grew uncertain and troubled. Choices, it seemed, had been taken from him. Almost, he felt that he was being prised out of the comfortable existence that he had enjoyed all his life. Scotland, despite his father's tales of tattie-hokers and the kindness of the people, was another world away and what might befall him amongst strangers, he dared not even guess. Here in Ballybeg he was safe. People knew him and he knew them. He could just as easily have remained amongst the gentle and mystical scenery and not ventured forth. No one would think any less of him whether he stayed or not. The farm would provide work and income. Declan, after all, was content to stay. Why did he, Oisin, have to go away? He thought if he remained just a little longer amongst the all encompassing security of Ballybeg, he would be safe, for the unknown was

275

a fearsome fear indeed. Over and over the uncertainties went round in his head. Over and over he read and re-read Mick's letter. He puzzled. He still found it incomprehensible that his uncle had entrusted the responsibility of the mysterious ebony box to him. Mick was forcing him to go; there could be no doubt of that. Forcing him to be the warrior and the poet...but how unworthy poor Oisin felt for such a task. If Mick, on his deathbed, had sent Frankie to Scotland with letters and a box, he would have accepted this without as much as a murmur. Frankie was always in charge. He was the obvious one, everyone would agree, including Oisin. But no, Mick had been adamant. Oisin had the key and the letter was addressed to him.

But what would happen to him when he obeyed the instructions and went to Silvio? He remembered the Italian as dramatic, flamboyant even, and the thought of meeting him again in the unfamiliar surroundings of an unknown city brought on more nervous imaginings. In his mind, he saw himself approaching Silvio with the box clutched in his hand. Silvio, eager, would snatch it from him and tell him to be gone and then he would be alone in a strange place, not knowing what to do or where to turn. The mystery would not be solved because Mick was the eternal enigma and Silvio Luchetta was a part of that terrible unknown. Oisin's stomach knotted once more as his imaginings grew more colourful. He had never heard Mick mention Silvio. Never once. Nothing made any sense anymore. "What am I to do?" he murmured to himself as the days passed. He stayed the summer to help on the farm and to earn enough money at Murphy's but autumn was approaching and he was running out of excuses. Mary's pleading that she could come along was tempting to say the least. He would have liked her to be with him but he passed off her suggestions with a dismissive shrug of his shoulder. No, he had to go alone. Why, he did not know.

He talked to no one about it except Bess. With his pony, he was free. One nudge and Bess was away, cantering along the sandy strand and he wouldn't stop her for a mile or so, not until the sand gave way to rocks. Then he would swing down from the saddle and settle himself on the black rocks while Bess stood silent, waiting. They would gaze out towards the sea and sometimes he thought Bess knew what he was saying. To Oisin, the country boy, it didn't seem like fantasy in the slightest that he could discuss his troubles with his pony for hadn't she always listened to him? She was more attentive than any human, Oisin thought, but she could not speak to him. There was only the splashing of the waves and the call of the gulls overhead.

One evening, they stood together and watched the sun, a fading glow behind thin clouds, drop below the line of sea and Ballybeg and the West of Ireland was the most beautiful, the most magical place in all the world, and why, oh why, did Oisin have to leave such beauty? He stroked Bess and leaned his head onto her shoulder.

"Oh, Bess," he murmured, "will I ever see ye or all this again?"

Deep within him, deep within his soul, it seemed, he was saying farewell to all that he knew and all that he had accepted just a short time ago, as permanency. A terrible hollow sadness passed through him in a kind of a wave, starting at the top of his head and flowing through his body and dreamlike, he felt pinpricks of tears behind his eyes. They threatened to spill forth and he told himself he was a coward and could never be the warrior of Mick's dreams. He looked at his leather boots with one black lace and one brown. The tide was coming in and he stood on wet sand. He shifted his feet slightly and the indentation quickly filled with water. The water crept to the soles of his boots and then retreated, ebbing and flowing, the coming and going of life, he thought. He studied the water as if in a dream seeing his life set out before him; almost a vision as the motion of the waves focused all his attention. He suddenly shook slightly. He viewed his life like the swing of a pendulum, like the flow of the waves, and he knew at that moment that he would leave this enchanted place where people lived out their days beside the sea.

He sighed. He stroked Bess along her neck and she stepped backwards as he did and away from the unstoppable tide. Oisin, the expert horseman, swung his left foot into the stirrup and with a confident movement, settled himself into the saddle. His hands held the reins ever so gently for Bess knew what to do. He made a clicking sound in his throat and the two of them set off once again back along the darkening strand. The night had descended by the time they arrived at the farmhouse and the evening meal was already on the table.

*****

The next day Oisin wanted to see Old Mother Fahy. He found her asleep in her chair beside the range; the son nowhere to be seen. Over the summer, the men of Ballybeg had worked together and thatched the roof of her cottage for she was known to them all and an old woman. She was warm and dry now. How Oisin longed to talk. Maybe she would listen to him and understand, for life had been hard for Old Mother Fahy. Wrapped in her crocheted shawl of red, blue and green she looked so frail and tiny. The colour of her shawl contrasted with the white of her old face. She slept with her mouth slightly open and a small dribble of moisture lay on her chin. Oisin gently shook her arm to awaken her. She opened her eyes, unseeing, startled and then focused on his face so close to hers. He could feel her breath on his arm. She travelled back from the world of the unseen to the present and her bony hand took hold of his.

"It is yerself, Oisin, me lad, the Saints preserve ye! I must have been asleep... sure, I must have been dreamin' it was ye. No. It *is* ye!"

Her pale blue eyes, dulled with age, stared into his and she smiled. The carriage clock on the mantelpiece ticked time away and all was still. Oisin sat on the chair beside her, beside the range while the faded print of Mary and Jesus looked down on them both.

"It's a wonder to me now, me boy," the old woman spoke and she mumbled her words in Irish, Bless ye all, the Kellys and my dear Padraig, God rest him".

There was comfort in her words. Comfort in the familiar. Comfort in the Irish. Then Oisin spoke in English:

"Mother," he said for the old woman had always been "Mother" to them all, "I'm after leaving ye. I'm off to Scotland in a week or so... and..." he paused. The words stuck in his throat but he wanted to hear them out in the open, in this room with Mary and Jesus and Old Mother Fahy for the old mother was kind. "And I don't think I'll be back... least not for a long time... and I don't know why I say that... no, I don't know but it's just a feeling I have inside myself and it will not go away..."

"Yer leavin' me, Oisin! Ah, me lad. It is the lot of the Irish to have to leave and there's the curse on them for don't they forever have the longin' to return... and sure, the longin' never leaves them. Four brothers I had and they all went to America and one sister, Ellen, she's dead now, God rest her, she was thirty years in Australia. But aye. Aye. Ye'll have to go... ye have the wanderin' in yer eyes, so. It's the curse on the Irish... the wanderin' curse. I would have had it meself but for the meetin' with my poor Padraig, God rest him and we stayed. Well, ye see, I just had me boy and Padraig and enough on the farm for the three of us. If we'd had more of the wee ones... maybe I would have left along with the rest of them but it's in God's hands, our lives, all our lives and it was not meant to be. No, there was just me and me boy and look at him. It is often I wonder what will happen to him when I'm gone. But yer a good lad, Oisin and the Kellys are a fine family, the best of neighbours. Ye hear others complainin' of their neighbours but the Kellys and the Fahys have always been friends... and that's how it should be. If we were all friends, lad, but what am I to say... I'm an old woman and no one takes any heed of me and me talk... an old woman's ramblings... but yer a good lad and ye'll go far. Far away from Ballybeg and the West. Did ye say Scotland? I've a cousin there these past forty years... as old as me she is, well, least I heard she was still with us... but who knows? Who knows? Now, Oisin, there's something for ye."

Across to the blue and white dresser she shuffled, tattered and bent, and opened the drawer nearest the range. She ruffled around amongst the bits and pieces of a lifetime, mumbling away in Irish as she did while Oisin remained seated, looking around the small room, taking in every feature for he had the feeling that he would never be in this place again.

"Ah, here it is, lad," the old Mother cried, pleased and thrust a silver egg cup into Oisin's hand. It was tarnished and very, very old, Oisin could see that. Around the rim and the base was the spiral border from the Book of Kells, he decided. He had once come across a book on Celtic Art with the various patterns and designs illustrated in detail. That was the day he remembered, that Baldy Lawrence had threatened to expel him from the school for not paying attention. He was just able to recall the spirals and they matched the ones on the egg cup. He held the cup closer to his eyes in order to read the words that were so carefully engraved around the centre. Written in the old Irish script, he could just make them out. It was difficult as the words were almost obscured behind the black of the tarnish. He had to rub his finger along them to reveal the words: *Gurb iad beannachtaí gach lá ba beannachtaí atá de dhíth ort –* May the blessings of each day be the ones ye need most.'

The "G" was an ornamental capital from the Book of Kells. How painstaking was its execution. Oisin had an eye for beauty and the shape of the egg cup and the details of the engraving fascinated him. He held the cup between his fingers, studying it. Suddenly shy, he looked at the Old Mother's face, weathered and weary. She spoke eagerly, patting his hand as she did. There was something of an urgency in her action.

"It's for ye, lad. Been in the family a long time since but it's for ye... on yer journey. When ye have yer boiled egg in the mornin' ye can remember an old woman... an' a blessin' on ye... don't look so... what would me boy do with it? An' there's no one left after I'm gone, leastways not around here. No one knows where it came from but it's fine done, ye can just make out the Irish. Now, will ye be havin' a cup of tea?"

Oisin, nodded, overcome. Out came the willow pattern cup and saucer and the tea pot with the crocheted cosy and the milk in the powder blue jug and matching sugar basin. Oisin was taking photographs in his mind of this room and this moment and Old Mother Fahy and the kindness of the simple life. In his mind, he was saying goodbye. He placed the precious silver egg cup beside his willow pattern cup and saucer. Thoughtfully, he ran his fingers over the egg cup feeling all the ridges and spaces of the engraver's work. Old Mother Fahy smiled, her faded blue eyes watered as her face lit up with gratitude.

"Aye. Yer a good lad, Oisin, my boy. Just like yer Uncle Mick, God rest him."

As she poured the tea, her hand shook and she had to put the pot back on the table. Oisin very gently took it from her and filled both their cups with tea. They drank in silence and then it was time to go. Oisin held out his hand but Old Mother Fahy took hold of him and her frail bony old body held him as tight as she could. He felt her heart beating against his chest and he breathed in the smell of age.

"May the road reach up to meet ye, dear lad".

"God bless ye, Mother," said Oisin, "and thank you. Thank you for everything, I'll treasure this, you know and I'll always remember you, that I will."

"God bless ye, lad. 'Tis the curse on the Irish to have to go away... Bless ye, bless ye. May all the saints look down on ye wherever ye may be... where was it ye said... America?"

Now Oisin could smile. He patted her arm, reassuringly.

"Aye. Aye. Somewhere like that," was all he said.

*****

The days slipped by and the time of Oisin's departure grew nearer and nearer. Annie, telling no one, settled into a ritual of sorts. Every day, even when the soft rain wet her face or the wind from the Atlantic blew across the farm, she would go to the vegetable garden and there she would spend a few moments. On sunnier days, she settled longer, sitting contentedly on the bench that now stood with its back to the wall. Here she would remain and her thoughts in the vegetable garden were precious. Here she felt at peace. Sometimes, she decided that she was as close to God there as she ever was within the sanctified walls of St Peter and St Paul's. If, for any reason, she was unable to go to the garden, she felt annoyed and out of sorts. She vowed the next day she would stay longer for it was here that the love of Mick remained strongest in her heart. For here no one intruded. No one noticed. No one questioned. Sometimes, she loved to sit and watch as the birds pecked away amongst the greenery of cabbages and kale and she would wonder at Nature's little miracles. She thought of Mick and Bernard, too, for her husband would often creep into her meditative moments, unbidden, for if the truth be ever told, she had loved them both. She was now the matriarch of An Teach Ban and her place in the wider community of Ballybeg had been accepted at last.

Mick's vegetable garden was no longer the well organised and productive piece of ground that it had been. The weeds grew high. Untended, they threatened to strangle the cabbages and kale but Annie, mindful of Mick's memory, would not neglect the patch of ground nearest the wall where she had planted two red climbing roses. Mick was here, she was sure of that. Not in the Ballybeg

282

Cemetery beside his brother but here, with her, for this was where she felt closest to him. After all, this had been his wish: "No priests! No priests!" even now Annie wondered. She had lacked the will to insist but now he was here and she spoke not a word of it to anyone. One day, in the early afternoon, her work almost done, she sat on the bench that Declan had positioned for her. The bench faced westward towards the sea but with a wall to the back and a wall to the side, it was protected somewhat from the prevailing winds. Annie had insisted that the bench face west. On days free from wind and rain, the dramatic sunsets lit up the clouds and to Annie, growing more philosophical as the years went by, this was a little taste of Heaven. She was certain Mick would have enjoyed the outlook and he would have approved of her choice.

Annie thought of her changing life. Mick's room had been cleared. There only remained his books carefully stacked into three boxes and ready to be taken to the Williamsons. Then it would be time for Oisin to leave. He would take Mick's precious ebony box and the letters to Silvio and that would be the end of it. He was curious. "Who is Concetta?" he had asked. Annie recalled his puzzled face for there was the letter and the photograph had to be of Concetta. She was such a beauty and it was no wonder that Oisin was curious. But Annie refused to answer his question and her reply was vague. "I've no idea," she had said and changed the subject quickly. She did not want to be questioned for still the wound was there and she wondered why. No, it would be easier if Silvio explained to Oisin. Surely that had been Mick's wish. Her thoughts turned to Oisin and she pictured him arriving in Edinburgh intent on his mission. She sighed. Her son was so different, not only in manner but in appearance as well. Frankie and Declan were strong and tall like all the Kellys. Handsome, too, both of them, with black curly hair and clear blue eyes but Oisin, well, he still looked a bit like a frog what with his flat nose and wide eyes. Even Mary was taller than him by a few inches and teased him when given the chance. No one could call Oisin Kelly handsome! His blue eyes were often troubled these days, she thought. But he was difficult and would not be approached. He would just shrug his shoulders and be silent and nothing would make him speak. Oisin. The poet and the warrior, how Mick went on about that and why did Oisin have to go? Surely, Annie reasoned, Frankie was the obvious choice. With his priestly demeanour and command of the situation, he would have been the ideal one to meet Silvio and even the beautiful Concetta. Even Declan would have gone off with a twinkle in his eye and his fiddle under his arm, happy to oblige. But Oisin was the least likely of her three sons and surely the least prepared for such a journey. What would befall the boy so far from the security of Ballybeg? Here his life was as predictable as the sun rising in the morning and setting in the evening. The sun still rose over Edinburgh, Annie mused, but over grey buildings and shone down on unfamiliar faces. Would Oisin miss all that was familiar? All that was safe? When she had taken him to London all those years ago, he had been talkative, a different lad almost, but after all, he was only ten then and over the last few years his attitude had changed. He was no longer the boy he was then.

"Ah, Mick," she sighed to herself, half-expecting in her dreamlike state that she would receive an answer. "What will become of the boy? You didn't want him to stay; it was you who sent him away. You and your mysteries..."and Annie grew vexed thinking on all this amongst the cabbages and potatoes where Mick had seemed so content. No matter how she tried to think otherwise and no matter how foolish she told herself she was, somehow and for some reason, Oisin always belonged to Mick and it was Mick, even from his grave, who directed the boy's path.

She stood up to go. The old Annie was there again and she laughed to herself. She told herself she was becoming a foolish old woman! If my mother could hear me now, she thought, what would she have made of all this?

"Mick Kelly," she said out aloud for there was no one to hear, "What would my life have been without you? What is my life now? Still, the boy will go and you will have your way. You always had your way, you old Irish rascal."

And at that moment, at that brief moment, Annie was Annie Smith again, the London girl who had given up her life to grow old in the West of Ireland. She chuckled at her own absurdity. Here she was talking away as if Mick was still there and the only living thing around was a solitary blackbird, intent on pulling a worm from the ground, and not taking any notice. Life goes on, she concluded silently to herself and I'm not afraid anymore. Mick will be with me until I die and Oisin, well, Oisin, who knows what will become of him?

*****

Annie and Oisin perched side by side on the sofa at the Manse. Around and about was even more of a muddle. Unable to lean backwards or forwards, the two of them sat upright because three of Effie's split cane fly fishing rods of various lengths lay along the full length of the sofa from arm to arm. Oisin had to position himself closer to his mother because various capes of cockerels, a fox tail, even a clump of badger's hair, an assortment of wings of mallard ducks, blackbirds and grouse were spread over the seat. On top of this motley heap lay an old hat, the ostrich herls destined to tie around the fishing hooks. "Old Bruno" tobacco tins, no doubt filled with even more flies and hooks lay scattered around the floor and competed for space with coloured floss, ribbing, gold and silver wire, silks, a moth-eaten pair of hare's ears, even hedgehog quills and what looked like grey dog's hair no doubt combed out of Sophocles and Aristotle. Even if Oisin could have moved backwards, he would have been trapped by Effie's green chest waders and her tweed jacket, now full of holes, which adorned the back of the sofa. Long-handled triangular nets, reels, fishing bags, a wading stick, were flung randomly amongst books and magazines. Even some of Leslie's watercolours lay amongst the fishing apparel. On the small coffee table in front of the sofa, a cup, its contents long forgotten, had an impressive furry mould growing along the dregs and Annie gingerly pushed it to one side as Effie arrived with tea and tray, to balance this on a layer of hazel nut shells. She pushed the fisherman's 'priest' off the table with her elbow as she did. The bronze object clattered onto the floor narrowly missing Oisin's foot. All these manoeuvres were no mean feat for Effie as she had to negotiate her way over Sophocles and Aristotle as well.

"Down, Sophocles," admonished Effie as the tray came dangerously near to the dog's head. The dog gave a noisy woof, a wag of his tail and then a deep sigh before finally resting his long nose against Oisin's leg. Sophocles's eyes closed and harmony was restored, if ever harmony could be found in the Manse. Aristotle, seeing his companion now lying flattened and stretched out, mimicked the position but he rested his head on Sophocles's belly so the two animals reclined at a kind of "T" shape angle in front of Annie and Oisin. Escape from the sofa was now impossible.

The behaviour of the two dogs did not concern Leslie one jot because he was enthusiastically engaged in pulling Mick's books from the three boxes, stacking each book one on top of the other so that the pile of books grew, each one adding to the height and each one threatening to cause the whole heap to descend onto the table or worse, the floor.

"Look, Effie," he cried with delight, *The Wit and Wisdom of the Nineteenth Century Music Hall* , that's one for you, my girl! What books that Mick Kelly devoured! Why, Hugh O'Connor once told me that Mick had read every book in the Ballybeg Library... now, that's something, isn't it? An enquiring mind the man had... catholic in his tastes. Look, here's another... *The Secrets of the Great Pyramid*!"

He turned to Annie and Oisin. "There was a genius in our midst," he said, "and not one of us knew." He peered at Oisin over his glasses, bobbing his head up and down as he spoke. "Now, my boy... the question begs an answer... are you going to follow in your Uncle Mick's footsteps?"

Oisin lowered his head and Annie reddened. But Leslie appeared unaware that his words had caused any discomfiture for he let out a great chortle of delight.

"Come here, Effie," he cried, "there's a letter here from Silvio."

At that, Effie deposited the tray with cups, tea pot and plate of chocolate cake onto the coffee table with a loud bang, scattering hazel nut shells and waking the dogs.

"Oh... a letter from Silvio Luchetta," she gushed. "Quick, Leslie, my love, what does he say? When was it written?"

Leslie looked at the postmark while Annie and Oisin looked on in awe.

"Ah..." replied Leslie, disappointed, "It's postmarked two years ago..." He held the letter up to the light and read the pages quickly, frowning slightly as he did.

"Silvio just says he will be in Dublin. The tone, alas, is quite threatening... it's almost demanding? Mick is being summoned by the padrone indeed! Ah well, all's past that's past. It would be presumptuous of me, dear Annie, if I were to enquire as to the contents of the mysterious ebony box which we so safely kept for so long for the dear departed Mick Kelly?"

Annie, her mind in a turmoil, managed a weak smile.

"There was a letter in it... and addressed to me!" announced Oisin, not waiting for his mother's reply.

"Was there now, young sir?" said Leslie. "I told you that you would follow in your uncle's footsteps."

"I don't want to," replied Oisin. He was slightly annoyed at the Reverend.

"Well, now, you are quite right, my boy. We all have our own path to travel."

"Was there anything more in the box?" asked Effie. She would have liked to have examined its contents.

"Jewellery, old photographs, that sort of thing, not much... said Annie quickly. She was anxious to change the subject.

"I'm off to see this Silvio... in Scotland... that's what my letter said to do," said Oisin, suddenly mindful of his mission.

"Ha! Ha! I thought as much. Why, my boy, this is your journey... you are Odysseus... off to conquer the world! To Caledonia, you go! Effie... an address... an address for the boy."

"Of course... an address. Silvio is in Edinburgh, that's right. My sister, Maisie lives there, too, with her husband..."

"The erstwhile Professor Potts," cried Leslie, gleefully, "A history man. Percy Potts, historian..." And with that he thrust a piece of paper into Oisin's hand. The address in Edinburgh of Professor Percy Potts and his wife, Maisie was written across the page and at the bottom, Leslie had scrawled:

"A contact if all else fails!!!"

"Don't look like that, boy," and he winked at Oisin, "why, they're as old as us and both as deaf as the proverbial two posts... only in an emergency, dear boy... only in an emergency!"

"My sister disapproves of my marriage," said Effie to Annie.

"Oh", said Annie, not knowing quite what to say. As usual, she never knew what to expect with the Williamsons. All she could think was that every encounter was different but each encounter gave rise to something more.

"They liven up Ballybeg," she said to Oisin when they were safely out of the Manse, "... and you have an address," she added, reassuringly.

Oisin didn't answer. The knot had returned to live in his stomach and it seemed to be turning in all sorts of circles. In a week's time, he would be leaving Ballybeg and the unknown was drawing closer by the hour!

****

Annie, tiny now between Declan and Mary, watched as Oisin climbed aboard the 7.45 am Ballybeg to Dublin train; final destination, Edinburgh, Scotland. Oisin's framed khaki knapsack was heavy. He had some difficulty getting himself and the knapsack through the narrow carriage door. When he put it on his back, it was so large over his small frame, that it gave the appearance of a knapsack with a body! He had packed the bag carefully ensuring that the precious ebony box was safe at the bottom. Worried lest anything should damage, what was after all the sole reason for his journey, he wrapped his knitted jersey securely around the box. Old Mother Fahy's precious egg cup received the same careful attention and it was safe. His green knitted scarf held it secure beside the box. Clothes and another pair of shoes were arranged on the top. Into his wallet, which he thrust deep into the pocket of his jacket, he folded a piece of paper with the three addresses – Silvio, Professor and Mrs Potts, and Frankie's phone number in England, the latter just to be used in case of an emergency.

He was leaving Ballybeg at last. Leaving behind the town, the sea, Slieve Geal, people, his entire known world. A mist lay heavy on the top of Slieve Geal and the autumn cold was in the air. As the train eased its way slowly out of the station, he caught sight of his mother's face. She held a handkerchief to her right eye. Beside Declan and Mary, she looked frailer and more alone than he had ever seen her before. An image flashed before his eyes and it was his mother again but this time she was lying, stretched over Mick's chest, and Mick was dead. He thrust the image out of his mind, shaking himself free of it. And in its place he held his last view of Ballybeg with autumn mist and dew on the ground. He thought to himself that this was goodbye to land and sea and people, too, for he viewed the scene as an

289

onlooker would, not part of himself, and he a stranger. Huddling together, the three figures grew smaller and smaller, finally disappearing from view as the train crossed over the bridge and headed eastwards across the flat landscape covered with granite rocks and walls made from those rocks.

"I'm Odysseus," thought Oisin, remembering the Reverend Williamson, "and I'm on a journey from Nowhere to Somewhere?"

*****

That evening, at Murphy's, Daniel O'Connor, Stationmaster and loyal servant of the people, sat beside Tommy Flynn, sometime labourer and faithful friend of the late Mick Kelly.

"The Kelly boy, ye know, Oisin, left on the 7.45 today for Dublin," Stationmaster O'Connor said. He finished the glass and laid it back on the bar counter.

"Remember, he used to help out here sometimes, clearin' tables and the like... ye know, he never said much? Short lad, with big ears, not like the rest of them. Ah, well, Tommy, I'll be off now, I've an early start in the morn."

"Be seein' ye, Dan. I'll be along soon meself. The nights are drawin' in, soon be Christmas. I'll jist have another... and isn't it grand to see ye man Declan over there, playin' away... jist like his Da, God rest him!"

*****

It was unfortunate for Oisin that he arrived at the Waverley Station at ten thirty at night. The journey from Ballybeg had taken two days and he was weary. Edinburgh was noise. It had rained during the day and the cobbled streets, their black cobbles wet and glistening under the street lights, meant that crossing over them was difficult. Oisin lost his footing, stumbling slightly and he almost fell back onto them. He managed to straighten himself, bowed down as he was under the weight of his knapsack, and he reached the safety of the pavement where he rested. People swept past him. No-one noticed the small Irishman with the huge knapsack on his back. His plan had been to reach the hostel, and in the morning get his bearings, but somehow in the confusion of the railway station, he had taken a wrong turning and now was completely lost. He was hungry, too. From his bag he brought out a soggy ham and tomato sandwich he had bought at Liverpool Station. He ate it slowly. It tasted horrible.

On both sides of the street, the tall buildings stretched towards the heavens and from countless windows high up and lower down, lights flickered on and off. The full silver moon scurried across the night sky shining on the lines of chimney pots and Oisin, far below, his imagination soaring, saw tall ships and ghostly pirate galleons from another age and another time. He shivered and pulled his coat collar up around his ears. In front of him, the dark outline of the Castle loomed and he decided to walk towards it. Time was passing and he began to despair that he would ever find the hostel and would be forced to wander the streets until the morning light. The Castle, he reasoned, gave him direction. He wearily lifted his knapsack onto his back once again.

"Watch it, mate," and a sailor with a bottle in one hand and a girl in the other, pushed him backwards. The two of them weaved in front and made Oisin's progress difficult. Suddenly, mindful of his situation, Oisin slowed his walking pace to avoid another collision but he needn't have bothered. The sailor lifted the bottle to his lips and with the other hand, clasped the girl around her waist. Sailor and girl, now giggling loudly, zigzagged across the cobbles and were soon out of sight.

Oisin, still confused and feeling hopelessly lost, found himself at the top of a series of steps that led downwards. The Castle still rose before him and he decided to go down the steps and thus reach a lower level. At least, then he thought, he would be going in the right direction. If all else failed, he would go back to the Railway Station where he could rest awhile. His legs ached. He had been walking around the streets for an hour and he was still no nearer to

291

the hostel. Halfway down the steps, he paused. A dim light lit up the steps, lighting the brick walls on both sides, and Oisin leaned hard against the wall for at that moment a youth about his own age came hurtling down the steps. He was closely followed by two other youths. All three were panting furiously.

"Slaw doon, Red!" one said.

"Weel, whit hav oo here...?" And the one called Red stopped in front of Oisin. He was at least a foot taller than Oisin and in the half light, Oisin could just make out the mass of red hair.

"Hae a leuk it this, lads," said Red, "a wee laddie wi a muckle bag, ye ken." The shorter youth pushed Oisin on the shoulder. Oisin stood his ground.

"Ye won't find a lot in there that would be of any use to ye," he said.

"Thon's a orra wey o speakin."

"A ken e's a Paddy, Red," announced the third youth, a gangly sort of lad with a thin face and he, too, gave Oisin a shove, harder this time.

"A Paddy, richt eneuch," said Red, "heez bag'll be fou o tatties than an heez heid is weel. Wull we tak a leuk, lads?"

The gangly youth giggled. From his hip pocket he produced a bottle of whisky. He took a gulp and handed the bottle to Red. Red drank and spluttered. He staggered slightly and had to put one foot on the lower step to balance.

"A dinnae lik Paddys'," he said, "I dinnae lik Paddys' ower here... Paddys' shid stey in Paddy-land."

"Wull oo sen im back tae Paddy-land, Red?"

"Ay. Yir richt, thare Shorty. Sen im back tae whaur e cam frae!"

The tension was rising. The three lads now surrounded Oisin and there was no way he could make a move. There looked to be another twenty steps or so down to the street level. Oisin, his heart pounding, decided to make light of the situation.

"Well, now, lads," he said, "If you'll just let me by... I'll be back in Paddy-land soon enough."

"Did ye hear thit, boys? Paddy can speak."

The three burst out laughing. Red stepped back

"Weel, Paddy. Aff ye go...," he said, bowing low. The elaborate movement caused him to topple slightly and he fell onto Oisin's chest. Oisin put his hand in front of him and in so doing, pushed Red back towards the wall.

"Ye shidnae hae dun thit, Paddy," cried Red and before Oisin could do anything further, Red punched him. The blow landed on Oisin's stomach causing him to lean over and gasp for air. But now he saw an opportunity to escape. Crouching forward, he pushed the gangly youth on the step below him. The lad staggered onto the wall and Oisin, holding his stomach, fled down the twenty steps as fast as he could.

He reached the bottom and steadied himself on the railing but Red was already there. His face was flushed and menacing and now Oisin, for the first time, felt real fear. There was no one about. The street lights and what he thought was Princes Street seemed a long way off. Along there, people strolled oblivious to the drama that was taking place so near to them. Along there, too, cars and buses stopped and started. Oisin could see lights and movement. He heard a police siren but it was too far away. People were spilling out of the pubs and making their way home.

Red was in no mood for joviality.

"Haud yirsel, Red," said Shorty.

"A'll fell im!!!"

"C'way Red, lea aff. E's ea a Paddy."

"A'm gonnae learn im a lesson, ken...!"

Red clenched his fists and thrust his head closer to Oisin. He smelt of tobacco and whisky and sweat. Oisin tightened his hands, too. The adrenalin rushed to his head and in his mind, he saw Mick – Mick, bleeding, his hand over his eye and the dark streets of Glasgow. In that split

293

second, he made up his mind to fight for there didn't seem any other way out. One of the lads, Shorty, took hold of Red's arm in an attempt to control him.

"C'way, Red," he pleaded, "Ye dinnae wint a ficht. Lat's hae anither dram..."

"Or a blaw," interrupted the gangly one as he thrust a pack of cigarettes into the face of the overpowering Red.

"Dinnae wint a dram! Dinnae wint a blaw! Wint tae fell im!"

"Listen tae whit Shorty's sayin? Hae a dram an lat's be aff. The polis'll be here... cum awa, Red..."

"A dinnae lik the Paddys'," mumbled Red but he stepped back and allowed Shorty to take hold of his arm.

Oisin relaxed slightly. Glancing to the side, he ascertained that he could reach the safety of the street and street lights in about two minutes given half a chance. A sudden stab of pain hit him like another blow in his stomach area and he tried to ease the ache with his right hand. In the dark no one noticed. Red was still breathing heavily.

"Lat iz it im!!" he said again. He lifted his arm to strike but at that moment, from out of nowhere, it seemed, a figure of a man leapt from the shadows and grabbed hold of Red's arm, forcing it tight against his back so that Red was unable to move. He yelped in pain. Shorty and the gangly one backed off. Shorty made a move to help Red but as he came forward, the figure holding Red, swept his other arm around catching Shorty on the chest. Shorty fell to his knees with a groan. Seeing his two companions wounded, the gangly one made his way off down towards the street below. Red struggled but he was no match against his assailant. Held in a vice-like grip, Red could only spew forth a variety of profanities of a sexual nature while his captor turned him towards the street lights and with a push, sent him toppling. Shorty, for his part, got somewhat shakily to his feet and, grabbing hold of Red by the arm, headed for the safety of the crowds and Princes Street.

It was now that Oisin could get a look at his rescuer. In front of him was a short man not much taller than Oisin himself. Oisin guessed the man was in his early fifties. He wore a dark Army jacket and on top of his head, set at a jaunty angle, was a tartan cap with a pompom right in the middle. Tusks of grey hair sprouted from beneath his cap and covered both his ears. He grinned at Oisin.

"Weel, noo," he said, "Ir ye alricht, laddie?" In the half-light,Oisin thought he looked a bit like Tommy Flynn from Ballybeg.

Oisin nodded but the pain still caught him around his middle.

"It's nae guid tae be aroond thir pairts if ye dinnae ken," the man said and then, seeing Oisin holding his stomach, continued, "Ir ye shair yir alricht, laddie? Did yon big yin git ye?"

Oisin nodded, grinning ruefully.

"Aye," he said, "Got me in the belly... up there," pointing to the steps, "I thought I was for it... glad ye happened along..."

"Ir ye Irish?"

"Aye. I got in at ten but somehow I got lost. Been trying to find the hostel for hours. Some place, this Edinburgh!"

The man laughed.

"Richt eneuch," he said, "Weel noo, A'll hae tae git ye hame tae Jeannie. Sha'll ken whit tae dae. Cannie hae ye traikin aroond lik this it this oor. It's gan twelve. Ye leuk hurtit. Can ye walk?"

Oisin nodded. He was beginning to feel nauseous from the blow and lack of food. His head spun slightly.

"I don't feel that great," he replied.

He could feel his knees wanting to give way and he had a vision of his collapse onto the wet pavement. A light rain had started to fall.

"Here noo, laddie. Tak haud o ma airm. A'll git ye hame tae Jeannie. It's nae ower ferr."

And at that, the little man took hold of Oisin who by now had bent forwards under the weight of his knapsack.

"Yon's an awfie bag yir cairin!"

"Aye. I think that's what the lads were after but there's nothing in it worth the effort... I'm called Oisin, by the way. Oisin Kelly, from Ireland."

The little man laughed.

"Pleased tae mak yir acquaintance, Oisin Kelly frae Ireland... an unner sic circumstances. Alloo iz tae introduce masel tae ye... A'm kent by aw an sindry is Wee Willie. Bit ma full name is Willie MacTavish, born and bred an leevin oot aw ma days in this fair toon. Noo, tak haud o iz, young man... an oo'll git ye hame tae Jeannie!"

CHAPTER FOURTEEN

Oisin awoke next morning to a shaft of light and the unfamiliar sounds of cars and trucks stopping and starting. He heard voices, rough voices greeting one another. "Braw day!" and the reply, "Bout time!" and the rattle of bottles. He glanced at his watch. It was a few minutes to nine. He had been asleep for hours. Outside his window, a pigeon cooed, its repetitious call louder than the humans below. Rubbing his eyes, he looked around the small room. A white painted dressing table took up most of the space along the wall in front of his bed. Two small drawers with brass handles fitted neatly beneath a rather ornate tilting mirror. Oisin could see himself in the mirror. He thought he looked rather wan; his black tousled hair stood on end and he was in need of a shave. He ran his fingers through his hair and, as he did, he noticed a man's hair-brush and a comb on the table in front of the mirror. Beside them in a gold frame sat a black-and-white portrait of a young man, about twenty, wearing an Army beret with a pompom. He looked well-drilled and disciplined.

The only other furniture, a painted white wardrobe, filled up the entire space in front of the wall near the door. On the only wall that didn't have furniture in front of it and near the window, a large coloured photograph in a wooden frame took up most of the space. Oisin assumed it was a view of some Scottish loch. The photograph, taken on a sunlit day, with blue sky and even bluer water, appeared somehow out of place secured onto a wall that was covered with blue and white striped wallpaper with rows of blue forget-me-nots embossed onto the white. The blue room, Oisin thought. He could see his green knapsack leaning on the wall beside the white dressing table and, as he eased himself out of the bed, he felt a slight cramp in his stomach, and he lay back onto the bed, groaning slightly. Then the memory of the night before came into his head. There had been an obnoxious youth called Red who had punched him

297

and a little man called Wee Willie who had saved him. Now he remembered. Holding onto the little man and walking, walking for miles it seemed and then climbing countless steps to a door on a landing that led into a hall and into a kitchen and then into a room. He felt stiff. He moved his body. Standing on the red, white and blue rag rug, his feet were cold and he dressed quickly, pulling his grey sweater over his head and zipping up his new black corduroy flared trousers. The ebony box with the egg cup beside it was safe. His wallet, with money and addresses, was just where he had left it, in his coat pocket. He opened the door quietly. A tiny grey-haired woman was busy washing dishes at the sink, her back to him. Oisin coughed slightly, to announce his presence.

"Ah... thare ye ir!" she said, turning around. Her hands, clad in bright orange rubber gloves, wet with water and suds, moved up and down rapidly. She reminded Oisin of a little sparrow which had somehow obtained orange wings, flapping and about to fly.

"Noo, than... did ye sleep weel?" She pulled the orange gloves off and wiped her hands on her floral apron. "A'm Jeannie," she said, smiling. Her smile was welcoming. "An ye maun be the laddie frae Ireland. Sit yirsel doon, laddie, an I'll makkit ye some brakefast... ye maun be starvin... comin aw thit wey!"

Oisin nodded shyly, unsure of what to say. Ballybeg and the familiar was a long way away. He sat down at the small neat pine kitchen table while Jeannie bustled around, darting like a little bird, in and out of cupboards and at the same time, frying eggs and bacon and talking non-stop all the time.

"Ir ye awricht noo? Yon's an awfie airt, thaim Closes, ye ken. Nivver gang nar thaim at nicht masel... Willie telt iz aw aboot it. E's a tae heez wirk the noo bit e'll be back aroond five an yir tae stey here... wi uz, ken... tull ye git yirsel redd up. Naw, e widnae say ocht mair. Whit a mannie is, that Willie! A'm tae see yir weel fed an comfine an tae

298

mak share yon reid-haired deevil didnae dae ye ower muckle hirm. That's whit Willie sayed. Noo, eat up... thare's onie amount... wadd ye lik tea... wi shuggar and milk... Ireland... noo whit pairt o Ireland did ye stey? Ma granfaither wis born thare... bit noo, whaur wis it? Nivver bin thare, ye ken... bit A'd luve to gae... whit wey, A tell Willie, whan heez feenisht wi heez wirk in a puckle years... oo go ower an veesit bit ye ken hoo it is... thare's ayeweys summit mair... mind hoo ye go, ee says, mind hoo ee go."

She poured them both a cup of tea. "Whit did ye say yir name wis? Willie wisnae richt share, juist sayed ye wur frae Ireland?"

"Oisin. Oisin Kelly and I'm from Ballybeg, in the West of Ireland."

He was beginning to feel more comfortable with this little woman whose tongue kept in time with her hands and whose body seemed connected to a puppet string for she was constantly up and down offering even more food. Oisin relaxed. He felt as if he had hadn't eaten for a week.

"Wondering could I be troubling ye for another cup of tea?"

Jeannie leapt in the direction of the pot in the manner of a rugby player leaping onto the ball.

"Ye juist tae what ye want, laddie. Thare's ocht maur whaur that cam frae. Eat up, laddie. Ye leuk as if ye are in need of a good feed! Now yer name... I've not heard that name afore... how do ye say it agin?"

"Oisin. It's an Irish name. The warrior and the poet though to be sure I wasn't much of a warrior last night, so. If yer man hadn't come along by...? I'm not used to cities... went to London once when I was a lad... my mother came from London... but Ballybeg... well, in Ballybeg everyone knows everyone. We get a few tourists in the summer and fishermen later on... but ye can hear the silence."

"Ocht, laddie. It sounds a treat but I'm been in the toon all me life... can't say I ken much aboot the countra. A bit

299

too quiet fae me, I daresay. Now, ye to mak yersel a hame here... I'll show ye whaur we keep the key."

Oisin glanced around. At home, he thought, at An Teach Ban the farmhouse was bigger than any other for miles around but compared to this flat, in the middle of a city, his home was small, indeed. Looking out from the bay window in the sitting room, he could see a green park and the craggy outcrop of what he thought must be Arthur's Seat. Directly in front of him the lines of elongated grey buildings sat side by side with the various church spires etched against a cloudless blue sky. It is indeed a braw day, thought Oisin to himself and a braw sight to behold. He was finding it difficult to understand Jeannie, so rapidly did she put her sentences together, but he liked the sound of the Scots and he was in no doubt that the perpetrator of the words was kindness incarnate!

"It's a braw day," he said, grinning at Jeannie for his spirits had lifted with rest and food.

"Ocht there laddie, we'll hae ye speakin the Scots afore the nicht's oot! Now, ye awa an get yer bearings... though ye won't find much of the silence hereabouts," she added mischievously as she wrote the address of the flat and the phone number on a piece of paper.

"Remember, Willie wull be in aboot five, he sayed. But ye juist go awa an enjoy the city sights. An I'll cook ye up a real treat... hae ye ever had the haggis?"

*****

A few hours later Oisin sat down on a bench in the Princes Street Gardens. His feet hurt. He had been walking for hours. He was glad to be away from the street and thankful to sit. A soft breeze blew over his face and the sun shone down. Wispy clouds had now appeared to block out some of the sun's rays, an autumn cool was in the air. All his life Oisin had looked out on sea and sky. The scene before him was so different. He was tired but there was an excitement within him, too, for there was energy all about him. He thought of the certainty of Ballybeg, of the predictability of the known for here in the city there was no certainty and, after last night danger in many places if he didn't watch out. Thoughtfully, he studied the bronze plaque fixed to the bench where he sat. The plaque, with two of its screws missing, looked as if it were about to come adrift.

"To the Memory of Colonel and Mrs...," but he couldn't read any further. Underneath the words were clearer. "Who Loved this View." Now he began to think that there were other parts of the world besides Ballybeg. Ballybeg was a microcosm of Life and within that small world was security, too, for everyone knew everyone and talked of nothing much else. The seasons, the farming, the appearance of strangers, births, deaths, marriages and above all this, an all-seeing God looked down, a merciful God but sometimes a wrathful one, too, if Baldy Lawrence and Father O'Malley, God rest his soul, could be believed. Ballybeg existed and its inhabitants lived and died and took heed of this divine mercy. Outwith Ballybeg, there was danger and the God who looked down on the small community might not be so accommodating elsewhere. Oisin thought he would make a point of attending Mass this coming Sunday just to reassure himself that this all-seeing deity was the same here as the familiar one who kept hold of the comings and goings of the Ballybeg folk. He guessed the MacTavishes would wonder but he sensed they would not judge. They were safe people to know and he was grateful for their hospitality. It had been a wonderful stroke of good fortune that Wee Willie had come to the rescue and that he and Jeannie had been so welcoming to a stranger. And there was still the matter of Silvio Luchetta and the ebony box. He decided that he would wait a few days before making any contact. After all, he reasoned, Mick had kept all his secrets hidden and his mother had, too. The two of them had been as one and there was no one around who guessed. Oisin set his mouth harder. No, he would stay. There was exhilaration, here, and he would be part of it. The MacTavishes were a godsend, indeed.

*****

Events now seemed to be working in Oisin's favour and he found himself doing things that just a few weeks ago he would have thought impossible. He began to transform his life. Wee Willie and Jeannie were the kindest of people and Oisin relaxed, convinced that whatever had guided him during his first night in Edinburgh, had indeed been providential. His altercation with the drunken Red and his equally drunken companions and the subsequent rescue by Wee Willie was most fortuitous. Had he not got lost and ventured somewhat foolishly down the Closes that dark evening, he would have probably found the hostel, delivered the ebony box to Silvio Luchetta and be gone. As it turned out, he fitted so completely and so neatly into the lives of the MacTavishes, that it seemed that he had known them all his life. Something had brought him from Ballybeg to Edinburgh and this something would hold him and bind him more closely than he could ever have imagined. Still he delayed making a move to visit Silvio and he did not mention any of his reasons for coming to Edinburgh to either Willie or Jeannie. Sometimes, at night, he would take the ebony box; unlock it with the ornate brass key he kept in his wallet for safe keeping, and sort through the contents once again. He wanted a clue to its mysteries but none came and Mick's letter to himself became more and more of an enigma until, puzzled and annoyed, he would thrust it back into the envelope. The two letters addressed to Silvio and Concetta troubled him even more and he was curious enough to wish that he could somehow open them, read what was inside and then quickly re-seal the envelopes and no-one would know. But Oisin was an honourable young man and deceit was not in his nature. So the letters remained at the bottom of the box, unopened. He delayed once more. His life was rolling along, day and night,

302

without a hitch. He had now been living with the MacTavishes for three weeks.

At night he lay in the blue room, as he called it, acutely aware of the sounds of the city outside his window. Ballybeg and the West dimmed as he listened to horns and sirens and voices. This room was reality for him now but the austerity of it troubled him somehow. The soul of the room was gone for there was no evidence of human habitation. Even the photograph of the young soldier with his grinning face, beret and pompom, had been removed along with the hairbrush and comb. In its place a white porcelain dish sat neatly on an off-white crocheted doily. All the drawers and wardrobe were empty, too. There was emptiness in the room, an unexplained emptiness. Oisin's few possessions took up little space and he kept the room tidy for this was where he slept but he was happier outside it, talking to Jeannie in the kitchen or to Willie in the living room. For Oisin now went with Wee Willie every day and worked beside him and enjoyed every minute of it. Willie drove a blue Bedford van with words printed in white on both sides:

WILLIE MACTAVISH JOINERY
No Work Too Wee for the Wee Man

The two of them worked around the city and once out as far as Bonnyrigg. Oisin loved the work for hadn't his father had a feel for the woodwork, too, and Mick as well, when he was able? As they drove along, Oisin chattered to Wee Willie about the carpentry and the carving, proud now, remembering the happier times and Willie nodded his head in agreement, his tartan cap bouncing up and down on his head, delighted with the company of the young man from Ireland who had such stories to tell. This young man was a good worker too and learned fast even though he was short in stature and odd-looking with his big ears and frog-like eyes? And Oisin told stories of the farm and the hard work, for all the Kellys were workers, even Mick when he had had a mind to it and that's why their farm had

303

prospered while other ones around them had sunk into decline. For the drink was an awful thing in the West, Oisin said and ruined many a man. But his father liked the Scottish people, had pulled up potatoes in Berwickshire until the work died out and there was more to do on the farm back home. His father had played his fiddle and left the drink alone, thank God. But now there was just his older brother, Declan who ran the farm and Oisin was pleased to talk of Declan but said nothing of Frankie for there was nothing to say of the brother who was a priest in England.

"Whit wey? E's a braw laddie tae hae aroond," Willie said to Jeannie and the two of them smiled.

"Gin ae Jamie wis here... the twa o thaim wad hae bin sae guid freends... A juist kent it."

"Thare, thare, lassie."

And Willie patted Jeannie's hand for they both missed the boy in the photograph so deeply. Somehow this young Irish laddie, well, he filled the gap just a wee bittie and Jeannie wiped a tear from her eye as she turned her head so Willie couldn't see. There are many thoughts a mother has that no man can ever know, even Willie, and he was one of the best.

"The wee soul," she said, "whit a airt yon Ballybeg maun be... A'm sae prood tae hae im here... an e's sae ferr frae hame, the wee mannie."

"Ocht, e's a wice fallie," answered Willie. He filled his pipe slowly and just as slowly lit it, flicking the match out and drawing the smoke into his lungs as he spoke. "Ay. E's a wise yin... gleg on the uptake richt eneuch... ye ae hae to shaw im the aince an e's gotten the hang ont... says e's faither an uncle wrocht in the widd back yonder in Ireland... ay, its guid tae hae im here, richt eneuch, tae its time for im tae gang... ye'll hae tae lat im gan, lass... oo cannae brung Jamie back, ye ken."

"A ken yon. De ye nae ken, A ken yon? Bit its guid tae hae the wee laddie here an heez nae tribble it aw... is e noo?

304

Willie shook his head but did not speak because in his mind he saw himself, on that dark night, with the whisky bottle and the park bench. He had drunk the bottle empty and sat all night, alone and undisturbed until the morning light when he went back home to Jeannie and crawled into bed beside her, cold sober even for all the drink. He had held her in his arms and felt her warm comforting body, made love to her and held back his tears for his boy had not even died a hero. Just an unfortunate accident, the letter had said. Somehow Lance Corporal Jamie MacTavish had lost control of his jeep as he drove around the barracks in England, hit a tree and been killed instantly. He was a good soldier, the letter had said, a credit to his Regiment and sadly missed by all. Commiserations to his family, the letter concluded. But Wee Willie MacTavish could not weep for his son. Whenever he thought of him, he thought of that night with the whisky and Jeannie, for Jeannie had known what to do. Jeannie had always known what to do; ever since they had first met, Jeannie had known what to do.

Jeannie did indeed know what to do. Everything came out of Jamie's room – his clothes, his shoes, his Boy Scout badges, his school achievement awards, everything, except his photograph and his hair-brush. These she kept on his dressing table. For Jamie in his uniform was her boy. How he had loved the Army and how proud he had been of his one stripe.

"I'll be a Sergeant one day," he would tell her and she believed him. There had been no reason to doubt until the letter came. After that, Jeannie took everything away but she hid a lock of her baby's hair, golden brown and soft, hid it along with his teddy bear and school reports and the silver cup he had won for winning the long distance swimming race. All these things she arranged in a shoe box, secured with a rubber band and kept the box hidden, safe in the dark attic and never breathed a word of it to any living soul, not even to Willie. She stripped the boyish lime green paper off the walls and, with her friend Jessie to help, cleared the room, turning her Jamie's room into a blue and white shell with no memory, laying it bare except for the furniture which she repainted gloss white. Yes, Jeannie had known what to do.

Oisin, lying on his back at night, gazing at the ceiling, knew none of this. All he felt was unease in the room and didn't know why. But here was a bed for him and outside, the city sounds. That was enough. He rang his mother to tell her what had happened and gave her his new address.

"Have you seen Silvio?" she asked and he fumbled a reply.

"I'll write," Annie said. "There's a lot happening!"

Annie wrote him a letter. A long letter, too, it must have taken her ages for she covered three pages with her neat handwriting. She wrote:

"The big news is that Declan has met a girl, English, from the south coast, near Hastings. She was over on holidays with her friend, an Irish girl from Co Sligo. Well, Declan is besotted with her and plays nothing but love songs at Murphy's. Ma teases him all the time. She's a lovely girl called Joyce." Annie sounded pleased.

"Effie and Leslie arrived at An Teach Ban one afternoon with a six-pound trout which they all enjoyed. Leslie is helping Mary with her art work because Mary has quite a talent apparently and has her sights set on Art School. She's sulking all the time about having to stay in Ballybeg but she does take Bess out nearly every day – along the beach as usual as far as Old Mother Fahy's. One of them looks in on the old woman every day. She's as well as can be expected and her roof is fine but she still thinks you went to America!

Father Byrne is well and as busy as ever. The parish is expanding and there's talk of a new priest to help with the workload. 'Oh Dear' still as worried as ever, don't think he will ever leave but be a curate forever!

Tommy Flynn is very ill with pneumonia, in the Ballybeg Hospital but they might have to take him to Galway. Doesn't look good.

Doctor and Mrs Ryan are away. She persuaded him finally to buy an apartment on the Costa Brava near the border with France. Might go with them one time, for a few weeks, it has been suggested. The Ryans plan to spend the winters there. Doctor Flannery is getting married – to a doctor too – and they intend to stay in Ballybeg. It will be good to have two doctors again.

It's turning cold and there was a frost the other night. Been a lot of rain, too, and the Owenbeg nearly burst its banks again but it was nothing like the big storm.

Have you heard from Frankie? When are you going to see Silvio? Hope you're going to Mass every week. What are you doing with yourself in Edinburgh and who are these MacTavishes?"

Oisin read his mother's letter carefully, word for word. The events from Ballybeg were other events, other people's lives. He viewed them now from a distance and was hesitant in replying too quickly. No, he would have to think about what he wanted to tell his mother. He was pleased for Declan though. He would make a good husband and father and look after Annie. If it had just been Frankie and Annie left, Father Frankie would have assigned his mother to a Home for the Elderly somewhere and called it performing his filial duty! No, Declan had always been the restraining force between Frankie and Oisin. Somehow, Frankie could always find Oisin's weak spot and would work on enlarging it and was almost gleeful as he did so. Then Declan would defuse the situation and Frankie would wander off, leaving Oisin alone, grateful to be left in peace. Oisin sighed. And Mary sounded ready to go to Art School. He hoped she didn't have her sights set on Edinburgh. He was quite enjoying being away from his siblings and all the family dramas. At least here with Jeannie and Willie he was his own man and didn't have to put up with the various crises, nor did he have to think of his mother and his uncle... together. He had tried unsuccessfully to distance himself from that knowledge but the thought of them would burrow into his mind and surface at odd moments. He could be working away quite happily with Willie or just walking along the street, when, out of the blue, the image of the two of them would disturb his thoughts and he wished he had never known. No one else knew... he was sure of that. His mother would stay silent because this was her way. No, Oisin thought to himself, I'm glad I'm not back there. It's exhilarating being away. I won't be missed, I was never missed. Even my mother mightn't miss me, he concluded with a certain amount of sadness, except to make sure I'm going to Mass and to find about Silvio and this Concetta. After all that's just curiosity.

"I have to visit someone," he said to Jeannie one evening when the two of them were sitting contentedly together. "That's why I came over... I've an address... I'll catch a bus... on Saturday!"

His heart beat a little faster as he spoke and he didn't know why. Just that he had this queer strange feeling that Silvio Luchetta was important, somehow, and that meeting him would transform his life. How, he did not know but he was almost certain of this and would have laid a bet on it had he been a betting man.

*****

42 Willow Crescent was a surprise. Oisin arrived outside the black wrought-iron gates at about ten o'clock on Saturday morning with the ebony box carefully packed into a small brown bag. The knapsack had proved unwieldy and the smaller canvas bag he had bought was much handier for his day-to-day life. He was nervous as he stood outside the gates. Ornate gates, too, with an intricate swirl of a design on both sides and meeting in the middle at the very top. No 42 was carved with much precision into the dressed stone which held them. The design was cleverly thought out and it took him a few moments to locate the

bolt. Having done so, he hesitated then decided, somewhat sheepishly, that the preferred entrance had to be through the smaller wrought iron gate further along the wall. This opened more easily and led up a gravel path to the front door. Four large cedar trees had obscured the view of the house from the street. If it had been a sunnier day and not a cold November morning Oisin would have taken more notice of the extensive garden, bare in the winter light but promising much in the springtime. The cold wind blew shafts of air across his face as he trampled over the wet orange and brown leaves. There were three stone steps, well worn in the middle, which led up to the front door. Two dressed stone Doric pillars stood on either side. This was a grand house –not at all the kind of dwelling in which he had imagined Silvio Luchetta to live. He had thought the mysterious Italian would reside in some inner city tenement, up a dozen steps or so, dark rooms and even darker surroundings. But here was a three-storey mansion with countless chimney pots, shutters over many windows and set in such a vast garden that the neighbours' similar dwellings were hidden by high shrubbery on either side.

Oisin hesitated. In front of him was the most impressive oak door that he had ever seen, making Doctor Ryan's grand entrance back in Ballybeg insignificant by comparison. The door was stained a dark brown and to add to the grandeur a rather flamboyant brass door handle in the shape of a wild boar's head completed the design. There was another bell, though, set next to the door and Oisin decided that this probably was the most obvious to ring. He pressed it hard and waited, then pressed it again, holding his finger down longer this time. All the time the wind swirled around and as it did, deposited droplets of rain and sleet which wet his face and coat. The weather conditions combined with his nervousness began to affect him and he was about to postpone his mission, to call again if he must, on another, more pleasant day, when the door was opened slightly by a young girl with curly red hair. She was about his age. She looked slightly amused at the sight of the rather odd-looking young man standing on the doorstep with his tweed cap over his eyes and his collar pulled up around his ears.

"Hello," said Oisin politely, "Does someone called Silvio Luchetta live here?"

The girl nodded but made no move to open the door any further.

"I have... something for him... is it possible to speak to him?"

At his words, the girl opened the door further.

"Wait here," she said, and shut the door again

Oisin was now left standing clutching his canvas bag tight in his right hand and trying to keep the rain from wetting him by holding the collar of his coat with his left. Rain, turning into droplets of sleet glistened on top of his cap. Finally, after what seemed an age, the girl opened the door again.

"Mr Luchetta wants to know who ye are?"

"Oh," Oisin answered, surprised, "Tell him I'm Mick Kelly's nephew from Ireland and I have something for him from Mick. My name's Oisin."

"That's a funny name," said the girl and shut the door again. A minute later she opened the door again.

"Ye'd better come in then."

Oisin entered a grand hallway with a highly decorated white plaster ceiling above and dark oak panels on the walls below. Directly in front of him at the far end of the hallway stood a marble bust of a man which sat rather confidently in the centre of a similar marble stand.

"Gie me yer coat," said the girl to Oisin.

Oisin's coat now hung beside other coats and scarves on a stand at the door. His coat looked rather shabby by comparison, he thought. He wiped his shoes on the coir mat at the door. He seemed to be dripping water everywhere and he tried to shake himself somewhat in the manner of Sophocles and Aristotle, back home. The girl giggled.

"Gie me yer bag," she said, giving him a cheeky grin.

Oisin swept his cap from his head exposing his curly black hair.

"No, I'll keep it..."

"Suit yersel then. Ye'd best come wi me... this wey."

He followed her obediently, delighted to be behind her. Her black mini- skirt clung ever so tightly to her body. Long legs clad in black nylons seemed to go on forever as she swung her hips confidently, well aware of the effect that she was having on this odd young man from Ireland.

"Here ye are then."

They were now closer to the marble plinth at the end of the hallway. A Coat of Arms with faded white background hung directly above it. Divided into four equal sections, a red cross on the top left, a black boar's head on the bottom right and above a crown, below a scroll. It was an ancient piece of craftsmanship and totally fitted its surroundings. The Coat of Arms was purposeful... somehow necessary above the marble and the two uncomfortable looking hall chairs, carved in walnut inlaid with olive wood that sat on either side. Oisin, his interest in wood aroused along with his preoccupation with the girl, noticed two heavily carved walnut tables along the wall. Four carved eagles, their wings outstretched, supported the tops and, arranged perfectly in the centre of each table, were two tall identical porcelain vases decorated with Chinese dragons breathing clouds.

How Mick would have liked the carving, thought Oisin as he passed by.

"Wait in here. Mr Luchetta will be along soon, he said."

Oisin looked around. Books filled the room. More books than he had ever seen. Mick had books but just three boxes and the Williamsons had hundreds hidden behind the clutter, but here was a library indeed. Leather-bound volumes, paperbacks, hard covers with dust jackets browning at the edges all arranged neatly on oak shelves and behind glass doors. A comfortable room this, thought Oisin, lit by three glass wall lights and an open fire where logs burned red and bright flames flickered through them. It was warm and cosy and Oisin relaxed slightly. On a mat in front of the fireplace, stretched out and asleep, was a grey cat with dark feet. Oisin had never seen a cat like it.

"What sort of cat is that?" he asked the girl. He couldn't help himself. The words just tumbled out.

"Ocht, that yins 'Ra'. Spoiled rotten if ye ask me. That's the Signora's cat. They're Italian, ye ken."

"What... the cat?" asked Oisin, surprised.

"Ocht, dinnae be silly! The Luchettas. Dinnae ye have cats in Ireland?"

"Of course we do... but none like that. It's got blue eyes!"

For at that moment, the cat opened its eyes, stretched and rolled over onto its other side. Then it stood up, arched its back and stretched its front paws in front of it and clawed the mat as it did.

"They used to be guard dogs in Ancient Egypt," said the girl knowingly.

"What do ye mean... how can a cat be a dog?"

"It's not a dog," replied the girl mischievously. "It's a cat and it's called Ra and if it likes ye, the Signora will like ye too!"

At this, the cat let out a loud yowl. Oisin had never heard such a noise and he giggled too.

"Sounds more like a dog now," he said.

"Leave it be. It won't harm ye. Too lazy, I say and too spoilt. Ye should see what the Signora feeds it. Why, my mother would have fed us all with the leftovers from that cat!!"

The cat sat on its haunches. Its clear blue eyes fixed on Oisin's face. It looked like a statue and viewed the two humans as intruders into its temple.

"Sit yersel doon... and forget Ra. He won't harm ye. I best be off now before the Signora calls." She grinned. "Might see ye again... ye never ken. I like yer accent, "she added and winked at him. She bent towards him slightly and Oisin caught a glimpse of her cleavage.

"Like yours too!" he said cheekily and the girl laughed.

Oisin relaxed more. He sat down on one of the chairs. All the chairs were covered with rugs presumably to prevent Ra from doing too much damage with his claws. The cat and Oisin studied each other. Neither appeared too sure of their next move. Oisin, despite his nervousness was curious. How could Mick whose mental state was always under discussion in Ballybeg, how could he have made the acquaintance of the likes of Silvio Luchetta? How could their paths have crossed and having crossed, what could their relationship possibly have as a common meeting ground? It seemed to Oisin, examining the room and the books around him, to be as much a mystery as the strange feline creature whose blue eyes fixed so determinedly onto his face and who refused to move from its position upon the hearth rug. Oisin was about to make a move to befriend the cat when the door to the library opened and in strode Silvio Luchetta. Here at last, and the reason for the visit, was the man who had made such an impact on the lives of the Kelly family so many years ago. He was older now but still held himself upright and as much in command as he had been then. Oisin shot to his feet and stood to attention much like a soldier who, seeing an officer about, stands rigid and expressionless.

"Sit," said Silvio. He sat down opposite Oisin and clasped his hands together. He fixed his eyes onto Oisin's face and it seemed to the poor lad that four eyes were upon him now for Ra still had not moved a muscle.

"I'm sorry to trouble ye, sir," he spluttered, "but I've something here for ye from my Uncle Mick back in Ballybeg. I'm his nephew, Oisin..." he faltered.

313

"Ah!" Silvio smiled. "I remember now. The honest man."

Oisin reddened. He reached towards his canvas bag and as he did so, Ra moved as well. With one gigantic leap the cat propelled himself from the hearth to the arm of Oisin's chair and then to the back where he sat, looking down. He proceeded to emit a most peculiar and noisy purr into Oisin's ear. Oisin, by now, was feeling decidedly awkward and wished desperately to be away from the room and the Luchetta mansion. He carefully lifted the ebony box from his bag and laid it gently upon his knee so that both man and cat could see. Silvio frowned. Ra purred even louder and Oisin cleared his throat.

"My Uncle Mick wanted ye to have this, sir. He said... well, he wrote me a letter... he wanted me to bring it to ye, the box, I mean, sure... he said ye would know what to do. I've a key for it and I've seen inside... there were photographs but he didn't want them to go, I mean, he just left letters and a few pieces of jewellery, sir..."

In his confusion, Oisin had not noticed that Silvio's expression had changed. The Italian now sat further back in his chair. He did not speak but tapped the fingers of his right hand onto the arm of his chair. Any further words that Oisin had wanted to say disappeared and he, too, fell silent. Only the persistent rasping purr of Ra broke the silence. The cat had settled quite comfortably onto the back of the chair and was endeavouring to reach out towards Oisin's head with his front paw, claws outstretched. Suddenly, Silvio smiled.

"Well done, young man," he said in his heavily accented English and he motioned Oisin to position the box onto the desk at the window. As Oisin got up he tripped over the canvas bag and felt even more foolish. But he managed to carefully place Mick's box onto the green leather of the mahogany desk and the box sat there, black, mysterious and majestic.

314

There was a bell positioned on the wall beside Silvio. He pressed it and a moment later the girl with the red hair appeared.

"Nellie," said Silvio, "the Signora, is she available?"

"Yes, Mr Luchetta."

Nellie was as servile as it was possible to be and did not look at Oisin.

"Ask her to come to the library. There is something to see."

It was now that Nellie glanced quickly at Oisin and grinned slightly. Oisin thought she winked at him but he wasn't too sure and all the time Silvio continued to stare at the box on the desk. His hair was grey, no longer greased and dark but softer now and there was no moustache upon his upper lip. He ran his fingers through his hair in a slightly distracted way and as he did, he thoughtfully nodded his head slightly as if he was recalling some long ago memory.

"Ah, Michael..." he murmured.

A moment later a small rather stout woman entered the room. There are some women who remain beautiful all their lives and, whatever the joys and sufferings they have encountered along the way, their faces stay as beautiful as in the days of their youth. Only the wrinkles and blemishes and thinning hair betray the increasing number of years. The woman who now stood before Oisin was one of those fortunate women. Although her hair was almost completely white and thin lines showed on her face, neck and around her mouth, her eyes were clear and bright. The shape of her head combined with the way she held herself upright and proud would have made her the perfect model for an artist with an eye for perfection in a woman's face. She must have been a stunning beauty at twenty. Forty or more years further on, she still had the same beauty, perhaps even more so after a lifetime of experience. Silvio rose to his feet and with a gesture of his hand announced:

315

"May I present my sister, Signora Cavellessi... and your name, young sir, I forget..."

"Oisin... It's Oisin Kelly."

The Signora extended her right hand to Oisin who clasped it in his. Her hand was light to the touch, a perfectly shaped hand; the fingernails elegantly painted with bright red varnish... and on the ring finger, an emerald ring surrounded with diamonds. Oisin was completed captivated. He wished he was an Italian and older. He would have loved to kiss that small hand, to press it to his lips the way the Europeans do for he had never set eyes on such an elegant woman before. He wished he had spent the time to run a comb through his black unruly hair and changed his Arran jumper his mother had knitted for a collar and tie.

"Pleased to meet ye, Signora," he mumbled and lowered his eyes. The Signora smiled gently.

"This is the nephew of Michael, Rosa," said Silvio.

At the mention of Mick's name, Signora Cavellessi drew in a breath and pressed her left hand to her cheek.

"Michael! *Grazie a Dio!* He is well?"

Eagerly she turned to Oisin... her soft brown eyes intent and Oisin was suddenly filled with apprehension, so surprised was he by the reaction that the name of his uncle had brought.

"No... I mean... I'm sorry," he faltered.

Both the Signora and Silvio and Ra too, stared at him, waiting on his next words. He was unsure and overcome. He blurted the words out clumsily, disjointedly and nervously.

"My uncle... he passed away a year ago... now... last November... I'm sorry."

"Ah," murmured the Signora.

"We do not know," cried Silvio. "That is why you come to us, of course... to tell us... that is why, Rosa... Michael wants us to know... and Concetta..." And he put his arm around his sister's shoulders.

"He is at peace now, Rosa. We are at peace, all of us... now."

The Signora sat down but there was an expression of such pathos over her beautiful face that Oisin, in his bewilderment, longed to know why. She sat down and as she lowered her body to the chair, her eyes caught sight of the ebony box in the centre of the desk. The shock must have been great for she rose again from her chair and, clasping her brother's arm, cried out in her native tongue:

"*È una scatola d'ebano di Papa. Ha ritornata a casa.*" (It's Father's ebony box. It's come back home)," and, turning to look at Silvio's face, she cried out: "*Dov'è stata? Dov'è stata?*" (Where is it? Where is it?).

Then Silvio took hold of his sister's hand.

"Michael is returning it to us... this boy, Rosa... he brings it back. At last. At last."

The Signora nodded and, as Oisin watched, her expression, which had in the last few moments gone from shock to sadness, regained the composure he had seen at first meeting. She turned to her brother.

"*Sì!* It is right, Silvio, it is right." She paused, slightly speaking now to Oisin. "My eyes have not looked upon that... the box of my father, Oh – sean (she faltered as she tried to pronounce his name), for forty years... it is a long time, *sì?*"

Now it was Oisin's turn to nod his head. Forty years was indeed a long time to have such a memory of a material thing.

"You have the look of your uncle... ah... it is Michael here... what fantasy! What fantasy! You think so, Silvio? He has the look of Michael. Say it!"

"*Sì,*" answered Silvio, softly, "It is a long time, *cara sorella.*" (dear sister).

At his words, Signora Cavelessi raised both her arms, palms outstretched in a gesture of finality, inclining her head to one side so that the light from the fire cast a glow onto her face. Her cheeks reddened in the dim light and

317

Oisin, quite overcome, would have fallen to his knees in front of her had it been another time and another place and he another man.

"Let me see inside the box. You have the key? Silvio. You have the key?"

She touched the top of the box with her right hand. That manicured hand travelled across the domed lid and down the sides. She caressed it as tenderly as a loving mother would stroke her child.

"I've the key here, Signora," replied Oisin, suddenly feeling brave. Now he was curious beyond belief. How would Silvio and the Signora view its contents? He fumbled in his bag for the ornate brass key that he had kept safe for months and handed it to Silvio.

"Ah... Rosa..."

Silvio lifted the pearl necklace from the box and handed it to his sister. She held the necklace in the palm of her left hand and ran her fingers over each pearl. It occurred to Oisin that the Signora had entered a distant world of memories, of secrets long hidden and carefully guarded and that each pearl told a story.

"There is more?" she asked. She clasped the necklace to her heart. Silvio delved once more into the box and carefully placed the jewellery – the Irish wedding ring, the brooch with sapphire and gold, the diamond ring – onto the desk and all this time, the Signora held the pearls to her.

"There are letters, Rosa. Letters from Michael..."

Now it was Silvio who looked puzzled. He sat down on the leather chair at his desk and ran his fingers through his hair once again. It seemed to Oisin that a drama was unfolding on stage and any minute the actors would expect the audience to applaud as the final scene was about to take place. Oisin by now was removed from the stage, he thought, a silent witness, with just Ra's front paws balanced on his shoulder as a distraction. The cat had

318

evidently decided that this boy was a friend and worthy of feline attention.

"Two letters, Rosa. Two letters. One, it appears is addressed to me and... the other to Concetta."

Silvio laid the two sealed letters beside the ebony box. From a stand that held bottles of ink and various fountain pens, he took a silver paperknife and carefully and slowly, opened the letter that Oisin had so longed to see for so many months. He unfolded three pages and read the words carefully before returning the letter to its envelope.

"I see you are a poet and a warrior, Mr Oisin Kelly."

Oisin hesitated.

"My uncle always called me that, sir... for as long as I can remember."

"Ah, and it appears that it is so. You learn much from your uncle, young man. There is much to tell. There are hidden lives and hidden secrets too long buried, is that not so, Rosa? But alas, we are here for so short a time... we keep our secrets guarded, we do not speak but then... poof... before we know..." and, as he spoke these words, Silvio raised his eyes heavenwards, shrugged and opened both palms of his hands. "Death, she comes... and the secrets we have kept so careful and so hidden for such a long time *per l'amore di Dio* (for the love of God) – then, we speak. Is that not so, young man?"

Oisin, by this time was hopelessly confused by all that had taken place, and he could only murmur:

"My uncle left me a letter, too, sir. I was to bring the box and the letters to ye. Don't know why me... I've an elder brother a priest... he would have been better to have asked, not me..."

Silvio smiled.

"Ah, yes. I remember now. The elder brother of the family Kellys... a bright young man, I agree. Destined to go far ... a priest, what do you think of that, Rosa? The nephew of Michael, a priest?"

"Do not mock, Silvio."

319

"You see, young man," Silvio said, "My sister, she thinks I mock. What do you say?"

"I do not know, sir... only that my brother, no doubt will be a competent priest."

"Ha – there you have it! You do not say 'a holy man' or 'a good man' or even 'a saviour of his people' but 'a competent priest'. No, young sir, Michael tells us the truth. You are the right man to return this box and the letters to us. Is that not so?"

"I do not know," answered Oisin, miserably.

"You are to be brave, Oisin Kelly. That is what your uncle wishes for you. You are a warrior, *sì*, I can see that and you have the soul of a poet. Do not die with your dreams still in you. And now, Rosa, we ask this young man – this nephew of Michael – this young man who returns to us the black box of Papa, we invite this young man from Ireland, the land of saints and scholars, we invite him to join us as our guest on Sunday." Silvio opened a leather-bound book which Oisin assumed was a diary. "*Sì*... you will join us a week now... on Sunday for dinner at the house of the *familigia* Luchetta. Concetta and Isabella, they will come on Sunday. You eat with us. You are remaining in Edinburgh?"

Oisin nodded. It was now that he rose from his feet, disturbing Ra. The cat leapt onto the arm of the adjoining chair and glared at Oisin. The Signora laughed.

"See how Ra likes you, Oh-sean. You will come to dine with us and Ra, he meets you once more. We eat at one."

She extended her hand graciously to Oisin. He shook it gently and smiled.

"I will come," he said, "and thank you. Yes, I will come and meet Ra again... and yourselves, too, of course."

Suddenly, he wasn't miserable anymore.

"Ah," answered Silvio, "You are a man who laughs, now I see that. One day you will see also that Michael was right – you are the one to come to the family of the Luchettas. *Grazie*."

And with those, words Oisin was dismissed. Escorted by both Silvio and the Signora to the front door and this time there were no summons for the red-haired girl called Nellie. Outside, the first snow of the winter was falling and Oisin, his heart pounding, ran from Number 42 Willow Crescent. He stopped at the black iron gate. Behind him the snow had covered his footsteps to the front door and the footprints were already disappearing from sight. He walked briskly and gaily with his empty canvas bag folded under his arm.

CHAPTER FIFTEEN

Oisin's thoughts were all of a muddle as he approached the Luchetta mansion for that, he decided was the right description of the building in front of him. For it was a mansion, indeed and gathered within its walls there was elegance and mystery, too. The light covering of snow still lay on the ground and the air was crisp and clear. Overnight, there had been a hard frost and Oisin's footsteps over the frozen ground disturbed the otherwise quiet scene, for the distant hum of traffic caused no problems in this garden. A robin, its spindly legs black against the white background, flew off as Oisin approached. Above, the sky was that soft pale blue of northern climes for there wasn't a cloud to be seen and the robin quickly disappeared from sight.

This time Oisin had taken greater care with his appearance.

"Ocht, wull ye tak a leuk at the wee mannie!" cried Jeannie when she saw him and just as mischievously she added, "Thar must be a lassie aboot!!"

To which Oisin replied with a cheery grin:

"I'm off to dine with the gentry. It's Sunday lunch and all."

And he straightened his wide floral tie and ran his fingers through his hair in a desperate attempt to smooth his black tousled curls.

He was thinking of Jeannie's remark as he rang the bell, more familiar this time. In the cold morning air his breath was a fog in front of him and he stamped his feet up and down on the icy step. He was anticipating Nellie with her suggestive demeanour and low cut blouse that promised much if he made the right moves. For days he had rehearsed what to say to her for he had decided to ask her out and hoped she would accept. Surely the soft Irish brogue would be as successful with the women as it had been for his father and he made up his mind to use it to his advantage. He moved his feet again as the cold penetrated his shoes for it seemed he had been waiting on the step for ages. He cleared his throat anxious now for a sight of Nellie.

"It is yerself," he planned to say, "and lookin' for all the world like the wild Irish rose back home. An' sure smellin' as sweet, so."

He thought this might just do the trick and hopefully her reply would lead on to pleasant things.

But when the heavy oak door finally opened it wasn't Nellie who stood before him but a black-haired woman in her late twenties with soft brown eyes. Perched securely on her hip was a small boy with the same dark hair and dark eyes. Seeing the stranger at the door, he leaned back onto the woman's shoulder and stuck his thumb into his mouth.

"Welcome," the woman said. "We have been expecting you. Come in. Come in out of the cold."

Oisin, who had the Irish ease with young children, immediately wanted to make the acquaintance of the young lad and also to be introduced to the woman whom he had to assume was the mother. He swept his cap from his head and ran his fingers through his hair in another futile attempt to appear tidy. The woman smiled at his antics. Her manner was familiar and relaxed. Oisin grinned. The small boy giggled and took his thumb out of his mouth.

"This young man is named Silvio," said the woman in perfect English when all three were safely standing in the hall. "And I am Concetta."

Before Oisin could utter a word she eased young Silvio to the floor and held out her hand.

"You must be Oisin," she said and she pronounced his name perfectly which surprised Oisin. Even Jeannie and Willie struggled with his name but this woman, who was obviously Italian, had no such problem. There was just the slight appeal of a foreign accent which added to Oisin's enjoyment on hearing his name. He smiled.

"Now, you must meet my family. We have been talking about you all week," Concetta said somewhat mysteriously.

She motioned for him to follow her and they walked slowly along the hall past the library where Oisin had been last week. Young Silvio ran ahead, his arms outstretched in the manner of a fighter plane and as he ran, he emitted a sound which possibly could have resembled the engine. He led them into a room at the end of the hall next to where the marble plinth and uncomfortable hall chairs were situated. Oisin looked around the elegant room with interest. He studied the ornate plaster ceiling and thick beige drapes. A log fire was burning away and various chairs were arranged somewhat randomly around the room. On one of these, Signora Cavellessi sat with a baby on her knee.

"Ah, Concetta... you bring Oh-sean!" she cried when she saw Oisin. "Oh-sean, we are so, so pleased to meet with you once more. Now you make the acquaintance of the family of Luchetta. You are surprised, perhaps? May I present my daughter, Concetta... and you have met my grandson, Silvio. This *bambina*..." and her eyes rested for a moment upon the face of the sleeping child," this is Sofia... is she not beautiful?"

Oisin nodded. In awe of his welcome, he almost turned his head to see if there was someone else in the room. After all, his life had been lived up to this point of time in the shadow of two elder brothers and an uncle whom no one understood. This was life, as far as Oisin was concerned, and to be suddenly made much of, with his tousled hair and less than handsome appearance, was novel. Here, it appeared, he was neither the object of ridicule nor judgement. He smiled.

"Sure," he answered politely. "Isn't she the most beautiful baby indeed?" and he knelt down beside the child, quite at ease, and studied her tiny face with the dark eyelashes and soft black hair. The Signora, delighted, clasped the small body even closer to her bosom. She inclined her head and placed the softest of kisses onto the brow of her sleeping grandchild.

"Now... it is time for my darling to go to her mother. Concetta..."

As Oisin watched Concetta cradled her baby to her. Baby Sofia murmured slightly but did not waken as her mother stood, her body swaying, and as she rocked the child, she hummed the gentlest of tunes. Here was love and Oisin cleared his throat – almost an intruder in a female world. But now he could study Concetta and it was at that precise moment as she stood in front of him that he remembered the black and white photograph in Mick's box. Here was that same beauty, older, but the same and his heart quickened. Concetta stood, her back to the window and past her he could see the pale sky and trees bereft of leaves, black silhouettes against the blue. It was mid morning but the winter light was weak. The glow from the fire reflected onto the dark-eyed beauty in front of him. Oisin felt himself growing mellow for the warmth of the room, and the security of the domestic contentment around him relaxed him. He had come to the Luchettas not knowing what to expect, half-expecting Nellie and little else but now he was captivated. He sat down, unbidden. He had entered a new world and the old world of certainties and expectations seemed to melt away in front of his eyes. Any minute now, he would burst into song. He, too, would be part of the scene. His heart leapt in his throat but shyness overcame him and he could not utter a word.

"Oh-sean." It was the Signora pronouncing his name in her peculiar fashion. She rested her hand gently onto his shoulder.

"Now I present to you Ramòn, the husband of Concetta. Ramòn Valdés. Ramòn... my friend, Oh-sean Kelly from Ireland."

The most unlikely-looking man to be a husband to Concetta extended his hand towards Oisin. He was of swarthy appearance with thick black hair, greying slightly at the temples and black eyes that did not look in Oisin's direction. Short of stature, his had the bearing of one whose home is the Iberian peninsula but when Oisin took hold of Ramón's hand he found it to be limp and moist and not at all what he would have expected. In fact, Ramón Valdés was neither forceful nor opinionated and preferred to remain in the background. Amongst the Luchettas, he was something of an oddity and was included in family gatherings because he was the husband of Concetta and the father of her two children. Ramón's purpose in life began and ended there and it became very clear to Oisin in a very short space of time that the doleful Spaniard simply idolised his wife. Concetta issued commands which her husband meekly obeyed and there never was such an unusual match it seemed. After all, not every man is a tyrant or every woman a slave.

Concetta laughed. She swung her hips gaily and all the time Ramón looked on adoringly, hardly noticing Oisin. Ramón did not encourage intimacy. He bowed to Oisin and then as quickly as he could, withdrew to the other side of the room. There, he sat, his small frame bent forward slightly in the large chair and his melancholic eyes fixed on his wife. The conversation flowed around him but he took no part at all except to nod occasionally. Life, it appeared to Oisin, passed Ramón by. Concetta talked unceasingly about people and events. Baby Sofia slept soundly in her cradle by the window while young Silvio, now the centre of attention, performed antics in front of Oisin who was relaxed enough to respond to the boy.

"We talked about you all the time," Concetta chatted on, "such excitement, wasn't it, Mamma? And the black box back. What joy!"

"My uncle had secrets," replied Oisin, "the box being one of many," he added as his mind shot back to his mother. "Yes, my uncle was a mysterious man, there's no two ways about it, God rest his soul."

"Michael was a clever man," the Signora suddenly said. She had not taken part in the conversation since her introduction of Ramón.

"Of course, Signora."

"We must respect the memory of Michael. There was no man like him."

Oisin frowned slightly. Upon hearing her words, he decided to be brave.

"There was a photograph in the box, Signora... was it Concetta?" he hesitated, uncertain whether to go on, "I don't mean to pry... but there was a letter too... and one for me as well... telling me to bring the box to you."

"*Sì*...," the Signora's voice was soft, "*Sì*, that photograph is of Concetta... my daughter... Time, how you say, goes by?"

Her expression was sad and it seemed to Oisin that he had opened a wound through no fault of his own; a wound that had to be opened for healing to take place. It still did not occur to him that there was any connection between Mick and Concetta. Puzzled, he frowned.

"No one knew anything about my Uncle Mick. He lived with me all my life and I never knew him. No-one did. My father used to get annoyed but Mick always got his way. That was Mick."

"You must tell me about him," murmured the Signora, "what life was like for him in Ireland. It is so long now. You see, Oh-sean, when Silvio comes, we explain but now, we wait."

The logs burned down in the grate. Soon there would be just the red glow of a dying fire.

"Ramón, the fire..." said the Signora.

At her words, Ramón rose from the darkness of his chair at the back of the room and knelt on the thick Persian rug beside the fire. He took a long handled ornate iron poker and re-kindled the fire. Soon the logs crackled into life and Ramón withdrew once more.

"Ho fame! Ho fame!" cried young Silvio in Italian, holding his stomach.

Oisin glanced at the solid Grandfather clock situated beside a green marble-topped table. Both the legs of the table and the face of the clock were covered in gold gilt. It was now almost one-thirty and there was no sign of either Silvio Luchetta or Sunday lunch. Oisin was hungry, too. On an empty stomach and in front of the warm fire, he felt himself succumbing to drowsiness. His eyelids grew heavy. Ramón had poured him a large sherry. He sipped it slowly so as not to appear impolite but he was not used to alcohol. Once, years ago when he was just sixteen, Liam Murphy had plied him with whiskey and Oisin had drunk half a bottle of the stuff. Annoyed that afternoon with Baldy Lawrence, he had wanted relief from his annoyance and the whiskey, he thought, would take the shame of the ridicule away. He forced the liquid down his throat. Gradually it worked its spell upon him. He became agitated. His head spun. His forehead grew damp. He stumbled and fell. Brown foul-smelling vomit spewed from his mouth onto the road and over his shirt. He was unaware of what was happening. In the morning he vowed he would never drink like that again as the reasons for his inebriation could never justify the effect it caused. No, sobriety was for him. He could never get drunk enough, he decided, to escape from himself and Baldy Lawrence would pass but a drunken man is a slave all his life.

The clock ticked on and on. Then suddenly there was movement in the room. At last, thought Oisin gratefully. As Silvio Luchetta entered the room, young Silvio leapt to his feet, Oisin forgotten.

"Uncle Silvio! Uncle Silvio!" he cried and held his hands in the air.

Silvio lifted the child and thrust him upwards above his head. Young Silvio, now high above the heads of the adults, giggled uncontrollably. His world took on a wonderful new aspect and when his uncle lowered him to the floor, he held his hands upwards to be lifted again. Silvio patted him affectionately on the top of his head and turning to Oisin said,

"Ah, Oisin, you have waited too long. Now, we eat. Rosa... Isabella cannot come."

"Com'è bruto... "(How cruel...) murmured Concetta.

"Senti, Concetta, non sappiamo..."(Listen, Concetta, we don't know...).

The Signora took Oisin's arm. She was completely at ease with him.

"They speak of Isabella, Oh-sean. She cannot be with us today. Isabella is the daughter of my brother, Silvio... you meet with her soon. Next time..." And she patted his hand. "Come!"

She motioned him to follow and the little group entered the dining room. Young Silvio charged ahead with eager shouts, "Food! Food!" much to everyone's amusement. Oisin smiled too for there is nothing more enchanting for adults than to observe the behaviour of the young.

If Oisin had expected a room smaller than the one he had just vacated, he would have been disappointed for the room he now entered was vast. Large casement windows extended from the ceiling to the polished wooden floor, and the thick crimson velvet curtains pinned back on either side hung so that the thin winter light barely penetrated into the room. It was necessary to have the three candles lit on the table and all the side lights on. Outside Oisin could see the garden, white with frost and beyond a huge chestnut tree, he could just make out the topiary garden – trees shaped to look like chess pieces, King and Queen and Bishop with the smaller trees in front, cut like the pawns, all with their leaves glistening in the winter sun. But it was the room that completely stunned him. Doctor Ryan's dining room back in Ballybeg was a modest arrangement by comparison and he had thought that a grand affair. The table was set for six. The thin white candles in their elegant silver holders burned brightly in the centre while above the table an ornate glass chandelier hung. Its splendour was reflected in the large mirror framed in white marble along the wall. So much silver and fine Venetian wine glasses, Oisin felt himself grow more nervous by the minute. The dark walnut sideboard under the mirror held trays of food and fruit, bottles of wine, serving spoons, fine bone china plates.

"And now we eat!" announced Silvio, grandly, and he sat firmly at the end of the table. Everyone obeyed. Oisin blushed furiously. He was quite overcome. Suddenly, unbidden, Mick came into his thoughts as he tried to move the heavy walnut chair with its white damask cushion attached to the seat. He longed to say, "Did my Uncle dine here?" for it seemed to him that the idea of Mick and the Luchettas was so incongruous as to be bordering on the fanciful. But he dared not speak and sat down awkwardly, folding his hands under the white linen tablecloth so as not to be seen.

"You eat with us, Oh-sean – you eat well. Today, Maria, she is inspired," the Signora whispered confidentially in his ear for it was she who sat at the opposite end of the table to her brother and it was she who insisted that Oisin sit next to her. All Oisin could murmur was a muted 'Thank you,' for his attention was focused on the correct procedure and, fearful lest he embarrass himself amongst such generosity, he lowered his head. His embarrassment did not seem to bother his hosts however, for they talked constantly, sometimes in Italian, sometimes in English and all the time Concetta's merry laugh brought smiles all around but when Silvio spoke, the chatter ceased. He was the patriarch indeed and as much in control of himself here as he had been, Oisin remembered, all those years ago in the kitchen of An Teach Ban. And how Concetta teased him, a favourite niece to a favourite uncle and Silvio's voice was kind.

"Ah Luigi, *grazie*," he said as plates of thick bean and pasta soup suddenly appeared carried expertly by Luigi, a thin faced man of about forty, who inclined his head as each plate was carefully positioned in front of everyone. He wasn't in the least servile. In fact, he seemed to be enjoying himself and he smiled at Oisin as if the sight of a young stranger for Sunday lunch was exciting and could have possibly made his day. Oisin, for his part, was surprised to see another servant for he was still looking out for Nellie who was nowhere to be seen. Must be that Scottish lassie's day off, he concluded, somewhat disappointed. He would have liked to enquire but he knew he lacked the courage. Out of the corner of his eye, he carefully observed which spoon the Signora took for the soup. He followed her actions and, as he did so, became aware for the first time that the silver spoon he now held in his hand, had the identical Coat of Arms that he had noticed a week before in the hall. Along the base of the spoon and etched on the other cutlery as well – the red cross, the boar's head, the crown, the scroll. Further examination revealed the same design on the label of the bottle of Merlot that Luigi kept pouring into Oisin's half empty glass. No sooner was the wine drunk than the glass was quickly refilled so that Oisin, enjoying both the wine and the soup and the crusty white round bread roll, decided that La Famiglia Luchetta was wealthy indeed. Now the riddle might include vineyards, for this wealth did not come out of nowhere.

Oisin relaxed more for it was impossible not to in such company. When Luigi whisked his soup plate away to be replaced with a huge portion of roast pork which seemed submerged in a rich tomato sauce with unknown strange black objects floating amongst the tomatoes and the herbs, Oisin hesitated. To not eat would have been impolite. He tasted the round black shape. It was salty and he was unaware of the stone inside. He held his hand over his mouth and expelled the stone into his hand, placing it carefully onto the side of his plate. No one noticed as a huge dish of potatoes followed by a dish of long thin green beans brought murmurings of approval from all. Everyone ate.

"Señor, what is your opinion of the war in Ireland?"

It was Ramón who spoke and he directed his question to Oisin. The Spaniard had finished his main course and he sat back in his chair, placing his hands together, prayer-like. Oisin was taken off-guard and surprised that it was Ramón who spoke. The Spaniard had not taken any part in the conversation up to that point and had seemed totally absorbed in satisfying his hunger. Oisin hesitated. It was a time of threats and hunger strikes and a peculiar kind of hatred. He was unsure of his answer. He took no interest in the agony of the North. Everyone in Ballybeg knew who belonged to the IRA and who sympathized but the Kelly family were aloof. No amount of persuasion would bring forth an opinion from any of them and his English mother spoke not a word. Conversation ceased around the table and everyone, including Luigi who was in the process of replacing the main dish with the most amazing tart, looked at him, expectantly.

Now Oisin chose his words carefully. It felt like a challenge. Almost as if a glove had been thrown down before a duel, he thought.

"I would say that if a man has convinced himself that to kill another for what he considers is a just cause... no amount of persuasion will convince him otherwise... I know no one in the North... but I am an Irishman."

Ramón nodded.

"Sì, Señor... you speak well. My father died fighting Franco and there was a medal on his chest."

At Ramón's words, Silvio raised his glass.

"We drink now to our dead comrades," he said sombrely.

Oisin drank and as the red wine slipped down his throat, his thoughts turned to his mother's brother, William and her father, both of whom he had never met because of a war.

332

No one spoke, not even young Silvio, for there are times when there is no need for an imposed silence. It comes as natural as conversation sometimes does. The Signora made the sign of the Cross.

"You are a wise young man, Oh-sean," she said softly. "We are pleased you eat with us today, and ah, Maria has made for us her speciality!"

"*Deliziosissimo!*" cried young Silvio, clapping his hands together. Everyone laughed.

Oisin looked on in childish wonder as a huge slice of honey and walnut tart was deftly placed onto his plate. He had already eaten more than he normally would have done in two days. Never had he eaten so well not even on Christmas Day when Frankie and Declan always got the turkey leg!

Suddenly, Concetta bounced out of her chair.

"Ah, there's my baby," she cried. "Time for Sofia to eat now! It is OK, Mamma, Ramón will bring Silvio! Oisin, thank you for dining with us – please come again!"

She smiled at Oisin and at her husband, too. Ramón rose obediently from the table, bowing towards Oisin and wiping his lips on the white linen napkin with the red 'L' embroidered in the corner. Concetta glanced briefly at her husband and, at that moment, Oisin, ever the observer, noted that she was as much in love with the mournful Spaniard as he was with her. It was a magic moment for Oisin. Here were two people in love despite appearances to the contrary – for is it not so, that the most unlikely of couples can often have the most enduring love?

"We go now to the library!" announced Silvio and with a wave of his hand, the Signora and Oisin followed obediently. It was just four o'clock but already dark and the curtains were drawn. Oisin noticed that the ebony box was just were it had been the week before and Ra was asleep on the rug in front of the fire. The cat did not move a muscle as Silvio, the Signora and Oisin settled down comfortably on the three armchairs. The Signora poured them all black coffee from an elaborate-looking pot and offered sweet almond biscuits. They were delicious and Oisin took two. The Signora smiled. It was Silvio who spoke first.

"Now, Oisin Kelly from Ireland, it is time that we speak to you of our family. You are curious, are you not and wonder how it can be that we speak so much of your Uncle Mick and we smile when he returns to us the black box?"

Oisin nodded and took another biscuit without being offered one. Silvio continued to speak. He waved his hands in the air and he was as much in control as always, it appeared.

"You understand, my boy... we are a family of the land. We have held our land in Bologna, lost it, fought for it, gained it back. For three centuries the Luchetta family own the land and the land, she owns them. We are of the earth. She runs like the red wine through our veins. Your family, the Kellys, you are of the land. I know. There is a common bond... this bond; it runs through all those who live by what the earth can give. Our land grows the red grape for the wine but the land, it is hilly and the soil poorer than in other places, so we grow the olive trees beside the vine." He paused, thoughtfully – his mind back with the vines and the olive groves.

"But now I speak of my family. It is, how you say, a paradox to feel ourselves separate and connected at the same time. I am Silvio Luchetta and through my veins runs three hundred years of Luchetta and yet, I am apart from them, is that not so, Rosa?"

Rosa who all this time had sat quietly in her chair, inclined her head slightly. She answered her brother softly as if she, too, felt the connection and the isolation.

"Sì, Silvio. I, too, have felt what you say. But now, we tell to Oh-sean the wonderful story of Great Uncle Bruno!" And the thought of that long-ago relative brought a smile to her face. Now Oisin was curious. Great Uncle Bruno sounded very grand indeed and just the name alone conjured up an image.

"My great grandfather is Silvio. I, too, bear his name. He fought against the Austrians. He was an idealist, or so the family say... a Don Quixote, perhaps, who charged at windmills! But for him the passion was a united Italy. So, you see, I was interested to hear you speak of Northern Ireland, Oisin and the sorrow there... but we live in different times and we are different people. Now, I think we are all Europeans, *sì*?, because of men like my Great Grandfather Silvio."

Oisin nodded. He had never thought of it that way before.

"My great grandfather has two sons, my Great Uncle Bruno and my Grandfather, Carlo. My grandfather was the second son. The glory belongs to the first born... would you not agree sometimes that is so, young man?"

Silvio's eyes rested with some amusement onto Oisin's face before continuing.

"Now, this elder brother, the inheritor of all the vineyards and the olive groves and yes, too, the ancestral home, was my Great Uncle Bruno. But Bruno, I suppose, was a rebel. Distant lands and distant people held more excitement for him than the land. Not for him the vineyards or the olive groves. All this he leaves to my grandfather. Not one word did the family hear of Great Uncle Bruno for ten years. They feared him dead. The priest had said a Mass for him. My grandfather is the head of the Luchetta family. He marries well – a Countess. Now the Luchettas are very rich and influence priests and politicians. Is that not so, Rosa? La familigia Luchetta is heard in Bologna. In English you say, 'Money talks' and it is so. But there are troubles in Italy and with my grandfather. He is ill. There is a son, my father, Carlo but only one son. No daughters. It is to Carlo that all the wealth of the Luchettas now comes but what happens... Great Uncle Bruno returns! With stories that fire the imagination of my young father. Bruno is a hero, an adventurer. He has fought wars in South America and lived in China. He now speaks

Spanish and Mandarin! He is the famous Bruno Luchetta. The women... they long for him... even my grandmother, the Countess, it is said. My grandfather is a good son but beside Bruno he is a dwarf to a giant. My Great Uncle Bruno brings the box – *la scotala nera* – to my father, young Carlo. This box with the mystery... with "Italia" carved on the base but it is Chinese, the family say. Great Uncle Bruno talks of China and my father listens to every word. How he would like to be like Great Uncle Bruno. He disobeys his father, my poor sick grandfather, Carlo."

"It is a story, *sì*?" murmured the Signora. "I think to myself sometimes, this is the story of the Prodigal Son but alas, Bruno has malaria and is dead. So there is left my grandfather, ill too and young Carlo, our father, inherits the land... and the Chinese box of Great Uncle Bruno, he treasures above all else. This is Bruno and the box has the mystery of distant lands. Our father longs to leave the vineyards and the olive groves to follow the dream of Great Uncle Bruno."

"But now, you see, Oisin," continued Silvio, "We have a war – it is 1914 and my grandfather fears we lose the land once more. So our father is sent to a relative in Edinburgh because my grandfather has an admiration for British democracy and Scottish education. So at the end of the war, my father stays and becomes a student at the University of Edinburgh. Ah, but now into my father's life there comes my mother. She is not the wife for my father but he loves her and they marry. They tell no one. She is Amy Harrison, our mother, a shop-girl but she has my father's heart. They return to live in Italy, to the land of the Luchetta, because my grandfather is dead and Carlo is the head of the family. But my grandmother, the Countess, she does not speak to my mother. No, Amy is a shop-girl and not the right social class for her son. It is a difficult time for Amy, our mother, I think. She longs constantly for Scotland and Edinburgh. Her heart aches for her homeland but it is duty and she has the name of Luchetta. I am born in 1924 and Rosa in 1928.

We are children. Now Mussolini, he is in charge and the "Black Shirts" are everywhere. My father is a proud man. My mother, Rosa and myself are to return to Edinburgh to be safe. We bring with us the box of my Great Uncle Bruno that was given to my father to remind us of them both. We live here in this home, this 42 Willow Crescent and, *sì*, we are safe but my heart is sad that I cannot fight beside my father."

A sadness passed across Silvio's face as he uttered those words and he fell silent. The Signora continued the story:

"You see, Oh-sean, the Fascists. They take our house, our lands, and my poor brave father they shoot on the steps of our castello."

She, too, went silent.

The unravelling of the story of the Luchettas was the most exciting story that Oisin had ever heard. There was excitement and drama. True life is far more interesting than fiction, he thought. He had known the black box he had brought so carefully from Ireland held a story. Soon, he thought, I will hear how Mick, my Uncle Mick, fitted into all this because now I am certain I am going to be told. The logs burned down in the grate. Silvio placed two more oak logs on the half dying embers and soon the red flames caught. Ra woke and, seeing the Signora, let out a yowl. With one leap, the cat was on her lap, purring loudly.

"Now we finish the story. This is what your Uncle Mick writes in his letter to me. I was to tell to you the story of the Luchetta family and the black box and then perhaps, you will forgive your Uncle Mick?" Silvio said thoughtfully. "But now, I am a young man like yourself, Oisin. It is 1945 and the war is over. I return to Italy. I am now the head of the Luchetta family. My grandmother, the Countess is dead. I have to reclaim my land for Rosa and myself. The Luchettas must live on. We are a proud family and have not bowed to the tyrant. I work hard. I am twenty-one and strong. Rosa comes with me. Now our servants return but it is a different time and we all must work hard. It is 1948 and I meet Maria. We marry. Rosa, too, she marries Cavellessi. But, Rosa, she tells you her story. It is not for me to speak." He hesitated. "Maria and I are happy. The vines grow again. Our wealth is returning with the land and then our joy. We have a daughter, Isabella. We think our world is perfect. But life is cruel sometimes. My Maria she dies in childbirth with our baby son. The worst thing that could happen to me, happened. I am alone... with just my daughter Isabella. Rosa she is with Cavellessi and my gentle mother, the shop-girl, is dead. But it is in that very worst time that I looked at the land, Oisin, I saw the leaves coming onto the trees and the grapes growing under the sun. I said to myself, 'Silvio, this is the worst time,' but within myself, within my inner being, a conviction grows that there was now for me the seeds of something precious to become the very best of times... and so it is to be... but now my sister talks. I leave you now, Rosa. Does not time heal all the wounds?"

The Signora sighed. She folded her hands together for Ra had moved from her lap and was now beside the fireside licking his front paw.

"Ah... Oh-sean... we speak too much of our family to you today, I fear but it is now that it is the story that has to be told. Silvio is right. Now I tell you the story of your uncle. You smile... *sì*, it is a love story! This, you find strange that I speak of love with your uncle? You are young. You think when you are old, you have no passion. But you are wrong... the passion burns still within me for Michael."

At these words, the Signora placed her right hand on her heart.

"Silvio, he tells you I marry Cavellessi. Ah, what fools women are, Oh-sean. I am young... and Cavellessi struts like a peacock into my life. '*Rosa, amore! Rosa, amore!*' he says and I believe him. He is handsome. He thinks always of his body. He is strong. I am caught like a moth in a trap. 'Marry me, Rosa,' he pleads. '*Sì... sì...* I will marry you!' I

338

am a fool. Cavellessi, he looks at the Luchetta family and thinks, 'Now I become rich!' Oh-sean, believe me, to this day I cannot say the first name of this man."

She raised her head slightly. In the glow of the fire, Oisin thought he saw a tear in her eye, threatening to spill onto her cheek but she took a deep breath and spoke again.

"He is cruel. He beats me... I, Rosa Luchetta, how dare he? I tell no one, Oh-sean. No one. Not even my mother and she wept at my wedding. She knew. She knew. But Cavellessi he is a Fascist in his heart... a bully, you say in English. Women are to him, playthings. He enjoys them and throws them away. And I, Rosa, am the same to him... but I have the money and Cavellessi, he spends it. He brings women into our home to taunt me. I am his slave, he thinks. But I do not submit. No, I do not weaken. The blood of the Luchettas runs in my veins. I am six months with child, Oh-sean, and Cavellessi hits me across the face. There..."

And she placed her hand on her left cheek.

"I push him away and he punches me, hard in my belly where my child grows..."

She was silent. This was difficult for her. Oisin clenched both his hands. He would have punched Cavellessi to a pulp if he had been there. How could a man hurt so beautiful a woman? Yes, Oisin thought, I would have killed him.

"Now... I say to myself, I divorce this man. My baby is lost. I am ill. I go to the priest in the village. I want to divorce Cavellessi, I tell him. But no, there is no divorce, says the priest and that one, he has fathered children all around Bologna. So much for the priest... would you say? But now, I am free to leave. I leave Cavellessi and our home in the middle of the night. I think of Great Uncle Bruno... he is beside me, I believe that to this day. There is my mother's home, Scotland, I will go to Scotland. I come to 42 Willow Crescent and I think no more of Cavellessi even though he tries to find me. And then one day I meet Michael..."

At the mention of Michael's name, the Signora clasped her hands and smiled.

"You wonder where we could meet? I go to Mass. Always I go... despite the priest... because the church is greater... this I believe. One day, at St Mary's, there is Michael...at Mass, too. And oh, he is handsome. Not like Cavellessi... his eyes were hard... but Michael, he has the soft blue eyes and the gentle voice... just like you, Oh-sean... you have his eyes. I see it when I first see you and my heart, it is glad."

"I'm not handsome," murmured Oisin. "My brother calls me 'Frog'"!

"Oh, oh, my dear... what nonsense is this?" and the Signora took hold of Oisin's hands and held them tight. She looked into his eyes and he sank into them. He felt he was entering into those eyes. If Uncle Mick had loved Rosa, he now knew why.

"But I continue... we are happy, Michael loves me. He comes often to Scotland now but I do not tell him... I do not say I am married to Cavellessi. I do not say I am rich. How can I? Michael is not like Cavellessi... he would not take my money. He is poor. He digs up potatoes and his farm, the land is stone. Nothing grows there like Bologna. We meet in secret. I long to see him but still I tell no one, not even Silvio. How can I tell Silvio? He is full of the bitterness for his poor Maria. And Michael he talks of Ireland and Ballybeg and his brother, your father and I long to be with him but I cannot. There is sadness when I think of it but no, I am glad for when I am with Michael, time ceases for me. Now he brings me a gift. This poor farmer from Ireland who has nothing brings to me, Rosa, who has all this... a gift... the pearls of his mother. 'Take them,' he says. 'Wear them.' I hold them to my heart and wear them to Mass on Sundays but then I place them, to be safe, in the box of my

Papa. *Sì*, always the box, it is with me. 'Michael,' I say, 'how I love you.' "

He is so gentle, so good, so quiet and when he speaks, I believe him. It is not like Cavellessi. When Michael speaks, he tells the truth. I know it. My heart knows it. But now, I have Michael's child inside me. *Sì*. I am frightened. How to tell him? How to speak of it, the honour of the familigia Luchetta?" And at those words, the Signora shrugged her shoulders. "I do not tell Michael. I do not answer his letters. He knows nothing. My Concetta is born and still I do not tell him."

Oisin, on hearing the name 'Concetta' sat upright in his chair. He could hardly believe what he was hearing. Concetta was Mick's daughter and that made her his cousin. She was a cousin to Frankie and Declan and Mary. She was family.

"But, Signora," he exclaimed, "what am I hearing? You are telling me that Concetta is Mick's daughter? Does she know? That was why Mick had her photo in the box... now, I understand. But... tell me, does Concetta know who her father was?" he asked again. He could not take it in. The Luchettas and Mick, the box and now, Concetta, beautiful laughing Concetta was his cousin.

"Ah, *sì*. She knows. We talk. This week we talk of nothing else. Of you. And Michael, he writes to his daughter from the grave."

"Mick knew then...?"

"Ah, *sì*. But that is Silvio to tell you... you have heard enough, I think for one day! *Sì*, Concetta, she knows... and you have met her. She thinks how wonderful it is to have a father from Ireland. Michael tells Concetta in the letter and gives to her the sapphire and gold broach of his mother. Concetta is happy. She laughs and she has Ramón. No, Concetta is not ashamed of her mother's love. I am blessed, Oh-sean with such a daughter. And now there is the young Silvio and my darling, Sofia... *sì*, I am blessed. And it is because of Michael. You tell me about him one day... but

341

now, I end my story. I think of Michael. What can I give him for I do not want him to know about Concetta? So I wrap 'la scatola nera' – Papa's black box of Great Uncle Bruno and I place the pearls that belong to the mother of Michael back in the box because I want not to hurt him and I know now he loved his mother. We do foolish things sometimes, Oh-sean, because at the time we convince ourselves it is right. I say to Michael in a letter – 'This is my gift to you – the black box of my father, Carlo and I must return to you the pearls of your mother'. The box is of no great value but it goes to Michael with my love... and I cannot bear to wear the pearls. I never see Michael again."

This time, the Signora wiped a tear from her eye and Oisin could understand her words. Why, if he loved someone as much as the Signora had loved Michael, he would have given Old Mother Fahy's silver eggcup away. That was all he could think to give for that was his greatest treasure and it, too, had little monetary value.

"I understand that, Signora," he said. "Yes, I can understand now why Mick kept the box safe... and why he wanted it returned to you. Now...," he said softly, "now you will wear my grandmother's pearls, won't you?"

The Signora laughed.

"Ah. You are such a young man! Sì. Sì. Give me the pearls, Oh-sean. They remain there in the box. Fasten them for me... around my neck... it is so long now since I wear them... but I know this is the wish of your Uncle Mick, my Michael. Grazie. Grazie. This is the day I remember."

Gently, Oisin held the pearls and just as gently he placed them around the Signora's neck. He fumbled awkwardly with the clip.

"Ah," the Signora cried. She stroked the pearls and now the tears welled up in her eyes. She was Rosa again, the beauty who had captured an Irishman's heart. She held out her hand to Oisin and very gently he kissed it – as the Italians do.

*****

342

That night, Oisin lay in his bed and the blue room never seemed so bare. He lay on his back and gazed at the ceiling in the half dark for in the city it is never the dark, dark of the country. He thought of his day – of Mick and the Luchettas, of the wonderful meal and the kindness of them all, but mostly he thought of Concetta and wondered if his mother, his English mother Annie, had known about Mick's daughter. He tossed and turned until finally he fell asleep to dream of Great Uncle Bruno dressed as a Samurai warrior holding a sword above his head and riding Bess hard along the strand at Ballybeg. Then Bess grew wings and landed as if by magic on the top of Slieve Geal. There was no Great Uncle Bruno but Ra as large as a tiger, with claws outstretched. The cat leapt at Mick and sunk its teeth into Mick's leg – and Annie was there and the Signora, too, but both were silent witnesses. Mick disappeared and Oisin, holding Old Mother Fahy's silver eggcup high in the air, rode Bess down the slopes of Slieve Geal to the back of An Teach Ban.

*****

"The Signor is waitin' fer ye," said Nellie when she saw Oisin standing on the doorstep, dripping wet. A thaw during the week had been replaced with rain for three days and the ground underfoot was wet. Oisin, with raindrops deposited on his nose, looked like the proverbial drowned rat and Nellie giggled.

"Now... dinnae ye be drippin all over my clean floor! Here... gimme yer coat! Look at ye! They've taken quite a fancy to ye, ye ken," she said as she took hold of Oisin's coat, scarf and cap, " 'Specially the Signora... anyways... he's in the library an I'm tae tak ye thare when ye arrive. Follow me, an I'll have none of yer Irish tricks..."

Oisin grinned.

"And what could they be? I'm just a lad from the West of Ireland all alone in the big city."

"Aye. That's richt... in with the toffs of Willow Crescent. Ye won't want to speak to the likes of me soon...

343

at the rate yer gaun with the Luchettas, ye'll be gaun places with them, off to the castle in Italy next, ye mark my words! 'Oh-sean this', 'Oh-sean that', that's all I've heard from the Signora this week."

"Ye'd better behave yerself then, hadn't ye? Never know what I might be wantin'!" laughed Oisin. He liked Nellie.

"Dinnae have any of yer cheek. Here ye are then, would 'Sir' require anything else?"

"Well, now... what a question to be askin' a poor Irish lad...," grinned Oisin and he winked at Nellie as he opened the door to the library.

Silvio was seated at the desk. The black box was nowhere to be seen.

"Coffee, Nellie please and some of those almond biscuits if Maria has some," he said. Nellie bobbed her head up and down, wrinkling her nose at Oisin when she thought the Signor wasn't looking.

"Now, young man," said Silvio and he indicated that Oisin should sit down. "You have heard some of the story of your uncle and the black box but now it is time for you to hear the rest. This week, my sister talks with me and we decide that it is right that the whole truth be told. We wait now for the coffee... a moment, please..."

He picked up his pen and wrote a few words while Oisin gazed around a room that was becoming more and more comfortable and just as familiar. The coffee came; the thick black coffee and the same delicious almond biscuits. Oisin wondered whether he should ask questions but thought better of it. Silvio was not the sort of man who liked to be interrupted. When he spoke, people listened, Oisin decided and a kind of admiration rose within him for the urbane and cultured Italian who now sat beside him, sipping his coffee politely.

"Now I confess to you, Oisin Kelly. A long time ago now it seems, I hear that Rosa no longer lives with Cavellessi but is here, in Edinburgh at the Luchetta house.

'What is this?' I say, 'My sister leaves her husband. What is happening?' "

So, I come from Bologna to speak with Rosa... and Rosa, she is not the Rosa of our childhood. She is to have a child, I see. And it does not belong to her husband. 'Where is Cavellessi?' I say. 'Why is he not here with you?' But she answers me, 'Silvio, I do not speak of Cavellessi.' We argue. But still she is silent. Then finally, she weeps. 'I love another,' she says. 'Ah,' I cry, 'who is this man who has done this to you?' And then she tells me, Oisin. She tells me it is an Irishman, Michael Kelly. He lives in the West of Ireland at a place called Ballybeg. A farmer, too, but she does not say to this man she has a husband or she has the wealth of the Luchettas. I am angry. So angry. The hate fills my heart. It is a madness within me. I will go to the West of Ireland and kill this man, this man, Michael Kelly. I think of my Maria and how I am alone and now I think my own sister is a whore. I cannot believe now I had so much hate in me, Oisin... but I was young and I had seen much cruelty in the hearts of men and their actions made me believe there was no good in the world."

He paused and took another sip of his coffee. It seemed to Oisin that Silvio found it very difficult to speak of these matters. No, he thought, no way can I ask questions. It is not my place and he kept silent.

"So," Silvio continued, "I go to Ballybeg and stay the first time at the Railway Hotel. Where is this man, this Michael Kelly? I go to the priest, Father O'Malley. 'Where is Michael Kelly?' I ask. 'Go out and ask anyone in the street,' answers the priest. So I see a man and I ask him. 'He might be here or he might not,' says the man. I think to myself... this is a crazy place! I ask another man, 'Where is Michael Kelly?' 'He is sitting himself on his bench looking at the sea.' So now I know and sure enough, there is a man sitting by the sea but not on a bench, on some rocks. 'Are you Michael Kelly?' I ask. 'I might be and then again I might not be. Who wants to know?' he says. 'Rosa Luchetta.'

345

There is a light in his eyes but I do not see it. I think… this is a perfect place to kill a man. I do not see the beautiful Ballybeg, I see only this man and how I will take him by the throat and squeeze the life out of him. No one will see and he can die here on the rocks. But what do you think he does now? He takes tobacco and rolls it into a cigarette and looks at me with a calmness I have never seen before. How do you kill a man who lights a cigarette in front of you? I am so angry. I clench my fists but I know I cannot kill him. No, Silvio Luchetta cannot kill a man who smokes a cigarette and has no fear. 'I come again,' I shout at him, 'one year to this day, I see you at the Railway Hotel and we speak then!' And I leave."

He was silent. Outside, Oisin could hear the rain beating onto the window pane and his thoughts went back to Ballybeg, to winter nights, to rain and wind. He thought of Mick, sitting on the rocks, smoking a cigarette and he thought, yes, that would be Mick.

"Now," said Silvio. "Now I think only of money. More money. I have the vineyards and the olives, now I return the wealth to my family. I have my Isabella to think of so I go back to Bologna and I work and work and think what I must do about this Michael Kelly and my sister Rosa. I try to find Cavellessi. No one knows. He has gone from the face of the earth. But Rosa, now, she has a daughter, Concetta. I say, 'Her name is Concetta Luchetta… she will be a sister to Isabella…' and Rosa agrees. You know, Oisin, many times I go to Ballybeg and the second time I meet Michael at the Railway Hotel. I know what I will do if I cannot kill him. He is poor and I am rich but he can pay. I will bleed him dry, as you say in English. 'You have fathered a daughter,' I say to him, 'and I am the brother of Rosa and you will pay me for the sake of my sister and her child. But you will never see Rosa or the child.' 'I will pay,' he says. 'What do you ask?' The man. I cannot understand the man. He troubles me. I take his money… all that he can give… I take it and give it to an Orphanage in Dublin. It is of no use to me…

but he pays and I tell no one not even Rosa. Can you believe that I would do that, Oisin young man? I think now that you can only give away what is in your heart... this I learn. When I had the hate in me, hate came back to me as sure as an arrow that penetrates the heart. I gave hate and hate was my burden. Hate held me down and would have killed me. *Sì*... I was a dead man inside with a dead heart."

He paused.

"But the next time I go to Ballybeg, I drive my car and I begin to see something. It is a beautiful place and I think, maybe this man has paid enough. Rosa is happy and Concetta is a beautiful child. We live in Italy. We are almost a family except I have no wife but my heart, you see, it is beginning to soften. The next time I see Michael he is ready to give me money and I take it but now I am not so sure. I say to him, 'Your daughter is beautiful. Her name is Concetta' and now I see the light in his eyes. The fourth time I see your uncle, we are at the home of the Protestant Minister, Leslie and his wife Effie and we have a wonderful time. I smile at Effie and Leslie laughs. We talk of art and music and life. Michael, too, he smiles but now he holds his hand over the eye with the black patch and I fear he is not well. 'What is wrong with Michael?' I say to Effie. 'Ah', she answers, 'he is ill... there is something wrong, I know.' I think to myself. This man has not done you any harm, Silvio Luchetta. Why do you want to harm him?' And now I forgive and we are friends. I think I hate him because I fear him and I am ashamed. It is something I want to confess. I hold out my hand to him in front of Leslie and Effie. They are my witness although they do not know. 'You are my friend, Michael Kelly', I say and he looks me in the eye and says to me, 'That I am. That I am.' So, now I write to him and send him books. He has a mind and I know now that Rosa loves him. I see him in Dublin and take the photo of Concetta to him. Ah, Oisin... if you could have seen that man's face..."

Silvio smiled.

"Then Michael writes to me to say the old priest, old Father O'Malley is dead. I think... I have known many priests like this old one. I will pay my respects to him for the sake of them all. I am not a very good Catholic, Oisin, but it is my religion and my heart is softer. I go to the funeral. 'Ah,' I say. 'The past is past', and I do not think any more of Ireland until you arrive at 42 Willow Crescent holding *la scatola nera* – the black box and you tell me and Rosa that Michael returns it to us... and that Michael, too, is dead. It is a story to be told, you think so, now? Your uncle was right to send you to us. Now you begin to understand?"

"Yes sir," answered Oisin for he didn't know what else to say and he wasn't so sure that he did understand.

"We are glad all of us that you come to us. I think you are like your Uncle Mick, young man and Rosa... she speaks of you all the time. We have to say, 'Stop Rosa!' and she laughs. It is good to see Rosa laugh again and the sadness goes. We thank you for that."

"I didn't do much."

"Ah... never underestimate what one person can do, young man... and you, you have the courage to come to see us... you are glad now? We go after Christmas to Bologna. There we stay the year. You are family now, Oisin... so you meet Isabella one day and then you meet us all. But Isabella, she is different. You see that when you meet... Isabella," he smiled, "my daughter is... how you say in English, 'Some woman!' That is right. 'Some woman!' But now, you are with us. You are like your uncle, *si*?"

Within Oisin, there rose a curious thought. Isabella... some woman? Yes, I would like to meet a woman like that, he thought to himself but now the thought of Mick came into his mind. Could he question Silvio now? Would Silvio answer truthfully?

"There is one thing I want to ask you, sir..." It was difficult. "Was my uncle mad? Always that's what they said in Ballybeg. It affected us all, you see... but I don't know..."

348

He hoped Silvio would listen. Yes, Silvio would tell the truth, he was certain of that. No one had ever listened to him before, except Bess, and she didn't count, but Silvio would.

The Italian shrugged his shoulders.

"What is madness?" he said, "When my father Carlo stands in front of twenty men with guns pointing at him, was that madness?"

"I don't know... I saw my father die, too, sir... but Mick, when Mick refused to go to Mass, awful things were said about him..."

"Your uncle hears a different tune, I think. Who are we to judge? When I see him, on the rocks, I want to kill him. Is that madness? No, the madness is within me. Michael has no fear of my madness... so which one of us is mad?"

And he frowned, shrugging his shoulders again, dismissively.

"No... we talk no more of this. We all make choices. This you learn. All life is choice and change. Michael... he makes the choice to love my sister... and that changes him. But this choice, this I believe, is not the choice of a madman?"

Oisin shook his head.

"Now, Oisin, we speak of other things. Do you like this Edinburgh?"

"Aye, that I do. Different from Ballybeg, that's for sure. But I like it here. Aye. I've a job and it's grand. I work for Wee Willie... says he'll make a joiner out of me one day... that is, when I don't go off dreamin'. But he's a grand fella, is Willie. And his wife, Jeannie... she looks after me. I'm very fond of the two of them, sir. Aye. I like it here and I like my work."

Oisin smiled. The thought of Wee Willie and Jeannie sent a warm glow through his body. They'll be wondering how it all went today, he thought. I can tell them some of it but not all. No, I can't tell them I've got a cousin called Concetta Luchetta whose very rich. Best not to talk of Mick, either, he decided. I'll just say I've friends now in Edinburgh... an Italian family and they are kind but I won't say anything about them being rich. Willie and Jeannie wouldn't know what to say about that.

Silvio stood up.

"And now, young Oisin," he said, "I think I drive you home to Willie and Jeannie. The rain... it does not stop... I have a Scottish mother but the rain, ah, I want the sun! It is cold and wet outside. *Sì*, I will drive. Have you ever been driven in a XKE Jag?"

Wow, thought Oisin.

"No sir," he said. "I'd sure love to though...!" And then he thought... life just gets better and better!

*****

It was a beautiful spring day in Ballybeg. The sun rose high in the sky. From An Teach Ban it was possible to see the outline of Inishmore, twenty miles away, so clear was the view across the sea. Silvio Luchetta stretched as he stepped out of the car. The dark blue Jaguar sports car with the white leather upholstery looked out of place at the farm. The ground was dry. It hadn't rained for a week. The red fuschia now grew right along the side of the front of the house and was already in flower. All was still and when Silvio knocked on the brightly painted red front door, the sound disturbed the silence. He knocked again. Annie opened the door and, seeing the stranger, she hesitated. She blushed slightly. I should have combed my hair, was her first thought. Her hands were covered in flour and she quickly wiped them on her apron. Why have I got this old dress on? She thought crossly.

"You remember me, Signora?" this elegant man asked. His hair was grey and there were lines on his forehead but how could she forget?

"Of course. You are Mr Luchetta?"

"*Sì*."

"Please come in," said Annie remembering her manners.

They entered the kitchen and the room was as it had always been. Newly baked scones sat on a wire rack in the centre of the kitchen table.

"Ah," said Silvio, "now I am back in the West of Ireland," and he sat down on the black leather armchair next to the range. Mick's chair. Annie took her apron and placed it on the back of one of the kitchen chairs.

"Would you like some tea?" she asked politely. "You've come at the right time!"

"Ah, Signora. Of course. Thank you. I drive from Edinburgh for two days and stay last night at the Ballybeg Hotel to rest. Such changes. And Ballybeg, there is change here too? Many more houses than I remember but the home of Michael, it does not change."

"No," replied Annie, "but people change. My children are all grown-up now."

She handed the Italian a cup of tea.

"*Grazie*," he said. "We all grow old. But in our hearts we are young, is that not so?"

Annie smiled. This man was so comfortable sitting there, eating her scone and drinking her tea. I should have brought out the fine china, she thought, why didn't I?

"I have met your son in Edinburgh. He comes often to our home when we are in Scotland. He is happy, I think to see us. A fine boy."

"Oisin... you have news then?" cried Annie. "Is he behaving himself?" she asked as a mother would.

Silvio smiled.

"*Sì. Sì*, Signora. You have no problem there. Oisin is part of our family."

"He is dreadful for writing," said Annie crossly. "I want him to come home for Declan's wedding but he won't tell me if he's coming or not!"

"Ah. He is young, Signora. Do not be hard on him. He is a good son."

"Aye," answered Annie, somewhat surprised. "Just wish he would let me know, that's all," she paused. "He told

351

me he had given you back... Mick's box... but he didn't say much..."

"Ah, *la scatola nera*... the black box, Signora. That is why I come to Ballybeg. That box... it does not let us go! Michael, he is a clever man, you see now, Signora."

Annie bit her lip. Mick had been dead two years but he was still in her thoughts.

"But what has Mick to do with all this?"

"You see, Signora, Michael writes three letters. One he gives to Oisin. Take this letter and the box to Silvio Luchetta. He will know what to do. I think it is a clever game he plays with us. The second letter he gives to me to tell me what to do. I read and say to myself, 'Silvio... this Michael is a friend. I will do what you ask.' And the third letter he gives to Concetta, the daughter he never sees. Ah, there is sadness, I know and I am ashamed. 'Silvio, you should not have been so cruel.' But it is past. I cannot bring it back that Michael and Concetta meet. Concetta weeps when she reads her letter. 'My Papa,' she says, 'he is an Irishman.' But Concetta, she is a happy woman now. 'Ah, Uncle Silvio,' she says to me, 'I am pleased to know. At last I know.' There you are, Signora. Three letters. And there are other things in this black box. Pearls. I give them to Rosa and she holds them to her heart and she, too, weeps. But it is a miracle. She is happy. The sadness goes and she talks to Oisin, your son. They talk and talk. I think, Rosa has found a son... you do not worry, Signora... Rosa and Oisin are friends. I think Michael knows that this will happen. Oisin, I think now is a son to Michael also. A warrior and a poet, he writes in this letter he gives to me. So I think Michael loves this boy. Am I not right, Signora?"

Annie's heart beat faster. This is the strangest thing, she thought and she was back there, for a brief moment, at the night of Oisin's conception. She reddened.

"You are right, Mr Luchetta," she said quietly.

"And now, Signora Kelly... there is one last duty that Michael tells me to do!"

He reached inside his pocket and brought out a small worn leather case. He stood up. He was tall in Annie's kitchen. She rose from her chair and they faced each other across the kitchen table piled high with scones. Silvio opened the box and held the gold Irish wedding ring which had belonged to Mick's mother. He held the ring between his long fingers and Annie thought of Father John back in Camden. Father John's hands were long and thin also and she wondered what on earth had made her think of Father John at this moment in time? Silvio took hold of her hand and slid the wedding ring onto her finger. It fitted perfectly and sat neatly beside the ring Bernard had given her on her wedding day all those years ago. Then Silvio took her hand in his. He held it and looked into her eyes. His brown eyes did not leave her face. Gently he kissed her hand... the hand that now held two wedding rings, side by side.

"Ah, Annie," he whispered softly, "I think it is possible, do you not believe, for a man to love two women?"

Now Annie's eyes never left the face of the Italian who held her hand in his and did not seem to want to let it go.

"Silvio..." she whispered.

Oisin's story continues...

FAMILIAR YET FAR

Young Irishman, Oisin Kelly, bitter and disillusioned leaves Britain vowing never to return. When he arrives in the outback Australian town of Kilgoolga his life is still haunted by past events. Struggling to come to terms with his new and sometimes frightening environment, he falls under the spell of the enigmatic Eleanor Bradshaw. Deception, intrigue and misplaced loyalty are at the heart of this work of fiction as Oisin discovers that things are not always what they seem. Publication in 2015.

Oisin's story concludes in the third novel,

HOMECOMING

Some other titles from Mauve Square Publishing:

For children:
SHADOWS FROM THE PAST SERIES by Wendy Leighton-Porter
NINJA NAN SERIES and WOLFLORE by Annaliese Matheron
THE RAINBOW ANIMAL and THE KELPIE'S EYES by Oliver Eade
THE GHOST WITHIN by Charlotte Bloomfield

For young adults:
FIRESTORM RISING by John Clewarth
THE TERMINUS by Oliver Eade

For adults:
MANHATTAN DECEPTION and THE MINERVA SYSTEM by Simon Leighton-Porter

Lightning Source UK Ltd.
Milton Keynes UK
UKOW04f1440300514

232604UK00002B/6/P